PITCH DARK

BROOKE LONDON

Cerridwen Press

What the critics are saying...

"Pitch Dark is one of the best romantic suspense novels I've read in a while. There's a nice easy flow to Brooke London's writing style and from this book, she has an ability to write well rounded, complex characters while keeping them from coming across as stereotypical and stale. Her ability to slowly build up on the plot and keep the tension going at just the right pace is just as fine. I'll definitely be looking out for more of her books." ~ *Madame Butterfly 90 Blogspot*

4 Nymphs *"Pitch Dark* is a good suspense story. I felt it started a little slow but picked up about halfway through to the point that I did not want to put it down. [...] I enjoyed reading the story." ~ *Literary Nymphs Reviews Only*

A Cerridwen Press Publication

www.cerridwenpress.com

Pitch Dark

ISBN 9781419959660

Edited by Briana St. James.
Cover art by Croco.

This book printed in the U.S.A. by Jasmine-Jade Enterprises, LLC.

Electronic book Publication March 2009
Trade paperback Publication June 2009

Cerridwen Press is an imprint of Ellora's Cave Publishing, Inc.®

Pitch Dark

Dedication

For my friend Nancee, without whose encouragement I wouldn't have started writing. Thank you for your unfailing support.

Trademarks Acknowledgement

The author acknowledges the trademarked status and trademark owners of the following wordmarks mentioned in this work of fiction:

Al Jazeera: Aljazeera International

Ben-Gay: Johnson & Johnson Inc.

Chevrolet Chevette: General Motors Corporation

CIA: Central Intelligence Agency

Cracker Jack: Frito-Lay

CSIS: Canadian Security Information Service

Dairy Queen: AM.D.Q. Corp

Google: Google Inc.

Gulfstream Corporation: Gulfstream Aerospace Corporation

Keystone Cops: Keystone Film Company

Learjet: Bombardier Aerospace

Lego: Kirbi AG

Mailinator.com: ManyBrain, Inc.

Second Cup: The Second Cup Coffee Company Incorporation

Semtex: Explosia, a.s.

Taser: Taser International, Inc.

Toyota Camry: Toyota Motor Corporation

WiFi: The Wi-Fi Alliance

Zamboni: Frank J. Zamboni & Co. Inc.

Chapter One

Connor Donnelly sighed in frustration. The CEO and President of Energy Unlimited tapped his long fingers on his desk and stared out the window at the surrounding mountains. He loved the view and normally it lulled him into sweet calmness. But right now his steadily growing annoyance obliterated any of the terrain's soothing effects. The cause of his mood? A cantankerous old curmudgeon named Douglas Tiernan, the CEO and President of Consolidated Banyan Energy.

"Mr. Tiernan, we've been negotiating a co-venture between our companies for the past two months. I think it's about time I actually get to see your process in action. If it's as good as you claim, then I'm willing to meet the majority of your terms," Connor said in as reasonable a tone of voice as he could manage.

"Young man, *we* haven't been negotiating anything! *I've* been dealing with your 'Keystone cop' lawyers. They all speak legal mumbo-jumbo. I don't deal with peons in any company, not yours, not anyone's. I don't just hand over my work to anyone, either. I've been working on this for five years and I want to be assured completely that I and mine won't get screwed in this deal," Douglas Tiernan's voice crackled over the telephone line.

Connor wasn't sure if the connection was bad or the old man's voice was cracking. A mental picture of Douglas popped unexpectedly into his head. Grizzly Adams. The old man sounded, and probably looked, like the grizzled mountain man of television fame in the seventies.

"Mr. Tiernan, *you* are the one who approached *me* about a co-venture. *I* did not approach *you*. I have no desire to screw you and yours. You've checked me out and know that I honor whatever contracts I sign. I've done some checking on my own. And I know that you've investigated a lot of companies, but mine is the only one you've approached. So let's just put aside the bullshit and get down to it," Connor said, but the words had little heat in them.

Connor wanted the co-venture, and if that required a little bit of a gamble on his part, then so be it. It would put his company at the bleeding edge of the emerging oil sands recovery technology wave.

Douglas fell silent for a few seconds before admitting, "You're right—I have checked you out. But if you want my process, then the only person I'll deal with is you. Not some useless, overeducated cracker jacks who don't know their ass from a hole in the ground!"

"Fine, Mr. Tiernan, fine. From now on, I'll deal with you directly, but I still want to see your process. I'll sign whatever confidentiality papers you want, but I need to see how the process works before I sink tens of millions of dollars into your oil sands project. I want to know that you can successfully extract oil from the tar sands less expensively than the current methods."

"Well, all you needed to do was ask nicely, boy," Douglas huffed.

Connor jerked the phone away from his ear, barely suppressing a loud sigh, and gazed up at the ceiling as if looking for salvation, or his missing patience, in the spackled surface. He waited a moment to compose himself before raising the telephone back to his ear. "Mr. Tiernan…"

"Call me Douglas, young man," Douglas interrupted, "especially if we are going to be doing business."

"Okay, *Douglas*, call me Connor. Now, when do I get to see the process?"

"Next week. You'll have to fly to Fort McMurray and take a car north from there."

"I have my own jet. I can be there on Monday around ten. How does that sound?"

"It sounds like a plan, young man, er, Connor. I'll meet you there at ten." Douglas banged the phone down.

Connor lifted the handset away from his ear and stared at it. He hoped that Douglas had just been having a bad morning and that he wouldn't always be so unpredictable. Connor cast a sidelong glance at his brother, Liam, who lounged on the couch off to Connor's right and had listened to one side of the conversation. "What else were you able to dig up about Douglas Tiernan on your journeys through cyberspace and other places thereabouts?"

Liam yawned, stretched and leaned forward to prop his elbows on his knees. "You've pretty well got everything. One Mister Douglas Edward Tiernan, born sometime in the stone ages in Edmonton, Alberta, Canada. At twenty, he scraped together everything he could to go to college, where he studied geology. Top of his class. After college, he tramped his way through the Alberta bush and discovered coal deposits. Staked his claim and became a moneyed member of society.

"Douglas married Josephine Sittler and had three children, Clarence, Rupert and Jonathan. To make a long story short, two of the children, plus the wife, died. Jonathan survived childhood, after which he went into business with Daddy. He married Elaine Ulrich and produced one child, Alyssa Serena Tiernan.

"Jonathan's wife died in childbirth. Jonathan died in a police shootout when the girl was twelve. It probably had something to do with the child because the police records were sealed. They would only seal the records if what happened somehow involved her as a minor. I tried to dig up more information about that, but I kept running into walls. Lots of death in this family," Liam observed.

Liam sank back into the luxurious comfort of the sofa. "Anyway, I know you're a stickler for detail when it comes to knowing everything about the people with whom we do business, so I dug a little further into Alyssa, since she's Douglas' only living relative.

"Alyssa's an interesting case. When her father died, she went to live with her grandfather and, from what I could piece together, it wasn't an easy relationship. She ran away a number of times in the first year of living with him and then things seemed to settle down.

"When she was fifteen, Douglas had her take a batch of IQ tests. She's extremely intelligent—she has an IQ of one hundred and forty-five. She took piano lessons from age six and, from all accounts, she was somewhat of a prodigy. She was heavily into musical training, but when she went to college at MIT, she took a degree in computer science and mathematics."

"Computer science and mathematics? Isn't that a long way from the piano?" Connor inquired, brows arching.

"Not as far as you'd think. The ability to decipher music and timing is mathematical. One can apparently lead naturally to the other. Researchers have found a link between music, especially classical music, with its complex patterns of evolving musical themes, and the ability to interpret complex visual-spatial problems. They believe music somehow primes some of the same neural circuits that the brain employs for these skills.

"Anyhow, she was at the top of her class at college and the Canadian government's intelligence agency took an interest in her. The Canadian Security Intelligence Service, or CSIS for short, hired her prior to her graduation from college. Her specialty was hacking computer systems."

"*Was* hacking? What happened?" Connor asked, curious. Not many women were into hacking—it tended to be more of a guy thing, unless you counted Trinity in The Matrix.

"Well, about two years ago, she apparently just up and quit. I know a couple of the guys she worked with and all they would tell me was that there was some kind of blowout between her and her superiors and she walked. When the American government found out she was a free agent, they were fast to approach her and, in not so polite terms, she told them to take a hike.

"So, with the exception of her grandfather's business, she's stayed away from technology. She auditioned as a pianist for the Calgary Philharmonic Orchestra about eighteen months ago and has been a part of the orchestra ever since then. Income is steady, but not spectacular. She keeps a low profile, no boyfriends or lovers that I could find."

"Is she involved with granddad's company?"

"She set up the computer system and the security for his company. 'To catch a thief takes a thief' kind of thing. After college, she never took a dime from the old man. She could have had it easy—the old man has enough money so she wouldn't have to work a day in her life." Liam grinned slyly at his older brother, his warm blue-green eyes laughing. He leaned forward and rested his elbows on his knees, pushing his overlong mop of golden brown hair out of his eyes. "She sounds like she's your type, bro."

Leaning back in his chair, Connor regarded his larger, younger brother with a mixture of affection and exasperation. Liam had been trying to set him up for the past few years and *that* had been always been a disaster. Connor rolled his eyes. "Okay, I'll bite. *Why* is she my type?"

"Well, she's brainy and has a checkered past."

"Yeah, right. Sounds like exactly what I'm looking for in a woman. Trouble." Connor laughed. "Next you'll tell me that she has a harelip, horn-rimmed glasses, speaks with a lisp, has crooked teeth, is hunchbacked and limps."

"Hey, man, don't knock it 'til you try it!" Liam shook with laughter for a minute. Wiping his eyes he continued,

"Seriously, you need to get out a bit more. We're worried about you growing moss on your north side. Turn south every once in a while. It'll help prevent tragedies like this from happening in the first place."

"Ha, ha. Very funny," Connor said, rolling his eyes. "You and Dillon are sniffing out new business leads all over the world, among other things, and constantly getting yourselves into trouble. You should be more worried about you." He rose from his chair and padded silently around the desk to look out the window at the panoramic view.

Connor loved living in the mountains of Colorado. It was a long way from the cloak-and-dagger world in which he had lived for so long. Peaceful and quiet and safe.

The fact that both the company headquarters and the family home had state of the art security systems made him feel even more secure. He wanted his family to be safe, and if that meant that they thought he was paranoid, then so be it. Connor protected what he loved and loved what he protected. He knew what was out there, even if they didn't.

Connor learned the hard way to be self-contained and cautious of new people. Most people, men that was, outside his circle of family and friends were reluctant to approach him. Women, however, seemed to be drawn to his dark good looks.

He dated sporadically, even going so far as to date some of the women that Liam had dug up for him, but no one had ever fired his imagination enough to think about a joint future. He wanted a woman, he wanted kids, but nothing ever sparked. There was a depressing thought. Connor sighed, turned away from the magnificent view and eyed Liam speculatively. "How long are you home for?"

"Only for a couple of days. I'm going to Venezuela to do some geological surveys. Find more energy sources for the good ol' U. S. of A. You're going to Canada on Monday, then? Make sure you don't freeze to death while you're there."

"It's June. Spring, nearly summer, you know? And I'm not going to the North Pole. It's a long way from freezing now in Fort McMurray," Connor said, smiling. "You feel like a little one-on-one on the basketball court? I feel like pounding on something and you seem to be available."

"I've already kicked your ass once this week. You're up for more humiliation? Brave man," Liam said. "Stupid, but brave."

"For your information, I *let* you win, little brother. C'mon. Let's go."

"Grand, I don't know," Alyssa Tiernan said to her grandfather, Douglas Tiernan, after he'd hung up on Connor Donnelly. "Are you sure this is what you want to do?"

"Lyssa, I don't have any options if I want to bring my oil sands extraction technology to market. I simply don't have the cash for that sort of venture." His coarse voice, roughened over many years of shouting at people, sounded surprisingly soothing.

Alyssa sighed, unwilling to reveal the hacker attacks that had nagged Consolidated Banyan's computer systems for the past two weeks. His grandfather, while not in his dotage despite his age of eighty-three, had enough to worry about without having to deal with things he wouldn't understand.

"So, this is it? You've perfected your technique to extract oil from the oil sands?" she inquired. "Does anyone else know about this?" If someone knew he'd hit the jackpot, it would certainly explain the hacker attacks. More to the point, she wondered if the Donnellys masterminded the attacks. Why pay for the process if they could simply steal it?

"Only Connor Donnelly knows about it and he's coming up Monday to Fort McMurray for a demonstration."

"Who else is going to be with you?"

"Just me and him."

"Grand, I really don't think that's a good idea. Someone else should really be there with you when you show him." She tried to make the words nonchalant, but she couldn't keep an edge of worry from her voice.

Grand peered at his granddaughter, shrewdness gleamed from his rheumy eyes. "What's this about, Alyssa?"

Alyssa pulled herself out the chair and strolled over to the sideboard to pour a cup of tea. She fussed with the cream and sugar before she replied in a steady voice. "Nothing, Grand. It's just that you don't know this guy and shit happens." With trembling hands, she poured the steaming amber liquid into the delicate cup.

Damn, she had to have better control over herself than this. She pasted a smile on her face and turned back to her grandfather, leaning one hip against the wooden server. She blew on the steaming tea, took a small sip and grimaced. Still too hot. She set the cup down with a clack and crossed her arms in front of her.

"I hired a detective and had him checked out. He's clean as a whistle. Nothing to worry about." He pried himself out of his chair and creaked over to her, his knees making crunching noises as he moved. "You worry too much." He stopped in front of her and grinned. "Besides, I've got my shotgun. I'll blow a hole in him the size of Texas if he tries any funny business."

Alyssa rolled her eyes—he was only half joking. "I'll go with you, then."

Grand's eyebrows snapped together, clearly affronted. "You will *not*. I'm not helpless, girlie. I can take care of myself," he puffed. He wagged a finger at her nose. "And if you roll your eyes again, they'll get stuck at the top and you'll be left staring at the ceiling for the rest of your life. It'll be very unattractive and then I'll never have great-grandchildren."

She concentrated on not rolling her eyes. Again he was only half kidding. She grabbed his head in both hands and gave him a smacking kiss on his bald pate. "Old man, you are incorrigible. If you want kids around, then you'd better have more children yourself."

"Too old. I just want to spoil them and send them back to you," he replied with a sunny smile.

"Yeahyeahyeah," she replied, unable to keep the smile from her face. "Dream on."

"I can always dream, girlie. You should give it a try," he said, his rough voice wistful.

"Ah, Grand, don't start this again. My life is fine."

"Yeahyeahyeah," he grinned at her, but sadness rimmed the grin. "I just want you to be happy. Have a husband, kids. More than just me."

"Enough, Grand. Most of the people I know with husbands and kids aren't any happier than I am. They just have more problems. Let's not do this, okay?"

"Okay," he grumbled. Then he brightened. "If this meeting on Monday goes as I planned and we decide to go through with the co-venture, I want you to go to Colorado and check out their computer systems. You know, make sure they're secure and we won't have any issues with connecting their systems to ours."

Alyssa stared at him. Yeah, he'd put her through school and, yes, she no longer did this sort of work for a living, but she couldn't refuse him. In actuality, he asked so little of her that denying him was out of the question. Maybe she should have stayed in the technology field, but she didn't want to think about why she'd left now. Too many painful memories. She pushed the unwelcome thoughts aside. "Sure. Just let me know when."

"I knew I could count on you, Lyssa." He beamed at her, his eyes lighting like a happy child's. "And to celebrate this new partnership with the Donnellys, I'll treat you to Dairy Queen. Anything you want."

Alyssa laughed. "Sure, Grand, you big spender, you, whatever you want."

Chapter Two

A week later, Alyssa found herself almost piercing the leather of an armrest on a seat in Connor Donnelly's Gulfstream jet with her fingernails. Her unlacquered nails bit into the soft leather, leaving deep quarter-moon impressions in the buff-colored material. She unclamped her fingers from the armrests and wriggled the fingers on both hands before carefully placing them gently back down. She took a breath and tried to reason with herself. *If I have to fly, at least I can do it in style.*

Ri-ight.

She took another breath and slowly released it. Gulfstreams were the gold standard of personal jets—Learjet owners could only dream of having a tricked-out Gulfstream at their disposal. Her eyes wandered around the luxuriously appointed cabin. Leather sofas and chairs neatly arranged around mahogany coffee tables, the plush carpeting making it cozy and inviting. The thing even had a fully functional kitchen larger than her kitchen at home. Money could definitely buy the finer things in life.

Still, she would rather have driven herself from Calgary to Colorado—visions of crashing into the ground flashed like a horror flick through her head. Uneasy, she looked around the cabin again and bit her lower lip. She glanced out the cabin window to the ground. Pretty soon it would be a lot further than ten feet below her. Her stomach rolled over sickeningly at the thought. She hoped she wouldn't embarrass herself by throwing up. She bit her lip harder, hoping the pain would distract her.

Her grandfather had asked for her help, and damn her, she would do anything for him. He may be a grumpy and unpredictable old bastard, but when it counted, Grand always stood by her.

So here she was, sitting on a plane, nauseated. *Crap.*

Since the hacker attack two weeks ago, she'd been trying to track down whoever had attempted to hack Consolidated Banyan Resources' system. Her mind drifted over the data she managed to gather from her Trojan horse. The hacker bounced his signal through a dozen countries and various satellites orbiting the planet. She managed to track him to the United States, but she'd been unable to narrow the field down any more than that. Her instincts kicked into overdrive.

What if this Connor Donnelly had paid someone to hack the system? After Googling the company, she knew that Energy Unlimited certainly had enough money to be able to afford that kind of talent. Maybe they wanted to take Grand's process and cut Grand out completely. With that in mind, Alyssa did a little investigating of Energy Unlimited and Connor Donnelly on her own. What she found out did not reassure her.

The brothers Donnelly—Connor, Dillon and Liam—had founded Energy Unlimited six years ago as a natural resources exploration, drilling and brokering firm. As time went on, they became interested in less conventional ways of producing energy, including wind power, hydrogen power and various other sources. Oil and gas became less important because new oil strikes were hard to find.

When Grand approached Connor with a process for extracting oil from the oil sands cheaply, efficiently and with less damage to the environment than conventional oil sands recovery processes, it must have seemed like a godsend for Energy Unlimited. Just add money, stir and presto—leap-frog past the competition in the oil sands.

Still, she had an uneasy feeling about Connor Donnelly. She called in a few favors from some of the people in the intelligence community with whom she still kept in touch and hit pay dirt. He was thirty-six years old, never married, possessed a degree in linguistics and political science from Yale University and had been an intelligence operative in his twenties.

The intelligence operative bit made her nervous. He'd know exactly how to extract information from people. A killer. Her lips quirked—he'd probably only killed people while he worked as a CIA operative, but still... Alyssa chewed on her lip again.

An involuntary shiver of dread peeled up her back, her hackles rising. Operatives. Charming. Manipulative. Without conscience. Cold as sharks, with about the same amount of compassion and humanity. She would need to find a way around him if she wanted to find what association, if any, he had with her hacker. Unfortunately, he probably wouldn't miss a lot of what went on around him.

Alyssa's stomach knotted tighter—she thought she'd left the world of covert operations behind her, only to be sucked back into it. She couldn't bring herself to tell Grand about any of it. He was getting old and he would just worry. She could worry just fine all by herself.

Alyssa jerked in her shoes as the cabin intercom crackled unexpectedly to life. "We're just waiting for clearance from the tower to take off, Ms. Tiernan. I expect our flying time to be approximately two-and-a-half hours at an altitude of thirty-two thousand feet," the pilot drawled with a Texas accent. "Nothing to worry about—forecasts say that we have clear skies all the way. You can help yourself to whatever's in the fridge, but wait 'til I say it's okay to unbuckle your seat belt."

"No problem," she muttered to herself. She doubted that she would take her seat belt off, period. "Why should I worry about being thirty-two thousand bloody feet above the planet?"

A leggy, blonde flight attendant in a fitted blue blazer with a thigh-high skirt and stilettos opened the cockpit door and stepped in to the main cabin. Smiling, she said, "I'm Krista. Is there anything I can do for you before we take off, hon?" The woman spoke with a slight Texas drawl as well.

"Aside from getting me off this plane, nothing at all, *hon*." Alyssa eyed the gorgeous woman speculatively. Connor Donnelly apparently liked beautiful, dumb women. She caught herself. Judging someone by her appearance snapped at her conscience. The woman could be perfectly intelligent. "Sorry, I'm a bit edgy. I don't particularly like flying."

"Well, don't you worry now, hon, we've got the best pilot in Colorado flying us today. He'll take us up and put us down as soft as a feather," Krista said, her voice exuded calm and serenity. "Why don't I get you a drink to calm your nerves? What would you like, scotch? Gin? Beer? Wine? We've even got Valium. You name it, we've got it."

"Actually, do you have any herbal tea? I'm not really up to alcohol right now."

"Sure thing. Tea's coming up."

The Gulfstream started to taxi down the airstrip. "Hon, I'll get the tea after take off. Right now, we need to belt up for takeoff." Krista settled into the jump seat by the exit door and fastened the seat belt. "Tell me a little about yourself."

As promised, the takeoff was feather soft, there was little turbulence, the flight took two-and-a-half hours and the landing was picture-perfect. Alyssa sighed in relief as the jet taxied to a stop. Slowly, she unbuckled her seat belt and stood, happy to be on solid ground again.

She ran her hands down over her form-fitting ruby-red turtleneck sweater and smoothed her hands over her jeans-clad hips. Her fingers wouldn't stay still, at least not steadily, so she ran her hands through her unfamiliar-feeling hair—she'd straightened her wavy locks into a flat style before leaving for the airport. She'd even applied makeup, an unusual step for her. She prayed that Donnelly would write her off as an old man's pampered, brainless granddaughter.

I should have dressed sexier to enhance the brainless effect. Oh well. She sighed—she really needed to think of these things in advance.

Krista opened the door and it unfolded in slow motion into a staircase to softly touch the ground. "It's been a pleasure to meet you, Alyssa. There's a limousine waiting for you that will take you to the Donnelly compound."

"The Donnelly compound? I, uh, thought I was going to a hotel or something," Alyssa said in a studied, casual tone of voice. *Am I going to be left alone with a man I think of as an enemy at worst and a conscienceless shark at best?* "Is that a normal arrangement for business guests of the Donnellys?"

"Depends. Some stay with the Donnellys, some stay at hotels. Quite honestly, honey," Krista said with a shrewd look in her eye, "you have nothing to worry about. The Donnellys don't get a lot of female business guests and they probably feel responsible for you."

"Responsible for me? Why?" Alyssa asked. She knew she could take care of herself in most situations. During the six years she'd spent at CSIS, she had taken various physical combat classes as well as weapons training. It hadn't been required, but she felt better knowing she could defend herself.

"I think it's sort of a chivalry thing. A 'women are to be protected' idea. But I'm not entirely sure. I only know that Mr. Donnelly has readied one of the guest cottages in the compound for you. Really, honey, you have nothing to worry about, he's a perfect gentleman." Krista read her tension very accurately. Too accurately. If this woman could read her so well, then to Connor Donnelly, she would be an open book, and that was the last thing she wanted.

"You're right, of course. I think it's just the stress of the flight that's getting to me," Alyssa said with as much nonchalance as she could muster. Krista seemed satisfied with the answer, nodding sympathetically.

"Your luggage will be taken to the compound and settled into your cottage. I suspect that Mr. Donnelly will greet you there. And welcome to Colorado. I'll probably see you here when you leave," Krista said.

Alyssa thanked Krista, stepped out of the jet, looked around and turned back to her. "Where are we anyway?"

Krista gave a short laugh. "This is the Donnellys' private airstrip. You'll be in the compound in thirty minutes."

"Oh, okay…uh, I'll see you later, I guess."

Alyssa turned around to tread carefully down the stairs to the tarmac and hurried toward the waiting limousine. An older man, dressed in a blue uniform, stepped out of the car to meet her. His stark white hair contrasted brightly with the dark green trees surrounding the landing strip. He opened one of the rear doors.

"Welcome to Colorado, Ms. Tiernan. My name is William. I'm here to take you to the compound." He gave her a warm smile, showing off his pearly white dentures.

"Thank you, William. Pleased to meet you. It's absolutely gorgeous here." She breathed in the crisp pine scent of the mountain air. It invigorated her, clearing out the cobwebs from the flight. She loved the mountains—pristine and fresh. She ducked her head to get into the limousine and slid over the black leather seat to sit in the middle of the car. William closed the door behind her.

William walked back to the driver's side door, opened it and slid in. "Have you been to Colorado before, Miss?" He placed the vehicle in gear and rumbled off the tarmac.

"No, this is my first time. I hadn't realized how similar Alberta and Colorado are, scenery-wise anyway."

As they drove along the steep road, Alyssa slid over to the right side of the car to gaze out the window as they ascended the mountain. The evening twilight filtered down through the pine trees and a light breeze gently rocked the majestic giants.

"This road must be really dangerous in the winter, William. How long have the Donnellys lived up here?" Alyssa asked.

"Well, young lady, they built the compound about four years ago. Mr. Donnelly, Connor, that is, got his company up and running successfully and they bought a side of the mountain and started building. I think you'll like it. It's a chalet-style house with a lake and a couple of guest cottages. Very cozy."

"Does the entire Donnelly family live there?"

"Mr. Donnelly's parents do a lot of traveling now that they're retired, but their main base of operations is the compound. They own a couple of homes scattered around the world. The boys mainly stay at the compound when they're in the country. It doesn't make a lot of sense of have a home and only be there for a few months of the year. But the family is rarely all together in one place these days."

"How do you like working for them?" Alyssa asked, curious. How people treated their employees, more often than not, indicated what kind of people they were.

"It's probably the best job I've ever had. It's like a big family. Mr. Donnelly knows the first and last names of all two hundred people that work for him, plus their families.

"Every year, the company throws a big bash for all the employees and the clients. They hire a band—everyone dances, has a little bit to drink, socializes and relaxes. It happens at the compound every year. My wife and I come to see the young folks have fun and have a little fun ourselves," William enthused. He looked in the rearview mirror and caught her eye. "In fact, it's coming up this weekend. Maybe you'll be here to see it yourself."

"Well, I don't really know how long I'll be here. I'm just taking a look at the computer systems." It sounded like fun, provided the Donnellys weren't her hackers. Alyssa's research into the Donnelly clan didn't exactly match up to William's glowing description of them. She would find out soon enough the truth regarding the Donnellys.

Twenty minutes later, William slowed down and took a right hand turn onto a gravel road. He drove for fifty yards before coming to a large wrought iron gate set into a six-foot stone-wall that disappeared into the woods on either side. An intercom and pass-card reader had been set into the stone beside the gate.

William took out a card and waved it near the reader. The imposing gate slowly swung open, moving without a sound on well-oiled hinges. William replaced the card in the driver's side sun visor and drove into the compound.

Enormous pine and spruce trees lined the driveway. A little further in, the trees had been cut down and in a clearing stood a large chalet and two smaller chalets to the right of it, arranged prettily around a small lake. Three stories high, the primary chalet's windows reached up from the first floor to the top floor, overlooking the lake a short distance away. She could see a small dock jutting out into the water.

The lake, more of a pond really, looked like a private swimming hole. Massive pines stood guard by the lake, some precariously dipping their toes into the darkly glimmering water. A riot of colorful flowers in meticulously nurtured beds and large expanses of emerald green grass surrounded the chalets. Stone paths led between them.

It's like a miniature Christmas village, mused Alyssa. A six-car garage sat off to the far left of the clearing and a curved gravel driveway led to the side of the big house. William stopped beside the house.

He looked back over his shoulder at Alyssa, his eyes twinkling. "What do you think of it?"

"It's beautiful. I've never seen anything quite like it," she answered truthfully. She could only imagine living in a place like this alpine fairy-tale.

William got out of the limo and ambled over to open her door. Alyssa carefully stepped out of the car and stood up. As she did, she noticed a large man standing beside the house, studying her carefully. William closed the car door behind her and the large man with the quiet, measuring eyes walked toward her.

The tall man moved like a large mountain lion, silent, muscular and confident. As he drew near, she looked straight into his ice blue eyes. A shock rippled down her spine and she stiffened in surprise, aware of the butterflies fluttering in her gut. *What the hell was that?* Confused, her gaze bolted to her feet to compose herself. At thirty years of age, she had never felt anything like *that* before. A second later, she lifted her eyes to his face and watched him approach.

Alyssa couldn't quite decipher the look on his face. He looked somewhat taken aback by her appearance—positively or negatively, she couldn't tell at first glance. But as he came closer, one thing became very obvious to her—he liked what he saw.

Connor had been waiting for Alyssa to arrive. He was surprised, to say the least. None of the technical people, or techies, that worked for him looked like she did. Well, first of all, most of them were men, and second, she was about five-foot-five, with a well-proportioned and shapely hourglass figure.

He didn't like bony women. He wanted a woman to look like a woman and this one definitely fit the description. He'd actually had to remind himself to go and greet her. One look at her had been enough to make every male neuron in his brain spontaneously combust.

At any other time and place, he would not have thought that the woman standing beside his house would have had anything to do with computers, let alone be a top-notch technology security expert. The word "geek" and this woman did not compute.

Appearances are deceiving, he reminded himself as he approached. He got about ten feet from her when their eyes locked. He saw her eyes widen fractionally before she broke eye contact and looked down momentarily before suddenly looking back up again, her hazel-green eyes neutral.

"Ms. Tiernan, I'm Connor Donnelly, you can call me Connor. It's a pleasure to have you here." Connor held out his hand and smiled.

Connor noticed that Alyssa hesitated for a split second before extending her hand to grasp his and her hand trembled almost imperceptibly, her face a polite mask. "Mr. Donnelly, uh, Connor, it's a pleasure to be here. You have a lovely home. But it wasn't really necessary to put me up here. I would have been quite comfortable in a hotel."

"Nonsense. I promised your grandfather I would take care of you and that's what I intend to do." He looked at William and smiled. "Could you take Ms. Tiernan's luggage and put it into her cottage? I'll take it from here. Thank you, William."

William nodded at Connor, smiled at Alyssa and climbed back into the car. He drove around them and headed for one of the smaller chalets. Connor came up beside Alyssa and, with a light hand guiding her elbow, walked toward the front of the main house.

"You…you can call me Alyssa," she said breathlessly, the words spilling out as she twisted her hands together into a knot.

Connor gave her a sidelong glance and narrowly avoided raising a quizzical eyebrow at her. *Hmmm, something's wrong with this picture—gorgeous woman who looks like she wants to be anywhere but here with me.* He shrugged it off. Any number of things could be the problem—fatigue, hereditary insanity, who knew? "Alyssa, then," he said gently. "You must be tired after your flight. It's nearly eight. It's too bad you couldn't make it until late in the day. Why was it that you couldn't come earlier?"

"I was in rehearsal until late afternoon."

"That's right, your grandfather mentioned that to me yesterday," he said. It hadn't slipped his mind—he had been casting about for a topic to ease the tension vibrating around her. "Your grandfather tells me that you're quite talented."

"My grandfather is overly enthusiastic," she said with a lopsided grin. "I could dance down the streets of Calgary with a bucket over my head and he'd still say it was wonderful." Taking a deep breath, she added, "I hope that you don't mind my being here to look at your systems. Grand is extremely cautious about anything that comes into contact with his stuff."

"No, of course not. I hope our security will stand up to whatever you can throw at it. We have some very good people," Connor said with pride. "But I guess we'll see tomorrow when we go down to headquarters. I understand you have specialized experience with security systems."

"Well, I do what I can," Alyssa said breezily as they trekked up the gravel path to the guest chalet nearest the main house. Connor released Alyssa's elbow and stepped up to the front door of the cottage. "Here we are. I hope you'll be comfortable." Opening the door, he reached around the door frame and flicked the light switch on. He stepped back and motioned for her to enter the cottage.

Alyssa stepped into the house and Connor followed closely behind. Her luggage already stood beside the door. Connor watched Alyssa as her eyes scanned the open-concept living area, pausing at the view of the lake framed in the floor-to-ceiling windows before sliding to the stone fireplace.

The softly burnished pine plank flooring glowed in the dwindling sunlight. Rustically furnished, the chalet was a warm, inviting retreat. At the far end of the cottage was a gleaming, black, baby grand piano. He smiled when he heard her gasp—her eyes had found the instrument.

"Do you always have a piano in here?" she asked, her eyes wide.

"No, but I thought that you might enjoy playing while you're here. One of my younger brothers plays a little piano, but mostly we only use it when we have dinner parties and hire a pianist to play. I've just had it tuned. Do you like it?" Connor asked.

Alyssa stared at the instrument, as if unsure how to react. "It's beautiful," she said finally before giving him a sidelong glance, biting one edge of her full bottom lip. Connor felt himself slip a little emotionally—she was absolutely adorable. "Do you mind if I give it a whirl?"

"Go ahead." Connor felt some of the tension drain away from her. Definitely the right thing to put her at ease. He gave himself a mental pat on the back.

Alyssa walked with fluid grace across the polished wood floors toward the piano while Connor watched in appreciation as her hips swayed. An hourglass figure—his mouth almost watered, pulled into the orbit of her femininity. She ran her long fingers lovingly along the piano's curved black side and drew out the bench. Sliding onto it, she shook her hands out and placed her fingers lightly on the keys. Closing her eyes, she took a breath and slowly released it.

Alyssa began to play the haunting strains of the adagio from Beethoven's Moonlight Sonata. As her head tipped slowly from side to side in time with the music, Connor saw the tension in her body release as she drifted into the music, note by note. She swayed faintly in time with the waves of poetry emanating from the taut strings of the instrument.

She ended the piece with a sigh, her head tipped back, eyes closed. She took a deep breath and slowly opened her eyes, pupils dilated. She almost seemed surprised to see Connor still there, staring at her.

"It's a lovely instrument," Alyssa said in a husky voice. She flushed slightly before she cleared her throat and said in a more normal tone of voice, "It was very nice of you to arrange for it to be here."

"That was amazing," Connor responded in a level tone of voice as he stared at her, unsure that the woman in front of him now was the same person he'd met not fifteen minutes earlier. His fingers itched to grab her and stroke her lovely body.

His gaze flicked to the slim digits that had so recently caressed the piano keys. Connor managed to tear his eyes away from her graceful fingers. He could only imagine what it would feel like to have those hands play *him* like an instrument. He could feel himself harden. *Stupid, get your mind off your dick already.* He had the feeling that if she knew about the detour his mind and body had followed, she would turn tail and run. And he couldn't afford for that to happen.

Alyssa stared back at him for a few seconds before she could make her jumbled thoughts behave and she could form words. "Um, sorry, I have a tendency to forget myself when I'm playing." Embarrassed by her side trip to nirvana, her face flamed with heat while Connor gazed at her as if she had sprouted another head. *Great, just great.*

She rose smoothly from the bench and pushed it back into place. Running her hands down her waist and hips, she smiled briefly at Connor, a pretty flush coloring her formerly pale cheeks. Her gaze dropped to the floor before looking him in the eye again, seeming shy. "You know, I've had, um, a *really* long day. I know it's early and this is a bit rude, but all I want to do is climb into a hot bath and then go to bed. Would you mind?"

Connor hesitated before answering, his gaze sweeping over her before returning to her eyes. She managed to suppress a shudder that threatened to rack her body. *Oh Mama!*

"No, no. Don't worry about it. I'll just quickly show you the rest of the cottage," he said, waving his hand vaguely, gesturing to the rest of the bungalow. "It's a single story and there are two bedrooms at the back, looking out into the woods. There is a bathroom attached to each of the bedrooms."

He walked toward the front door and picked up her luggage with ease. Alyssa could barely keep her mouth from dropping open—she'd had problems simply dragging the large suitcase to the airport limo in Calgary. And here he was, handling her luggage like it weighed as much as a pillow.

"The bedroom has been made up for you. I'll just show you where you'll be," he said, gesturing with the suitcase as he strode to the back of the chalet where he paused and threw a curiously blank look at her.

"Thank you." Alyssa sidled around his bulk and, at his urging, down the hall to the last room. Keenly aware of how silently he moved behind her, she suddenly felt pint-sized—he was so, well…large. She opened the door and walked in.

The bedroom had a rustic charm that matched the rest of the chalet. Sliding glass doors on the far side of the room led out to a small patio with a fountain, bistro-style table and chairs. Beside the entrance to the bedroom and to Alyssa's right was another door that led to an adjoining bathroom.

In the bedroom, a plaid coverlet lay over the huge king size bed. A clear-stained cherry wood chest of drawers with a matching mirror stood across from the bed. A full-length chevalier mirror stood beside the chest of drawers. He obviously had a thing for mirrors, she thought inanely, even as a flash of heat rocketed through her body.

An image popped into her head unbidden. Her and Connor, in front of a mirror, making love, driven by primal needs, wild and desperate. She shook her head to clear the vision. God help her, she was being turned on by *mirrors*. Or, more accurately, by the combination of Connor and mirrors. She'd never even looked askance at a mirror before now.

As Connor moved past her into the room, he brushed her shoulder with his arm, sending another shock of electricity through her flesh. Perplexed by her reaction to him, she stared at his back, wide-eyed, as he placed her luggage on the valet stand and crossed over to a table to deposit her laptop computer case. She managed to plaster a neutral look on her face just before he turned toward her.

"Is this okay?" Connor asked. His smooth, rich voice coated her stretched nerves like warm honey.

"Perfect," Alyssa replied, continuing to glue a smile on her face.

Connor smiled back at her. "Just one more thing. It's unlikely that you'll need it. We've never had any problems here. But I've had panic buttons installed in the cottage."

"Panic buttons?"

"Yes, there's one just to the left of the bed on the wall. See there? It looks like a little red doorbell," Connor explained, pointing at the button. "There's also one above the piano on the wall in the great room. If there's trouble and you need help, just press one of these buttons and an alarm will sound in the main house. Someone will come out to check on you right away."

"Trouble? What kind of trouble would happen here? It seems very safe." Alyssa cocked to head to one side in puzzlement...Oh, right—a former intelligence agent would be paranoid about safety.

"Oh, it *is* safe. We just like to make sure it stays that way. And one last thing." Connor presented a key to her. "This is for you. Just remember to lock up at night and before you leave the compound."

"Thank you." Alyssa inwardly shrugged. Extra security certainly couldn't hurt.

"I'll come get you tomorrow morning around nine and take you down to headquarters. It's at the base of the mountain. It's about a thirty minute drive from here." Connor glanced around the room and then looked back at her. His face unreadable, he asked politely, "Can I get you anything else before I leave?"

"No, I think I have everything I need, thank you," Alyssa said. "Everything looks absolutely lovely."

"Well, then, I guess I'll see you tomorrow morning," Connor said as he moved toward the bedroom door. Alyssa followed him down the hall and to the front door. She couldn't help but watch him as he walked. He moved so gracefully, with such assurance and power in his gait. He also had a cute butt and she wouldn't have minded walking behind him all day.

"Sleep well, Alyssa, and welcome to Colorado," Connor said, turning around at the door.

"I will. You too. Thank you," Alyssa repeated.

"Do all Canadians say 'thank you' so much?" Connor asked, a teasing note in his voice.

Alyssa snorted and laughed. "Probably. It's a very Canadian thing to do. It would be sacrilege to deviate from the norm," she said, smiling at him openly for the first time.

Smiling back at her, he said "Goodnight, Alyssa. Remember to lock up."

"Goodnight, Connor. I will." She bit her tongue on the "thank you" that threatened to come out.

Alyssa closed the door behind him after he left. She didn't hear him crunch down the path until she slid the deadbolt on the door home.

As he strode away from the guesthouse, Connor reflected that he had not expected Alyssa Tiernan. He hadn't expected to find her so attractive. He hadn't expected to feel this fierce physical pull toward her.

When she had been playing the piano so passionately, he'd had a nearly overwhelming urge to sink his fingers into her silky hair, slowly make his way down to the spot just behind her right ear, down to her neck, to her breasts and even further and make her respond to him the way she responded to the music. Just thinking about it now tightened the fit of his trousers.

Get a hold of yourself, man, you have to work with this woman. He laughed. Might that be the relief he needed? His aching dick, however, refused to listen to cold reason—it wanted to be held. Tightly. Wetly. Skin to skin. He shook his head to clear from his mind the erotic image of what it would be like to sink into her honeyed warmth. *Maybe a swim in the lake would help.* Icy water sounded like the perfect prescription for his current condition.

Connor jogged down to the small dock and started peeling off his clothes. Darkness had fallen and no one else was in the compound now, anyway, except for Alyssa, but she had already gone to bed. Once undressed, he dove straight into the lake, not bothering to dip in a toe to test the temperature.

The frigid water shocked his body and he broke the surface of the water, gasping. Well, at least "Dick" has retreated like a frightened turtle, he thought grimly, treading water. The coldness of the lake clawed at him. A little more than one hundred yards in length, the pond provided enough space for a decent swim.

He swam two complete laps of the lake before muscling his naked body up onto the dock, shivering with cold. As he bent down to grab his pants, something caught his eye. He would have sworn that the drapes on a window of the guest chalet shifted slightly, as if someone had been watching his nude performance. And been caught in the act.

He managed to suppress a smile. This will work nicely, he decided as he leisurely pulled on his clothes despite the shivering. Baiting the hook was always the first step.

As soon as Connor had left the guesthouse, Alyssa had locked the door behind him and turned off the lights in the great room. She wasn't sure what had made her do it. Instead of returning to the bedroom, she'd lifted a bit of curtain on the front window to watch as he walked away. She had been more than a little surprised when he jogged to the dock, doffed his clothes and dived into the lake.

She'd been unable to pull herself away from the window, not during his swim and certainly not after. That was, not until he lifted his head and stared at the cottage. Rattled, she'd dropped the curtain with a start, fully aware that her reaction resembled that of a fifteen-year-old girl in a girls-only Catholic school—naked eye-candy had been there for the taking, er, looking. And so she had looked. Long.

She covered her eyes with her hands, but that only made it worse—she could still see him in her mind.

Oh hell.

Beautifully built, Connor's lean, muscular and powerful physique must have caused more than one woman to throw herself at him. Alyssa shook herself. She wasn't here to find a man. He could even be the enemy, for God's sake. *Stop letting your hormones do your thinking for you,* she thought disgustedly, rolling her eyes.

As her heartbeat settled down, exhaustion reasserted itself and sucked remorselessly on her body. She decided against doing laps in the enormous tub and opted for the bed instead. Stretching, she walked back to her room, slipped off her clothing, left it piled on the floor and climbed naked into the enormous bed. She felt lost in the wide expanse.

Closing her eyes, she sighed deeply and consciousness eased away from her.

* * * * *

On the other side of the world in Saudi Arabia, a man in his fifties tried to wait patiently for the battered telephone to ring. He had waited all morning. *Insh'Allah,* the man would call him soon. He was tired of waiting. But he supposed that Allah, the all merciful, the all knowing, would make His plans known to him soon enough. The time had come for the despoilers of Islam to be judged as Evil and destroyed. But, he shrugged—he was a simple soldier in Allah's divine army. His feelings and thoughts did not matter.

Getting up from the rickety chair, he walked over to the stove where sweet tea simmered. He poured the steaming liquid into a time-etched glass tumbler and went to sit back down by his window, looking out onto the dusty courtyard. Once, before World War Two, his family had been great, even feared by others. Now they were reduced to this state of poverty.

He thought about the history of his sacred country. Since the early part of the twentieth century, the Saudi government courted the spoiled westerners, especially the Americans, with crude oil. The Saudi Royal family, who ran the government, tried to take the soul, the blood, of Arabia and sell it off to the Americans. The blasphemers contaminated Saudi Arabia. The government must be destroyed. The government must be replaced with righteous men who would know how to deal with the Americans. The government made him sick.

The ancient phone croaked. He snatched the phone and listened intently. "When do you want this done?" he asked.

"Tonight. You have all the equipment and instructions. You will set the charges as discussed," the second man said, his Arabic containing the whisper of an American accent.

"I am ready to die. I am thankful to be in Allah's service at last. I will not fail."

"Allah waits for his faithful with open arms. He will surely gather you to his bosom. You will be in paradise forever," the caller assured the Arab and the telephone went dead.

Chapter Three

At precisely nine the next morning, Alyssa heard a knock at the front door and she felt her heart thud frantically in her chest. Well, at least he's punctual, she thought uneasily. She hoped like hell that he hadn't seen her watching him the night before. *Oh God, what if he had?* She couldn't deal with this kind of guilt first thing in the morning.

She had barely managed to get up twenty minutes earlier, take a quick shower and throw on some jeans and a form-fitting olive green tee shirt. She'd fallen asleep the previous night as soon as her eyes had closed. Normally, in a strange bed it took her forever to get to sleep. Maybe the mountain air did it. She stumbled toward the door and fumbled with the lock.

Finally able to manipulate the mechanism, she opened the door to find Connor standing there in faded blue jeans and a white tee shirt, smiling brightly at her. "Good morning!" Connor said as he gave her a quick once-over and smiled a bit more broadly. "Not a morning person?"

Damn, did he know? He looked so…so…she couldn't place the look exactly, but if she had to, she would have guessed that he looked smug. Her stomach knotted into a great big bow. She smoothed one hand over her hair self-consciously.

"No. Not a morning person. Give me another hour and I'll start functioning. Oh, right, uh, good morning. Come on in. Can I get you some coffee?" she said, stepping back into the hallway, waving him in lazily. He accepted the negligent invitation and stepped inside.

"No thanks. Are you ready to go?"

"Actually, I thought I'd try running a test from here first," Alyssa said slowly.

"From here? Why?" Connor asked, his eyebrows scrunching a little, leaving a little furrow between them. She had a sudden urge to smooth out the line with a fingertip, but she clenched her hand at her side to ride out the impulse.

"Well, I want to try to break into your computer system from outside your offices. And here is as good a place as any. I didn't want to do anything until you were here and I got your okay. And since you're here and I'm here and my computer is set up over there..." Alyssa drifted over to the sunny desk where her laptop sat humming happily. She looked back over her shoulder. "Do you mind?"

"Don't see why not. Just out of curiosity, have you tried hacking into the system before?" Connor asked with a note of doubt in his voice.

Alyssa smiled thinly at him. "*No,* I have not *hacked* into your system *before*. If at all possible, I try to avoid computers." She paused before adding tiredly, "If you don't trust me, I can go back to Calgary."

"Sorry, sorry." Connor held up both hands in a placating gesture. "I didn't mean to insult you. Touchy in the morning, aren't you?"

"I just don't deal well with people in the morning. Let's just do this, okay?" Alyssa turned back to the computer, her annoyance in direct proportion to her guilt at having obtained his personal profile, unbeknownst to him.

She thought she heard him mutter something under his breath and she turned back to him, eyebrows raised. "Sorry, what did you say?"

"Uh," he asked casually, "how long do you think it will take?"

Her mouth twisted and she glared at him for a moment—he'd said something else and didn't want to repeat it. *Fine. Just fine.* She probably didn't want to hear the original version either. "Depends on your system. It can take seconds or it can take minutes, hours or days. Most systems have really pathetic security. And contrary to what a lot of people believe, any computer system can be hacked. It just takes skill, knowledge and patience." Alyssa plopped down in front of the computer and started typing. "Let's just see how it goes."

Very aware of Connor watching her, Alyssa brought up Energy Unlimited's website and fed a CD into the laptop. "I wrote a program a while back, I call it the 'Hack Master'. Corny, I know, but it rolls through an extensive algorithm to gain access to a system. Most of the time, it takes about two minutes to hack into someone's system. I'm just going to set it up now."

Alyssa stared at the screen and typed a few more gibberish commands. "Okay, the time is 9:07 am exactly and I'm starting it....now. Now we wait and see." Alyssa leaned back in her chair. She wanted to apologize for being crabby earlier, but he would probably take it as a sign of weakness. The apology, not the crabbiness.

"I think I will have that cup of coffee. No, don't get up, I'll get it myself," Connor said, waving her back down into her seat as she started to rise. "Can I get you a cup of coffee?"

"Uh, sure," Alyssa responded as he started to move off. "And, uh, Connor?"

"Yes?" he said coolly.

"Sorry for being so bitchy. Mornings are not good for me," Alyssa said uncomfortably, annoyed that she felt guilty about chewing on him.

"Don't worry. I don't normally accuse people I've just met of criminal activity. Let's just call it even," Connor said, his voice steady and a touch cool.

"Fair enough. I take cream and sugar."

"Cream and sugar? Oh yeah, right. Coffee's coming up." Alyssa's eyes tracked Connor, unable to help herself, while he strolled to the kitchen to the waiting coffeepot. He found two fresh mugs and poured steaming caffeine into each. He drizzled cream into one and cream and sugar into the other. Picking up the two mugs, he wandered over to the desk and put one mug down beside her.

"How does it look so far?" he asked, taking a sip of the coffee. He choked, gagged actually, and then sputtered, "Hell! This stuff is like rocket fuel. How many cups of this stuff have you had so far?"

"Oh, only two." Alyssa ignored his evaluation of her coffee-making skills—no one was forcing him to drink it. Examining the screen, she said, "Well, I've made it past your proxy server and your firewalls here and here." She pointed out the different areas of his network she had compromised so far. She typed in a few more commands and text scrolled by on the screen. After a few minutes, the scrolling stopped and the screen flickered to a halt.

Connor stared at the display, appalled, before turning his head to stare at her. "This is the secured area of the system—only a few people in the whole company have access to it. How the hell did you do that?"

Great, I've sprouted another head again. She remembered how he had looked at her the previous evening—realized now he'd watched her play the piano with a look in his eyes that'd had nothing to do with music and everything to do with attraction. She felt a warmth course through her body in a primal response and took a breath to steady herself. "To be fair, the program took seven minutes to run. Most systems roll over after two or three minutes. You've probably got better than average security on your system. Your technical people have done a reasonable job."

"Better than average. A reasonable job," he repeated dully, wincing.

"Yes. Better than average. That's nothing to be embarrassed about. However, in order for this co-venture to go through, you need to upgrade your systems," Alyssa spoke in a matter-of-fact tone of voice. Her voice softened. "Connor, you must have done a background check on me. Am I right?"

Connor hesitated before he carefully nodded and fixed his eyes on her face.

"What exactly did you find out about me?" Alyssa asked, her eyebrows furrowing slightly.

"I know you worked for CSIS for six years as a security analyst before leaving two years ago. I know the American government approached you to work for them after you left CSIS," Connor said. "That's about it."

Alyssa nodded. "Well, I guess that's true enough. " She paused. "Look, Connor, this is something I am very good at. I don't like doing it, but I can if I have to. You need to upgrade your security."

"I agree. Will you do it? I can't think of anyone better," Connor said simply.

"Me? I didn't really think that I would be down here for that long. I still have commitments to the orchestra and then there's Max." His proposal conjured up a twisted pit in her stomach, panicky that she'd have to spend more time with her would-be hacker.

"Max?" Connor echoed, sounding oddly perturbed by this piece of information. She eyed him curiously.

She rested her hands on her hips, raised an inquiring eyebrow. "My iguana. It's hard to find anyone willing to look after a lizard. People are so squeamish," Alyssa said, cocking her head to one side to gaze at him intently. She sensed something had upset him. And he'd implied *she* was moody.

"Ah, well, uh, perhaps you could speak to the orchestra and see if you could get some time off."

"It would probably take me a good month or two to set this up. I'd really have to take a close look at your system. I suppose I'd be able to swing it, though. I guess the orchestra is sort of used to me taking off at weird times, and I'm only the second pianist for them," Alyssa thought aloud. Grand really needed this to happen. Damn. She sighed, knowing she didn't have a choice. "Okay, fine. But I need to find someone who will take Max for however long I'm here."

"I'm, uh, sure I can find someone to take care of Max," he replied and then his tone became brisk, business-like. "Now, we should talk money."

"Money?" Alyssa asked, confused. "What money?"

"The money I'll pay you to fix the security," Connor said, as if explaining the concept to a very young child. He sounded more amused than condescending.

Alyssa wasn't sure if she wanted to be in Colorado for that long. She supposed that it would give her a good excuse to snoop around the Energy Unlimited computer systems, but being in close contact with Connor could be difficult.

Connor made her uncomfortable in a way she had never felt before and it scared her. Men were not her strong point. They seemed like alien beings with motivations that were entirely foreign to her. She had briefly dated two men over the six years she had worked at CSIS. She hadn't been particularly attracted to either one, but she had been naively flattered by their attentions.

One was a techie, the other an intelligence operative. They'd been more interested in using her than knowing her. The techie wanted to pick her brain and present any findings to his boss as his own ideas. The operative thought she would supply him with endless information to advance his career, despite the fact that doing so would have put Alyssa into a compromising position at work. She'd rapidly seen through both men, painfully coming to the conclusion that love and family wouldn't be in the cards for her.

It seemed that men saw things in her they didn't like. She wondered if the problem was hers or theirs. Probably hers.

Looking at Connor, she realized he attracted her at a very basic level and frightened her a little at the same time. Her choices in men to this point had been a total loss. And on top of it all, he could have been behind the attempted hacking into Grand's system. She groaned inwardly. *How do things get messed up so fast?* Apparently, the more things changed, the more they stayed the same.

Despite trying to keep her expression neutral, she saw something flare in Connor's intent eyes as he watched. With his intelligence background, he'd probably picked up on all the signals she inadvertently fired off—her slightly tensed shoulders and she conspicuously hadn't been looking him in the eye. No wonder he looked suspicious of her.

Alyssa realized that Connor was waiting for an answer. Definitely a little rattled, she said, her voice breathy and high, "Right. Why don't we talk about money later? I'll need to take a closer look at your system to determine what it'll take. I can give you an estimate once that's done."

Damn, I sound like I'm having an asthma attack. That or a fit of the vapors. How girly of me. Disgusted with herself, she barely stopped herself from whacking her forehead with her palm. Or with the nearest wall. Either would do, really.

"Okay. Fair enough. Why don't we go down to the office and I'll show you around?" Connor asked.

"Sounds good." Alyssa looked wistfully out the window at the sun-drenched sky-blue lake in front of the cottage. "Are all your spring days like this?" she asked as she shut down her laptop and got up to go.

"Only during the day. It can be very cold at night, even in midsummer. As well, being in the mountains, we can get a lot of rain during the summer because we're so high up," Connor answered.

"It's gorgeous. I've always loved the mountains. The border between Alberta and British Columbia follows the Canadian part of the Rocky Mountains. You can see the mountains from Grand's acreage. He and I used to hike in the mountains every summer before I left for college." Alyssa sighed with pleasure at the memory. She stood at the window, staring out at the lake. Connor moved to her side and gazed at the lake as well.

A minute passed before Alyssa became fully aware of his covert study of her person and she stiffened in response. He looked back to the lake. "Ready to go?" he asked casually.

"Yes," Alyssa said, relieved that he was no longer looking at her as if she was a lamb-chop and he was a hungry wolf. Nervousness made it difficult for her to think straight. Her stomach rolled, performing back flips without the benefit of a safety net. She had an urge to rest her head against his well-muscled arm and close her eyes.

Oh for God's sake, get a hold of yourself. He's beautiful, but honestly, just pull yourself together. She shouldn't have had that third cup of coffee. It was only nine twenty and she could barely see straight because the caffeine had hot-wired her for takeoff.

Alyssa turned to leave, stopping short as Connor barred her way by shifting his body in front of her escape path. She raised her eyebrows quizzically. "Is there something else?" she asked.

"No. Yes." Connor grimaced as he flip-flopped. "I was just thinking that my brother Liam should be here for your evaluation. He's the one who originally designed the security, although the techies take care of it now. It would be good for him to see how the system can be breached."

Alyssa didn't particularly want anyone hovering over her shoulder while trying to discover if these people had tried to hack her system. But she couldn't think of any plausible reason not to have his brother tag along. She tried for a casual shrug but the motion felt jerky, unnatural. "Sure. Whatever you want. Is he around?" she asked.

"Actually, he'll be back from Argentina tonight," Connor answered and then grinned. "We can explore today. I'll take you around and show you the sights and tomorrow you can start fresh. Besides, the Telluride Bluegrass Festival started yesterday. Telluride is a pretty town about an hour from here. Would you like to go?"

"This isn't a working day for you?" Alyssa asked, hoping to awaken his work ethic and settle the butterflies in her stomach at the same time.

"That's one of the perks of being the boss," Connor said, smiling. "I can make my own hours."

Alyssa couldn't see a way to gracefully decline his invitation. "Sounds good," she said, smiling as encouragingly as she could. "Is it a very large festival?"

"It's big for Telluride. People come from all over," Connor answered enthusiastically.

Connor's enthusiasm was contagious. "It sounds great." Alyssa found herself smiling back at him with genuine pleasure. Well, why not?

Fifteen minutes later, Alyssa and Connor were tucked into his arctic silver Porsche 911 Carrera Coupe, rumbling over the gravel drive toward the main gate. He glanced surreptitiously at her. Alyssa was small compared to him. He knew his big hands would encircle her waist. Her wrists and hands were petite, as were her feet. A study in contradictions.

Drop-dead gorgeous without knowing it. Smart as hell without being an egghead. Technical, yet artistic. Passionate, yet distant. Perceptive, yet unsure of herself. The women he normally dated were polished and sophisticated, always aware of who they were and what they wanted. Personally, he thought that it was all bullshit—all the pretense of perfection, but none of the substance.

Connor liked Alyssa's vulnerability. Her way of moving. The soft clipped rhythm of her speech. The razor-sharp mind. Hell, he liked the whole package. But now was not the time. She was too uncomfortable with him. He was a patient man. He could wait.

As they approached the compound's gate, Connor took out a remote control to click a button and the entranceway slowly opened to let them out. Ten minutes later, they were laughing over trying to decide whether or not Superman would kick The Flash's butt in a fight when Connor noticed something that had his old instincts kicking into high gear. In the rearview mirror, he observed an ancient gray Fiat following them too closely for safety.

Connor hadn't seen the car behind him until this moment. The hair on the back of his neck rose in response. He accelerated to put some distance between themselves and the other car, but it continued to keep pace with them. Alyssa gave him a strange look.

"Is there a problem?" she inquired, a worried note in her voice.

"No, no problem. Do you have your seat belt on?" Connor looked over at Alyssa. She had her belt on. "Good." Connor glanced in the rearview mirror.

Alyssa stared at him before she scooted down in her seat and checked the passenger side mirror to spot the gray car. "Friends of yours?"

"Not mine. I was hoping they were yours," Connor said grimly. "Just the same, I'm going to try to lose them." Memories of his former life came flooding back, but with a determined effort, he refocused his thoughts on the present.

The steep and winding road unraveled more quickly in front of the Porsche as Connor opened up the throttle as far as he dared on the treacherous road. His eyes flicked to the rearview mirror every few seconds. Their pursuers evidently had a souped-up engine under the hood of their car and easily stayed with their quarry.

Abruptly, the gray car accelerated and rammed the rear of the sports car. The impact threw Connor and Alyssa back in their seats and then forward. They were screaming toward a hairpin turn that peeled off to the right. Alyssa gasped aloud and braced her hands against the dashboard, knuckles white, fingers clawed.

The Fiat accelerated again so that the two cars ran parallel to one another. It slammed into the driver's side of the Porsche. Connor yanked the steering wheel violently to the left, smashing into the other vehicle.

Although concentrating on driving, he saw Alyssa try to get a look at the other car's occupants, but the Fiat's windows were opaque. She wouldn't be able to see anyone through the impenetrable glass.

The hairpin turn roared toward them at breakneck speed. The Porsche's brakes were four times as powerful as its massive 3.6-liter engine, so Connor knew that he would be able to cut it closer than the other car. Twenty yards from the corner, he slammed into the side of the gray car again and then stomped on the brakes.

The Fiat lost control and fishtailed wildly before hurtling off the cliff into the clear blue sky beyond. The car sailed out fifty yards before gravity took over and slammed it down onto the jagged boulders at the bottom of the canyon. The car exploded into a huge fireball, tongues of flame licking far into the air.

Connor managed to stop the Porsche a few scant feet from the edge of the cliff, the back end of the car swinging to the left a hair as the vehicle finally halted.

Noisily gulping in air, Alyssa fought with her seat belt and bolted from the car. She bent forward at the waist and put her hands on her knees, her body shuddering as she struggled to breathe.

Enraged, Connor's first thought was that someone from his past had come back for vengeance. As an operative, he'd caused many problems for many people in many countries. His second thought was that Alyssa stood beside by the car shaking violently. He tore out of his seat belt and vaulted over the hood of the car to reach her in record time.

Adrenaline blazed through his veins. Without thinking, Connor levered Alyssa up from her bent position, more roughly than he had intended. He grabbed her by the shoulders and half-frantically searched her eyes. "Are you okay?"

Alyssa looked through him, her eyes wild and unseeing. She swayed away from him.

"Alyssa, are you okay?" Connor repeated, shaking her gently.

Alyssa snapped back to reality and stared at him. "What?"

"Are you hurt?"

"N-no. W-w-what the h-hell was that?" she managed to stammer through the tremors flooding her body.

"Concentrate on breathing or you'll keel over before I can find out," Connor coaxed, his voice soft. "C'mon, in and out."

Alyssa nodded at him, but her breathing continued to be comprised of short gasps of air.

Connor had seen this reaction to fear before. Hell, the first couple of times that he had slammed headlong into an adrenaline rush hadn't been any easier for him than it was for her right now.

Connor slipped an arm around her waist. She flinched once, but didn't resist the contact. From experience, he knew she was probably starting to feel lightheaded from the buildup of carbon dioxide in her blood attributable to her hyperventilating. Connor inched her close to his body, hoping to calm her. She smelled faintly of vanilla. He breathed her scent in deeply, comforting himself as well. She was unhurt.

Connor used his other hand to lightly stroke her shimmering hair and her shaking back. Slowly and methodically. Again and again. Gradually, Alyssa relaxed into him, something he relished more than he should have, given they had a working relationship. She laid her cheek against his chest with her hands rested lightly at his waist. He enjoyed holding her. She fit him nicely. He wondered how long she would let him hold her.

Probably not long enough.

Eyes closed, Alyssa felt Connor's heart thud in a measured beat against her cheek. His muscular body, his strong arms felt wonderful around her. Somehow, it felt…right, as if she belonged in those arms. She snuggled in closer to his warmth without thought and he tightened his arms around her.

Slowly, Alyssa returned to herself. The tremors faded, although she still felt a bit shaky. She was finally able to take a full breath of air and steady herself even more. It felt so good, just standing here, having him touch her. It had been so long since a man had touched her so…gently. Actually, no man had ever touched her like this, so profoundly soothing.

The soothing feeling, however, started to change, morphing into something…else. Too late, she recognized the sensation and stiffened in his arms.

Alyssa slowly backed away from Connor, embarrassment caused heat to rise in her face. His hands dropped slowly from her body. "Sorry, I, uh…sorry. I didn't mean… I hope I didn't…." She couldn't even look him in the eye. Coming apart like that. Her body responding to him so quickly, so completely. She didn't want to show weakness. Especially to a man she wasn't sure she could trust not to use it against her.

Connor manacled her right wrist gently with his left hand, stopping her retreat, placed his right hand under her chin and tenderly tipped her chin up to look into her eyes. "You have nothing to be sorry about. This was scary. No one could have done any better."

"You did better than I did," Alyssa retorted, mortified to feel her face flame even hotter—she probably looked like a Macintosh apple. She hoped he didn't realize that her physical response to him had been sexual. And her acting sucked, so with her luck, her reaction was probably emblazoned across her face like a road sign.

Sin City – 1 mile.

Lovely.

"I've also hit the wall many more times than most. I've got more experience in handling the effects of adrenaline overload," Connor said as he watched Alyssa closely. "You have nothing to fear from me, Alyssa. Nothing," he emphasized. "It's over now."

"Is it? Is it really?" Alyssa said, her voice rising in volume, embarrassment pushed aside. She looked over at the smoking wreckage of the car that nearly killed them. "Do you know who the hell that was?" she almost yelled, pointing wildly into the canyon. "Because I sure as hell don't!"

"No, not yet," Connor said calmly. "But I will."

Alyssa stared at Connor. Blood pounded through her head, roared in her ears. The initial jolt of terror and weakness had passed, leaving a cold fury in its wake. Connor studied her for a minute before taking out his cell phone and making a call to the local police. He didn't take his eyes off her during the call.

Connor pressed the End button on the cell phone and flipped it closed with one hand.

"The police will be here in about twenty minutes," Connor informed her.

Arms wrapped around her body, Alyssa nodded briefly and turned toward the canyon to gaze at the smoldering wreckage. Her mind worked furiously. She wanted to examine the other car and she didn't think that the police would let her near it once they arrived. With a backward glance at Connor, she carefully baby-stepped to the edge of the precipice and looked down.

This is doable.

Before he could fully react, as she had intended, Alyssa sat down with her legs dangling off the precipice and slipped out of sight. "Hey! What do you think you're doing?" Connor skidded to a halt on his knees by the edge to peer down at her.

"I'm going to take a look," Alyssa responded as she balanced against a large boulder under the edge of the drop-off. She looked down for her next move, peering under her arm at the rocks below.

"A look? Has anyone ever told you that you're insane? What do you think you'll find when you get down there?" Connor inquired, his voice reverberated with a hint of temper.

"Okay, in order then. Yes, a look. And yes, someone has. And lastly, I don't know. When I see it, I'll know it," Alyssa responded with exaggerated patience, looking up at him. "You can either stay up there and bitch about it or you can come down with me. Take your pick." Alyssa switched her attention back to the task at hand. She proceeded to delicately pick her way through the boulders and debris strewn over the steep slope.

"Women!" Connor muttered loudly enough for Alyssa to hear. She looked up to see him staring at her for a moment before he lowered himself over the edge and followed her down.

It took twenty minutes of concentrated effort to reach the car. Alyssa and Connor were both breathing heavily from the exertion.

The car lay on its left side, the nose propped up on a huge boulder, gently roasting in the yellow flames that licked at it ravenously. Black smoke plumed upward to the sky. Alyssa walked around the car in a wide circle, searching the surrounding ground for any clues as to the reason for the attack. Connor followed suit and circled around in the opposite direction around the car. The bodies of two people, now charred husks, toasted in the burning hunk of twisted metal. Ick!

Definitely dead.

"Do you see anything?" Alyssa asked, standing with arms crossed, surveying the wreckage.

"*No,*" Connor said, biting out the word.

Alyssa overlooked his tone and threw another question at him. "Do you have any idea why someone would want to run you off the road?"

"As I recall, you were in the car with me. Do you have any idea why someone would want to run *you* off the road?" Connor snapped.

"I'm not the one who used to work black ops for the government."

Connor's head whipped around. "What the *hell* do you know about that?"

Alyssa ignored his question. She had only guessed that he had been involved in black ops, but his reaction confirmed her suspicions. "What do you take me for? I didn't just fall off the turnip truck. Did you really think I'd come down here without first checking you out?" Alyssa flung back at him.

"You know *nothing,* lady. Absolutely *nothing,*" Connor growled through tightly clenched teeth.

"Oh, nothing, is it? I should have known. Every single person I've known to be some sort of covert agent for any government is, without exception, cold, calculating, merciless, a liar, a manipulator and totally amoral!" As soon as the words were out of her mouth, Alyssa wanted to whack her head against the nearest boulder—there were plenty to pick from. She closed her eyes and silently swore. *Shit. Sure, just alienate the guy who is helping to save Grand's company. That'll help the situation lots.*

Alyssa opened her eyes and looked up into the air above her head. She took a deep breath to calm herself. "Look," she said in a more conciliatory tone, "I'm sorry. That was way out of line. I shouldn't have said it. All I was trying to get at is I can't think of a reason why someone would come after *me*. The only thing that makes sense is someone going after *you*."

Connor breathed heavily, trying to contain his emotions as he stared at Alyssa out of half-closed eyes. He'd never experience this particular combination of emotions before—royally pissed and totally aroused. He silently cursed himself, unsure of what to do about it. Back in the day, this would never have happened. He had always been in control during his operations and the realization that he wasn't in absolute control now gave him an unpleasant jolt.

Her eyes glowed in the sunlight. Her full, pink lips tempted him to taste them. The skeins of her chestnut hair danced softly in the light breeze. He had an overwhelming urge to grab her and kiss her to within an inch of her life. His fingers twitched as he overrode the impulse to touch her. *Hell*. He was thinking with the little head instead of the big head. Thinking with the little head *always* led to trouble.

He wanted this trouble.

"Connor! What the hell do you think you're doing down there, buddy?" A voice boomed from a bullhorn up on the road, the owner of the voice clearly unimpressed.

Connor welcomed the distraction. He had nearly done something really dumb. He took a step away from Alyssa to focus on the person calling down to him. Roy Jenkins. The local sheriff.

"Just taking a look, Roy," Connor shouted to the man. "We're coming back now."

Connor turned back toward Alyssa. "This discussion is *not* over." He took Alyssa's left arm firmly by the elbow. "Let's go."

Alyssa looked down at his hand as if it were a snake slithering up her arm. Very quietly, with a deadly calm, she spoke softly, emphasizing each word. "I am perfectly capable of climbing back up to the road. If I need your help, *I'll* let you know. Remove. Your. Hand. Now." Her lips trembled as she shifted her body into a more defensive stance.

Connor saw the fear and the anger in her face and recognized the danger in her stance. *What the hell had happened to her?* Very carefully, Connor lifted his hand from her arm and slowly backed away a couple of steps, hands held up at the elbows. She looked like she would happily rip out his throat, warily eyeing him as he retreated.

"Alyssa," Connor said, "I'm sorry. I didn't mean to scare you. I was not going to hurt you. I would never hurt you." She did not answer him. "Alyssa, please. We've both just had a real shock and things got a little crazy."

Alyssa studied Connor for a fraught moment before relaxing slightly, her eyes still wary. "Fine. I guess you're right. We're both wound a little tight right now," Alyssa conceded. "Let's just go back up to the road. Okay?"

"Okay."

Negotiating the steep slope, Connor climbed ahead of Alyssa. Going up was definitely harder than coming down. When they came to a more difficult portion of the climb, Connor looked back at Alyssa and held out his hand. She hesitated for a moment before taking it. Connor noticed the hesitation, but didn't remark on it. He had to build her comfort level around him. Pushing her was definitely not the way to do it. Something had happened to her in the past that made her very nervous of him.

After thirty grueling minutes, Connor and Alyssa finally reached the road. Connor leaned his butt against the nose of his mangled 911 while Alyssa lay on the ground, both trying to catch their breaths.

Roy stood surveying them with obvious amusement, his arms crossed in front of him. "Connor, man, you need to do some more climbing. You're getting soft in your old age. My ten-year-old could do that climb and chew bubblegum at the same time," Roy said, pride puffing out his chest.

"Yeah, but she's part mountain goat, just like her old man," Connor retorted with a smile.

"Well, I do say she gets it from my side of the family. She got the brains from her mother's side," Roy said, smiling. The smile dimmed a little. "On a more serious note, I guess neither of you is hurt. Or at least I don't think so. You wouldn't have made it down there and back otherwise." His eyes brows lowered in clear suspicion. "You didn't mess with my crime scene, did you?"

Roy looked down speculatively at Alyssa, who blinked innocently at him. Wow, that batting eyelash thing really did work—Roy smiled at her, dazzled.

Connor looked to Alyssa, then to Roy. "Alyssa," he said, looking back at her, "this is Sheriff Roy Jenkins. Roy, Alyssa Tiernan."

Roy held his hand down to Alyssa. "Ms. Tiernan, it's a pleasure. Can I help you up?"

Alyssa reached for the proffered hand. "Just Alyssa. And yes, thank you." She grasped his hand firmly and he levered her up into a standing position. Dust from the gravel of the road clung to Alyssa's clothes and hair. She ran her fingers through her hair, trying to fluff out some of the dust. "I didn't disturb your crime scene either," Alyssa responded to his question with a smile. "I was just curious."

"Curiosity killed the cat, if I recall correctly," Roy said, his mild voice holding both an edge and a smile.

"Yes, but cats have nine lives and I have about seven of those left."

"What happened to the other life?"

"Puberty," Alyssa said, deadpan.

Roy sputtered, laughed. He shot Connor a glance, a look of devilry in his eyes. Connor knew what the look said, "You've been looking for a woman, what about this one?"

Connor glared at him and Roy sighed. "Okay, okay, tell me what happened."

As Connor described the details to Roy, a second police cruiser pulled up beside the sheriff and a uniformed man of about twenty-five emerged from the car. Big and burly with a shaved head and a black handlebar moustache, the man looked more like a member of the Hell's Angels than a cop.

"A couple more cruisers are on their way, they should be here in about five minutes," the officer reported in a deep, rumbling voice the consistency of sandpaper. He walked around Connor's 911 Carrera and let out a long, low whistle. "Man, hate to see a car like this all messed up." He proceeded to walk toward the cliff to stare down at the smoldering car in the gully. "I guess he got the worse end of it. He must have just been flying when he went over." He looked back at Connor.

"He was," Connor responded, but didn't offer any details. He just wanted to get the hell out of there, but his car wasn't safe to drive. Just as the thought crossed his mind, William pulled up in the black limousine. Connor looked a question at Roy, brows raised.

"I called William when I was waiting for you two to get back up here. Your car isn't going anywhere except the station," Roy stated.

"You're the best, Roy," Connor said with a grin.

"All part of the service," Roy said sardonically. "You're not thinking of leaving the area anytime soon, are you?"

"No, I'll be sticking around if you need me," Connor replied.

Alyssa slid into the back of the limousine. As Connor followed her in, she moved over to the far side of the bench seat and sank back into the soft luxury of the leather seats. She closed her eyes as if she had been robbed her of strength by their ordeal.

Connor studied Alyssa as William drove off before sliding closer to Alyssa. He hesitated a moment before he carefully lifted a hand and settled it lightly on her head, stroking her hair gently. What made him do it, he wasn't sure. He just felt…a need, to make sure that she was okay, to make sure that she hadn't been physically harmed during their misadventure, to make sure that he hadn't scared her off. Why that was so important, he didn't know. It just was.

Alyssa's brow furrowed for a moment at his first touch, but she didn't ask him to stop. As he continued, the muscles in her forehead relaxed beneath his fingertips and she drifted off.

Fifteen minutes later they were back at the compound.

"Alyssa, we're here," Connor murmured as his fingers stopped their mesmerizing movements.

Alyssa's eyes fluttered open to meet Connor's focused gaze. She blushed faintly, a pink hue coloring her cheeks as she stared at him with a hint of horror in her eyes. He could sort of understand the horror. After all, what *does* a woman say to a man who pets her like a house cat and she falls asleep?

Connor gave her a sympathetic smile and slid from the backseat without waiting for William to come around. Alyssa scooted over the seat toward Connor's outstretched hand, grasping his fingers with hers as he handed her out of the car. The bright sunlight was a shock after the darkness of the car. Connor squinted and shielded his eyes with one hand while holding her hand with the other.

Connor looked down at Alyssa. There were large dark circles under her beautiful eyes. He felt a tug of guilt. Today wasn't supposed to be stressful. He wanted to gather her up in his arms and rock her gently. Soothe away all the tension. Stroke her softly curving body. Plunge deep into her secret depths until all they both felt was an exploding, throbbing ecstasy. He shook himself mentally. The stress of the day was getting to him too.

"Why don't you climb into the tub and relax? I'm sure there are candles and whatnot in the cottage's bathroom," Connor murmured, making his voice as soothing and calm as possible. "We can discuss everything later."

Alyssa looked at him wearily and nodded. Connor knew enough from experience that she was headed for an even larger emotional crash once the reality of their near miss sank in.

"You should eat something first, though." Connor eyed her critically. Food could help ease the body past a stressful experience. And as long as it didn't become a habit, it was far less harmful than other ways of relieving stress.

Sex was also good, but he stopped short of suggesting that remedy. Just what she needed—she'd nearly been killed on the road and the words, "Do you want to have a little sex to help you get over it, babe? Your room or mine?", were on the tip of his tongue. Biting said tongue, he managed, "Are you going to be okay?"

Alyssa smiled crookedly. "Connor, one of the things you'll learn about me is that nothing knocks me down for long. I may bitch and complain and whine to no end, but I get back up and brush myself off. Every time. I promise."

"I'm starting to realize that," Connor replied, smiling back at her. "Once you've had a chance to recuperate, why don't you come over to the main house and I'll make dinner. That'll give you the afternoon off. I make a killer steak. You're not one of those women who turns her nose up at beef, are you?"

"Are you kidding? I'm from Alberta—beef country. I like my beef very rare. Most people get queasy looking at it, but I figure it needs to be struggling a little for it to be good. A few moos out of it are also a good thing."

"Ah...a woman after my own heart," Connor replied, grinning. He looked at his watch. "It's about one-thirty now. How 'bout seven for dinner?"

"Sounds good. I'll see you then." Alyssa walked away only to pause and turn to him. "Connor, I didn't know you were in black ops. It was a guess. I only knew that you worked for the CIA. You don't have to worry about who told me anything. No one ratted you out, if that's what you're worried about, and I keep secrets to myself."

Silent, Connor appraised Alyssa. He believed her. She wasn't the type to flaunt the laws that governed the privacy of operatives. That still left the question as to how she knew he worked for the CIA. He supposed that there must have been some kind of record of his employment there, but still..."How did you know I worked for the CIA?"

"I'm very good with information. Finding it. Interpreting it. Manipulating it." She gave him a lopsided smile, tilted her head to one side and shrugged. "I'm a bloodhound. I sniff out all sorts of things. You're just one of the things I happened to sniff out."

Connor wished that Alyssa would sniff *him* out in a more physically immediate way, but he didn't voice the thought. "I guess I'll just have to be satisfied with that answer. For now. Go and take it easy. If you need anything, just call the house and ask."

Alyssa nodded, then turned and walked toward her chalet. Connor noticed that her ass swayed nicely under her close-fitting jeans. He watched her until she disappeared inside, then he sauntered to the main house, feeling remarkably chipper for a man who had just scraped by death.

Alyssa had felt his eyes burn into her back as she'd returned to the cottage. He'd awakened something primal in her, something wild. It made her nervous and hot, blazing wisps of desire coursed through her body. Entering the cottage, she tapped the door shut and leaned her head against the doorjamb.

She wanted him. She wanted him so badly that it clouded her judgment. She turned and rested her back against the door, slowly sliding down until she was on the floor, knees drawn up in front of her, head tilted back to rest against the wood.

Alyssa lightly tapped the back of her head against the door. She had to find a way to look at his computer in the main house. He had never mentioned it, but she knew he would have one there. She might be able to do it at dinner tonight. She would simply ask to see it on the pretense that if he accessed the company system from home, then another security risk had presented itself. She could also check out his corporate system at the same time.

The more she thought about it, the more she liked the idea.

Chapter Four

Connor stood in his expansive, high-tech kitchen, slicing juicy tomatoes with the skill and rapid-fire expertise of a Japanese chef. Liam sat on a high stool at the breakfast bar and watched him work to get dinner ready in time for Alyssa's arrival.

"You know, Li, if you got off your butt and helped, this would go a lot faster," Connor observed good-humoredly, lifting only his eyes from the task at hand to glance momentarily at his brother.

"You look like you're doing just fine. I burn water, remember?"

"Yeah, yeah. Excuses, excuses," Connor teased. He knew Liam felt like death on his feet, but a little needling was always in order for his youngest brother.

Liam rubbed his hands vigorously over his face and then massaged his scalp with his fingers, as if trying to stimulate blood flow to his head so that he would stay awake. He had about two days' growth of dark stubble on his cheeks and, with the dark circles under his bleary red eyes, he looked downright menacing.

"You're looking rough, bro. Maybe you should just skip dinner. Snoring at the table isn't exactly a good thing and neither is scaring the guest," Connor said, eyeing Liam doubtfully.

Liam snorted. "You turn into Martha Stewart or something? You'd look rough too if you spent eighteen hours on a plane. Besides, I'm curious to see the woman who decimated my security in record time," Liam said with a sly grin. He paused before adding, "So, what's our Ms. Tiernan like?" He yawned and stretched his muscular frame, then leaned his elbows on the breakfast bar.

"*Our* Ms. Tiernan?" Connor stopped slicing and glared at his brother. He loved his brother, but he had a tendency to go through women fast and Alyssa was *his*. Even if she didn't know it yet. "Our Ms. Tiernan is somewhat of a mystery woman. She's gorgeous, smart, a little aloof and a lot of everything else. I don't know what it is, but I get the distinct feeling that all is not as it seems. I think she's hiding something."

"Hiding something? What would she have to hide?"

"That's what's bothering me. Whenever I'm around her, she seems nervous, on edge. It might just be her personality, but I don't think so," Connor replied, his eyebrows furrowing. In his former line of work, he had developed the ability to size up anyone within a few seconds of meeting him or her. It had kept him alive on more than one occasion. This same ability made him very successful in business—he could tell whom he could trust and whom he could not.

The doorbell rang. Connor glanced at the clock on the wall. Seven o'clock on the button.

"Showtime," Connor said, smiling at his exhausted brother. "Remember, no snoring." Connor grabbed a white tea towel and wiped the tomato juice from his hands. He threw it at Liam as he walked by. Liam caught it in one hand and threw it back at Connor's head. Connor ducked. It missed its target and landed on the floor. He scooped it up from the floor and flung it over his shoulder as he sauntered to the front door.

Connor could see Alyssa through the stained glass panels set into the cedar door. He grabbed the handle of the door and swung it open. Alyssa had changed her clothing from that morning. She wore a cherry red summer-weight turtleneck sweater and black slim-fitting jeans with medium-heeled black boots.

Her hair was down and looked slightly mussed-up. She looked stunning. He realized she always seemed to look like she had just fallen out of bed, all soft, warm and sexy.

"Any problems finding the place?" Connor asked, teasing her with a smile.

Alyssa's stomach did a back flip. Her reaction to him never seemed to settle down. He made her very aware of herself as a woman. And of him as a man. "Nope. I'm part bloodhound, remember?" Alyssa answered with a grin, hoping that he couldn't tell what was going on in her mind and her body. It was damn embarrassing that she continued to react to him as strongly as she did. And she found it impossible to control.

"Right. I forgot," Connor replied, smiling. "My brother, Liam, just got in a half hour ago. He'll be having dinner with us. Is that okay?"

Damn. "Of course," Alyssa said, covering up her disappointment with a bright smile. She didn't want anyone around when she examined Connor's computer, especially not someone who would know enough to suspect that she was doing something irregular.

"*Entrez-vous, mademoiselle. Vous êtes la plupart de bienvenue,*" Connor said, bowing slightly as he stepped aside, sweeping his arm in a graceful gesture to welcome her into his home.

"*Merci, monsieur,*" Alyssa responded, dimpling at him as she stepped past him. "*Vous parlez français très bien. Là où vous avez étudié*?" she said, complementing his excellent French and asking where he had studied.

"À Montréal et à Paris."

"I *love* Montreal and Paris. Have you spent a lot of time in both cities?" Alyssa asked, reverting back to English as she noticed a man of Herculean proportions rise from his seat at the kitchen's breakfast bar.

He was even taller than Connor, with beautiful, albeit bloodshot, blue-green eyes. A few days' growth of stubble clung to his sculpted jawline and made him look dangerously sexy instead of merely unkempt as most other men would. He looked exhausted, but entirely capable of pandemonium should the need arise.

"A fair amount," Connor replied. He looked back and forth between Alyssa and Liam, who was now moving toward them. Connor spoke to Alyssa as he gestured toward his brother. "Alyssa, this is my brother, Liam. Liam, Alyssa."

Liam held out his hand with a smile that transformed his face from that of a predatory wolf to a friendly puppy. Alyssa gave him a lopsided smile and grasped his hand. Her hand disappeared into his big paw, his touch amazingly gentle. *Maybe it runs in the family—large men who had the lightest of touches.* "Pleased to meet you, Alyssa."

"Pleasure. You've just got back home?" Alyssa asked, trying to size him up. Whenever she met new people, she automatically assessed whether she would be able to defend herself if the need arose. More often than not, it had very little to do with the other person. She doubted if either man was a physical threat to her. If they had nothing to do with hacking Grand's computer system, that is.

"Yeah. I, uh, heard about your little run-in on the road earlier today. Conn, you're supposed to be taking care of her, not getting her killed. Now she's going to think that Americans are violent," Liam teased.

Connor grimaced slightly, but before he could respond, Alyssa spoke.

"I actually lived in the US for four years while I went to college. I doubt very much that most Americans are violent.

And besides, if I had been driving that car this morning, we would both be dead. So your brother has been doing his job," Alyssa said, tilting her head toward Connor. She turned toward Connor with an impish grin. "Good job. Well done."

Connor gazed at Alyssa, his surprise at her defense of him evident in his raised eyebrows. He probably hadn't expected her to defend him, especially not after their heated exchange of words beside the smoldering wreckage of their attackers' car that morning.

Alyssa felt his scrutiny and looked up into his speculative blue eyes. "Have you heard anything from Sheriff Jenkins?"

"Yes. Apparently the car that ran us off the road was hot. Stolen a week ago in Denver," Connor answered. "They haven't been able to ID the occupants yet. That could take some time. Roy feels it was probably a couple of drifters and we just got unlucky."

"Unlucky?" Alyssa echoed, her eyebrows furrowing slightly. "I *guess* you could call it that."

"Yeah, you *could*," Connor agreed, his lips thinned and tightened a little.

Alyssa's eyebrows shot upward. "You don't sound convinced either."

Connor shrugged. "We'll have to wait and see what happens once it's investigated."

Alyssa clasped her hands together nervously and tried to steer the conversation away from what she didn't know to what she wanted to investigate—if the Brothers Donnelly were her hackers. "Yeah, well, uh, you know, I should have thought of it this morning, but I want to install a sniffer on your network. Tonight, if possible." *Yeah, that was smooth.* Alyssa winced inwardly.

"A sniffer? What's a sniffer?" Connor asked, his expressive eyes alight with curiosity.

"It's just a little program I created a while back. If someone tries to get into your network, I'll be notified. It shouldn't take me more than ten minutes to install. You have a connection to your network from here, don't you?"

"Well, yes. I guess we've got another fifteen minutes 'til dinner. Are there any risks involved?"

"No, this is perfectly safe," she answered, trying to project a calm she did not particularly feel.

"What do you think, Liam?"

"If it can't hurt, it's probably a good thing," Liam responded.

"Great!" Alyssa smiled reassuringly at Connor. "If you'll show me your computer, I'll just nip in and quickly dump this in."

"Doesn't it normally take longer to install a program than that?" Liam questioned.

"It does if you buy the program off the shelf. This is a custom program that goes through the computer system and network, detects all your settings and comes up with a recommended setup. It's very fast and, for the time being, I'll take quick, dirty and secure over what you have now."

Liam shot Alyssa a distinctly un-amused look.

"Sorry, I really need to learn how to be more diplomatic," Alyssa awkwardly excused herself, wincing. "I just meant that I want to know if someone is scoping out your system. This will allow me to catch anyone before they can gain full access. If I got into your system this morning, then someone else can do the same thing."

Liam leveled an impenetrable gaze at Alyssa for a few seconds. "Do you mind if I watch?"

"No, of course not," Alyssa responded with a smile, but she narrowly avoided groaning aloud. "I tend to be a lot like that myself, you know. I try to absorb as much as I can, whenever I can." *Don't start babbling. Don't start babbling.* She zipped her lips shut against the urge.

"Li," Connor said, "why don't you show Alyssa the PC and get her connected and I'll check on dinner?"

"Sure."

Liam prowled to the far end of the great room, with Alyssa trailing behind him, and he pulled open the first door in the hallway that led off the kitchen. The office space was immaculate. Fragrant cedar-lined walls gave the room a cozy, rustic feel. A large mahogany desk sat before a large window, which had a beautiful view of the nearby forest. A monitor sat on the right side of the desk with a keyboard tray concealed under the main desk area.

Liam sat in the luxurious chocolate leather chair facing the monitor. He powered up the computer and logged into the company network. "I'm just going to set you up as an administrator so you have full access to the network and systems." Liam swiftly typed in some commands, rose from the desk and gestured toward the chair "You drivin', ma'am?" He drawled lightly.

Alyssa smiled crookedly and drawled back, "Shore am, suh." She settled herself into the vacated chair and gazed at the screen for a minute. She grabbed her handbag from the floor, opened it and withdrew a compact disc. She slid the disc into the computer's drive and brought up the command screen. "Here goes nothing," she muttered. The screen flashed a number of times and then presented her with options. "Your proxy server is outside the DMZ?"

"Yes."

"Nice choice. A lot of companies put it too far back into the system. You actually have fairly tight security," Alyssa commented.

"But not tight enough to keep you out," Liam answered, his tone flat, emotionless.

"There's not much I can be kept out of. In general, I don't try to break into systems," Alyssa responded matter-of-factly. "Anymore."

"Anymore? You used to do a lot of this stuff?" Liam asked artlessly. A bit too artlessly.

Alyssa slanted a sharp glance at him. "Used to. Don't now. Ancient history," she said shortly, slamming the door shut on that topic.

Liam took the hint and remained silent.

"I'm just going to poke around the system for a few minutes while the program is installing. See if you've had any break-ins recently, aside from me." Alyssa started typing before Liam could respond. He'd never know what she was actually looking for. She knew exactly where her Trojan horse would be if it were in the system.

Alyssa accessed the registry information on the company network and carefully scanned it for her beacon. Nothing. She switched her attention back to Connor's computer and searched its directories. Nothing.

Relief swept over Alyssa in a huge wave, making her a little lightheaded. These people were not her hackers. She swayed on the chair a little.

"Alyssa? Are you okay?"

"Hmmm? Uh, yeah, I'm fine. Just a little dizzy," Alyssa said, closing her eyes for a moment and then re-opening them.

"When's the last time you ate?" Liam asked, his head cocked to one side as he studied her.

"Ate? I think that would have been this morning. Just forgot, I guess."

"Is that program of yours nearly finished? We should have done this later, *after* you had something to eat."

In answer to his question, the computer let out a squawk and sat waiting for more instructions.

"Perfect timing," Alyssa answered him. "All done. I guess this could have waited until later, but I tend to have a one-track mind. I think of something, I want to do it and I want to do it *now*." Stretching her tired limbs, she smiled at him. "Let's eat." She popped the disc out of the computer, slipped it into its protective sleeve and dropped it back in her bag. She pressed the power button on the computer to shut it down and turned back to Liam.

"What just happened here?" Liam asked, leaning forward to look into her face, suspicion clear on his.

Alyssa regarded him for a moment before deciding to turn in herself. If they wanted to get rid of her once they found out what she had been doing, then that was their choice. "Why don't we go find your brother and I'll tell both of you."

Chapter Five

"Hackers? You thought we were hackers?" Connor asked, incredulous, staring at Alyssa across the breakfast bar. He carefully lowered the knife he had been using to chop parsley, now forgotten. Liam stood beside Alyssa, silently looking at the expression on Connor's face.

"Yes. Hackers," Alyssa confirmed, her eyes unwavering as she surveyed him. She rested her hands on the cold granite countertop.

"Why?" Connor sounded totally baffled.

"I found out about your business dealings with my grandfather two weeks after we were hacked, or at least, after someone tried to hack us. From my perspective, you would have known something of Grand's process. Maybe you didn't want a legit business deal. Maybe you were trying to get the process without having to go through the trouble of dealing with Grand. I didn't know you, or Liam, from Adam."

"Why didn't you say something?"

"Yeah, right," Alyssa snorted mirthlessly. "Like that was going to get me what I wanted. What was I supposed to do? Get off the plane, meet you, and while I'm shaking your hand, ask politely if you've hacked my system? C'mon. Get real."

"Why admit to this now?" Connor asked.

"I know you're not my hacker."

"Why would you think it was us in the first place?"

Alyssa paused. "Connor, I worked for CSIS as a hacker. I know what it costs to hire that sort of talent, especially if you don't want any attention drawn to yourself. My system, while not unbreakable, is very, *very* secure. I put years of experience into that security.

"There are *maybe* a couple of dozen people in the *world* who would know how to get past my security. Someone was knocking my security down as if it were a pile of Legos. The amount of money it would take to do that is easily into the tens of thousands, if not hundreds of thousands, of dollars. Energy Unlimited has that kind of cash. It was as simple as that. You had the motive. You had the resources. You had it all."

"What would you have done if you had discovered we were your hackers?" Connor asked in a faintly puzzled tone. "How did you think you'd get out of here in one piece?"

As Connor watched, Alyssa picked up her handbag and rummaged through it. Her first trip into the bag yielded a metal cylinder with a spray nozzle, which she dumped onto the breakfast bar. "Mace." Her second foray into her bag produced an object that looked like a television remote control with fangs and she plopped that down beside the mace. "Taser." She went back to digging through her bag. Out came a switchblade, dumped next to the taser.

Connor stared at Alyssa in amazement. She had a whole arsenal in there. He gingerly picked up the stun gun and turned it over in his hand. It was a top of the line model. He looked back at Alyssa ransacking her bag. "Any real guns in there?" He asked, leery of what she would pull out next.

"No. I don't like guns," Alyssa replied distractedly, her nose in her bag.

Connor looked at Liam. Liam looked at Connor. Liam smirked. Connor grinned. They erupted into gales of laughter. For a person who didn't like guns, she sure had enough weaponry to make up for it.

Alyssa stared at the convulsing brothers, her head dropped to one side like a puzzled puppy to survey the now near-hysterical brothers. Twenty seconds went by before

Connor, leaning against the breakfast bar, could gasp, "Okay, so you could have *possibly* fought your way out of the house, but how did you think you would get down the mountain?"

"I thought I'd hotwire one of your cars," Alyssa replied, a small smile flirting at the corners of her mouth. "Okay, so it wasn't the best of plans. And I didn't think your brother would be here, and so…large, like you. Which, quite honestly, scared me a little. Is your whole family huge or something?"

"Pretty much," Connor replied, wiping his eyes. His vision cleared. "Hotwire a car? Where'd you learn that?"

"Product of a misspent youth."

"Alyssa Tiernan, you are nothing like what I expected when Douglas said he wanted you down here," Connor declared, smiling broadly. "Oh Lord, I didn't think this would be the result of dinner."

"It's not something I generally do when I have dinner with someone. It just sort of happened that way."

"Is that why you were so nervous around me?" Connor asked.

"I can see my acting abilities have *not* improved." Alyssa smiled briefly and then sobered. "I was envisioning having to seriously maim someone to get out of here. It was not a comforting thought."

Connor sobered as well. "Why'd you agree to come down here at all, then? Didn't you tell Douglas of your suspicions?"

"I didn't tell Grand anything. He's getting old and his heart isn't strong. I came down here to protect him. I can take care of myself. If it had turned out that you were my hacker, I would have figured out something. But I don't want him worried over this. You can't tell him anything. Promise me." Alyssa straightened and stared intently into Connor's eyes.

Connor stared back. He nodded slowly.

"It's your choice, Connor. If you want me to leave, I'll leave. No harm, no foul. I'll understand if you don't want me here," Alyssa said softly.

Connor looked at Liam, who nodded at him. "Alyssa, I…we want this partnership with your grandfather to succeed. We've done a little checking up on you of our own, and it's unanimous that you're one of the best. How about we start over? "

Alyssa nodded. She was about to say something else when her stomach yowled like a cat in heat. Her face turned a charming shade of pink and she placed a hand over her abdomen, whispered, "Oops. Sorry."

"Dinner it is, then," Connor said mischievously.

After dinner, Alyssa curled up in a wing chair beside the fire blazing in the fieldstone fireplace and lazily declared, "That was amazing. Where'd you learn to cook like that?"

"I like to eat good food. I hate to eat bad food," Connor replied, hunkering down on the rug in front of the fire. He considered it for a few moments and then goosed one of the logs with a wrought-iron poker. The tongues of flame danced over the burning logs, crackling and popping loudly, echoing in the great room. Liam had excused himself after dinner, having narrowly avoided ending up face down in his garlic mashed potatoes part way through dinner.

"Well, you're hired. I've never had much interest in cooking." Alyssa closed her eyes and settled her head on the armrest of the chair. Her silky hair hung down over the armrest, sparkling in the light of the fire. He itched to touch her hair and find out if it was as soft as it looked.

Connor gazed at Alyssa, at her delicately featured face and the mane of her hair. She looked very sweet, curled up in the oversize chair. Like an angel. A very sensuous angel. A wave of desire flooded his body.

It had been a while, hell, who was he kidding, more like forever, since Connor had been interested in both a woman's mind and body. He had been on a few dates in the past couple of years—he was no monk. The women he saw, although extremely attractive, had left him feeling empty and cold. It seemed to him his checkbook had one up on him in terms of being the target of their interest.

And here, in front of him, was a woman who seemingly didn't care about his bank balance. A woman who braved her fears to protect someone she loved. A woman with smoky eyes that threatened to consume him whole. A beautiful, talented woman with the body of a Venus. An exhausted woman, he reminded himself, who'd been traumatized earlier in the day.

"Alyssa," Connor said huskily, gently.

"Hmmm?" Alyssa murmured. She sounded like she was nearly asleep.

"You're exhausted. Did you get any sleep today?"

"No. I was too anxious to sleep," Alyssa said distantly. She smiled, but kept her eyes closed. "I thought I was going to have to manhandle you and hightail it out of here." She shook with a small soft laugh.

Connor chuckled, amused by the image of her successfully attacking him. He had nine inches and a good ninety pounds on her, but given all the hardware in her purse, she might have been able to pull it off. Of course, the thought of her touching him brought…other things to mind. He wondered what her hand-to-hand combat skills were like. He'd definitely volunteer for a trial run on that one. Desire tightened his body deliciously.

"Manhandle me? That would have been interesting," Connor said in a deliberately seductive voice.

Alyssa opened her eyes slowly and fixed them on Connor kneeling a couple feet away, focused entirely on her. Alyssa's breath came faster, harder, but she didn't speak. He wasn't sure if she was thoroughly terrified or thoroughly turned on.

"Would you?" Connor asked softly, not breaking eye contact.

"Would I what?" Alyssa responded, her voice shaking.

"Manhandle me," Connor answered, his heart beating heavier in his chest.

"I, uh…" Alyssa whispered. "I…"

They both heard the ring of her pager, buried in her purse where it sat on the breakfast bar. Alyssa's eyes widened in surprise.

"What the…" Alyssa exclaimed, swinging her legs around and sitting up in the chair. Her body tensed, as though under attack.

"What's wrong?" Connor asked, trying to keep the frustration out of his voice. He swore inwardly. He had been so close…

"Only Grand has that pager number. The only other access points are from Grand's system and your system. I set both systems to alert me when there's suspicious network activity." Alyssa rose and ran to her purse, leaving Connor staring at her in consternation. She unzipped the bag, pulled out the pager and examined the display window. "It's you! Damn!"

"*Me*?" Connor got up off the floor and walked toward Alyssa.

"No, not *you*. Your *system*. Someone's rattling the door handles," Alyssa said impatiently, staring at the readout. She lifted her eyes to meet Connor's. He stood very close to her. She backed up slightly, gesturing a bit wildly. "I need to log on to your system *now*. I want to be at least able to stop them if I can." Alyssa started to push past him.

Connor lightly grasped her upper arm. "Do you need me to do anything?"

"Yeah, if I can find the guy, I'll need to know if I should fry him or not."

"Fry him?"

"I'll explain later. Right now I need to get into the system." With that, Alyssa strode off in the direction of the study, Connor shadowing her.

Ensconced in the leather chair and logged into the system, Alyssa stared at the activity on the monitor, occasionally typing something and waiting for other things to happen.

"It looks like he's just taking a look around the system. I don't think he's actually loading anything into it yet. But he will. Hackers generally break into a system and then leave behind little goodies that allow them to get back into the system at a later date. They'll overwrite passwords, assume administration accounts and come back when it suits them. I'm going to see if I can ping him."

"*Ping* him?"

"It's a submariner term. One submarine sends out a sonar burst to bounce off the hull of another submarine. Lets them know how far away the other guy is. In this case, if the guy's on your network, I can ping him. If he's not on your network, I might be able to get an IP address, unless it's been spoofed."

It sounded like gobbledygook to him. "Sorry, you lost me." He watched her mouth open to explain, but he held up his hands in surrender. "I don't need to know the specifics—I trust you to do what needs to be done."

She smirked. "Okay—sounds good to me." She continued to type at light speed, not moving her eyes from the screen.

"Can't ping him—he's not an internal intruder. He's spoofed his IP address. But I might just be able to trace the messages he's sending out," she muttered more to herself than to him, he suspected.

Connor watched her work without comment, impressed.

"Okay, okay, I need a Trojan." Alyssa looked around quickly for her bag.

Connor looked at Alyssa quizzically. She needed a *condom*? He wished she did, but it didn't *look* like she had sex on her mind.

Alyssa caught the look and looked puzzled at his bewilderment. "Why are you looking at me like that?"

"And a Trojan is …?"

She did her lopsided grin thing, finally understanding which track his one-track mind was on. "Oh. A Trojan is a program that you dump on someone's computer system to do any number of things. Not a condom. I'm going to see if I can send this guy into cyber-hell. I want to trace the responses from your system to wherever he is and dump my Trojan onto his computer so I can eventually try to come up with a geographical location for him. And *then* I'll fry him," she concluded gleefully.

Connor smiled to himself in spite of the circumstances. She looked like she was having a lot of fun as she typed.

"Okay, I know what port you're coming in on, pal." Alyssa smiled devilishly, still talking to herself. "I've got your number and you're going to wake up with one hell of a headache."

Alyssa made a grab for her bag and dumped the contents out on the desk. A whole mess slithered out in a heap and she quickly ran her fingers through it, swiftly finding a compact disc. She whipped it out of its protective cover and popped it into the disk drive of the computer. She typed a line of gibberish into the keyboard and hit the enter key.

"Uploading the program now. A gift from me to you. Choke on it. And. Have. A. Nice. Day." Alyssa typed a letter for each word she spoke. She finished off by hitting the enter key. "Okay, my little fly, tell me where he is."

Connor waited for her to start rubbing her hands together and cackling over her witch's brew of electronic wizardry. A scary, sexy lady.

"Now is fry-time. I'm going to shut him down and block the rest of the attack," she said.

A few more keystrokes, a lot more muttering and she turned to Connor, smiling. "Okay, I've fried his connection, he probably won't be back again tonight, but we need to start a comprehensive evaluation of your system as soon as possible."

Connor stared at Alyssa. Why wasn't she doing this for a living? She had lit up like a Christmas tree when she had bobbed and weaved around the hacker, stinging like a bee. This is what she was meant to do. What had caused her to give it up?

Under his scrutiny, Alyssa grew fidgety. He just stood there and stared at her. "Hello? Is anyone in there?" Alyssa joked, nervous with his silence.

Connor blinked. "Alyssa, why aren't you doing this for a living? It's obvious that you're not only good at it, but also you love doing it."

It was Alyssa's turn to stare at Connor. The manufactured mirth leaked out of her eyes, leaving them wary. He saw the doors clang shut behind her eyes. Carefully, not breaking eye contact, she said, "I have chosen not to pursue this as a career." Her tone did not invite discussion.

Connor ignored the tone. "But you were enjoying it. Why give up something you enjoy?"

"It's none of your business," Alyssa responded, her shoulders drawn down and tight, her voice matching her body's defensive posture. "I don't want to talk about it."

Connor heard the tension in her voice, vibrating a little with emotion. Alyssa quickly turned her head away from him, but not before he saw the gleam of tears in her eyes.

With trembling fingers, Alyssa pressed the eject button on the disc drive. The drive stuck its tongue out at her, mocking her, and presented her with the fragile disk. As she reached for the disk with quivering fingers, Connor leaned past her and caught her digits, encasing them in his steady hand.

Alyssa closed her eyes. "Connor …"

Slowly, Connor pulled her hand toward him, swiveling the chair and Alyssa to face him. She let out a shuddering breath and opened her eyes. He offered her refuge, if she would only take it. He knew what it was like to carry a grief so deep it scarred one's soul, what it was like to need the warmth and understanding of another human being, what it was like to want to let go of the guilt and the pain, but fearing it was the only thing keeping your life together.

Gently, Connor pulled her to her feet and wrapped his arms around her. She stiffened. He didn't let go. He just stroked her hair, murmuring unintelligible words of comfort.

Alyssa's arms lifted to encircle him as she rested her cheek against his chest. Connor rocked her gently in his arms, willing her to release the agony that she kept trapped inside. Slowly, softly, silently a single tear wet his shirt as it flowed into him. More followed and she began to sob quietly as Connor absorbed her pain and lent her his strength. He gathered her closer, offering all the comfort and forgiveness she had denied herself.

Alyssa began to sob in earnest, uncontrollably.

Still holding her, Connor carefully edged toward the chair that she had vacated and sat, pulling Alyssa onto his lap. Her sobs gradually quieted to jarring hiccups under his stroking hands. She leaned heavily against him, her eyes closed, her legs curled up tight against her body. As the last of the tears fell, she began to speak softly.

"About two years ago, I was directed to hack into a system where I found information that pointed to someone taking major kickbacks from a terrorist in the former Soviet Union. I handed the information over to my superiors, standard procedure, telling them that I needed to recheck the information. I had been detected midstream and had to get out quickly before the signal could be traced back to me.

"Without my knowledge, my *superiors* handed the information over to the government in question and they proceeded to torture the man and his family. I was too naïve, too stupid to know what would happen. I just thought they'd question him, perhaps imprison him pending a trial. But they tortured him to death. They brutalized his wife and family. When I found out what was happening, I was horrified.

"On my own time, I broke back into the system I'd hacked and found that the information had been a plant, perpetrated by the eastern European government. They'd needed an excuse. He'd been publicly critical of the government and they wanted him gone." Alyssa took a shaky breath. "So they killed him. Murdered him. His wife was so brutalized that she'll be in a mental institution for the rest of her life and his kids have all disappeared.

"I couldn't prove that CSIS knew what would happen once that information was handed over, but I couldn't disprove it either. I couldn't live with it, so I left.

"Someone died because of me. Someone is out of her mind because of me. Children have been orphaned, or worse, because of me," Alyssa spoke harshly, her voice shook with emotion. "I should have known, I should have been able to stop it, I should—"

"Alyssa, hush. There's nothing you could have done and you're only hurting yourself more." Gently, Connor rested his lips against her temple. He realized that they had, each of them, left the game for the same reason. People got hurt. Innocent people.

It was a soul-sucking, dehumanizing experience, which had threatened to overwhelm him six years ago. But he'd had his family. They had been there for him, supporting him when he needed it, seeing him through the dark days. Making sure he faced his fears and pain to help him to move on.

But Alyssa hadn't had that kind of support. No doubt she hadn't wanted to burden her grandfather with this, leaving her alone with her demons. Connor's heart ached for her. He wanted to take away the pain, pain with which he was all too familiar. He rocked her slowly, knowing that she didn't need words. Not right now.

Gradually, the tension in Alyssa's body unwound and she relaxed in Connor's arms, her head resting against the hollow below his shoulder, calm. He looked down at her face, slightly red and swollen from crying, and gently kissed each of her closed eyes. Those beautiful, red-rimmed eyes opened and gazed at him intently. And as he watched, he saw a flicker of desire in her eyes, felt the sudden tension in her body as she held her breath.

His body pulsed savagely in response to hers. He wanted her more than he had ever wanted any woman, but he didn't want to take advantage of her. She was too vulnerable.

Damn it, it's not right. He pulled away from her slightly.

Alyssa reached up a shaky hand to prevent his retreat. She feathered her fingers over the stubble covering his jaw and smiled faintly. "It's like stiff, prickly velvet," she whispered. Slowly, she wrapped her hand around the back of his neck, teasing the short, dark hairs there and gently pulled his head toward her.

"Uh, Alyssa…" Connor didn't think he'd be able to stop once he started. Once again, he tried to pull back from her.

"Don't say anything. I just…want…" Alyssa's voice trailed off as she lifted her lips to his. Her lips touched his, perhaps a little uncertain, gently exploring.

Connor returned the kiss with care, heedful of Alyssa's fragile emotional state. She shifted her body closer to his and caught his lower lip between her teeth, softly tugging at it. His body responded with a huge throb of lust. His jeans fitted him too snugly, almost painfully. He pulled his lip out of her gentle capture and traced her lips with his tongue. He smoothed his hand down her body, lingering at her breast, moving down to her stomach, working his hand up under her tee shirt, splaying his fingers outward over her softly curved belly.

They both stopped fighting their minds and surrendered their bodies to pleasure.

Alyssa felt a stab of pleasure radiating outward from where his hand touched her body and she arched her back to welcome his caress. His hand burned on her flesh, sending pleasurable shocks stabbing down through her abdomen into her womb. Her hips undulated upon his lap, inviting him to take more. Clearly, he got the message.

Connor moved his hand upward to her breasts, pushing up her tee shirt above her chest. Undoing the snap front of her bra, he gently cupped a breast, stroked the nipple as a shaft of fire lit her body from within. Rising heat dewed her skin and he shifted her slightly to lean down to suckle one nipple, his tongue laving the sensitized areola. She arched her back, encouraged him to feast.

His hand moved downward, undoing the button of her jeans and unzipping her fly. Her hips moved languorously in response. Tucking his hand beneath her lacy white panties, he sought her sex with inquisitive fingers. Delicately stroking the folds of her labia, a warm liquid rush drenched his fingers, filling the air with her scent. It was dizzying. She felt so tight, so wet, so soft.

Alyssa shivered at her wholehearted response to his expert touch and her mind went blank. No words, no thoughts, just sensations. His clever fingers moved inside her, lighting a fuse deep within her body, sending delicate pulses radiating outward to the tips of her toes and to the hairs on her head.

She writhed on his lap, helplessly moving her hips to better feel his fingers playing her. She wanted to wrap him around her, feel him deep inside her and plunge toward ecstasy together. It felt wonderful, but it wasn't enough. She wanted it all.

His fingers moved, driving to a rhythm, pushing her toward the brink of ecstasy. Before her release came, he pulled her back, teasing her. She groaned, "Connor, please..."

Connor laughed softly. "Sweetheart, take off your clothes and show me what you want," he said in a low, seductive voice.

Alyssa slowly opened her eyes and saw the raw need in his. She climbed off his lap, shaking in excitement. Her body ran along in front of her mind like a puppy excited by the prospect of a walk, pulling her forward, eager for the coming experience.

Her mind tried to pull back on her body, but her body was so far ahead that there was no reining in her unruly responses. She pulled her tee shirt over her head, shaking her chestnut hair loose. She dropped her opened bra to the floor and took a deep breath. Connor's hands reached up to her breasts, softly stroking them, his eyes dark with passion. She pushed her jeans and panties down to her ankles and slowly stepped out of them.

She was completely vulnerable to him. She was naked. He was not. She found it amazingly arousing. His big hands traced down her body. As he gently explored her petal softness with his fingers, no doubt feeling the wetness of her response around his fingers, she caught her breath and grabbed onto his broad shoulders as he found an exquisitely sensitive nub and tormented it sweetly. She bit her lip to stop the moan building in her throat, not wanting to give it voice.

Sweat beaded his upper lip and he inhaled raggedly. He rose from the chair, discarded his shirt and quickly pulled off his jeans and underwear. Alyssa inhaled sharply. My God, he was ready for her and then some. A thrill shot down her spine.

Sinking to his knees in front of her on a slow descent, he kissed her mouth, her neck, her shoulders, her breasts, her belly and then her sex. Alyssa groaned and shifted her legs into a wider stance to enjoy his tongue gentling her, tasting her, exciting her. The exquisite sensations between her thighs made her knees wobble precariously. Connor wrapped his arm around her buttocks to support her while he built that fire higher and higher.

At last, when she was aching and wild, beyond thought, beyond words, he commanded huskily, "Come to me."

She stepped back shakily, placed her feet on either side of his thighs, rested her fingertips on his shoulders and then, oh so slowly, slid down his body, enjoying the skin-on-skin friction created by the passage of her soft body against his. He grasped her buttocks with both hands as he lowered her down to within a fraction of an inch of her goal, her vagina a hair's breadth away from his penis. She squirmed in impatience—she wanted him inside her *now* and he was making her wait.

"Please," she whispered against his mouth as she undulated against his rock-hard body, gently catching his lower lip between her teeth.

Connor pulled back and whispered, "Do you invite me in?"

"Oh, God, yes..." Alyssa breathed. Heated pulsing built steadily in her body. She wanted him as hard and as fast and as deep as he could go. She moved her hips against him in invitation. He carefully lowered her until his penis nudged into her satiny fire. With infinite patience, he slowly sheathed himself to the hilt in her softness.

Alyssa gasped, and rolled her hips to take all of him, shivering slightly as the sensation of his presence within her body pricked her into hyper-awareness. The marvel of the smoothness of his skin, the heat of his body, the subtle abrasion of his chest hair against her swollen breasts, his musky, masculine scent. All swamped her senses, overwhelming her. His hips started moving rhythmically, slowly, thrusting powerfully into her welcoming body.

He anchored her more securely on him by wrapping both arms around her waist. She would have screamed if she'd had the breath, but all she could do was arch her back and shake as he drove her higher and higher. He drove both of them relentlessly to the edge and tipped them over into mind-numbing, anything but senses-stealing, bliss.

Chapter Six

Disoriented, Alyssa slowly came to her senses. It was just barely light outside the window. She was in a bed with a very large man, who was holding her closely and studying her, his head on the pillow next to hers, his gray-blue eyes washed to the color of shadow by the dim light. Memory flooded into her sleepy brain cells and she flushed.

"You're beautiful. You know that?" Connor said softly, raising his hand to trace her eyebrow with his thumb, sinking his fingers into her silky hair. He drew a handful of her hair gently away from her scalp and let it run through his fingers like water. She could see the beating pulse at the base of his throat speed up.

"I wasn't before you," Alyssa said simply, feeling a bit awkward, but pleased all the same. She had never woken up in bed with a man before. In her two previous sexual relationships, the men had never stayed the night. As if sex without tenderness was adequate. As if she hadn't been worth the effort. It was very reassuring to be treated like someone special. It was a new experience.

Hoping to look less awkward than she felt, she dropped her eyes and casually played with the curly black hair on his chest. "Sorry for all the hysterics last night. I didn't mean to jump you like that and all." She lifted her eyes to his face and her fingers stilled, an unasked question in her voice.

Connor's eyes were full of compassion. "No apology needed. You've had a rough go of it." His lips quirked into a wicked smile that spoke volumes. "And as for the jumping part of it, in case you didn't notice, I thoroughly enjoyed that. You can do *that* anytime you like."

Alyssa felt the heat rise in her cheeks again, the ones on her face, and dropped her eyes. Connor gently put his hand under her chin, making her look at him again. "There's nothing to be embarrassed about, Alyssa. You're a beautiful, talented, passionate woman. I'm lucky to have you in my life."

Alyssa studied Connor. He was telling her the truth. There was no hardness, no falseness to his words or in his eyes. And he wanted her, even knowing what she had done. Her heart squeezed almost painfully, her breath catching in her throat. He accepted her, warts and all. She wound her arms around his neck and molded her body to his. "I'm the lucky one." She lifted her lips to skate across his lips, rolling her hips against his groin.

Connor's breath came hard and fast as his phallus rose swiftly to the occasion. "Are you sure?" He molded her body to his with firm strokes of his hands upon her back.

Alyssa felt the blunt evidence of his desire and her hand snaked down to find him hot and urgent. "I want you. I want to feel you deep inside me. Now," Alyssa murmured, kissing him deeply. Her tongue tangled with his, tasting his salty masculinity, drinking it in. It was a heady sensation. He, hot, hard and hungry. She, warm, soft and demanding.

For Alyssa, sex had never been anything like this. She was caught in a whirlwind of desire. It spun her so fast she felt dizzy. She closed her eyes and concentrated on the ambrosial sensation of Connor exploring her sensitive neck with his tongue. She tipped her head back in pure enjoyment.

She'd thought she was frigid, but she'd been wrong. Her sexuality had only needed to be stoked, awakened. Connor had shown her things about herself she never knew existed. Needs. Wants. Desires. She had to have more.

It was a long time before they left the bed—the sweet, earthy scent of sex perfuming the air.

*****

Connor strolled into the great room of the chalet and spied Liam sipping a cup of coffee in the kitchen wearing a tattered green terry robe. Liam blinked and squinted at his older brother before he flicked his eyes to the wall clock and shook his head like a confused puppy.

"Hell must have officially frozen over. It's ten in the morning and you're just getting up? You're normally like a rooster, up at the crack of dawn." Liam frowned at Connor. "You look good—all relaxed. What's up?"

"I decided to go into work late. Problem?" Connor responded shortly, eyeing his youngest brother warily.

"Nooo. It's just unusual," Liam answered, clearly unconvinced. "I've never known you to be the sleeping-in type."

Alyssa entered the room, wearing Connor's cherry-red silk dressing gown. She had rolled up the sleeves numerous times and had wrapped the gown around her narrow waist as tightly as the belt allowed. She should have looked ridiculous, but she didn't. She glowed.

Liam's jaw dropped as he all but gawked at her. Under his breath, he muttered, "Jesus, you're still a rooster and you *were* up at the crack of dawn."

Connor arched one eyebrow at Liam, which silently said, "Shut your mouth and don't say anything stupid." Liam snapped his jaw shut and arranged his face into a less shocked façade as Alyssa approached them with an uncertain look on her face.

"Uh, morning, Alyssa. Sleep well?" Liam tried.

Connor kicked Liam under the table. Liam shot Connor a woeful sidelong glance.

"Uh, morning, Liam. Yes, thank you. And you?" Alyssa responded, the fingers of one hand running through her hair.

"Like a rock." Connor delivered another kick under the table to Liam's leg. Liam shot him a wounded look and sighed.

"You know, I need to get my ass in gear and take a shower. I'll see you later." He got up, smiled at both of them and strolled toward his room carrying his coffee cup, disappearing down the hallway.

Connor's eyes riveted on Alyssa as she watched Liam leave.

"Your brother must think..." Alyssa said softly as she turned back to Connor, her eyebrows furrowed.

Connor slid his arms around her waist and kissed her hard. "You don't have to worry about what anyone thinks. My brother doesn't pass judgment, if that's what you're worried about. You want coffee?" Connor released her, his fingers loosening in slow increments, reluctant to let her go, and walked to the coffeepot. "I don't think it's as powerful as your regular brew, but it should do."

Connor rummaged around in the cupboard and pulled out two mugs. He poured the steaming black liquid into the two cups, doctoring both with cream and sugar. Walking back toward her, he bent down to give her a swift kiss before presenting the steaming mug to her. She took a careful sip of the hot liquid.

"Not bad. Not strong enough, but not bad," Alyssa said, sighing.

"Sort of like the system security?" Connor joked, grinning.

"Sort of like the system security," Alyssa agreed with a smile. "And speaking of the security, I should really get to work and see what we're looking at."

"All business, and first thing in the morning too. Why don't we spend the day in bed and forget the security?" Connor asked. He put his cup down and wrapped his arms around her tightly. He was still totally up for it.

"You're insatiable, "Alyssa whispered just as his lips touched hers.

"Only for you," he murmured as he molded her body to his and let his hands wander possessively over her curves, his tongue leisurely explored her mouth, the actions designed to pull her under the spell of his desire. It took a minute for him to realize that she was quivering. He pulled back and frowned at her in concern. "Everything okay? You're trembling."

"I just realized that you're not the only insatiable one here," Alyssa gasped unsteadily, staring conspicuously at his lips. She took a deeper breath, shook her head and pulled away from him as far as he would allow, which wasn't far at all. "You're dangerous." She laughed. "But we need to take a rain check.

"Connor, someone tried to hack your system last night. Your systems aren't safe. Your data isn't safe. With any luck, I'll be able lock it down, at least temporarily. Tracking down your intruder will be harder."

Only half-teasing, Connor groaned and complained, "I finally meet the woman of my dreams and she wants to play with a computer instead of with me."

"Don't worry. I'll play with you very, *very* soon," Alyssa purred, her voice husky and inviting. Her eyes closed halfway and a visible shiver coursed through her. Her nipples hardened, becoming erect, outlined by the thin silk of the dressing gown.

Connor, staring at her responsive body, felt the blood pounding through his head. Both heads. It was all he could do not to drag her down to the floor and take her. Right here. Right now. "Sweetheart, unless you want to do it on the kitchen floor, you need to get dressed. Aside from which, you hadn't had sex for a while and I don't want to hurt you—and you're probably a little tender now." He released her, still reluctant to relinquish her, and took a step back for good measure. If he kept touching her, nothing would stop him from acting on his desires.

Alyssa hesitated and sighed. "You're right. I am kind of sore right now."

"Then go. Now. Fast. Get showered and dressed." He paused while she hesitated, gazing at him. "Did I mention *go*? Before I forget my good intentions and take you here in the kitchen?" Connor managed to make the lighthearted comment sound like a threat. She didn't look threatened—she looked intrigued. He must be losing his touch. That, or she enjoyed the kind of trouble he "threatened" to unleash.

Alyssa continued to look fascinated, evidently seeing something…else in his eyes before she backed off and held up her hands. "Going. I'm going. I'll just grab my clothes and I'll meet you back here in forty-five minutes, all right?"

"Good," Connor responded, relieved and disappointed at the same time.

"Connor! Something's happened in Saudi Arabia. One of their oil refineries exploded last night. They don't know if it was an accident or sabotage." Liam emerged from the far hallway, barefoot and still wearing his tattered green bathrobe. He strode toward the television set in the far corner of the great room. He grabbed the remote control from the coffee table and flicked the television on to the news channel.

Both Connor and Alyssa went to stand beside Liam.

"Again, from file photos, this is what the refinery looked like before the explosion. We're told it was a state-of-the-art facility, with most of the technological expertise coming from America," the anchorwoman intoned. The television showed gleaming metal towers jutting skyward, coughing out acrid smoke and surrounded by huge circular white storage tanks that held the refined oil, ready for export to the world.

Connor stared intently at the screen, knowing this latest news could affect Energy Unlimited's business. Any slowdown of oil flowing out of the Middle East could mean price hikes for oil—and more money poured into alternate energy sources.

"And now I think we have footage of what the refinery looked like last night." The television footage had been shot a couple of miles from the refinery. The night sky lit by an eerie orange glow, the shot showed one of the remaining steel spires listing precariously to the left. Another explosion rocked the complex and a series of huge, orange fireballs chased each other into the black starless sky. Shock waves hit so hard the camera bounced wildly, the noise likely deafening to anyone near enough to hear it.

"And this is a live shot of what's left of the refinery this morning. As you can see, all the smokestacks are gone. The fire crews have been trying to contain the blaze, using fire-retardant foam to coat the nearby storage tanks hoping to keep them from exploding. They've been at it since very early this morning, yesterday afternoon our time, but it looks like they're losing the battle." The anchorwoman raised her voice. "Frank, are you there? Can you tell us what's happening?"

For a few seconds, Frank didn't respond. Finally, his voice came through crackling and distant and the live feed from the camera looked grainy and jerky. "Yes, Mary. I can hear you. The fire crews are losing ground and are pulling back from the storage tanks. From our vantage point, we can see the fire drawing closer to the tanks. If the oil in those tanks blows, it'll be a major burn."

The television showed eight or nine fire crews shooting away from the refinery. The fire trucks kicked up plumes of dust as they roared out. "Yeah, it looks like that's it. They're all pulling out now," Frank verified.

"Frank, do you have any more information on what precipitated this event? Was it a terrorist attack?"

"No one has been able to give us a definitive answer about that. As you know, the security around the oil fields and refineries has been very tight since 9/11. It was a major fear both in Washington and here in Saudi Arabia that the terrorists would go after the Saudi oil production machine.

"The White House, knowing that the Middle East is so politically unstable, has been weaning America from Middle East oil for sometime now. Twenty years ago, we counted on the Middle East for up to twenty-five percent of our domestic consumption of oil. Now that percentage has dropped to eight percent, which provides some insulation against political fluctuations in the Middle East situation. But it doesn't cushion us enough.

"Saudi Arabia has a massive surplus of approximately two million barrels of crude oil a day. That surplus has brought a measure of security to the oil industry. The Saudis have the capability to step in and stabilize the oil market because of this huge surplus. They did it after the World Trade Center attacks, which helped the world oil market immensely… Wait a second, Mary." Frank paused. Voices could be heard in the background. "Mary…we're being waved off. They want us to move further away from—"

A massive explosion drowned out Frank's voice. The live feed went dead. Liam flinched. Connor registered no reaction, except to glance at Alyssa as she covered her mouth with one hand. He took her other hand in his and held on firmly, comforting.

"Oh my God," the anchorwoman's voice quivered, but the screen remained blank. The screen suddenly leapt to life, showing a dark-haired woman with light blue eyes staring at the camera.

A moment passed before she spoke. "We've just lost our live feed at the refinery in Saudi Arabia. We're working on getting it back now." The woman suddenly pressed her fingers against her left ear, as if listening for instructions. "We have another breaking story coming in now." She continued to look straight at the camera for another five seconds before speaking.

"There's been an explosion at an oil refining facility outside the city of Fort McMurray, Alberta, Canada. Fort

McMurray is home to the world's largest oil sands deposits. We're getting more information in now."

"What is going *on*?" Alyssa asked. The beginnings of panic infected her voice and it shook.

Connor drew her into his side and wrapped an arm around her waist. "Let's just see what they say," he said softly as he breathed a kiss into her hair.

The anchorwoman, having paused, continued. "The province of Alberta contains the second largest proven reserves of oil in the world, behind Saudi Arabia, and most likely has more oil than the rest of the world combined. The main issue with most of the oil in Alberta is that it isn't in liquid form. It's contained in vast tracts of soil and sand. The combination of sand and oil is known as bitumen, or oil sands. Improved technology in addition to the skyrocketing price of oil in recent years has made extracting and processing the oil economically feasible.

"The American government has been looking to Alberta to supply America with oil, replacing Middle East oil as much as possible. The reasons for this are obvious. Canada is a very stable country—economically, technologically and socially similar to America."

Mary hesitated again. "Do we have a feed from the area yet? No? We have very little information at this time for you. We're not sure if the two explosions, one in Canada and the other in Saudi Arabia, are related at this time, but we will continue to monitor the situations in both countries."

Connor glanced down at Alyssa and she looked up to meet his eyes. He could see the fear and the anger in her eyes. She radiated pent-up emotional turmoil. He could almost see the waves of anxiety pouring off her body.

"I've got to get a hold of Grand," Alyssa said tightly.

"Was he in Fort McMurray?" Connor asked.

Alyssa shook her head and then scraped her wrist across her forehead. She shook out her hands, clenched and unclenched them a few times and then wrapped them around her waist. Grand might very well have been near the explosion. "I don't know. He may have been. He isn't supposed to be, but Grand does a lot of things he's not supposed to do," Alyssa said, her voice low, grim.

She spun around and hurried to the kitchen counter where her bag sat. She dug through it and finally extracted her cell phone. With slightly shaking fingers, she dialed the eleven digits of Grand's telephone number. Putting the cell phone to her ear, she listened. The phone rang once. Twice.

"C'mon, *c'mon*, Grand. Pick *up* the phone," Alyssa whispered urgently into the device, dragging her free hand through her hair. The phone rang a third time, then a fourth time. Alyssa rolled her eyes and shifted her weight onto her right leg. If he were going to pick up, Grand would have done so by now. She wanted to throw the phone on the ground and stomp on it for good measure. "Damn!"

Connor came up behind Alyssa and massaged her tense neck muscles. She ignored him.

She cut the phone call off savagely and dialed again. Someone picked up. "Hello?"

"Mrs. Brody? It's Alyssa. Have you—" Alyssa's voice shook with strain, agitation.

"Alyssa, my dear! How nice to hear from you. How are you doing, love? It's been such a long time since you've been to see me," Mrs. Brody pouted. She was Grand's next-door neighbor, if you counted next door as two miles down the road in his rural community. One would think at seventy-five years old, she would be over the "crush" phase of her life, but apparently not. "Are you coming to see me soon?"

Alyssa wanted to reach through the phone and shake the sweet, annoying woman. "Mrs. Brody, I'm sorry to be rude, but I really need to know if you've seen Grand today or if you know where he is. It's very urgent."

"He's here in my kitchen right now, dear. We're just having a nice spot of tea with some scones."

At Mrs. Brody's words, Alyssa sagged against the kitchen counter, relieved. Her heart, which until now had been threatening to jump out of throat, threatened to stop altogether. She slowly leaned forward until her forehead rested against the cold granite countertop. It felt wonderful against her overheated skin.

"Alyssa, what is it?" Connor asked, his hands resting motionless on her shoulders.

Alyssa tried to speak, but nothing came out. A deep breath and a few croaks later, she managed to mumble, "He's okay. He's with Mrs. Brody, a long way from Fort McMurray. Thank God."

"What's that, dear? You really should speak more clearly. It's hard to hear you," Mrs. Brody scolded her.

Alyssa snorted, amused. She levered up into a standing position, feeling lightheaded. "I'm sorry, Mrs. Brody. May I speak to Grand, please?"

"Of course, dear," Mrs. Brody said. In the background, Alyssa heard, "Dougie, Alyssa's on the phone for you. Yes, you." Silence. *Dougie*? She called him *Dougie*? "No, I don't know why. You'll just have to talk to her yourself." Another silence. "Here he is, dear. I'll talk to you later. Bye, sweet-pea."

Alyssa spoke to Grand for five minutes, explaining what had happened in Fort McMurray. After ascertaining that he wouldn't go anywhere near the oil fields, she told him about her progress with Energy Unlimited's technological security.

"Is it fixable?" Grand asked.

"Don't see why not. It could take a while though—perhaps a month, give or take a little," Alyssa responded.

"And how are you getting along with Mr. Donnelly?" Grand asked.

"Uh, fine," Alyssa answered. "*Mr.* Donnelly and I are getting along just fine." She wasn't about to tell Grand exactly how well she was getting along with Connor. She didn't know how he would react to that. Grand was never one to mix business with pleasure and he probably wouldn't approve.

Connor smiled wickedly behind Alyssa. Forgetting that Liam was still in the room, Connor slid his hand under the soft drape of hair to lift it away from her neck and gave her pecking kisses on the now-exposed column. Goose bumps rose on her neck. She tried waving him away like a pesky fly. The fly kept landing.

Alyssa turned around and placed a blocking hand against his chest. "Okay, Grand. I gotta go. Yeah, I love you too. Bye."

Alyssa snapped her cell closed as she narrowed her eyes at Connor. "What am I going to *do* with you?"

"I've got a few ideas." Connor smiled at her enticingly, wrapping his arms around her waist, drawing her close.

"I'm sure you do. But that's not going to get you better security, is it?" Alyssa leaned back to get a better look at him, her eyes laughing.

"It might," he responded in a low voice as he leered at her playfully.

Alyssa disentangled herself from Connor's grasp, laughing. "I'll meet you back here in forty minutes."

And she slipped out the front door.

"Well, well, well, *Mr. Donnelly*, I must say I am truly shocked. Your security expert there is quite a woman. It seems you've recruited her for yourself," Liam said, mischief lighting his eyes. "I thought you said she sounded like trouble."

Connor cast a despairing glance at Liam. Of course the circumstances would be too irresistible for Liam and his brother rarely got such a ripe opportunity plunked into his lap. No doubt he would relish his good fortune to be around when Alyssa proved to be such a distraction.

"This kind of trouble I'll take." Connor lifted his eyebrows at his brother.

Liam cocked his head to one side and studied his older brother for a moment. A lopsided grin appeared on his face, his eyes laughed. "I don't think I've ever seen you like this."

"Like what?"

"If you were a woman, I'd say you were smitten."

"Smitten, is it?" Connor asked dryly. Here it comes, he thought ruefully.

"Smitten. Definitely." Liam's voice changed into falsetto, supposedly imitating a woman. "Oh, Romeo, Romeo, wherefore art thou, Romeo?" Liam brought fluttering hands to rest theatrically over his heart and batted his eyelashes at Connor.

Connor laughed in spite of himself. "You're nuts, you know?"

"I may be nuts, but I'm *also* right." Liam proceeded to flutter a few steps away, his hands still over his heart. He coyly rested one foot on the toe and turned his knee inward, all the while blinking bashfully back at his brother. The sight of his decidedly masculine, very large, unshaven younger brother attempting to look like a fragile, delicate flower of femininity was laughable. Delicate, Liam was not.

Connor tried unsuccessfully to suppress an amused smile. "You keep that up and some nice burly woman is going to sweep *you* off *your* feet."

"Yes, but not before Alyssa sweeps you off yours, Romeo. Oops! Too late. Already happened."

Connor grabbed the nearest tea towel and flung it at his brother's head. A direct hit. Liam grabbed both ends of the towel and pulled it down to surround his face. He blinked becomingly at Connor. Connor rolled his eyes upward in defeat.

Liam whipped the tea towel off his head and tossed it back at Connor, who caught it with one hand. "Don't worry, bro. I won't tell anyone you're a human being. It'll just be *our* little secret." He winked conspiratorially at Connor. "No one would believe me, anyway."

Chapter Seven

Ten long hours later, Liam sat down heavily on the sofa in Connor's office at Energy Unlimited. He leaned forward and buried his hands in his hair, pulling it back from his face.

"That bad?" Connor inquired, eyeballing him.

"That woman is a whirlwind. She's doing an inventory of all the major systems, servers, firewalls and routers. Everything." Liam heaved a sigh.

"Where is she now?"

"In the network room down in the basement, crawling around the network connections. She said she wanted to see if the system has been physically compromised."

"Is she down there alone?"

"Bill's with her. You know, the roundish, *happily married* network guy," Liam said pointedly with a smile. Meaning, of course, that he posed no threat to Alyssa. Or Connor's plans for her. Connor relaxed his tensed shoulders.

"How much longer will she be down there?" Connor asked, looking at his watch. It had been a long day for both of them.

"She said maybe another half an hour or so." Correctly reading his brother, Liam said gently, "She's not made of china, Connor. She's a techie. She's used to long hours." And she's more equipped to deal with anything than I've seen in any single person, other than you."

"That she is." Connor sighed and changed the subject. He ran his fingers through his hair, trying unsuccessfully to pull Alyssa out of his mind. He took a deep breath. "I received more information on the two explosions today. My sources in the government say that the Saudi refinery was definitely bombed. They found traces of Semtex, a powerful military-grade explosive, in the wreckage. A little goes a long way, as they say.

"Unfortunately, the Saudis are being very tight-lipped about the whole thing. At this end of the world, the Canadians think the Fort McMurray explosion is suspicious. It could be days before they have anything conclusive.

"The problem with the Canadian situation is that any number of people or groups could want to damage oil sands production. Part of the problem is that the Alberta government has ordered producers of natural gas to stop operations in and around Fort McMurray in order to keep sufficient pressure in the ground to be able to extract the oil from the sands. So the natural gas producers have motive.

"As well, the current methods for extracting the oil are extremely damaging to the environment. The Alberta government currently has a shitload of outstanding lawsuits from citizens claiming adverse health effects. So the environmentalists have a motive.

"Then there's the possibility of terrorists and I don't even want to get into that one right now. The short and the long of it is that there is a whole whack of people who have motives for wanting to shut down the oil sands."

"Great," Liam said sarcastically. "And we're wading into this mess why?"

"Because Douglas' process would solve one of those problems, the environment. Or at least alleviate it tremendously. Instead of using water to separate out the oil from the sand, it would use a heated chemical compound, with any dangerous chemicals being trapped and dumped into empty oil wells where it would be of no danger to the environment. It's a once in a lifetime opportunity for us. We would be at the forefront with this new technology. Alberta will be the next Saudi Arabia and we'll be right there along with it."

"Is the bleeding edge really worth the risk?" Being out on the bleeding edge of any technology brought larger risks than just being on the leading edge of technology. The bleeding edge meant that you were so far out in front of the pack that if something went wrong, you were totally on your own. If the gamble paid off, the rewards were huge. If you failed, well… Liam continued, "I know you've dealt with terrorists, but the rest of us haven't. This sounds like it's getting out of hand."

"This is nowhere near out of hand."

"I'd hate for you to be wrong. You'd be pulling all of us down with you."

"Don't worry. I'm not wrong. The smoke signals all point to us getting out of this in one piece."

"Are you sure you're thinking with the head with the brain? As opposed to the other one?"

"I know what I'm doing, Liam." he said softly, irritated. "Do you really think I'd put the business and our family at risk without a solid idea of the problems and how to circumvent them?"

"Under normal circumstances, I'd say no. But these aren't exactly normal circumstances, are they? You've got a very personal interest in all of this. I'm worried that it may have…compromised your objectivity," Liam responded mildly.

"Look," Connor said and then flinched as he heard a light knock on his office door. "We'll discuss this later," he said in an undertone. "Come in."

The door opened and Bill poked his balding head through. "Alyssa's done in the basement. She asked me to tell you to come down. She says she wants to introduce you to the guts of your system." Bill looked amused.

Connor shoved back from his desk and walked toward Bill, ignoring Liam. "Let's go."

Five minutes later, Bill and Connor arrived in the bowels of the building. As the elevator doors opened, Connor saw Alyssa standing off to the left waiting for them, an impish look on her face. She had a streaks of dirt splayed across her left cheek and forehead. "Bill, it's been a long day. You've been great about everything, but you must be tired. Why don't you go home to your family?"

Bill looked uncertainly at Connor, who nodded at him. "She's right. Go home. We'll see you tomorrow, and thanks for everything."

Connor stepped out of the elevator as Bill stepped in. Bill waved at them as the door slowly closed. Connor looked at Alyssa, puzzled. The amused look on her face had vanished, leaving in its place a worried one. "What's wrong?"

Alyssa gestured with her head to follow him back into the dark. "I found something. I spotted it before Bill saw it. I sent him up to find you so I could have some time to look at it. You've got a problem."

They came to a door in the corner of the building. Alyssa opened the door and a blaze of light poured out into the hallway. The room was air conditioned, sparkling white and clean. It almost glowed. "This is where the main connections for your network meet the outside world."

Attached to the far wall about three feet off the ground was a metal box with a mess of cables leading to and from it in all directions. It looked like an unruly, mutated octopus. She walked toward the mutant and gingerly selected one of the tentacles. It had been spliced open and a small pillbox size contraption had been inserted into the cable.

"You've got a saboteur." Alyssa whipped out a tissue and carefully lifted the transmitter with it. "It looks very new. You can tell by looking at the cable—it's slightly covered with dust. Around the 'addition', the dust has been disturbed and there's no dust on the transmitter. I'd say this has been in place maybe a couple of days, max." She turned to look directly at Connor. "How well do you know your staff?"

"We vet everyone who comes in. A full background, credit, personal and security checks are performed."

"Are any of your employees having financial problems, any personal gripes with you or the company?"

"Financial problems?"

"If someone in your company has serious financial or gambling problems, it makes them easy pickings for a competitor, or someone, to take advantage of him or her. Blackmail, threats can all be used to obtain cooperation. Likewise, if someone's pissed off at you, they're more likely to be receptive to an invitation to play."

"I know everyone in this company personally. I'm having a hard time believing that one of my people could have done this."

"If it's not one of your people, who else has access to this room? Whoever it was knew exactly where to look, where and how to place the transmitter and how to get out without attracting attention. And that doesn't necessarily mean it's one of your tech staff. Anyone can be instructed on how to carry out this sort of thing."

"Did the hacker use this to get into the system last night?"

"No, I would have been able to ping the guy and I couldn't." Alyssa took a deep breath and ran a hand through her hair. "Connor, if I had to guess, I would say that this probably happened last night. Maybe the day before."

Connor gave a long, low whistle in comprehension. "Can you tell where the transmitter came from? Who was the manufacturer, that kind of thing?"

"It looks like it's a personal job. I can see solder marks on it. Someone probably assembled it by hand from various components."

"Maybe we should take it apart and see."

"I'm not sure if you want to do that," Alyssa cautioned. "If we take this thing out of commission, whoever is using it will know that we're on to them."

"But if it's there, then someone has access, *internal access*, to the system. Right?"

"Yes, someone has access. But we might be able to use it to track them down. And I might be able to transfer the transmitter to a standalone box and mimic network traffic so it doesn't give away the fact we know about it."

"Disinformation." Connor gazed at her in admiration. "I like how your mind works. We put dummy information on it and yank their chain." He grinned. "How do we accomplish this without tipping them off?"

Alyssa squirmed, knowing that he would probably agree with some of what she said and knowing he would disagree with the other.

"I can simulate a network crash and bring all the systems down. When it's down, I can transfer the transmitter to another machine. The problems are, number one, finding an adequate machine on short notice, and number two, setting it up will take some time, especially since I don't want to involve any of your people."

Unsure as to how to phrase her next question, she studied Connor and bit down on one edge of her lower lip, worrying it. Family was always a touchy subject, especially when a family member's loyalty and motivations came under scrutiny. She couldn't see any way of avoiding the question.

"What is it?" Connor asked. "Sweetheart, what's going on?"

Alyssa looked at him warily, trying to decide how to proceed. "Uh, well," Alyssa managed to get out and stopped. A moment later, she resumed speaking very carefully and slowly. "It's one thing to suspect one of your employees is on the take. It's another thing altogether to...to question whether or not the people who are...close to you are capable of this sort of thing." Alyssa hedged. She chewed one edge of her lower lip and hazarded a look at him out of the corner of her eye.

"Close to me? You mean Liam." Connor looked icicles at Alyssa. "My brothers and I built this company up from nothing and *you're* questioning *them?*"

"I mean *anyone* who's close to you. At this point, you've got to make up your mind as to who to trust. That means Liam. That means anyone and *everyone,*" Alyssa shot back. "You know the people in your life. I don't. You tell me because I can't tell you."

Connor stared at Alyssa, trying to put a chokehold on his anger. His family was everything to him. They had seen him through the dark times and, come hell or high water, he would stand by them. Alyssa took a step back from him, tension filling her body, her eyes challenging his.

Connor continued to stare at her as he dug through his jeans pockets, searching for his cell phone. When he retrieved the phone, he punched in a few numbers. When Liam picked up, he said, "Get down here. We're in the main network room in the basement."

Hanging up, Connor said very softly, with a chill in his voice, his eyes cold and icy blue, "I trust Liam with my life. You, I'm not sure about."

Alyssa flinched as if he had slapped her. She took a deep breath and spat, "Great—just great. I am such a freaking idiot! You'd think I'd learn. Someone dangles a carrot in front of me and I run after the damn thing. *Shit.*" She closed her eyes and rubbed her eyes with her hands.

Liam walked through the door and stopped short. "What's up?" he asked cautiously.

Alyssa opened her eyes and flicked them over to Liam, avoiding Connor's scrutiny. She explained the problem, the solution and the desired outcome.

"What do you need me for?" Liam asked curiously. "I mean, you're going to be here, so why—?"

Alyssa cut him off. "I'm not going to be here. You've got enough experience to do this on your own. If you run into trouble, you can give me a call and I'll walk you through it."

Liam switched his attention to Connor. "What do you have to say about all of this?"

"She's a big girl. It's a free country. Her decision," Connor answered, his voice hard and unyielding.

Liam lifted his eyebrows, looking bewildered. "Look, I don't know what happened between you two, but this *really* isn't the time to be— "

Alyssa cut him off again. "You want to know what happened? Fine. I don't have a problem with that. I just told Connor that he's got a very wide range of suspects for this little caper. Everyone connected with this place is a suspect. Including family. Including friends. Including *me.* Your brother has just decided that I'm the enemy. Quite honestly, I don't give a rat's ass. You're on your own. I'm out of here. Any questions?"

"Me? I'm a suspect?" Liam sputtered.

"Grow up. Everyone is," Alyssa snapped. With that, she stalked out of the room toward the elevator.

Connor jumped to the entrance of the door and called after her. "You don't have a car. You'll have to wait until we can drive you back to the compound."

"I'll walk," Alyssa bit out as the elevator door closed behind her.

The elevator took Alyssa to the third floor where she had left her bag and leather jacket earlier in the day. The doors opened onto a dark floor. *Great, just great. This day just gets better and better.* She dragged her fingers along the wall to guide her down the hall to Connor's office where she had left her things.

Reaching the office, a soft illumination of moonlight lit the room. At least she could see now, she thought sourly. She looked at her watch, which glowed a touch green in the dark. Nine o'clock. Maybe she'd be able to hitchhike to the compound. Or maybe she'd just hotwire his car and drive herself back. The thought made her smile bitterly. She shrugged on the jacket and flipped the collar down.

She picked up her bag from the sofa and managed to upend it onto the plush carpet. Rolling her eyes, she dropped to her knees in front of the Connor's table. Her lipstick sat under his leather chair, glinting in the watery moonlight. As she crawled toward it, reaching with one hand, another glint caught her eye. She froze.

Alyssa's heart jolted hard. She was eye to eye with a masked intruder. With a gasped cry, she shot back from the desk, whacking her head and landing on her butt. She scuttled away from him, crab-like, clawing her way backward. The intruder bolted forward and grabbed one of her legs. With her free leg, she kicked him as hard as she could, her foot landing solidly on his shoulder, breaking his hold on her leg. He gasped in pain, but rolled quickly to his side and stood, towering over her.

Being in a weak and nearly indefensible position on the floor really didn't help. She had to get out, fast. He reached down to grab her again. She lashed out with her leg, nearly tripping him. In the split second before he recovered his balance, she scrambled to her feet and ran for the door. He grabbed her around the waist from behind, lifting her up off the floor slightly, her legs dangling. She drew in breath to scream when a gloved hand came down hard over her mouth.

Twisting frantically, she managed to sink her teeth into the restraining hand. He didn't let go. She bit harder and he tore his hand away from her, swearing in an unintelligible language. Breathless, she swung her booted foot wildly and managed to score a hit on his lower leg. He gasped in pain, staggered and dropped her.

Alyssa bolted out of the room, the intruder hard on her heels. She couldn't get enough space between them to escape. He grabbed her by the shoulder and she twisted out of his grip. She screamed as he caught her around the waist and yanked on her hair like a leash. His hand, this time grasping a damp rag, descended over her nose and mouth. A sickly sweet odor filled her nose and head. She tried wrenching her face away from the rag, but his hand stuck like glue. She felt a wave of dizziness pass over her, melting her resolve to escape.

Connor, Alyssa thought dimly and checked out of consciousness.

Chapter Eight

In the elevator with the doors opening on the third floor, Connor heard a strangled scream. Alyssa! He felt himself slide effortlessly into operative mode—he darted to the side of the elevator doors as they opened. Connor shot a quick look down the hallway.

In the darkness, he could just make out a large man holding the limp form of Alyssa. Cursing the lack of a weapon of any kind, Connor stepped into the hallway, his weight balanced on the balls of his feet, ready for combat.

"Let her go," Connor called out. Rage burned through his veins at the thought of Alyssa being hurt by this animal.

The man didn't respond, only backed up a step, then another, dragging Alyssa with him.

Connor approached slowly, his eyes flicking between the man and Alyssa. Connor stopped six feet away from the pair and held up his hands "There's no reason for anyone to get hurt. Just let her go."

The man appeared to be thinking over Connor's words. Without warning, the man shoved Alyssa at Connor, hard. Connor managed to catch her before her slack body hit the floor. The man took off running down the hallway and disappeared into the fire exit stairwell. Connor fought the impulse to go after the man, knowing that leaving Alyssa vulnerable and undefended wasn't an option. Not one that he would consider anyway. He scooped her up in his arms and strode into his office to gently arrange her on the sofa.

With practiced, professional hands, Connor skimmed her unconscious body, looking for any signs of damage. His fingers were probing her scalp for lumps or gashes when he caught a whiff of the sickly sweet aroma. He leaned closer to her face and inhaled more deeply. Laced in with her normal vanilla scent was another scent. Chloroform. She'd been drugged. He breathed a sigh of relief. She'd feel sick when she eventually woke up, but he didn't think she had been physically hurt.

Connor retrieved his cell phone and made a call to Liam in the basement. Quickly explaining the situation, Connor asked him to call the police. Hanging up, he sat and watched Alyssa, her breathing deep and slow.

Connor knew she wasn't his enemy. He'd known that all along. She had hurt him, had attacked his "blind" devotion to his family, rightly or wrongly, and he had lashed out at the thing that had caused him pain—her.

Connor sat in a chair close to the sofa, head in his hands, thinking of what had just happened. Alyssa moaned and shifted on the sofa, one arm flopping out to hang over the edge. His head came up to study her profile. Very carefully he extended his hand to stroke her hair. The contact seemed to calm her.

Minutes later, Alyssa's eyes fluttered open to reality. It was dark. Horror flooded back into her body and she bolted upright on the sofa, looking around wildly. From behind her, she felt someone reach for her, touch her shoulders. With a throttled cry, she tore away from the unwelcome grasp and landed on the floor with a thud. Her head pounded. Her stomach rolled over sickeningly. She was dizzy. She had to lie down on the floor before it came up to hit her.

Someone knelt beside her and picked her up off the carpet. He held her closely, but she struggled weakly against him, not knowing who he was.

The person, the man, gathered her up in his arms and carefully placed her back on the sofa. He sat close to her as he stroked her hair. Alyssa's head rested on the back of the sofa, eyes closed, breathing jaggedly. Still stunned by the attack and chloroform, she wondered with some confusion why her attacker would be stroking her hair.

After a few minutes, she found she could open her eyes without the room turning upside down and she rolled her head toward the hand's owner so she could get a good look at her captor. Her eyes widened in surprise to find Connor.

"What happened?" Alyssa croaked. Nausea swept over her in a massive wave. She closed her eyes.

"I was hoping you could tell me. I was in the elevator when I heard you scream. When the doors opened, you were out and a man wearing a balaclava was holding you up. He threw you at me and lit out of here."

"Well, at least you're timely, if nothing else," Alyssa whispered, her voice shaking and faint.

"Can you tell me what happened?" Connor asked, his voice battened down and quiet.

Alyssa swallowed hard, trying to push the nausea down and briefly explained. She slumped forward weakly. "I'm going to throw up."

Connor leaned back and snatched the trash bin from beside his desk and placed it next to Alyssa's legs. "Just try to breathe in and out through your mouth. It'll help with the nausea." Connor stroked her back. "Did he hurt you?"

Alyssa did as she was instructed. She started to shake her head in reply and stopped, thinking better of it. "No. Can you get me a glass of water or some ginger ale?"

"Sure," Connor answered. As he made his way over to the bar fridge, the office lights blared on. He looked back at Alyssa to see her wince and cover her eyes with trembling fingers. Liam must have found the controls. Connor grabbed a can of ginger ale out of the fridge as something caught his eye.

He glanced out the window. A police cruiser and an ambulance rolled to a stop in front of the building, lights flashing. Liam met them as they got out of their vehicles.

Connor could barely contain the rage that welled up in his body. If he'd behaved like a civilized human being, she wouldn't have been up in his office, alone, at the mercy of a predator. It wouldn't happen again, not while he drew breath.

"The police are here." Connor strode over to Alyssa, opening the can of pop. He handed it to her and she grasped it with shaky hands, nearly dropping it. He wrapped his warm hands around her cool ones and helped her to drink.

Alyssa swallowed a sip of the sparkling soda. "Thanks."

Connor slowly let go of her hands, checking to make sure she wouldn't dump the liquid on herself. As Alyssa leaned back against the cushions and closed her eyes, he evaluated her condition. She hadn't been physically hurt in the attack, only shaken. The chloroform didn't help matters. Still, he'd feel better once a doctor checked her over before sending her home with him.

Liam and Roy Jenkins appeared at the door, a paramedic behind them. The paramedic brushed past Liam and Roy and headed to Alyssa.

Squatting beside her, the paramedic gave her a reassuring smile. "Hi, I'm Mike. For starters, I'm just going to take your pulse and we'll go from there." He gently lifted her limp wrist to find her pulse. "Your pulse is a little elevated. How do you feel?"

"I've had better moments," Alyssa responded dryly. "I'm a little dizzy, a little nauseous and a lot tired."

"Did the guy hit you?"

"No. He just grabbed me and yanked on my hair."

Connor added as the paramedic examined Alyssa, "He used chloroform on her. I got a whiff of it after the guy took off."

The paramedic whipped out a small flashlight. "I want you to look just past my shoulder and focus on the far wall. I'm just going to shine this in your eyes to make sure your pupils respond normally."

As Alyssa concentrated on the far wall, he quickly flipped the light into her left eye and then away. He repeated the procedure for the other eye. "Eyes are responding normally." He took out a stethoscope and listened to her chest. "Your lungs sound fine—chloroform can depress respiratory functions, at least temporarily, but it's not a problem right now."

As he rose to his feet, the paramedic spoke to everyone in the room. "Offhand, I'd say she's okay. A good night's sleep and she'll be fine. But to be on the safe side, we should take her to the hospital to be checked out."

"No doctors, no hospital," Alyssa said firmly. "I'm fine. I've had more than enough commotion for one night without dragging it out indefinitely."

"Alyssa," Connor said in a gentle voice, "maybe—"

"*No*. No more," Alyssa snapped. Her voice softened as she addressed the paramedic. "Thank you for your help." The paramedic nodded in understanding. He gathered up his equipment and left.

Roy took over. After conducting a thorough interview, he went over to Liam and Connor, who looked on anxiously. "I think she surprised the guy. Otherwise, he wouldn't have been hiding under the desk. If she hadn't dumped her bag, it probably wouldn't have happened. No one would have known anything. She just got unlucky." Roy looked back at Alyssa, who had curled up on the sofa, knees drawn up into a fetal position, arms wrapped around her body, eyes closed.

Roy dropped his voice further. "What's going on, Connor? First someone tries to run you off the road and now an intruder is hiding in your office."

Connor followed suit and dropped his voice as well. "I don't know what's going on."

"You were looking around when I was questioning her, can you tell if anything is missing?"

"Not that I could see."

"You wouldn't be holding out on me, would you?"

Connor gazed steadily at Roy. "No. Nothing."

"Then keep your eyes and ears peeled, because something smells rotten. I'm going to step up patrols around your house and your office, just to be safe. If you see anything, you let me know. Take her home and see that she rests." With those last instructions, Roy departed.

Alyssa had fallen asleep on the couch. Connor knelt beside her and gently ran his fingers over her cheek. Her skin didn't have the normal warmth he had come to expect. It was cold, clammy. His heart squeezed guiltily. It was his fault. He grabbed the afghan quilt that hung over the back of the sofa and tucked it around her. Liam's reassuring hand squeezed his shoulder. "C'mon. Let's take her home."

Connor nodded, gathered Alyssa up in his arms and rose from the sofa. She didn't even stir. Liam tucked the afghan around her more securely and grabbed her purse.

Liam drove the Mercedes carefully up the mountain to the compound. In the backseat, Connor held Alyssa as she slept peacefully wrapped in his arms. They arrived at the compound and Connor maneuvered out of the backseat with Alyssa, careful not to disturb her slumber.

Depositing her on his bed, Connor stripped off her boots and socks. She'd be warmer if he put her in his flannel nightshirt, but he hesitated. When she woke up, she wouldn't be impressed. He hemmed and hawed for a few more minutes—it just didn't feel right to take off her clothes while she was unconscious.

Screw it, he thought. He carefully and clinically removed her clothing, leaving on only her white cotton panties, and wrapped her in his thickest flannel nightshirt. She didn't stir. He tucked the fluffy goose-down quilt up around her chin. She still felt cold. He went over to the gas fireplace in the corner of his room and flipped the switch on. It crackled to life, casting both warmth and light into the darkened room. If she woke up in the middle of the night, she'd at least be able to see where she was.

Connor drew an overstuffed chair up to the bed and sat next to her as she slept. He gazed at her profile and couldn't resist gently dragging a forefinger over her dirt-smudged cheek.

He'd reacted instead of thinking things through. And she'd paid the price for his error. There was nothing he could do about what was past, but he would sure as hell try to make it up to her.

If she let him.

Chapter Nine

Alyssa awoke as she did most mornings—slow and confused. She was not in her bed at home. She was not in her bed in Connor's guesthouse. She peeked under the covers to see what she was wearing. She was not wearing the clothes she remembered wearing. She had no idea where her clothes were. She had no idea where her oversized flannel nightshirt came from or how she had come to wear it.

She cast her eyes about the room and spotted Connor sleeping in a chair beside the bed, his long legs stretched out in front of him.

Her stirrings woke him. She eyeballed him, eyebrows arched, when he opened his eyes. He smiled at her. "Sleep well?"

Alyssa didn't bother to answer. "Where are my clothes?" Her eyebrows arched in question as she sat up in bed. She would have swung her legs over the side of the bed, but she would have crashed into his long legs.

"I dumped them in the washing machine last night."

"Who took *off* my clothes?"

"I did."

"You did," Alyssa repeated in a flat voice. "Just who the hell died and made you God?" Her voice low and angry, she glared at him. How dare he touch her in such a personal way? He'd made it very clear he considered her to be the enemy.

"You did. When you passed out at the office, someone had to…manage…your affairs."

"Manage my affairs," she repeated angrily. "Manage my affairs? You son of a bitch. What makes you think you have the right to do anything for me, with me or to me, for that matter? You made in abundantly clear that I am *persona non grata* as far as you're concerned. Move your damn legs."

Connor didn't move except to lean toward her more closely. "I'd like another chance, Alyssa," he murmured, seeming sincere.

Alyssa stared at him in disbelief. "Another chance," she repeated.

"If you're going to repeat everything I say, it's going to be hard to hold a conversation." Amusement lurked in his eyes.

In response, Alyssa whipped the bed covers off her body, bounced over to the other side of the immense bed and hopped off. The nightshirt's sleeves were about a foot too long for her. She tried to push her riotous hair out of her eyes with one shirtsleeve. It flopped back into her face. She ignored it. She waved the other sleeve at him vehemently, flapping it up and down wildly. "You want conversation?" Her voice squeaked in outrage.

"As I said, if you're going to repeat everything I say, this is going to take a long time," he said with a smile in his voice, his lips twitching.

Alyssa stood staring at him, breathing heavily, angrier than she could ever remember being. She desperately wished she could smite him down with a look. Her hands curled into fists under the long shirtsleeves. She leaned both sleeve-encased fists on the bed and snarled, "Hell will freeze over before I *ever* hold another conversation with you."

Alyssa stomped around the foot of the bed and made for the door. Connor blocked her exit. She moved to her right. He moved to his left to block her. She moved to her left. He moved to his right. She glowered at him. "Get out of my way."

"We need to talk."

"Like hell we do." Alyssa smiled death-rays at him, her eyes burning. She snorted. If he wanted to play, she could play. He wouldn't like it though.

Alyssa watched Connor's eyes narrow. Good, he was wary of her. Alyssa backed up a step, then another. What followed was a blur. Using her tae-kwon-do training, she tried a forward jump kick aimed at his midsection. She assumed a fighting stance, one leg forward and one leg back. She thrust her rear leg forward and upward, gaining enough momentum to lift her body off the ground. She snapped her other leg forward to connect with his body.

She hoped.

Connor knew what she was doing in the instant before she did it. She might be fast, but years as an agent had honed Connor's reflexes to razor sharpness. He easily sidestepped her attack and snatched her out of midair, grabbing her around the midsection. He whirled her around and dumped her unceremoniously on the bed, partially lying on top of her, his leg flung across both her legs, holding her down. Alyssa froze, staring daggers at him. "Get. Off. Me."

"Not until you calm down," Connor replied, impressed by her nullified attack. Not many women could have even attempted that move. It required a lot of strength. "Alyssa, I'm apologizing. I was wrong. I should never have lost my temper with you. I know that now."

Alyssa breathed heavily. "How *wonderful* for you. Do you think that makes everything all right?" She spat the words at him. "I should've known better. Trusting you was a mistake. I won't make it again."

"It wasn't your mistake. It was my mistake." He took a breath and searched her angry eyes. "Alyssa, last night, when that animal grabbed you, all I could think of was how wrong I was. I wanted to kill him where he stood, erase him off the face of the planet."

No response.

"Alyssa, what do I have to do to convince you I'm sorry? Fall on a sword?" Connor asked.

"That would be a start."

Connor tried another tactic. "Alyssa, you can't leave anyway."

"I can't while you're on top of me."

"What about the partnership I have with your grandfather? You know he looked for a long time before deciding on me. You leave and the whole deal sinks."

Alyssa hated to admit it, but he was right. Grand had searched high and low for a compatible company, and because of her stupidity, he'd have to start all over again. She didn't relish the thought of having to explain to Grand why she couldn't fix the security system. *Oh, and by the way Grand, the reason your deal fell through was that I screwed the CEO. Sorry.* Yeah, that would be good. She'd never be able to look him in the eye again. She rolled her eyes, disgusted with herself and him. "You bastard."

"It's not the first time I've been called that and it won't be the last."

"Fine. *Fine.* I'll fix the security, just get the hell off me."

Connor cocked an eyebrow at her. Alyssa gave him an exasperated look in return, raising her eyebrows. "I promise I won't try to eviscerate you again. Better?"

"Better." Connor gave her a last look and released her. She scrambled off the bed and out of his reach with as much dignity as she could muster. Dignity was hard to come by when your ass was freezing cold. She eyed him balefully before turning on her heel and stalking out of the room. Connor followed closely behind her.

Liam sat at the breakfast bar, slowly ingesting his caffeine fix, when the procession came out of the hallway. Looking from Alyssa to Connor, he shook his head. "Morning all," he hazarded.

"Liam." Alyssa clipped out his name as she spotted her bag resting on the bar beside him. Without stopping, she grabbed for the bag, swung it over her shoulder and headed for the door. "See ya."

Alyssa was nearly at the door when Connor called out after her, frustration making his voice rough. "Alyssa, what about your boots? You need to put something on your feet."

Alyssa couldn't see her boots in her line of vision. Not bothering to look back, Alyssa spotted a pair of Connor's size twelve sneakers by the door and stuffed her feet into them. It didn't help that her feet were only size six. They swam around her feet as she clomped out the door and shut it firmly.

Liam looked a questioning at Connor, eyebrows raised. "You have a real talent for pissing her off, bro. What'd you do now?"

"Simply pointed out that she couldn't leave without scuttling the deal Douglas worked so hard for."

"She must have enjoyed hearing that."

"Oh, yeah. Tons." Connor sat down heavily beside his brother.

"I thought I'd have to come in there and pull you two apart. I could hear the hissing from out here."

Connor eyed Liam's cup of coffee covetously. Liam picked it up and gestured to the waiting coffeepot. "Pot's over there. We have the party tomorrow, in case you've forgotten." Liam reminded Connor as Connor filled his cup. The party was the high point of the year for the Energy Unlimited staff and clients.

"Great. Perfect timing," Connor said, without enthusiasm.

They still needed to set up a computer to fool the transmitter Alyssa had found yesterday. Work still needed to be done. Connor didn't think Alyssa would want to be anywhere near him for the next while. Well, he thought, she would just have to get over that.

He sure as hell wouldn't let her get over him.

Chapter Ten

Alyssa arrived at her cottage, shaking from both cold and anger. She had tripped and shuffled her way from the main chalet, Connor's shoes like barges on her feet. She fumbled with the guest keys, dropping them twice before finally sliding the key home and opening the door. She stumbled inside and promptly fell on the floor. She kicked at the door to shut it, swearing in exasperation.

The stress of the past two days came crashing down on her and she broke. Wave after wave of anxiety wrung the last vestiges of control from her grip, leaving her shaking and unsteady.

Alyssa knew she had "problems", as her grandfather liked to call them. She lay on the cool floor, limp. That coolness soothed a balm over her tightly strung nerves. Bitter, she snorted. Control. Always a fleeting, slippery thing that flowed freely through her fingers like water. The harder she tried for control, the harder it was to hang onto.

Alyssa used to think that if she could just be still enough, quiet enough, that she would be able to ride out any storm. In fact, growing up, the other kids had nicknamed her the "Ice Queen". Never one to socialize, she was more of an outcast than anything else. She had had a few friends, but kids were cruel, and if it came to a choice between her and their own status, she lost.

Never let the bastards know you're hurt or they'll circle around for the kill. It was a harsh lesson she learned from her father. Now there was a *shining* example of good mental health. Hardly.

Jonathan Tiernan. Alyssa supposed at one time that he'd been a decent human being. Before her mother died giving her life. The gift of which her father had never let her live down. He'd loved his wife, Elaine, to distraction. Elaine had been his whole life. Her grandfather told her that when Jonathan had found out his spouse was pregnant with Alyssa, the man had been over the moon. Rapturous.

That all ended with the beginning of Alyssa's life. He was responsible for a squalling, tiny scrap of humanity and, without his beloved Elaine, he couldn't find the energy to nurture his daughter. His daughter reminded him of the happiest days of his life—days that were gone forever. He would look at her in despair and pain and turn away.

Oh, he'd given her the bare essentials of life—sometimes—food, shelter and education, but never love and acceptance. The daughter who wished desperately for a father, a family. Someone who would care about her no matter what. Someone who would be there for her when she needed help or reassurance. And love.

Alyssa had been beneath his notice for her entire life. Until the last day of his life. No, no, no. She wasn't going to do this. Not here. Not now.

Alyssa rolled her head on the floor in frustration. The all or nothing approach to life had gotten her nowhere. She had to trust someone. She just didn't know if she could. What would happen if someone she trusted turned on her? Would she cease to exist? Be so shattered she'd never recover from it?

Alyssa dragged herself up off the floor and sat down at the piano. This was her solace, her release, her only true companion. Music never let her down. She placed her fingers on the keys and bowed her head. She closed her eyes and took a deep breath, letting some of the tension flow out of her body.

Alyssa launched one of Chopin's Nocturnes. The music suited her. She had found that the trick to playing Chopin was to play the emotion, not the piano. The piano was merely the means for expressing the emotion. Alyssa gave herself over completely to the melody, for it said all the things she was afraid to say herself.

This music was soothing and uplifting, as always. Whenever she played this piece, she would imagine dancing with a tall, dark and handsome man, who would whirl her expertly around an elegantly appointed ballroom. The man never had a face, but now as she played, the man slowly came into soft focus. Connor. She didn't fight the imagery and she let it capture her until the final strains of the music died in the air.

Alyssa opened her eyes and stretched fully, wiggling her fingers and toes. Playing piano was almost as good, if not better, than a session with a therapist. The music had imparted its calm to her. It had done its job.

Now, Alyssa had to do her job.

She pushed back from the piano. She glanced toward the kitchen, suddenly hungry, and as her gaze swept over the area, noticed that in her earlier fit of pique, she hadn't quite managed to kick the door shut. She made her way to the door, only to find Liam standing just outside, leaning against the doorframe.

"Liam?" Alyssa asked warily. "What're you doing here?"

Liam had the good grace to look a little abashed. "Sorry, I came over to arrange a time to take you down to the office and heard you playing. I was going to leave, but…" Liam shook his head. "Connor was right. You belong in a concert hall."

It was Alyssa's turn to look a little taken aback. "Well, I've had a lot of practice. I've been playing for nearly twenty-four years now."

"Yeah, but you're not *just* technically very good. The mechanics can be learned, but it takes a special person to communicate that kind of emotion." Liam said, his voice radiating sincerity. "I've seen musicians from all over the world. You've got talent to burn."

Alyssa studied him for a moment and then smiled somewhat shyly, her eyes dropping momentarily to the ground in embarrassment. "Thank you. That's about the nicest thing anyone's ever said about my music." The brothers Donnelly were full of surprises. So many unexpected facets kept being revealed. It kept her off balance. She was used to putting people into categories and they rarely surprised her.

"Actually, while I've got you here and smiling, I forgot to mention that we're having the company party tomorrow. We hold it here and you are definitely invited."

"Company party?"

"Don't say it like *that*. Every year we have a different theme and this year's theme is Celtic Ceilidh."

"Really?" They didn't look like the Celtic Ceilidh type of people. "I've been to a few of them myself. They're great. Do you have a band playing?

"Yeah, we've booked the Barra McLeahys."

"Really?" Alyssa repeated herself. "I saw them in concert once in Toronto at the Harbourfront Center. They were amazing! I can't believe you're having them here."

"I take it that you'll be coming, then?"

"Try to stop me."

"Good. We look forward to having you there."

"Thank you."

"So, when do you think you'll be ready to go?"

"It's a bit early for the party, isn't it?" Alyssa asked, surprised and a little confused.

"To the office," Liam responded, his voice amused.

"Oh. Right. Forgot about the work part," Alyssa answered with a crooked smile. "Just give me a half an hour."

Drumming his fingers against the countertop, Connor waited at the breakfast bar for Liam to return. When Liam strolled into the chalet with no apparent sense of urgency, Connor glared at him.

"Well?" Connor barked.

"Well, what?" Liam responded, innocent as sin.

Connor rolled his eyes. Little brothers were a pain in the ass. "Is she coming?"

"Yes."

"Good." Connor had no doubt that if he had asked her, she wouldn't have agreed to go.

Liam eyed his older brother, a smirk on his face. "I hope you're as good as you think you are."

"Why?"

"After what I saw here this morning and hearing Alyssa playing piano just now, you're going to have your hands full." Liam ran his hand through his mop of golden brown hair. "Fire and ice, man. Fire and ice. You're either going to be a smoldering pile of ash or frostbitten."

"Speak *English*."

"I just heard her play Chopin. The pure, raw emotion that pours out of that girl when she plays is astounding. I think that she bottles up all her emotions and it explodes in her music. And this morning, before she stomped out? Pure ice. It's amazing that it's all contained in one person. And here I thought you were too lazy to want a relationship with a woman. Hell, you pick a woman where it's all work."

"Yeah, but the rewards are worth it."

"As long as you're up for it. 'Course being around you is enough to make anyone spit bullets."

"Drop dead," Connor said without any real heat in his voice. He smiled devilishly. "She's coming and I have a plan. Watch and learn, grasshopper. Watch and learn."

Chapter Eleven

Alyssa had managed to avoid Connor for the entire day. Truth be told, she was a little embarrassed about her behavior that morning. *The guy possibly saves your life, treats you like good china, watches over you while you sleep and you attack him?* She closed her eyes and shook her head, her pony-tailed hair swinging from side to side. *I must be getting more stupid the older I become.* She winced.

"You okay?" Liam asked. They were in the network room at the office. They had been there for the last ten hours, setting up the decoy computer system without anyone noticing.

"Hmm? Oh, uh, yeah, just a little headache," Alyssa lied as she rubbed her temple for effect. Liam didn't need to know the details, as far as she was concerned. "What time is it anyway?"

"About seven."

"So most people are gone for the day by now?"

"Yup, just us mushrooms left in the dark."

"Well, I think we're ready to roll then. If you could call Connor and let him know we're ready, he can see if anyone is left in the building."

"Sounds like a plan." Liam dug through his jeans and found his cell phone. After a quick conversation, he hung up. "Connor will go through the building now. He thinks everyone is out, but he'll check anyway."

"Good."

An awkward silence ensued. Alyssa developed a fascination with the floor, staring at it awkwardly. Liam picked up the conversational ball. "So, uh, how much do you know about your grandfather's oil sands extraction process?"

Alyssa looked at him curiously. People didn't generally ask her about Grand's experiments. Of course, Liam was a geologist, so it would be natural for him to be curious. "I know some."

"Not to be nosy or anything, but I'm assuming that the process is on Consolidated Banyan's computer system. Aren't you worried that someone may try to hack your system again?"

"I would be if it were there. It's been moved to a…safer location. I may be good, but my system is not un-hackable."

"I guess I won't ask where."

"No, you won't," Alyssa agreed. "Until there's a rock-solid contract, nobody knows where it is."

"Fair enough."

Connor walked through the door, interrupting the small talk. "Okay, checked with security, everyone's out of the building." He eyed Alyssa thoughtfully. "What's next?"

Alyssa's heart pounded, his nearness nerve-racking. Taking a deep breath, she tried to smile politely at him. Her face felt like it would crack from the strain. "Your system is going to have a heart attack and collapse. Liam will need to go up and cover the system from the main computer room upstairs. As soon as he's crashed the system, an automated message will be sent to Bill.

"Liam will call Bill, tell him he's got it under control and that there's no reason for Bill to come in. At that point, we move the transmitter from your real system to the dummy system and cross our fingers. We'll have to power up your system and the dummy system at the exact same time. If we're off, even by a couple of seconds, they'll probably suspect something is wrong. We've got one chance at this and we have to get it right."

Liam moved toward the door. "I'll call when I'm ready, Connor." As he left, he shot Connor a warning look, which Alyssa happened to catch.

Great. Just love everyone to tiptoe around me.

After Liam left, Alyssa felt Connor's eyes on her, so once again she developed a fascination with the floor. She never knew floors could be so interesting—all those white tiles. So…square. Connor's presence filled the room and her senses. His very male scent pervaded the room, as did his presence. It was an intoxicating drug, making her dizzy.

"You, uh, don't have to stay. I can take care of this," Alyssa said without looking at him.

"I'm staying right here. After last night, you'd be nuts to think that I'd leave you down here by yourself. Someone's already been in here leaving that little doodad on the system."

"Suit yourself." Alyssa shrugged, hoping to look unconcerned.

"I will."

"Fine."

"No problemo."

"*Stop* already. Let's not make this harder than it has to be."

"I'm not making anything harder that it has to be."

Connor's cell phone rang. "Yes. Okay…hang on." Connor looked at Alyssa. "Liam's ready. Are you?"

"As I'll ever be. Tell him to go." Alyssa walked over to the main network router box, the one with the tentacles protruding from it.

"It's a go," Connor spoke into the phone, before disconnecting the call.

The humming of machines that was ever-present in the network room began to grow dimmer, and eventually, the behemoths were silent. Alyssa opened a small roll-up toolkit and began to work. Carefully, with tweezers, she meticulously separated the wires that ran to and from the transmitter. "Nice bit of work, this. Very professional," she muttered more to herself than to Connor.

"Professional admiration? You like what this guy did to my system?" Connor sounded indignant as he stood behind her and watched her work.

"More like professional appreciation. It's hard not to admire the handiwork. This transmitter may be a homemade jobby, but it's a well-done homemade jobby. This guy really knew what he was doing." Alyssa fished her magnifying glasses out of her toolkit and put them on. "That's better." She took a closer look.

"Uh oh." Alyssa abruptly stepped back from the transmitter and crashed into Connor. His hands descended on her shoulders to steady both of them.

"Uh oh, what?" Connor asked.

Alyssa looked back up at him over her shoulder, her heart shuddering from the unexpected physical contact with him. It was hard for her to think straight, but she dragged her mind away from his touch to the job at hand. "It looks like it has an anti-tampering feature built into it. This is going to be a lot harder than I thought."

Connor stared at the offending electronic intruder. "How much longer is it going to take?"

"Originally, I thought that it'd take about ten minutes. This could take me an hour, maybe more."

"Why so long?"

"I don't want to trigger any sort of alarm to alert whoever put this thing here. It going to be very delicate and I have to make sure I don't set it off."

"Do you need any help?"

"I'm not sure. Maybe." Alyssa bit her lower lip. "You'd better let Liam know I've run into a snag. And we need to make sure that no one comes into the building unexpectedly."

"Right." Connor released Alyssa's shoulders, somewhat reluctantly it seemed to Alyssa, and turned away from her quickly, as if hiding something. "Do you need anything else from upstairs? I'm going to call Liam."

"No. I'm just going to get started on this." Alyssa turned around to see his back to her, phone held to his ear. With a sigh, she turned back to the transmitter and started pulling it apart slowly. She didn't relish the idea of picking though the mind of the creator of this little baby.

She pried the outer casing off the transmitter and placed it on the table they had set up beside the router. She took a careful look at the naked components and shook her head. Computer geeks were the worst. The creator of this one apparently had a god-complex. He'd wrapped every conceivable piece of hardware into the damn thing. She wasn't even sure if she could remove it undetected.

"Connor?" Alyssa said, feeling him stare at her back as she worked. She shook her head.

"This doesn't sound good already—do I really want to know what you're thinking?" Connor asked.

'This is going to be tricky. I don't know if I can remove the transmitter without being detected. It's going to be a fifty-fifty split. What do you want to do?" Alyssa turned her head to look at him as he approached her.

"I'll take the odds. Just do the best you can and we'll deal with the consequences later."

"You're the boss," Alyssa said, doubt coloring her voice. She hoped she could do it. She'd never seen anything like this sucker. She turned back toward the transmitter. Connor was so close that the warmth radiating from his hard body stroked her back, his breath softly caressed her neck, bared by her upswept hair, causing goose bumps on her unprotected flesh. He smelled of sweet mint and virile man, distracting her from the job at hand. She sighed. Loud. "You're making me nervous."

"Nervous?"

"You don't have to stand right behind me and breathe down my neck. I'm trying to concentrate and you're making it difficult."

She craned her neck around to look at Connor. His smile would have done justice to a pirate.

"Nervous?" he whispered into her ear. "Let me help then." He placed his hands on her shoulders and started to massage her tense neck muscles.

Alyssa froze solid. "What are you doing?" She braced herself, wanting to melt into his hands. It felt so-o-o good.

"I'm helping you relax."

"You're helping me relax." Clearly unconvinced, Alyssa swung around to face him. His hands lifted from her shoulders and he smiled down at her.

"This is not helping me relax." Alyssa arched her eyebrows at him. She breathed in his delicious male scent, a combination of soap, mint and a pleasant masculine musk.

"What about this?" Connor slid his arms around her waist and pulled her close. She stiffened in response. He ignored that and bent his head to nibble on her sensitive ear. Why was it that the man always seemed to know exactly where to touch her for maximum effect? Her ears and neck were two of her own erogenous zones.

Shivers of pleasure rode down Alyssa's spine. Her eyes rolled back into her head. She relaxed into his arms involuntarily and her mind went blank. "Connor?" she whispered.

"Is it working?"

"I can't think when you're doing that."

"What about when I do this?" Connor pulled her around to face him and opened her mouth with his, plunging into her without hesitating. She met his pleasure with her own. She kissed him back long and hard. His hands traveled over her body, stroking and exploring. He grabbed her butt with both hands and pulled her up his body. She wrapped her legs around his waist, desperate to be closer to him. Transmitter forgotten, they wrapped themselves in a blanket of passion.

Connor pushed Alyssa against the wall beside the router box. Their bodies and mouths melded together in raw passion. Bolts of pleasure shot through her body and she desperately wanted one very personal, hot bolt inside her right *now*. Gasping, spiraling out of control, Alyssa opened her eyes and froze.

Oh crap.

Liam stood at the entrance to the room with an embarrassed, yet oh-so-amused look on his face.

Alyssa went rigid in Connor's arms, and he asked, "What is it, sweetheart?"

"Uh, Connor, I came down to see if you needed any help," Liam answered from behind him. "But apparently you have everything well in…hand."

Alyssa's head dropped to Connor's shoulder. She unwound her legs from around his waist. He let her slide slowly down his body—she enjoyed every last sweet bit of contact. She leaned against the wall, legs shaking, as Connor edged his fingers and hands from her body and turned around to face the music.

"What do you think you're doing?" Liam inquired politely.

"I was, uh, helping her relax." That didn't sound even vaguely true, not to anyone in the room.

"Were you." Liam flicked his eyes over to Alyssa, who ran shaking hands over her head. She could barely meet his eyes. He turned to Connor and shook his head. "You might think of helping her *relax* later, stud," he said dryly, his eyebrows rising in decided high spirits.

Alyssa felt a flush rise on her face in embarrassment and closed her eyes. *Oh God, this just keeps getting worse and worse. What was I thinking? Apparently nothing, that's the problem.* Alyssa spoke up. "Let's just get on with ripping this thing out and leave everything else alone." She brushed past Connor and picked up the tweezers with trembling hands, turning her attention to the transmitter. Maybe if she ignored them, they'd go away.

Connor flung Liam a disgusted look. Liam shook his head, half-amused and half-annoyed. Liam slowly crossed his eyes at his brother and snorted in grudging amusement. "Let me know if you need anything. I'll be upstairs in the main computer room." Liam turned and left.

Connor turned back toward Alyssa. "We need to talk."

"Right now, all I need to do is get this thing out of your system. I can't think straight when you touch me and I can't talk to you about this right now. Could we please just get on with this?"

"You're right. Now is not the time." Connor crossed the room and sat down on a chair by the opposite wall. Silently, he watched her work and wondered. She was a veritable volcano of passion. Why was she having such a hard time trusting him?

Maybe she was still mad about the argument they'd had yesterday. Maybe she was one of those people who had a hard time letting go. Maybe she didn't have a lot of experience with men. Maybe it wasn't just him she didn't trust. Maybe she didn't trust anybody. Which meant she didn't trust herself.

A half an hour went by. The silence was starting to get to him. He fidgeted in his chair, crossed and uncrossed his arms, tried to calculate the coming budget for the remainder of the year. Nothing helped. And she still hadn't said a word.

"I need your help here," Alyssa spoke for the first time, her voice a little strained.

Relieved at the loss of silent inaction, Connor came over and stood beside her. "What do you need?"

"You see this wire? I need to bypass it. I need you to attach two leads onto the wire while I cut it and re-route the signal."

Connor nodded and grasped one tiny clamp in each hand. At a nod from Alyssa, he carefully maneuvered them onto the wire. Alyssa attached a second tiny cable to the main wire and ran the cable to the waiting decoy computer.

Working quickly, she cut the wire that Connor had clamped off and removed the transmitter, handling it like an explosive device. She attached the device to the decoy machine and closed the lid with a faint snap. From her pocket, she produced an identical reproduction of the transmitter and attached it to the place where the original transmitter had previously resided.

"I think we're ready. Let me have your cell."

Connor handed it over silently. Alyssa punched in Liam's number.

"Liam, I'm ready. Yeah. Okay, on the count of three, power up the network and I'll do the same on the decoy box." Alyssa stood by the decoy box, hand poised over the power button. "One, two…no. I'll count one, two, three and then go…okay…one, two three, go!"

The machines in the room started humming like bees in a hive. Alyssa sat down at the decoy's monitor and keyboard and stared at the incoming information. Ten more minutes went by with Alyssa performing more checks. She finally heaved a heavy sigh of relief and smiled, looking up at Connor next to her. "I think we're clear." She looked back at the monitor as she dragged one hand around the back of her neck.

Connor took over the massage and started kneading her tightly corded neck muscles. She shrugged his hands off and stood, her butt tight against the edge of the desk.

"Connor, this is moving too fast."

Connor wasn't ready for her to back away from him, not now, and with a sudden realization, not ever. He swore inwardly. He'd pushed too hard, too fast and was in danger of scaring her off permanently. Forcing a smile to his lips, he raised his hand to gently tuck a wayward piece of hair behind her exquisitely shaped ear. "Sweetheart, we can go any speed you like."

Alyssa studied him. "Thank you."

"No thanks necessary." Connor's voice softened. "I can wait." If he had to, he could, and would, mark time forever.

Alyssa nodded, the dark circles beneath her eyes a testament to the long, stressful days. He brushed her cheek with gentle knuckles of one hand. Her eyes closed and she moved her cheek against his fingers as if craving his touch.

"Time to get you home before you fall over," he said softly.

Chapter Twelve

Alyssa tossed and turned restlessly, alone in bed at the guest chalet. She just couldn't get comfortable. She knew that the problem wasn't so much the bed, but the incessant replay in her mind of her earlier tryst with Connor. The memory was enough to cause the heat to rise in her body, demanding appeasement.

Connor just had to touch her and all semblance of sanity flew out the window. She hadn't experienced that with any other man. She had never allowed it. Strict rationality was more her style. Or at least the pretense of it. It allowed her to put distance between herself and the world. But she wasn't able to maintain any sort of distance from Connor.

She felt like a yo-yo, running away only to return to him on the roll back. She fought it unsuccessfully. Maybe it would be easier if she stopped fighting herself, stopped fighting him. Every fiber of Alyssa's being shrieked in horror at just letting things happen.

Control. CONTROL. She'd drummed it into her head every single day. It was her mantra, her religion. The issue of control permeated every corner, every facet of her life. Logically, Alyssa knew that control was an impossible state to achieve—a fiction created by those too afraid to accept life as it unfolded. Those who wanted to predict down to the last second how their lives played out. And God, she was afraid. Of everything.

Now the iron control Alyssa tried to exercise over her life was slipping away like water through her fingers. The more she tightened her grip, the faster it leaked out between her desperate fingers. Because like life, she couldn't contain water in her hands without spilling it.

Alyssa sat up in frustration, pulling at the neck of the thigh-length tee shirt she'd worn. Not only was she not going to get any sleep if the riot in her head continued, but she'd be tied up in knots from sexual frustration. Damn Connor for winding her up like that. Swinging her legs over the bed, she made her way to the bathroom in the dark, feeling her way around the room like a blind person.

Alyssa reached to turn on the tap for a glass of water when she heard something from the living area of the cottage. A faint, sharp crack. Alyssa flinched and then froze. Things going bump in the night made her nervous. She didn't even like things going bump in the daytime.

Alyssa tried to write off the noise as something that houses did on occasion. The house was probably settling. Houses did that all the time. Just the same, she decided to take a quick peek around the chalet to satisfy the butterflies churning in her gut.

She quietly made her way to the bedroom door when she heard another sound like someone walking or tiptoeing across the floor. This was definitely so not her imagination.

Too afraid to confront whomever in the hallway, remembering the previous night's attack, she backed away from the door as quietly as she could and moved swiftly toward the sliding glass doors. She had drawn the vertical blinds closed before going to bed. Something stopped her hand before she drew the blinds aside. Instead, she carefully pulled aside one panel a fraction of an inch and looked out.

Alyssa almost fell over backward, barely choking down the shriek that rose in her throat. There was a man standing with his back to the glass. He was tall and very, very frightening. She was trapped.

Heart pounding wildly, Alyssa pushed down rising hysteria. Running her hands through her hair, she tried to think straight. Someone was in the house. Someone was outside the chalet, guarding the glass door. *Okay. Deep breath. Just keep breathing.*

The guy outside was probably waiting for the guy inside to let him in. Maybe she could lure the guy outside her door inside the chalet. She looked around the room in a near panic, the chamber barely visible in the dim light provided by the night-light in the bathroom.

Think. I have to think. Her bag. She had mace. And the stun gun. The bag sat on the bureau. She slunk over to the bag, being as soundless as possible, and retrieved both coveted items.

Alyssa returned to the sliding glass door and, without opening the blinds, scraped the latch to the unlocked position and opened the door a fraction. "Hssst," she hissed softly at him as she would a cat. She positioned herself along the wall to the side of the door. The man wheeled around quickly and, seeing the door open, no doubt assumed that his partner was letting him inside. Softly spoken foreign words accompanied his actions of sliding the door further open, softly batting aside the blinds and stepping in.

Alyssa took her only chance. She activated the stun gun and jammed it with all her strength into the man's neck. He cried out and turned his head to look at her in shock as he fell. She tried to grab him, but he was too heavy and he hit the floor with a loud thud. *Damn.* She had to get out of there *now.* She was climbing over his inert body when she remembered the panic button in the room. She turned back quickly, not bothering to be quiet anymore, and slammed her fingers clumsily into the glowering red eye on the wall.

Stumbling over the man's body as she fled through the sliding door, she heard someone shout as they entered the bedroom behind her. Finally out in the night, she ran straight into the table and tripped over one of the chairs on the small patio, landing hard on her knees.

She scrambled up and bolted into the woods on her bare feet. She knew there was a method to moving silently, but she didn't know what it was, and at this point, she didn't particularly care. In the dark, she constantly stubbed her toes on rocks as she barreled over the forest floor, strewn with dead branches and other crackling debris. She was making one hell of a racket.

As the realization hit her, Alyssa stopped. Hell, she was making more noise than a bear on a rampage. She was probably fifty yards from the chalet by now. She moved behind a tree and looked back at the path she had just blazed. She couldn't see anyone. Straining, she couldn't hear anyone either. But they could quite possibly be much better at this sort of thing than she. Make that probably. Actually a total certainty.

Alyssa refused to stay in the woods waiting for someone to catch her. She needed to get to the main house. Connor and Liam were there. Relative safety was there.

Taking deep breaths to calm her rattled nerves, she made her way to what she thought was the basic direction of the main house. She didn't backtrack because someone might be lying in wait for her. It seemed to take ages for her to find the lights of the main house flickering through the trees.

Alyssa came to within ten yards of the edge of the clearing, but didn't enter it. She surveyed the area. Off to her left was her cottage. To her right was the main house. She saw two men crouched by the right corner of her cottage, and even from this distance, she could see they were holding weapons. She'd never seen machine guns, but in the movies, that's what they looked like. Fear shot down her spine, nearly paralyzing her. She tried to see what had captured their attention.

Alyssa felt nauseous. Liam and Connor, wearing boxer shorts and t-shirts, were jogging to the guesthouse. She saw the intruders' weapons trained on the brothers. Ready to shoot them down in cold blood.

The pressure in Alyssa's head skyrocketed, stars shot across her field of vision dizzily and she screamed louder than she had ever done so in her entire life. "Get down!!!"

Time slowed down. Liam and Connor dived for cover behind a large boulder as one intruder started emptying his loaded weapon at the brothers. She saw the second intruder swing his weapon in her direction. As she dove to the ground, she heard bullets slam into the trees around her and dig into the ground beside her, spraying her with dirt. She scrabbled wildly on the forest floor, trying to get behind a tree. More bullets pounded into her position. She curled up into a tight ball, head down.

After twenty seconds or so, an eternity to Alyssa, the onslaught of bullets was no longer directed at her. The majority of the noise didn't seem to be coming from the location of the intruders now. With a shock, she realized that someone was firing back at the miscreants, drawing their fire away from her. She chanced a peek from behind the tree, crouched against it. Liam had a hand weapon of some sort and was firing at the gunmen. Connor wasn't with Liam anymore. She couldn't see him.

Alyssa scanned the clearing, fear poisoning her mind. Where was he? He wasn't lying on the ground anywhere. Please don't let him be dead, she prayed desperately. *If he's dead, I've lost everything. I've been so stupid. Why do I wreck everything?*

The firing stopped. There was an eerie calm in the air. Not even crickets chirped.

Alyssa gathered her courage to take another peek around the tree when a hand descended over her mouth and an arm encircled her waist. As she jolted violently, she heard a familiar whisper, warm lips brushing against her cold ear. "It's me, Alyssa. Don't scream."

Alyssa nodded jerkily. The hand lifted from her mouth. She whimpered in relief and turned quickly in Connor's arms.

She threw her arms around him. His lips pressed against her temple before he pulled her away from him.

"The police are on their way. They should be here any minute. Are you okay?" Connor searched her eyes in the moonlight.

Alyssa nodded unevenly, like a bobble-headed toy, unable to form words.

Connor looked at her critically. Twigs and pine needles decorated her hair, which stood out from her head at odd angles. Dirt smudged her face and a nasty-looking bruise marred her forehead. He ran a gentle forefinger over the bruise and kissed it with care. He eased Alyssa down to the ground behind the tree and peered out from their shelter.

Liam sat on the ground on the other side of the boulder. He swung his eyes over to the corner of the guesthouse. Only one intruder was there. The other guy must be circling around for a better shot. They'd pinned Liam down.

"Stay here until I come for you. Do you understand?" he whispered urgently.

"Y…yes."

Connor kissed her hard. "I'll be back," he said in his best Terminator voice.

Connor silently made his way toward the lone intruder. From the waistband of his boxer shorts, he drew his handgun and carefully screwed the silencer into place. He lay flat on the ground, took careful aim and pulled the trigger. The intruder collapsed to the ground without a sound. One down, one to go. He hoped.

Connor circled around the guesthouse, his movements camouflaged by the trees. The second intruder seemed to have vanished. Connor made his way down to the corner of the guesthouse to the prone body lying there. Crouching down, he placed two fingers on the man's neck, searching for a pulse. Dead.

Connor edged around the side of the house nearest to Liam. When he was about ten yards from Liam's position, he picked up a pebble and lobbed it at Liam's boulder. The pebble bounced off the large rock.

Connor softly whistled the opening notes of Beethoven's Fifth Symphony. Liam peeked around the side of the boulder and smirked. Connor motioned for him to leave his position and move out of harm's way. Liam nodded and half-crawled, half-sprinted to Connor's position by the house.

In a voice barely a whisper on the breeze, Connor said, "I've taken out one guy by the house. He's dead. We need to check the house. I couldn't see the other guy anywhere. I need you to stand guard."

Carefully, they crept to the sliding glass door of Alyssa's bedroom, which was wide open. Connor flattened himself on the wall outside the door. He moved a panel of the closed blinds aside a fraction and peeked inside. He didn't see any motion. He did see a man lying motionless on the floor. Entering the room, he noted that the man was still breathing. Alyssa had managed to knock the guy out cold, but he didn't know how much longer the guy would be out.

"Liam," Connor whispered.

Liam poked his head into the room.

"Tie this guy up using the duct tape in the closet. He's out, but there's no telling when he'll wake up."

Liam slid to the closet and brought out the tape. Bound and gagged, the guy was going nowhere.

Connor cased the inside of the house next. No one. Nada. Maybe the other guy had taken off. Connor left the house, Liam trailing behind him, covering his exit. Little, or not-so-little, brothers did have some use after all. They were making a sweep of the perimeter when flashing red lights lit up the dark trees, announcing the late arrival of the police. Connor heard a number of cruisers rolling over the gravel road to the main house. One, two, three cruisers pulled up. Roy got out of the lead cruiser.

Connor jogged over to Roy. "Nice of you to join the party."

Roy swept a look over Connor's attire, or lack thereof, his eyes concentrating on the weapon held in Connor's hand. "You shouldn't have started the party without us. What's going on?"

"Looks like three, maybe four guys broke into Alyssa's cottage. She somehow managed to knock one guy out before hitting the panic button and escaping into the woods. Liam and I were alerted by the panic button in the cottage and came out to see what the problem was, when all hell broke loose. We would have been dead if Alyssa hadn't screamed. Anyway, the bastards started shooting with automatic weapons fire. While Liam returned fire, I made sure Alyssa was safe and then went after whoever was shooting at us.

"I killed one of them, Roy. He's outside the corner of the guesthouse, one guy is taped up in Alyssa's bedroom and we don't know where the other one is. Liam can fill you in while I get Alyssa. She's still in the woods. I told her not to move."

Roy turned to his officers and they fanned out over the grounds in a standard search grid.

Connor strode into the forest to find Alyssa.

Alyssa hadn't moved from where he'd left her. She'd probably seen the flashing red lights and knew that the police were in the compound. As Connor approached her, he knew that all she'd be able to see of his approach would be a dark shadow moving toward her.

Connor held out his hand as he approached and called out to her. "Alyssa, it's okay. It's me."

Alyssa sagged against the tree that was holding her up, shaking violently.

"Sweetheart, I'm here." Connor wrapped strong arms around her and held her tightly. He nuzzled her prickly hair. Alyssa's arms wound around him just as tightly and she pressed her body against him hard.

"I thought you were dead," Alyssa said in a strangled voice.

"I'm not going anywhere." Connor brushed his lips against her hair. "You're safe now. Safe." He rocked her back and forth gently for a moment, hoping to reassure her with his physical proximity, willing her mind to slow and her body to relax.

Connor stepped back from Alyssa, hands on her shoulders and looked down at her. In the moonlight, Connor could see her forehead was bruised and that her legs were scraped, bruised and bleeding. Her feet…were bare and bleeding, for chrissake. She didn't look like she'd be walking anywhere without pain being a factor. "I'm just going to pick you up, honey. You don't look like you're going to make it too far."

Connor swung Alyssa up into his arms. She wrapped her arms tightly around his neck and burrowed into his warmth, evidently any token need to protest her capability dying a quick death.

"You're freezing, girl. We need to get you inside," Connor murmured as he nuzzled her hair with his nose and nearly sneezed on a leaf. He took off downhill through the forest, sure-footed as the spy he'd once been. As he entered the clearing, Roy looked over at the pair coming toward him and swiftly opened the trunk of the cruiser, where he grabbed a blanket.

Roy walked toward Connor and threw the blanket over Alyssa, tucking it in around her. He looked into Alyssa's eyes. "Your feet and legs are kind of battered. You people are having a really *bad* week. I've got a first-aid kit in the car. Get her inside and we'll take care of it."

Connor's concern for her grew with each passing second. She'd barely spoken a word since bringing her out of the woods, probably in shock. He entered the main house with her clinging to him, her head down against his chest. When he tried to ease her onto the sofa, she stared at him with wide eyes and refused to release him. So he sat down still holding her and cuddled her in his lap. He stroked her hair and made soothing noises to calm and reassure her.

Roy came into the house with the first-aid kit. He appeared to be thinking of treating her himself until he got a little closer to Alyssa. He hesitated and then handed the kit to Connor. "Connor, maybe you should do this."

Connor nodded at him and took the kit with one hand. "Give me fifteen or twenty minutes to take care of her. Then we'll talk."

Connor pulled back to survey Alyssa more clinically. She was in shock, in pain, confused and scared. He brushed his fingertips over her cheek—she was also as cold as the snows of Kilimanjaro. It was going to take more than a little antiseptic lotion to cleanse her wounds and abrasions. She had dirt everywhere. It was also going to take a lot more than a little empathy to tend to her emotional wounds. Alyssa stared back at him, her eyes huge and black in her ashen, grimy face.

"Sweetheart, we need to get you cleaned up and the best place for that is the bathroom." Alyssa nodded vaguely, still on autopilot, released him and got to her feet. She winced. Connor picked her up again, she felt as light as air, which worried him more, and walked toward the bathroom.

Connor's personal bathroom, tiled in sparkling white, had a huge whirlpool tub at one end and a large open shower stall with a tiled bench at the other. Connor chose the shower stall and lowered Alyssa to the heated bench. Next to the bench was a faucet. He turned the faucet on and adjusted the temperature to lukewarm.

Connor wet a sponge and squeezed it to trickle water down her battered legs before patting her wounds clean. He moved down to her feet and cleansed the abraded skin. Alyssa winced now and again as he thoroughly, but gently, cleaned her cuts and bruises. She leaned back against the shower wall tiredly and closed her eyes.

"Can you take the shirt off, honey? We really need to get you cleaned up and a sponge bath just isn't going to do it." Connor reached for the hand-held shower wand.

Alyssa opened her eyes and looked at Connor, kneeling in front of her, looking worriedly at her. He wasn't trying to be cute, getting her to take off her shirt for his personal ya-yas. She grasped the bottom of the shirt and peeled it up and off her body, tossing it on the floor outside the shower, leaving her naked.

The water from the wand sheeted over her hair, her head and her body. She closed her eyes as Connor squeezed a dollop of shampoo on her head. He massaged the shampoo into her scalp and neck with great care, as if she would shatter with the wrong touch. He soaped the rest of her body and then rinsed it off with the shower wand.

Turning off the water, he reached for a fluffy white towel and patted her dry. He grabbed his heavy terry bathrobe from the hook and wrapped her in it. He picked her up, cradled like a baby, and sat her on the countertop.

Connor opened the first-aid kit and pulled out the antiseptic cream. "This is going to sting," he warned her. Alyssa nodded.

Connor was right. It did sting. And she had a lot of cuts and scrapes, so it took some time. Eventually, he finished. He looked up at her and smiled. "All better." Getting to his feet, her gave her a soft kiss on the undamaged portion of her forehead, just like she'd imagined she would receive from her mother, if she hadn't died at Alyssa's birth.

Alyssa almost burst into tears but managed to give him a wobbly smile instead. "Thank you." No one had ever treated her like this. Amazingly gentle, incredibly tender and totally concerned. She moved to slide off the counter, but Connor laid a cautioning hand on her arm.

"Just wait here." Connor left the bathroom and returned with a pair of white cotton socks. "You don't want to get your feet dirty." He slipped the huge socks onto her small feet and nearly rolled them up to her knees. "These only reach a couple inches past my ankles. On you they're more like stockings."

Alyssa carefully dismounted from the countertop and tried out her newly repaired feet. A little sore, but not too bad. "Anyone ever tell you that you should've been a nurse?"

"Not recently, no." Connor smiled as he touched her face with his fingertips. Then he grimaced. "Unfortunately, we need to talk to Roy about all this. Are you up for this?"

Alyssa nodded. Connor swung her up into his arms again and walked out of the bathroom. With Alyssa settled comfortably on the sofa and a quilt tucked up to her chin, Connor brought Roy into the house.

Roy studied Alyssa for a moment, before speaking. "You are having the world's worst week, Alyssa." He smiled at her, sympathy in his eyes. "Can you tell me what happened?"

Alyssa took a deep breath and rattled out the blow-by-blow account of the ordeal.

Roy scribbled notes on a pad. "Where'd you get the stun gun?"

"I brought it with me from Canada. I bought it from a company in the States a couple of years ago."

"And you thought you'd bring it with you on your trip here? Why?"

Alyssa hesitated. She wasn't sure how to answer him. The truth?

Connor answered the question. "Her grandfather's company's computer system was nearly hacked a couple of weeks before she came down here. She thought that we were her hackers, so she came prepared."

"Prepared, was she? You know, I'd like to think that all this crap, excuse me, that's been happening to both of you lately is coincidence, but I don't think so. *Someone* tried to run both of you off the road. *Someone* was snooping around your offices yesterday. *Someone* came after Alyssa directly tonight. I'd like to know why."

"I don't know why," Alyssa answered truthfully. "It's possible it's related." She hesitated, unsure of how much she could tell Roy about the co-venture. "My grandfather's company and Connor's company are in the beginning stages of a partnership. My grandfather has created a technology, but doesn't have the finances to bring it to market himself. That's why he approached Connor.

"I guess there are a number of groups who wouldn't want to see this co-venture work," Alyssa thought aloud. "But I can't see that they'd resort to attempted murder and God knows what else." She looked up at Roy. "I mean, why come after me?"

"You tell me."

"Maybe someone thinks I know something. Maybe someone thinks that I..." Alyssa's voice trailed off. God, she hadn't thought of that before. Cold fingers of unease crept up her spine and she felt the blood drain from her head. She swayed and her vision clouded.

"Alyssa, what is it?" Connor asked, concern colored his voice.

Alyssa swallowed hard. "Maybe someone thinks that if they can get a hold of me, they can somehow intimidate Grand or get access to his research. I could be used against him."

Alyssa threw off the quilt and got to her feet, wincing in pain. She took a few tentative steps, running her hands through her damp hair. "Maybe they think *I* know the process."

"*Do* you know how the process works?" Connor asked.

Alyssa's heart pounded as she studied Connor. She supposed he would know sooner or later, but still… Alyssa closed her eyes, took a breath and handed her life to Connor. "Yes." She opened her eyes.

"You know the whole process? Beginning to end? The whole shebang?"

"Yes, yes and yes."

"You have notes," he stated.

Alyssa shook her head. "After the hacker attempted to get into Grand's system, I downloaded all the schematics and formulas and memorized them. I took all of Grand's notes off the system and put the only other copy in a safe place. No one will find them. Only Grand would be able to figure out where. If he needed to."

"You memorized them? That must be thousands of pages of research."

"Twenty-five hundred and twenty-one pages, to be exact. I, uh, have a photographic memory."

Connor whistled. "Does anyone else know you have a photographic memory?"

"CSIS knows about it, so does Grand. Aside from you two, that's it."

Roy interrupted. "Who or what is CSIS?"

"The Canadian Security Intelligence Service. I worked for them for six years as a security analyst."

Roy whistled. "And here I thought that mountain patrol would be nice and quiet and uneventful. What did you do as a security analyst?"

"I hacked computer systems."

Roy stared at her. "You're kidding."

"I wish I were."

"Why'd you stop?" Roy asked.

"That's a whole other issue that I am *not* getting into now. It isn't relevant to this."

"Are you sure?"

"As certain as I can be at this point. If that changes, I'll let you know."

Roy considered Alyssa for a moment. He shrugged before turning to Connor. "All I can tell you, man, is that you need to increase your security. These guys managed to disable your security perimeter and get into the guesthouse undetected. The main house security is better than the guesthouse security. Make sure she stays here with you. With all this excitement going on, she shouldn't be left alone."

"No shit."

"I'm going to leave a couple of the guys outside the house for tonight. If anything else happens, they'll let me know."

"I will. Thanks, Roy."

"Next time, don't start without me. I hate missing the beginning of a party. Don't get to mingle with all the guests." Roy turned to Alyssa. "Do you have any other weapons in your possession that I should be aware of?"

"I've got some mace and a switchblade. I don't know where the stun gun is. I can't remember if I dropped it in the house or I lost it in the woods."

"One of my guys picked it up. We'll need to hold onto it for a couple of days."

Alyssa nodded. "That's fine. Hopefully, I won't need it again."

Connor walked Roy to the door. Roy nodded his head toward Alyssa and lowered his voice. "She's going to be okay? She's been through a lot since she arrived. "

"I think so. She's a lot tougher than she looks. I won't let her out my sight."

Roy studied Connor a moment before smiling. "I guess she's safe enough then. I'll check in with you tomorrow. The guy Alyssa zapped is still out cold. We'll have to take him to the hospital to be checked. I'll let you know in the morning when he's awake."

"I want to be there when you question him."

"Does that mean Alyssa will be there too? Is she going to be up for that?"

"I'll see how she's doing tomorrow. If she's not good to go, then I'll get Liam to keep an eye on her."

"Fair enough." Roy hid a yawn. "We all need some sleep. My guys will be here all night, keeping an eye on things and going through the crime scene. If you see anything, let them know."

Roy opened the door to leave and Liam walked into the house. He had changed into a green sweater, jeans and runners. "Hey, Roy. Leaving so soon?" Liam asked.

"I hate to be the last pathetic guy left at a party that's already over. You know how it is," Roy replied with a smirk.

Liam grinned. "Not these days. Take it easy."

Alyssa's bruises ached, her cuts burned and she felt like she'd been run over by a Zamboni. An icy feeling crept into her soul. Someone was after her. All the things that had happened since she arrived in Colorado were because of her. It was only dumb luck that no one had been injured or, worse yet, killed. She knew what she had to do, but it tore at her mind and her heart.

Connor's glancing touch on her shoulder brought her out of her reverie. She quickly took his hand and brought it to her lips, kissing it. It would be better, easier, if she did this quickly. She lifted her gaze to him. "Connor, I have to leave. I'm going to go back to Canada tomorrow."

Connor flinched. "Why?" he asked, his voice raw with tension.

"All this is happening because of me. It's only a miracle that no one's been killed. You and Liam nearly *died* tonight because of me. I can't be responsible for your deaths. I won't have more deaths on my conscience. I can't take it. Not again." Alyssa's voice shook with emotion.

Liam took the opportunity to drift away from Connor and Alyssa, edging toward his room.

Connor looked down at her. "I'm a big boy, Alyssa. I can take care of myself."

"And what about Liam? What about the rest of your family? What about the people who work for you? You're all in danger for as long as I stay. The sooner I leave, the safer everyone will be."

"What about you? If you leave, you'll be alone, defenseless. If you think I'm going to throw you to the wolves, you're crazy."

"Do you think I want to?" Alyssa's voice broke. She struggled to her feet and limped away from Connor, shaking with emotion. "God help me, but I don't want to leave," she whispered. Tears traced down her cheeks and she brushed them away impatiently with the back of her hand. She tilted her head back, willing the tears to stop, but they just came harder.

Connor came up behind her and turned her around to face him. "Then *don't*." He took her face in his hands and kissed her softly, thoroughly. "Don't leave. Not when I've just found you." He pulled her against his warm body, willing her to change her mind. He kissed her hair, her eyes, her neck, as if to inhale her very essence, her very being. He cupped her face in his hands and stared into her eyes. "You can't go. I won't let you go."

Alyssa took a jagged breath as the tears squeezed out of the corners of her eyes. She missed him already and she wasn't even gone yet. Awash in a sea of pain, physical and emotional, she closed her eyes and tried to shut him out of her mind. It didn't work. He was everywhere, a part of her, mind, body and soul. "What about your family, your employees, you?" she asked raggedly.

"I'll look after it. I *promise you.* Everything will be fine, sweetheart. I'll make it right." Connor's voice grew just as ragged as hers. "Alyssa?"

Alyssa gasped and nodded. "Okay." She wound her arms around him and held on hard, feeling all the ridged muscle mold to her curves. "Okay," she whispered. She lifted her wet face to his, placing her trembling lips against his, drinking him in.

Connor groaned and buried his tongue in her mouth. Her addiction to the gentle, hungry mating of lips and tongues grew. He dragged her as close to him as humanly possible without a transplant operation. His hungry hands explored her body, teasing her relentlessly but softly. He placed both hands on either side of her neck and pushed them up into her damp hair. Alyssa shivered violently. Her head fell back as he nibbling on her neck. She went boneless as waves of pleasure shimmered through her body.

Connor lifted Alyssa into his arms and, still kissing her, walked to his bedroom. He placed her on the bed, breathing heavily with building passion. He leaned over and flipped on the switch for the gas fireplace. The light of the flames danced exotically over her face. Kneeling over her on the bed, he slowly opened the terry robe to reveal her lush body, her skin glowing in the firelight.

Alyssa arched her back as a shiver rippled through her body, making her rosy nipples tighten inviting Connor to lean down and suckle hungrily, first one and then the other. Pleasure rocked her body from the inside as her sex engorged wetly in arousal. The musky scent of her arousal perfumed the air.

Connor slowly licked and laved one breast, taking his leisure to coax the sensitive nipples into a stiff, velvety peak. He playfully inhaled the breast into his mouth and ran his tongue around the edges of her areola. Her breast swelled a minute amount in his mouth, obedient to his, and her, pleasure. He released the breast in his mouth with a miniscule popping sound, causing Alyssa to snicker in amusement and then gasp as he indulged the other breast with the same loving attention.

Releasing her breasts, his hand caressed her forehead, her nose, her cheeks and lips. Her eyes opened to find his two inches away, gazing at her with such intensity that her breath locked in her throat. As he lay beside her, his strength both protected and sheltered without overwhelming her. His hand feathered to her breasts, tweaking the nipples to remind them of his presence and then coasted down to her belly and to her navel.

He shifted down her body only to be welcomed by her parted thighs. He lowered himself into the cradle of her body, his mouth at the same latitude as her navel. He wrapped his arms beneath her lower back, arching her slightly into his mouth, and bathed her navel with repeated licks, making her shiver in pleasure.

The amazing sensation felt like he had physically reached into her to stimulate every erotic receptor in her entire body and mind, creating an unrelenting buzz of anticipation in her primed flesh.

When she was gasping within the fire of ecstasy he had nurtured so carefully, he slid further down and placed his lips to the softest of her flesh. She cried out softly and bucked under his ministrations. He lapped up and down her labia, carefully avoiding her clitoris, creating an almost unbearable anticipation.

The very act of avoiding her clitoris caused it to become ever more insistent for direct contact. Trembling, as if stretched on a rack, she groaned as he bypassed her clit yet again. And again. Gasping brokenly, she was about to demand relief when he took the sensitized nub of flesh gently between his lips and sucked on it delicately. He released her captive flesh almost immediately, before she could climax.

Wild and sobbing, Alyssa twisted on the bed and rent the bed sheets with her hands, desperate for him to finish what he had started. He unwound her clenched fingers from the Egyptian cotton linens and held her hands down by the sides of her body. Open for his delectation, he continued his single-minded pursuit of her pleasure, teasing her to the edge of release, but no more.

Finally, Connor released her hands and slid his naked body up hers, brushing her body with his. Alyssa didn't know how he managed to get naked without her knowledge and she didn't care. She needed him as she had never needed another human being. He captured her wrists in his hands and drew those outward from her body, as if tied to either side of the bed.

Alyssa shivered and wrapped her legs around his waist. She could feel his penis resting at the entrance to her wet, soft core. She moved her hips rhythmically, trying to lure him. To share her body. To own her body.

Connor gasped as Alyssa whimpered. "Now." She squirmed desperately against him.

"Your wish is my command," Connor whispered back as he drove into her welcoming body. Alyssa gasped, her body arching yet again to take him into her flesh. Her vagina clenched spontaneously, joyously, around her welcome visitor. Her whole being was focused on where flesh met flesh intimately. The pulses radiated outward, leaving her poised on the razor edge thin precipice.

Connor thrust hard into her. She took all of him, wanting more, wanting it all. Her body heaved upward as she was dragged over the edge into the throbbing oblivion, her body convulsing tightly around him, pulling him over the edge with her.

Connor collapsed on her body, breathing heavily. She liked the feeling of having him deep inside her body, physically and spiritually connected to her. She wrapped her arms around him tightly. He groaned and tried to shift his weight off her. She held him where he was. "Don't go," she whispered.

Connor wrapped his arms around her and rolled over onto his back, taking her with him, still buried deep in her body. "I won't." He tightened his arms to hold her closer and whispered, "Sleep now, Alyssa. Sleep."

They fell asleep still joined deeply, peaceful.

Chapter Thirteen

A shaft of light lanced through a crack between the curtains and tried to pierce Alyssa's closed eyes. She winced and tried to move away from the offending dawn. She found she couldn't. Slowly, oblivion left her mind. She was in the same position in which she had fallen asleep. On top of Connor, who still held her possessively even in his sleep.

Her stirrings woke Connor.

"Hey, sleepyhead," Alyssa said softly, leaning back to look at him. She drew a light finger slowly down his nose to his lips. Connor took her finger into his mouth and sucked it into his mouth greedily. Her breath hissed inward as he watched her with hooded eyes.

Connor groaned and released her finger. He flipped them over so that he was lying on top of her, between her legs. His morning erection was at full attention. He growled softly, deep in his throat, as he nuzzled her neck with his nose and bit her gently. She sort of liked the growling. And the biting. It sent shivers chasing down her spine. She wrapped her arms around him in welcome.

Slowly he pulled his face away from her neck and settled in nose to nose with Alyssa. He shifted so that his penis rested quietly at the entrance of her vagina, still soft and slick from their lovemaking the night before. Deliberately, meditatively, he sheathed himself in her heated, wet softness, holding her eyes captive with his. Her eyelids fluttered in pleasure and she shuddered some more.

Connor and Alyssa moved gently to their own rhythm. Quietly, purposefully, they made love with absolute deliberation. The world did not exist. Words did not exist.

They existed in a world of their making, only speaking the language of their bodies, of ecstasy.

The growing shudders in each of their bodies didn't change the pace of their loving. And still their eyes did not waver from one other. As their mutual climax hit, Alyssa's vision dimmed with pleasure. She cried out softly and unraveled in his arms. Connor groaned as he poured the last of himself into her and lay, spent, on top of her. Nuzzling her neck.

Alyssa was shaken. She'd felt like she was the center of his universe and he hers. The bone-deep intimacy was unlike anything she'd ever experienced.

"Good morning," Connor said softly. His insides were mush. He'd never made love like that before—it had been so...personal. An elemental joining of minds and of bodies and all that metaphysical stuff. Yikes! But it was a good "yikes". He could never have prepared himself for what had transpired between them. His feelings toward her were protective and possessive in the extreme.

Last night's events had brought the protectiveness out into the open, even though his years as a spy had allowed him to function clearly and logically. The slightest thought of Alyssa in jeopardy had left him panicked, had compelled him to possess her in the most primitive, the most physical of ways. Their lovemaking hadn't been about overpowering lust. Or not only about lust. It had been about possessing and protecting that which he loved—her. And that wasn't something he had expected to actually feel, not now for the first time at the age of thirty-six.

"Good morning," Alyssa answered softly. "I like waking up that way."

"I'd be happy to wake you up like that everyday, if you like."

"I like. I like a lot."

"I'm also available for other occasions. Weddings, bar mitzvahs, weekdays, weekends, mornings, afternoons, evenings, nights and so on."

"Do I book in advance?"

"I'll pencil you in."

"Deal."

Connor furrowed his brows at her. "How do you feel?" The question was about twenty minutes too late. She must be sore from her bumps, bruises and cuts from last night and he'd forgotten about all of that upon waking and finding her nakedly near.

"Strange. Wonderful. Awful. Sort of the good, the bad and the ugly, all rolled into one."

Connor lifted himself off Alyssa, taking care not to brush her battered legs. He leaned on his shoulder, head propped in his hand. He brushed the hair off her forehead. Alyssa turned her head to look at him, then rolled over onto her side to face him, wincing as she did so.

"What about you?" Alyssa asked.

"The good, the bad and the ugly pretty well covers it for me too," Connor said, his smile crooked. "Alyssa, last night I meant what I said. I want you here. Not just now. Always."

Alyssa ducked her head to avoid his eyes. "Let's just take things one day at a time for now. That's about all I can handle at this point."

Connor fastened his eyes onto her face. Warning bells went off in his head, but he held his tongue. She hadn't outright rejected the idea of staying. She hadn't said she'd leave. He forced a smile to his lips. "I'll take it. " He paused. "And you, my dear, must be starving. Nothing like good, old-fashion terror with a dollop of sex on top to build an appetite," he said in a light, playful manner to get past *that* awkward moment.

Alyssa snorted. "Now that you mention it, I could eat a horse."

"Horse is definitely not on the menu, but I'm sure I can come up with something just as satisfying." Connor rolled out of bed naked, closed his eyes and stretched his arms above his head, groaning with the pleasure of it. As he opened his eyes, he caught Alyssa staring hungrily at his body and at one appendage in particular. He smirked, smug in the knowledge he pleased her.

Alyssa caught the smirk, felt her face heat, but smiled back at him. "I'm allowed to look."

"You can look, touch, taste. *Whatever* you'd like."

Alyssa rolled out of bed in his direction. Connor backed up a hair to give her room to stand. She glanced up at him out of the corner of her eye. Slowly, she brought her hands to his chest and she ran her palms over the taut muscles. Her curious fingers slid up to his broad shoulders and down his well-muscled arms.

"What is this? An inspection?" Connor arched his eyebrows at her.

"You said I could touch. *Whatever I like* was how I heard it."

"Then by all means, continue."

She did. Connor enjoyed her caresses, his eyes closed, smiling.

Alyssa sighed. "Inspection over, I guess. You need to feed me before I start eating something else."

"If I didn't feed you, what would you be snacking on?"

"That's best left for another time." Alyssa smiled, arching one eyebrow with a touch of wickedness infusing her expression. "You'll just have to wait to find out."

Connor laughed. He couldn't wait.

In the kitchen, Alyssa sat at the breakfast bar, elbows on the countertop, chin resting on one palm, and watched Connor cook. Pancakes were on the menu. He didn't even need a cookbook. She sighed inwardly. Damn, that just made the man more attractive. He took out a large bowl and poured the flour into it freehand, eyeing the measurement. He then sprinkled some other dry ingredients over the soft pile and started mixing.

"You do this a lot?" Alyssa asked.

"What? Cook?"

"Yeah."

"There aren't any restaurants nearby. And as I've said before, I like to eat. You cook?"

"Not if I can avoid it."

"That's why you're so skinny."

"Skinny? You call this skinny? Another twenty pounds and maybe, but hardly skinny now."

"You'd be too thin. I like a woman I can hold on to. And you've got just the curves I like. You could even add to those curves."

"Don't even tempt me. I can turn into a blimp in no time."

Connor laughed. "Well, maybe not blimp proportions."

"Don't feed me too well then," Alyssa warned, smiling.

"After the past few days, I don't think you need to worry about calories. Stress burns a lot of energy. As does sex." Connor dumped eggs, vanilla and milk into the dry mixture in the bowl and started stirring lightly with a large wooden spoon. He eyed her curiously. "Was the hacker attack at Consolidated Banyan the first of the unusual occurrences?"

She cocked her head to one side to think. "As far as I know. Grand never mentioned anything to me about any other odd occurrences. I didn't tell him about the hacker." Alyssa leaned forward, rested her elbows on the granite and cradled her chin in her hands, fascinated by his display of domesticity.

"Who else would know about the process?" Connor poured the batter onto a hot griddle. The future pancakes sizzled as cold batter met hot metal.

Alyssa raised her eyebrows and blew out her breath forcefully through pursed lips. "I suppose a few people have different bits and pieces of information. Grand couldn't physically do all the work himself, so he had to hire a few people here and there. He may have told them what he was looking for, but I doubt it." She shrugged. "Someone may have figured it out, though.

"The oil sands in Alberta are a huge project now. Everyone and their dog are trying to find a way to extract the oil cheaply. People would have known that Grand was working on a process, even if they didn't have the details."

"You said that there were a number of groups who could possibly sabotage the project. Who are they?"

Alyssa rattled off the same suspect groups that he had come up with originally upon learning about the Saudi and Alberta oil field explosions—environmentalists, natural gas producers, oil patch competitors and terrorists. She sighed and looked down at the counter.

"It's the terrorist angle that has me worried the most. Until recently, the general consensus was that the Middle East held all the cards when it came to oil production. Now, with Alberta holding the world's second largest proven oil reserves, I can see that it would produce a little uncertainty, especially for the Saudis.

"They're still top dog, but they're in a downward spiral. Corruption is rampant, the Saudi family is totally out of control and their people know it. There've even been rumblings about a revolution, restoring Islamic law full scale and wiping out the excesses of the Saudi family. I wouldn't put it past any terrorist not to make the decision to wipe out Saudi oil production in an effort to return to traditional values.

"Unfortunately, if that happens, it takes the world's economy and flushes it down the toilet. If al-Qaeda or other terrorist groups have jumped into the fray, I can definitely see them going for the Alberta oil sands, making sure that no one has access to any oil." Alyssa dropped her head into her hands and closed her eyes. "God, what a mess."

Connor touched her shoulder and she brought her head up to look into his eyes. "We'll figure it out." She watched as he lifted the corner of one of the bubbling rounds of batter and then flipped all the pancakes over. They sizzled in unison.

Alyssa raised her head, her eyes worried. "I wish I could believe it, Connor. I saw a lot of intelligence information while I worked for CSIS. I just hope to hell that this has nothing to do with terrorists. Canada is not prepared to deal with terrorists," Alyssa said with a note of disgust in her voice.

Connor didn't know what to tell her to make her feel better. She knew the players and the angles. You could sugarcoat the truth if you wanted, but a smart person didn't and Alyssa was a smart person. He watched her as she struggled to swallow the possibilities. "You need food. Everything looks better on a full stomach."

Connor lifted one of the pancakes. Perfect. He shoveled them all onto a plate and put it on the counter in front of Alyssa. He walked around to perch on the high barstool beside her. Leaning over, he gave her a hug and kissed her ear. Straightening up, he proceeded to dump five pancakes onto her plate.

Alyssa looked at him in surprise, eyebrows arched. "If I eat all that, I'm going to explode. Full is one thing, dead because I've exploded is another."

Connor smirked. "Eat up. This is going to be a long day. You're going to need all the energy you can get." He dropped some pancakes onto his own plate, slathered his stack with butter and maple syrup and dug in.

Alyssa picked at one of the pancakes.

"I'll feed you myself if I have to." Connor glanced at her. "You barely ate yesterday, except for some toast and Coke, so eat."

"It's the geek diet." Nonetheless, Alyssa picked up her fork and slowly started to eat. "Mmm, you make great pancakes." She ate a bit faster, smacking her lips on the maple syrup that clung to the flapjacks.

The phone rang. Connor wiped his mouth on a napkin and picked up the extension telephone placed on the breakfast bar beside him.

It was Roy. "Our boy is awake, but he's speaking some weird-ass language. We're not even sure if he understands English."

"Where is he?"

"He's here in one of the holding cells. I'm not sure how we're going to question him."

"I speak a few languages. I may be able to communicate with him."

"He's not really the talkative type, but you can try," Roy responded.

"We'll be down there in about an hour or so."

"See you then."

As soon as Connor hung up the phone, Alyssa asked in a tight voice strung with tension, "He doesn't speak English?"

"They're not sure. Did you hear any conversation last night between any of the gunmen?"

"When I lured the one guy into the bedroom, he was speaking some other language. It didn't sound like a European language, but aside from that, I don't know."

"You can't repeat what he said?"

"Sorry."

"No problem. Let's get dressed and see what our mystery man has to offer. Maybe he'll be a little more talkative when I get there." It sounded like a threat.

Alyssa looked up at him warily. "What exactly are you planning to do?"

"You don't want to know."

Chapter Fourteen

The gleaming new police station glowed in the bright sunlight as Connor's hunter-green Jaguar pulled into the attached parking lot. Connor turned off the engine and looked at Alyssa, sitting silently beside him. She felt his gaze. She'd been staring out the window for the past ten minutes, silent. She turned her head to look at him.

Connor looked controlled, but beneath the control a whisper of worry clouded his eyes. Again.

"Alyssa, you don't need to do this. I'll take care of it."

"No. I want to look this bastard in the eye." Alyssa drew a deep breath. "They came after *me*. I want to know why. I want to hear it for myself."

"This could get ugly. I don't think you want to see it."

"Connor, I'm in this up to my eyeballs. I own it and I'm going to see it through. Wherever it takes me, I'll go." Her jaw set. She was going. There was no way in hell she'd be left behind.

Connor blew out a breath. He brought up his hand to stroke her hair and leaned closer to her. "Just remember you're not alone. I'm with you all the way."

Alyssa's eyes softened. "Thank you."

Connor leaned even closer, cupped her face and kissed her softly, lingeringly, his eyes searching her face. "Let's go."

In the station, Roy led Connor and Alyssa to an interrogation room. The room was bare except for a long table with a single chair on one side and two chairs on the opposite side. A long expanse of mirror lined the wall behind the table.

Alyssa retreated to the nearest corner of the room, crossed her arms and waited for the man to arrive.

Connor sat down in one of the chairs facing the door, his face carefully schooled to blankness. She'd seen that exact same look on many operatives' faces. She knew what he was feeling because she was feeling it herself—it was like stepping into a well-worn pair of shoes that were just a little tight at the toe. A little painful, but familiar.

The door swung open and a man in orange prison coveralls was partly shoved, partly led into the room by Roy and one other officer. In the reflection of the mirror, Alyssa saw a man chained hand and foot. The chains rattled as he was pushed down onto a chair. His short, midnight black hair, a medium-length black beard and moustache all contributed to hiding his face. His cold black eyes stared defiantly at Connor.

Connor eyed Roy speculatively. Roy took his silent cue and, taking the other officer with him, left the room.

Alyssa stared at the man in the mirror. Her heart pounded furiously. She knew she was safe, but his physical proximity made her uneasy. Irrationally, she felt like knocking him over the head. Hard. Unfortunately, there was nothing really handy to hit him with. *Except* the extra chair. She eyed it with interest for a moment before shaking her head. She doubted if anyone would let her hit him anyway. She settled for glowering at him, staring daggers at his head.

The man, seeing her reflection in the glass, swiveled his head in her direction, his eyes drilling malevolently into hers. Her eyes narrowed as she picked up the challenge in his eyes. *You bastard. You're not going to get the best of me.* She mustered as much coldness into her eyes as possible. The man sneered condescendingly.

Connor rapped his fisted knuckles sharply on the table to get the man's attention. Connor spoke softly, a razor fine edge to his voice. "I know you speak English, asshole."

Alyssa didn't see the man react. Connor, his instincts honed by years of spookdom, apparently saw a tiny something in the man's eyes and snorted. "You just gave yourself away, slick."

The man cocked his head to the left and shrugged. In heavily accented English, he said in a deep baritone voice, "It is of, how do you say, no matter." He gestured with his head to Alyssa. "She should not be here, my friend. Women are…unsuited to the business of men."

"Unsuited? You son of a bitch. If I were so unsuited, you'd be free now," Alyssa said, angered by the man's insulting attitude. "Maybe you're *unsuited for the business of men.*"

The man smirked. "She is a, uh, handful?" he said to Connor. Before Connor could reply, the man sneered at Alyssa. "Go home, *Jane Bond*. This does not concern you."

Alyssa flinched at the insult. "You're hardly one to be giving orders," she retorted. "You're the one in chains, not me. And if it doesn't concern me, what were you and your pals doing in my cottage?"

"Protecting you."

"Protecting me from yourselves?" Alyssa asked acidly, all but spitting out the words. "How *kind* of you. I feel all *warm and fuzzy* inside."

The man rolled his eyes and turned his attention back to Connor. "Your good friend Joseph Taylor sent me."

"Joe sent you," Connor repeated, skepticism laden in the voice. "I don't believe you."

"Call him. He will confirm my identity."

"Which is?"

The man leaned forward and spoke very softly, in Hebrew, more mouthing the words than saying them. "I am Ari Alyashar. I am an agent of the Mossad. Israeli intelligence." Ari's dark eyes held Connor's narrowed blue eyes.

Connor abruptly got to his feet and walked around the desk. He grabbed Alyssa by the arm and walked out of the room with her in tow. Alyssa acquiesced until the door was closed.

"What are you doing?" Alyssa whispered in a heated tone, hands moving in exclamation. "That guy's Mossad."

"Since when do you speak Hebrew?" Connor asked, startled, and caught her hands in his.

"Another of life's great mysteries," Alyssa snapped, her eyebrows arched in question. "Answer me."

Connor considered her for a moment. She had the right to know. "If this guy is Mossad and Joe sent him, then we're in a lot more trouble than I thought."

"Who is Joe?"

Connor looked around the hallway. He lowered his voice even though no one else was in the corridor. "Joe was my handler when I quit the CIA. He's not supposed to have any contact with former agents. It's too risky."

"So, you believe Ari whatshisname?"

"No. I need to get a hold of Joe before I talk to this guy again."

"I thought you said it was too risky."

"I don't have much of a choice. But I can't do it from here. I—"

Roy stepped out from a room a door down from the interrogation room and walked toward them. "What's going on?" Annoyance invested his features. Connor knew that in the dark was not Roy's favorite place.

"Throw the guy back in his holding cell."

"Why?"

"I can't tell you. Don't push me on this one, Roy." Connor's voice held a measure of steel.

Roy considered Connor, speculation rife in his eyes. He spoke slowly. "I need to charge him with something. I can't just keep him indefinitely."

"Charge him with breaking and entering. Assault. Hell, picking his nose in public. I don't care. Whatever the hell you can think of. I need more time."

Roy considered Connor and raised his eyebrows doubtfully. "I didn't catch the last thing he said to you before you stomped out. What was it?"

"Roy, all I can tell you is that there's more to this whole thing than meets the eye. I can tell you he speaks English. You can do your own interrogation. I can't tell you anything else."

Roy looked decidedly under-whelmed. "You're not helping me much, man."

"Sorry. Can't be helped. Just keep a close eye on him. He's dangerous."

"What if he gets bailed out?"

"Let me know the second he lawyers-up. I'll deal with it then."

Roy sighed, clearly unhappy. "Fine, but you owe me. Big-time."

"You're a prince, Roy."

"Yeahyeahyeah. Another name for a sucker."

Connor and Alyssa climbed into his Jag and left the station. Alyssa stared at Connor's profile. Feeling her scrutiny, he looked over at her and sighed. "There's no need to look at me like I'm green or something."

"Connor, if that man in there is Mossad, I need to warn Grand."

"Why would you warn Grand?" The woman was too quick by far. He could see it would be impossible to hide anything from her.

"*If* he's Mossad and *if* he is protecting me, which, by the way, I don't believe for a moment, then it means that everything that's happened has something to do with terrorists. Islamic terrorists. The blast at the plant in Saudi, the explosion in Fort McMurray. All related. I mean, think of it.

"Why would the Mossad be involved?" Alyssa answered her own question. "*Because* they've caught wind of someone trying to permanently shut down world oil production. The reason the Israelis would be involved is that if the world economy tanks, the Arabs will overrun and slaughter every Israeli they can find. America won't be in any position to defend Israel, much less itself."

"That would be a reasonable hypothesis. If he's Mossad."

"What are you going to do about it?"

"I have to find a way to get to Joe Taylor. I don't know if any of my old channels are still open."

"What kind of channels did you use?"

Connor glanced at her out of the corner of his eye. Alyssa rolled her eyes at him.

"Connor, as I've said before, I'm in this up to my eyeballs. I've been in the intelligence community and I can help. Look, if I'm going to trust you, you're going to have to trust me too. It goes both ways."

"It's not an issue of trust, Alyssa." Connor sighed. "Various drop points in DC. Coded messages sent over the Internet, in newspapers, satellite links. All the standard stuff."

"Drop points I can't help you with. Coded messages over the Internet and satellite links I can do," Alyssa said, sounding determined, but reluctant.

Connor reached over and took her clammy hand that lay on her lap. "Alyssa, how do you know Hebrew?" Jesus, why would she learn Hebrew?

"CSIS receives a little intelligence from the Mossad. I was curious, which was a bad thing. I only know a little. Enough to recognize the word 'Mossad' when I hear it, let's put it that way."

"Okay, I can accept that." He considered her for moment. "You said that Ari spoke a little yesterday. You didn't recognize it?"

"He may not have been speaking Hebrew. We don't know who he is. He may have been speaking some other language. On my part, as I've said, my spoken Hebrew is weak. I was terrified at the time, so I didn't stop to ask him what language he was speaking," Alyssa answered tartly. "Why does this make a difference?"

"It doesn't, really. Just curious."

Alyssa eyed him. "Why do I have the feeling you're storing this information away for future reference?"

"Just want to know everything there is to know about you. And it's not just you. I squirrel away all sorts of information." Connor gave her a winning smile, the sun coming through the sunroof glinting off his blue-black hair. The look was designed to simultaneously fire every female neuron in her brain. He knew it worked when she blushed.

Alyssa laughed. "Fine. You're a squirrel. I get it."

"And so much more. You'll just have to stick around and see."

"I'm starting to see that." Alyssa paused. "When do you want to contact Joe?"

"I'll try a few things when we get home. It's Saturday, so I may not hear anything until Monday or Tuesday."

"What channels are you going to try?"

"With your help, I'd like to go for a secure satellite transmission. You've done those before, haven't you?" Connor glanced at her.

"Please." Alyssa snorted derisively. "In my sleep."

"Well, Ms. Technology, you're going to get a chance to do it while you're awake."

Connor expertly maneuvered the Jag onto the gravel road that led to the house. As they approached, they could see that the caterers and the band for the ceilidh were setting up on the opposite side of the lake from the house. Connor glanced at his watch. Eleven a.m. Entering the garage, he parked the car, coming around to Alyssa's side and opening the door for her. He extended a hand to her help her from the car. Retaining her hand, he pulled her close.

"Alyssa, you don't have to do anything you don't want. I know that being sucked back into this world is not what you want. I *can* handle it myself," Connor said softly, searching her eyes with his. He wanted to protect her from all the nastiness that he knew was coming. It was almost overwhelming, this…need…to protect her.

Alyssa reached up to brush his cheek gently with the back of her hand. She furrowed her brow at him. "In for a penny, in for a pound. It's not what you want either. You can't protect me from this, Connor. If anything, I should be protecting you. This isn't your fight. Not really. It's mine. And Grand's. He just doesn't know it yet."

"You're wrong. It's our problem," Connor said fiercely. He caught her hand and pressed his lips to her palm, keeping his eyes on hers.

Alyssa's breath caught in her throat. Her mind emptied, staring at him. Whatever happenstance had brought him into her life, she didn't know. She didn't care. She cared only that he was here. Now. Warmth flooded Alyssa's body. She relaxed and leaned into his body, wrapping her arms around his waist. Tears pricked at her eyes and she let out a ragged breath of relief.

"Hey, hey, hey," Connor murmured, drawing her away to look in her eyes. He smiled, "Did you really think I'd tell you're on your own?"

"You wouldn't be the first." Alyssa took a steadying breath and smiled weakly, her gaze skittering away from his.

"They were all idiots. Every single last one of them," Connor muttered darkly. He tucked a lock of her hair back behind one ear, his hand lingered on her jawline and tipped her face up to his, making her look at him. A dawning look of discovery flew over his face. "That's it, isn't it?"

"What do you mean?"

"You expect to be hurt and so you have a hard time trusting other people."

"Something like that," Alyssa whispered, nearly in a panic that he'd seen through her walls and subterfuge, feeling her chest tighten. She forced air into her lungs and changed the subject. "Do you know which satellite you want to bounce your message off?"

Connor let the topic slide after a moment of silence. "It's a military satellite in high orbit around the forty-ninth parallel." Connor wrapped an arm around her waist and they moved out of the garage into the blinding sunlight.

Alyssa put up her hand to shade her eyes, adjusting to the sudden brilliance, and looked up into the sky. It was a clear azure that seemed to go on forever. She felt her spirits lift. The beauty here nearly stopped her heart. She could almost imagine living here… The pined-scented clean air, the snow-capped mountain peaks and sparkling lake. She smiled. "You know, I—"

"Ali? Ali Tiernan?" a voice called out from the bandstand. Alyssa looked for the voice in the distance. Shading her eyes, she made out a tall blonde woman in jeans and a white tee shirt. Alyssa smiled even more broadly. Teresa Sumner.

Teresa was a bubbly, outgoing woman Alyssa had met in college. Teresa had been a singer in a bar band back in Massachusetts, which was how they met. She had sung her way through a liberal arts degree, managing to pay off most of her school costs in the process. Their mutual love of music had been the touchstone that bound both women. They'd become fast friends and had kept in touch through the years.

Alyssa slipped out of Connor's arms. "Girl, what you doing here?" She called as the woman bounded toward them. As Teresa reached them, she flung her arms around Alyssa and hugged her hard, laughing. Alyssa hugged her back, joining in her laughter.

Teresa released Alyssa and stepped back. She curled up her hand, fogged up her fingernails with her breath and shined them up on her shirt. "I am the *new* manager for the Barra McLeahy."

"You're kidding! When did this happen?"

"Two weeks ago. That's why I called you, but you didn't return my call. Now I know why you haven't been at home." Teresa glanced around Alyssa at Connor and nearly purred. "And *who* is this gorgeous hunk of man you've found?"

Alyssa laughed and turned to Connor, who surveyed them with undisguised amusement. "Teresa Sumner, this is Connor Donnelly. Connor, this is Teresa. We met while we were at college."

"The boss man himself," Teresa teased as she shook his hand. "I hope you're treating my Ali right. I'd hate to have to take a round out of you."

Connor laughed. "Yes, ma'am. As much as she'll allow." Which wasn't enough as far as he was concerned, but some things were out of his hands… He'd wondered what Alyssa was like around people she knew. Her normal reserve had slipped away to be replaced with a buoyancy, a lightness. He'd seen glimpses of that light over the past couple of days, but with current circumstances, she had held her reserve to her like a shield. Now she radiated happiness. He liked it. A lot. Enough to want to see it repeated many, many times.

"What are you doing here? It was quite a shock to see you wrapped around Mr. Donnelly here," Teresa asked, an impish light to her smile.

"Grand's company and Connor's company are going into business together. I'm here to check out Connor's security system."

"You're *checking* out the *security*, are you? Tell me, what is the *security* like? Satisfying?" Teresa leered comically at Alyssa.

Alyssa choked and then laughed. "You're incorrigible."

"Yes, and it's sooo much fun. You'll have to tell me all about the *security*." Teresa eyed Connor with laughing, sky-blue eyes. "A bit later would be better."

"Yes. Maybe later would be better," Alyssa agreed. She sighed. "Unfortunately, I need to do a couple of things first. You're going to be around?"

"With bells on my toes. When you're finished, come find me and we'll hang." Teresa gave Alyssa another quick hug. "Bye, babe." She took a quick look at Connor and waved at him. "Nice to meet you." Teresa bounded off toward the bandstand.

"Now I feel guilty for monopolizing your time," Connor said, one corner of his lip pulled down. She should be having fun—not having to deal with asshole terrorists. His hands tightened into fists and he had to concentrate on wriggling his fingers loose, one by one, so as not to alarm Alyssa.

Alyssa lifted her eyebrows, apparently not noticing his hands, and shrugged philosophically. "You're hardly monopolizing my time—I'm really monopolizing your time when you think about it. We might as well get this thing done. It's going to take a little time to hack the satellite. I don't suppose you have any of your old access codes?"

"I might. " Connor took Alyssa's hand as they walked toward the house, away from the noise and bustle across the lake.

An hour later, Alyssa was ready to link to the military satellite. Hands poised at the keyboard, she hesitated. "Just remember to keep it short and sweet, we've got about one minute before they detect us. I'll count down." She gave Connor a sidelong glance. "Ready, Freddy?"

Connor smiled. "Freddy's ready."

Alyssa selected a few more keys and quickly vacated the chair. Connor swiftly sat down and started typing ferociously.

"Forty seconds," Alyssa said softly, gazing at her watch.

Connor nodded and continued to type.

"Twenty seconds. I need five seconds to kill the connection."

Connor typed faster.

"Ten seconds. Nine, eight, seven…" Connor scooted off the chair and Alyssa replaced him. Alyssa made a few swift keystrokes. Four, three, two… And smacked the Enter key hard. The screen went blank.

Alyssa heaved a sigh of relief. "Not bad. One second to spare." She turned the chair around to look at him. "Say everything you needed?"

"Yes. Now we wait."

"How long?"

"Probably Monday, so we've got a couple of days."

Alyssa nodded and lifted a hand up to rub the back of her neck. Connor nudged her hand aside and started running his fingers up and down her neck. Alyssa groaned in pleasure and closed her eyes. "You're hired."

"Sold." Connor coaxed her head forward and slid his fingers into her hair. He massaged her scalp and lightly pulled on her hair to relax the muscles beneath. Alyssa shivered and her nipples tightened under her olive-green tee shirt. He eyed those points speculatively, wondering if she wanted to have a complete body massage, with full benefits, when she looked back to find him eyeing her breasts. "Cold?" he asked.

"Nuh uh. It feels amazing. You have *the* most amazing hands." Connor laughed. Alyssa flushed in embarrassment. "That sort of came out wrong."

"You mean I don't have the most amazing hands?" Connor asked, all innocence.

"No. Yes. I don't know." Alyssa stumbled over the words, seeming to be embarrassed with his friendly, sexual camaraderie. She closed her eyes. "God, I am such a geek," she muttered.

"Believe me, you're no geek." Connor swung the chair around so that she faced him. He pulled her up into his arms, wrapping them around her waist. "You know, I don't think I thanked you properly for saving my life last night."

Alyssa pulled back and looked at him in surprise. "Saving your life? Because of me, your life nearly ended. And Liam's."

"If you hadn't warned us, we'd be dead now. Simple."

Alyssa raised her eyebrows. "Simple?"

"Simple," Connor answered. "Let it go, Alyssa. You've nothing to feel guilty about. None of this is your fault. None." He paused. "Why don't you go and spend some time with Teresa? You've had a hell of a week and I'm sure some girl time will do you a world of good. Relax. Let loose. The rest of today is fun only. No more serious stuff. Okay?"

She grinned. "Okay."

Chapter Fifteen

The warm sun shot white sparks off the rippling waves of the lake, temporarily blinding Alyssa. She raised her fingers to shield her eyes from the brilliance and looked sideways at Teresa. They sat side-by-side on the small dock that jutted out into the lake, dangling their feet in the cold water.

"Jesus, Ali. What're you going to do?" Teresa asked worriedly, leaning forward and looking back over her shoulder at Alyssa.

"I don't know. I don't know anything anymore. My life has been turned upside down in the space of three weeks," Alyssa said unhappily. She shook her head. "It's kind of surreal. It feels like it's happening to someone else. I never knew I could be so scared and so... I don't know how to describe it...happily scared, all at the same time."

"Well, at least *some* of the life on the flip side seems to agree with you. Connor's gorgeous. Judging from how he was wrapped around you when I first saw you, he has no intention of letting go."

Alyssa laughed. "I don't know about his intentions. I only know that he's a definite toe-curler."

Teresa smirked. "I see that you've found my favorite phrase when it comes to men. I'm glad to see you've discovered the pleasures of sex. I told you so."

"Yes, you told me so. I just never believed you."

"Hmmm." Teresa eyed her appraisingly. "So what are you wearing to the ceilidh tonight?"

"Jeans. Sweater."

"Just as I thought—you didn't come prepared. Luckily for you, I did."

"What do you mean?"

"Well, a sexy Celtic lass needs some sexy Celtic duds."

"I thought Celts wore tons of wool and dead furry things."

"That's only if you look for historical fact. I'm talking about present-day fiction. You know, sexy peasant girl wearing next to nothing. Something to really get Connor's motor running."

"I'd say it's running pretty well already."

"Oooh, is it now? Let's just kick it into high gear then, shall we? He won't know what hit him."

"Will I know what hit *me*?"

"Just leave it to me."

"That's what I'm afraid of." Alyssa laughed. She glanced over at Teresa and sobered. "I'm glad you're here."

"So am I. Honestly, leave you alone for a couple weeks and you go out, attract hackers, attackers, terrorists and a hunk-a-hunk-a burnin' lu-uv." Teresa counted off the points on her fingers. "Not bad. Can you show me how to do it? Just the last bit, though. The hunk-a-hunk-a burnin' lu-uv part only."

Alyssa snorted, laughing helplessly. "I wish I knew. It just happened."

Teresa gazed at Alyssa for a moment. "C'mon." She got to her feet and dragged Alyssa to hers.

"What?"

"You've got clothes to try on."

"Teresa, I'm hardly going to fit into your clothes. You've got three inches on me and I think we're the same weight." Alyssa eyed Teresa wistfully. Teresa's willowy body fit well into anything.

"That's the whole point. My clothes will show off every curve."

An hour later in Connor's bedroom, Alyssa stood in front of a full-length mirror with her eyes closed. The police had still cordoned off the guesthouse, so they'd confiscated Connor's room. Teresa stood behind Alyssa, holding her shoulders.

"Babe, he's going to have a heart attack when he sees you in this," Teresa purred into her ear.

"I think I'm going to have a heart attack when I see me in this," Alyssa retorted.

"Open your eyes."

Alyssa sighed and opened her eyes. She wore a midnight black, off-the-shoulder cropped knit top that hugged her like a second skin. An airy, long, black skirt hung low on her hips. Alyssa's jaw dropped as she gaped at herself. She looked, well, sexy as all get-out. "This is a little too much. It's the mountains. It's going to get cold tonight, you know."

"Then you'll just have to cozy up to tall, dark and handsome. Believe me, he'll like it. We'll just put your hair up like this." Teresa gathered Alyssa's wavy hair and piled it high on top of her head. Tendrils of hair escaped her grasp and flirted temptingly with Alyssa's cheekbones. "A little come-hither makeup and Bob's your uncle. Or, at least, Connor's your *very* close kissing cousin."

Alyssa stared at her reflection. Even she had to admit that the person in the reflection looked amazing. Definitely more revealing than anything she owned. Still, she felt bare. "I don't know."

"C'mon already! You look great. Don't you think you look great?"

"Well, yeah, but—"

"Yeah but nothing. *This* is the ticket. You've got it, use it."

Alyssa considered her reflection for another minute. Maybe it was time for a change. Stretch her boundaries. See how the other half lived. She took a deep breath. "You're right. Why not?"

"That's the spirit." Teresa released Alyssa's shoulders and stepped back, eyeing her watch, wincing. "Oops. Forgot. Have to do the sound check. Why don't you change into your regular clothes and give me a hand? I could use someone on the keyboards. The band should be here in about a half an hour or so. We can entertain the crew."

Alyssa was already shrugging out of Teresa's clothes. "No problem." She folded the top and skirt and pulled on her jeans and shirt. "Ready."

Teresa and Alyssa jogged up the steps to the bandstand. The setup crew had just completed the jigsaw puzzle-like parquet dance floor. The dining area, filled with white cloth-draped tables, sat to the right of the dance floor.

Alyssa stood behind the keyboard and, at a nod from Teresa, started playing a medley of bluesy jazz tunes. The keyboard cried out its anguish as she massaged the keys softly. Teresa ran around, making sure the sound was right while conferring with the sound crew.

"Ali, why don't you sing?" Teresa called out from the sound setup area.

"Sing? Nuh-uh." Alyssa continued playing.

"No one here but us deaf chickens. No one cares if you can sing. Besides, your voice isn't that bad. I just want to see how the mics are set up and balanced."

"Yeahyeahyeah," Alyssa muttered to herself, but not quiet enough to escape being heard over the microphone.

"C'mon, Ali. Sing," Teresa called out.

Alyssa leaned closer to the microphone and spoke clearly into it. "Fine. But if dogs start howling and birds fall dead from the sky, it's your fault."

Teresa laughed.

Alyssa flowed into a Blue Rodeo tune, *After the Rain*, a bluesy, angst-ridden piece with a slow, deliberate beat. Alyssa began singing in a smoky, contralto voice. Although untrained, her voice had a sensual appeal despite its rough edges. The words spoke to her of making the wrong decisions in love and living to regret them. As she ended the song, she looked up to find the caterers and the setup crew, who had stopped working to listen, erupt in applause.

She saw Connor and Liam striding toward the stage, applauding enthusiastically. Connor mounted the steps to Alyssa and threaded his arm around her waist, standing beside her.

"That was amazing." Connor leaned down and whispered to her. "And not-a-one bird falling dead from the sky." She felt a blush coming on and smiled shyly at him.

Connor smiled down at her. This is what she needed after the past week—fun, and lots of it. Truth be told, when she was singing, it was almost if she were speaking to him. He wondered if the song had been subconsciously picked with him in mind. A song of coming to terms with her own fears and hopes about love.

Walking back toward the house, Connor whispered into Alyssa's ear, "You didn't tell me you could sing."

"I can't. I hardly have any range at all. I'll stick to my piano, but thanks for saying so anyway," Alyssa responded, smiling ear-to-ear.

"So, you're all set for tonight, then? Maybe you'll do an encore."

Alyssa snorted. "Don't count on it."

Connor stopped and pulled Alyssa around to face him. "So, why *were* you and Teresa hiding in the bedroom earlier? All I heard was giggling and laughing."

"That's for me to know and you to find out."

Connor gathered her close and gave her a soft, suggestive kiss. "Sure I can't convince you to tell me?"

Alyssa heaved a sigh, leaned into his body, looked up into his face and nodded. "Positive. All good things come to those who wait."

Chapter Sixteen

Connor knocked on the door to his bedroom, glancing at his watch. Seven o'clock. Why was it taking Alyssa and Teresa so long to get ready? Honestly, you have one woman trying to get ready for a shindig and you waited *forever,* but two women? *What's longer than forever*?

"Alyssa, you about ready?" He spoke to the door.

Muffled laughter came through the door. "Uh, yeah, we just need another minute."

Connor sighed and walked to the great room where Liam was waiting. Liam looked at him and Connor spread his arms wide in hopelessness. "She said another minute."

"What are they doing in there anyway?"

"I have no idea."

Moments later, as Liam and Connor killed time by shooting the breeze next to the fireplace, Liam abruptly looked behind Connor in the direction of the bedroom. In mid-sentence, Liam stuttered to a halt and his face took on a somewhat stunned look. Connor swung around to see the cause.

Connor's jaw dropped. Lust shot through his body like lightning. He looked Alyssa up and down hungrily. "It was worth it," he said, his voice husky with approval.

Her skillfully applied makeup looked very natural, hid the nasty bruise on her forehead and enhanced her best features, her wide eyes and generous mouth. Piled carelessly atop her head with various tendrils escaping to curl around her face, her chestnut hair gleamed.

The body-conscious black knit top and long skirt clung becomingly about her curves. She wore a pair of black strappy low-heeled sandals to complete the ensemble. The look somehow managed to marry innocence with smoldering sensuality.

Alyssa flushed at the stark hunger he didn't bother to hide from her. "What was?"

"The wait. It was all worth it." Connor slid up to Alyssa and gallantly offered her his arm. "May I?"

Alyssa beamed at him and then dropped her eyes. "You may." She took his arm and he drew her even closer. He bent down and brushed a light kiss across her lips. She ran a trembling hand over her stomach as if to settle her nerves against his obvious interest in her appearance.

"Hey, handsome, do I get an escort too?" Teresa teased Liam, who still stood there gaping at Alyssa.

Liam recovered his composure and looked at Teresa, a slight red tingeing his cheeks. "Absolutely." He smiled broadly at her as he offered, and she accepted, his arm.

They left the house for the party. The higher-than-average night temperature warmed the party-goers. The black velvet sky overflowed with sparkling diamonds, glimmering in the far reaches of the universe.

Dreamlike, Alyssa gazed up to the glittering points of light. How many loves had those stars witnessed? How many loves had started with a starlit walk down a beach or a winding country road or on a high mountain? Alyssa didn't know. Time indeterminate. Incalculable. Forever. Now.

The party area buzzed, literally, with happy, mildly intoxicated people. Connor, Alyssa, Liam and Teresa strolled through the milling crowd, stopping occasionally to chat with someone. The buffet table overflowed with every kind of food imaginable. Chefs in white hats and tunics manned various stations, serving everything imaginable—steak, roasted chicken, seafood, salad, pizza, even Asian and French cuisine.

Leaving Liam and Teresa to mingle, Connor pulled Alyssa with him up to the bandstand. He fastened his arm firmly around her waist and didn't seem to have any intention of releasing her. Alyssa gave him a questioning look. She knew he would address the crowd, but she couldn't see a reason for her being up there with him. He gave her a slow, hot smile. Her body tingled in response and her breath caught her throat. She allowed herself to be escorted onto the stage.

Arm still around her, Connor grabbed the microphone. "May I have your attention? I promise this won't take too long." The crowd groaned good-naturedly and then quieted. "I welcome all of you to the Energy Unlimited Sixth Annual Summer Bash. We've got everyone from everywhere here tonight. Of course, we have our valued employees."

Connor paused as hoots erupted from the crowd and he grinned. "As well as some of our very special clients, suppliers and the local law enforcement, just to make sure you hooligans don't take the place down," Connor joked. He spotted Roy next to the dance floor, nuzzling his smiling wife's neck as she squirmed. "Apparently, the local law enforcement has other things on its mind right now, *Roy*, so don't let us disturb your fun."

Roy looked up as people snickered around him. Roy, not be outdone, called out, "I used to be able to say 'at least one of us is having fun', but that's not the case this year. How about a kiss?"

Connor lowered his voice suggestively. "Sorry, Roy, you're not my type."

The crowd laughed.

Roy smirked. "Not me, Romeo. Alyssa. You know the one, she's the woman you're wrapped around."

Alyssa stiffened and flushed. But the faces looking up at her from the crowd were nothing but friendly. The heat left her face as she relaxed and smiled wryly at Roy.

The crowd started clapping and raucously chanting, "Kiss. Kiss. Kiss."

Alyssa turned her newly flaming face into Connor's shoulder. He turned his head and whispered, "Whad'dya say? Just one kiss to hold me until later?" His arm tightened around her, jostling her.

Alyssa glanced up at him from out of the corner of her eye and one edge of her mouth kicked up. She nodded, glancing at the exuberant crowd.

Very slowly, Connor lowered her mouth to hers as she closed her eyes and lifted her hand to gently caress his cheek. It was a very chaste kiss by any standards, but it made Alyssa's breath come fast. Connor ended the kiss as gently as it began, to the hoots and clapping of the crowd. Heat prickled her skin from head to toe.

Connor took a deep breath. "Well, " he said to the crowd, "with the pre-show entertainment adjourned, the last thing I'll say is eat, drink and be merry, for tonight we won't let you drive if you're drunk. For those of you who didn't know, my name is Connor Donnelly and I am the president and CEO of Energy Unlimited. And the lovely lady by my side is Alyssa Tiernan. Have a good time."

A smattering of clapping rippled through the crowd as they returned to the serious business of partying. Connor led Alyssa to the curtained-off backstage area of the bandstand, unnoticed by the crowd. Connor nudged Alyssa against a wall and murmured, "I don't think just one kiss will hold me after all. Have anything else for me?" Pressing his body against hers, his fingers skimmed her body, exploring and provoking.

Alyssa shivered in pleasure. Being kissed on stage by Connor, she hadn't expected to feel the primal pulse of desire they'd experienced in private. Her response to him on stage took her by surprise. Exhibitionism generally wasn't her thing, but it had lit a fuse that burned hot within her body. Her fingers trembled as she started undoing his belt.

"You little minx. You *do* have something else for me," he said, his voice husky and amused.

"Do you want me to stop?" Alyssa asked breathlessly, her hands stilled.

"Hell, no," Connor responded, looking around. A mountain of boxes was piled high off to one side of the stage behind the curtain. He pushed a few boxes aside and pulled her inside his impromptu fortress, rearranging the boxes quickly so they were completely hidden. The area was just big enough for the two of them.

"Good." Alyssa managed to undo his belt, pushing his trousers and underwear down to his knees. His erection bobbed stiffly. She breathed in his masculine scent. Slowly, teasingly, she knelt in front of him, whispering her fingertips lightly down his body. He slid his fingers into her hair, his fingertips tensed against her scalp. She ran a delicate tongue around his exposed and incredibly sensitive, rigid flesh as if he were the best ice cream known to woman.

Connor's breath hissed out as she teased him. Sweetly tormenting him, she slid his erection part way into her mouth, lightly sucking before withdrawing. He groaned. She smiled, pleased with his reaction. She continued the gentle teasing until Connor grabbed her by the arms and drew her up to him, kissing her deeply.

His hands slowly dragged the long black skirt up her legs to her warm buttocks. He froze. "You're not wearing any underwear," he groaned happily, hoisting her up and wrapping her legs around his waist.

His fingers played with her slick, wet center. Tempting and teasing. She moaned and tried to get closer to those playing fingers. A thread suspended her over a molten sea of ecstasy. It wasn't enough. Nothing but him filling her would ever be enough. She whimpered her desire softly.

"You want me?" he whispered, teasing her.

"Yes," Alyssa whispered, arching against the pressure of his clever fingers.

"How much?"

"I want you so far inside me that you'll never leave," Alyssa whimpered, her voice ragged. "Now. Do it now."

Connor grabbed her firmly by the hips and drove himself into her soft body, hard and deep. She arched her back against the onslaught, struggling to breathe, struggling to take even more of him. The first waves of pleasure rocked her. She teetered on the brink of climax, breathless, when she heard people speaking, coming closer.

Connor must have heard it too. He continued to move his hips, pushing her closer and closer to the edge. He shifted her a bit and his fingers closed around the hot, wet lips that clasped him so tightly and massaged gently. Alyssa's eyes rolled back in her head. She bit her lip to silence her ragged breathing before she betrayed their presence.

"I don't know, Liam. Maybe they went back to the house for something," Teresa said.

"I guess. I'm just going to do another sweep of the area," Liam answered.

Footsteps and conversation moved away from their hiding spot.

"You are so bad," Alyssa gasped.

"Yeah, but I'm so good at it," Connor breathed.

"No argument here," Alyssa whispered, and a delicious tension filled her body. Her release pulsed outward, she gasped and a tiny cry escaped from her lips. Her eyes went blind, the shock waves slamming into her body as she rode him.

Connor came with a violence that strained all the muscles in his body. He staggered a little, breathing as heavily as a winded racehorse, and gasped, "You're going to be the death of me."

Boneless against his chest, except for her legs, which wound tightly around his waist, she lazily turned her head to suck on his chest through his shirt and murmured, "Yeah, but what a way to go."

Alyssa felt a ripple of tension course through his body. Still ultra-sensitive where they were joined so snugly, she breathed heavily as the ripples spread through her body, like a stone tossed into water, the rings of sensation moved away from the center. With shock, she realized she was coming again. She leaned back in his arms as he pumped her against his hips again, drenching him. Still shaking, she climaxed violently before slumping against him, exhausted.

Connor laughed silently. He'd just made love to a goddess and all he could think of was more. Much, much more. "Why don't we go back to the house? To hell with the party."

Alyssa sighed, exhausted and disappointed. "You know we can't do that. Everyone expects to see you," she breathed.

Carefully, Connor lifted her off his body and placed her on her feet in front of him. Her knees buckled. Connor caught her with ease and gathered her close to his chest. He pulled back his head so he could look into her eyes. "You okay?" Maybe he'd pushed her too far. The past week had been hell, and heaven, on roller blades. A stab of guilt sliced through him.

Alyssa laughed. "I'm fine. I feel like I could sleep for a week, but I'm fine."

Connor arched an eyebrow at her.

Alyssa arched an eyebrow back at him. "Honestly." She reached a trembling hand up to caress his cheek. "You are just, so much…more than I ever expected."

"I could say the same of you."

"Then I guess the feeling's mutual, isn't it?"

Connor smiled down at her and held her until the shaking subsided. After a few moments, Alyssa heaved a long sigh and pulled back from him. She gave him a lopsided grin.

Connor gave her a crooked smile in return and let his hands fall from her, making sure she wasn't going to keel over.

Alyssa's eyes wandered down to his trousers, which were still open, and raised an eyebrow. "Mr. Donnelly, your guests would be shocked if they could see you now."

"This is for your eyes only. And your hands. And your mouth," Connor said as he pulled himself together. He managed to straighten his clothing and then looked at Alyssa, who gazed at him in amusement. "You're looking a little…windblown yourself."

"Really? How windblown?" Alyssa asked. She dug through her tiny handbag and pulled out a small compact. She flipped it open and examined her makeup. Her lipstick was smudged. She took a tissue from his outstretched hand and blotted at the smear. She reapplied powder to her face and refreshed the lipstick.

She took another look, holding the mirror further away from her. Her makeup looked a little haphazard, but not too bad. Her hair had a tumbled look to it. "Oh well, it was kind of windblown to start with. Am I presentable?"

"Always," Connor said, smiling at her. "Now we've got to find a way to blend in with the crowd and we're set."

Feeling like a teenager hiding a tryst, Connor took Alyssa's hand, peeked out from their curtain and pulled her toward the back of the bandstand. Jumping down to the ground, Connor held his hands up to grasp Alyssa's waist and lowered her down beside him. They made their way through the forest to the compound's gravel road.

They walked out of the forest, hand in hand, into the clearing where the party rolled and stopped to look around. Liam spotted them from the corner of the buffet area and strode over to them.

"Where'd you disappear to? With all that's been going on lately, I didn't know what happened," Liam asked, concerned.

Liam took a closer look at his brother and then at Alyssa. He rolled his eyes as understanding hit him. "God save us from puppy love," he muttered with a sardonic smile, shaking his head. "Next time, just let me know. I was about to send out a search party and there *are* some things I don't need to witness firsthand."

"Promise," Connor said laughing. He clapped Liam on the shoulder and held on. "Let's eat. I'm starving."

Chapter Seventeen

After dinner, the Barra McLeahys kicked off the ceilidh, luring the diners onto the dance floor to burn off the excesses of the buffet and bar. Reels and jigs ruled the evening.

Toward the end of the evening, the pace slowed down and the band struck up a slow, sweet-tempered waltz. The music from the fiddle and piano melded effortlessly, one picking up effortlessly where the other left off, intertwining seductively. Connor pulled Alyssa to her feet and, holding her hand, spun her gracefully onto the nearly deserted dance floor before drawing her close.

Alyssa realized that Connor's waltzing had a very European flavor. He held her very closely with his hand pressed firmly against her mid-back. He propelled her expertly around the floor. She didn't have to think about where to put her feet—they seemed to follow Connor's without conscious thought.

Alyssa sighed, closed her eyes and rested her cheek against his broad, warm chest. The soft music played before her closed eyes, with shades of greens and yellows and whites, like the softly undulating curtains of color of the northern lights. The rhythm transported her far, far away to a plain of existence where only she and Connor existed.

A shiver of sensual pleasure ran up Alyssa's spine. This was perfect. Beautiful music, beautiful man, beautiful night. She snuggled closer to Connor, who tightened his hold on her body. They moved as one. They danced, aware of only themselves, selfish in their joy with one another, expressing in motion all the words that would not or could not be said.

Alyssa had no words to describe what she was feeling. She'd quite simply never felt anything like it before. The physical and emotional sensations flooded her body and mind like a tidal wave crashing down upon an unprepared and undefended coast, overwhelming her.

Connor wished the dance would never end, that he and Alyssa could dance on forever under the starry skies. His eyes closed and his chest tightened with something close to pain as a wave of emotion rocked him. With no small shock, he realized that he truly loved this woman he was holding on to, as if his life depended upon her presence, her touch.

Connor loved his family, but this…this was completely different. He wanted to crawl inside Alyssa's skin and never come up for air. He wanted to feel her emotions, know her thoughts and understand every molecule of her body. Blood pounded though his head and roared in his ears.

Both he and Alyssa seemed to realize, nearly simultaneously, that the music had ended and they were still dancing. The people surrounding the dance floor were looking at them, bemused. Alyssa flushed as she tried to draw away from him. Connor grasped her lightly around the waist, preventing her retreat. Their eyes locked. Alyssa's breath caught in her throat and a shiver threaded through her body.

"Connor?" Alyssa managed to whisper.

Connor forced a small smile to his lips, as he lifted his hand and brushed his thumb over her full lips, silencing her. Lightly capturing her face between his hands, he soothed a feather-soft kiss over her lips. Her hands reached up to hold onto his wrists and she looked questioningly at him. Connor shook his head a fraction before releasing her, smiling mysteriously. He grasped her hand and they drifted from the floor.

It was late. Most of the party guests were drifting off to home and bed. Shouts of departure bounced through the clearing. The band had stopped playing and was packing up. The takedown crew would be in tomorrow to handle the final breakdown of the tables, dance floor and bandstand.

Connor stood behind Alyssa on the dock jutting outward into the black lake, his arms wrapped around her as they gazed at the dark water reflecting the lights of the stars. His chin rested on her head and she leaned her head back to look at him. He looked down at her seriously.

"What is it?" Alyssa asked.

Connor took a breath. "Marry me." He'd never asked any woman that question before and it came out before he had time to think about it. It seemed right, somehow.

Alyssa's eyes widened as she took a quick step out of his arms and swung around to gawk at him. "W...what?" she stammered.

"Marry me."

Alyssa's eyebrows shot up. Her lips moved for a moment without speech. She shook her head, as if trying to clear the shock from her system. "I c...can't," she gasped. She tried to run her fingers through her hair, but it was still done up and her fingers snagged on the tumbled curls. Connor's body blocked her only dry exit off the dock.

Connor studied at the now-panicked woman standing before him. Pain lanced through his chest and he closed his eyes. He opened his eyes and stared at Alyssa. A moment passed before he managed to ask, "Why not?"

Alyssa only shook her head. She looked into his eyes and whatever she saw there caused her to tremble. Alyssa took a step back and then another. She looked down behind her. Already at the end of the dock, one more step back and she'd be in the drink. She looked back at Connor.

Connor didn't realize how he looked to Alyssa until she looked down at the water behind her and then back to him. Shocked, he realized that to Alyssa the icy cold water looked more appealing than he did. With another shock, he realized she was terrified of him. Or what he represented.

With a concerted effort, Connor forced his hands to unclench, letting the blood flow back into them. He took a deep breath and let it ease out through his mouth, relaxing his face. The thought of terrifying the woman he loved horrified him. He looked at her more closely. She was even having difficulty breathing.

Connor slowly held out his hand to her. Alyssa flinched, watching him as if he were an unpredictable and dangerous wild animal who hunted her. He'd heard of many reactions from women who had received proposals of marriage. Most women were happy to be asked, as far as he knew. None of the reactions included the intended bride diving into the water to escape the hopeful groom. Alyssa behaved as if she had been sentenced to death.

"Alyssa," Connor said his voice soft, his hand dropped. "I just want to know why you can't marry me."

Alyssa started at his words. She gasped. "I can't marry you," she breathed. "I can't marry anyone. Not ever."

"Why not, Alyssa? I don't understand. Help me to understand." Connor's mind raced. Had he done something? Said something? Smelled bad? What was it?

"I'm not fit to marry."

"What?"

"I can't give you what you want. I can't give you what you need."

"You're not making any sense."

Alyssa's hands clenched and she shouted at him, "I don't trust you! I don't trust anyone! I don't even trust *me*!"

Connor knew the truth when he heard it, but the knowledge didn't take the sting out of her words. "What happened to you?" he asked softly.

Alyssa stared at Connor in a hopeless panic. How could she tell him that she was so totally screwed up that there was no hope of even a semblance of normal life? She always lived inside her head, carefully observing other people and judging if they would hurt her or not. Always expecting to be rejected. Reading more into people's actions than there generally was.

She lived behind the wall for most of her life—letting the drawbridge down to admit someone into her refuge was unthinkable. Crazy. Suicidal. Alyssa inched her head from side to side, the tendrils of her hair languidly following the motions of her head. "No."

"No, nothing happened to you or no, you won't tell me?"

"I can't do this."

"Alyssa, you can walk away from me. You can walk away from us. But you can't run fast enough, or far enough, to get away from yourself. Believe me. I've been there. I know. Sooner or later you're going to have to stop running and face yourself. If you don't, then you'll always be running. There'll be no comfort for you, no refuge and no *peace*."

Tears ran unchecked down Alyssa's face. She didn't bother to wipe them away as she stared at him, through him. She was so tired of hiding. So tired of being scared. So tired of being a freak of nature. So tired, period. He was right, but she didn't know what to do, other than her time-tested reaction of running away.

Her mind skittered back to the night eighteen years ago, back to the childhood that had scarred her so deeply, charted her every move and reaction even now. She began speaking so low that Connor had to move nearer to hear her words.

"My mother died giving birth to me. My father never forgave me. I lived with my father until I was twelve. I was beneath his notice and care for all those years until the last night of his life." Alyssa took a ragged breath to steady her against the onslaught of her memories. Her eyes squeezed shut. "That last night I told him that I hated him, that I would tell Grand how he treated me. My father snapped.

"I knew that the only reason we had a roof over our heads was because of Grand. He began to strangle me before he changed his mind and threw me in my bedroom, locking the door. It was so hot in there, so stuffy I could barely breathe. I lay on the bed and came up with a plan to get to Grand during the night.

"It took a while, but eventually my father fell asleep, drunk and snoring. I picked the lock to my bedroom and tried to sneak out of the house in the dark. I knocked over a lamp and he woke up, more crazy than I'd ever seen him. He said he'd had enough. He said he'd kill me. I ran out of the house and he followed me with his hunting rifle.

"I ran into the street and nearly got run down by a police cruiser. One officer grabbed me and dragged me to the other side of the car and tried to force me to the ground, but I saw my father point his shotgun at the other cop and they shot him. Suicide by cop."

Alyssa shook her head, her eyes closed. "I remember seeing the bullets slam into his chest. I remember him staggering back and looking down at the blood pouring from his chest. I remember him *smiling*," her voice shuddered, "before he fell to the ground dead.

"The one person in my life who should have loved me hated me with an all consuming passion. The one person I should have been able to trust, I couldn't ever trust.

"Even Grand I couldn't trust. He knew what my life was like and he left me there with that monster. I don't understand how he could have left me there. I must have been so worthless to be left like that. There must have been something so wrong with me that everyone could see it but me," Alyssa whispered brokenly in anguish. "What's wrong with me?"

Connor stared at her even as his own eyes burned, tears running down his face. Now he understood, as he hadn't before, her skittishness and reticence in their relationship. Trusting someone, anyone, was more than she could handle. Asking her to marry him had been totally premature. She hadn't even accepted herself as a worthwhile person. A person worthy to love and to be loved without reservation.

Connor wanted to bundle her up and protect her against everything bad that had ever happened or would happen to her. His chest ached from not being able to hold her close and soothe away her pain. He wanted to be able to bestow self-esteem and self-worth upon her like a gift. But he knew he couldn't. Self-esteem only came from within, not from without.

Alyssa slowly opened her eyes and lifted them to Connor's face and froze, as if astonished and unable to absorb the change in him.

"There's nothing wrong with you, Alyssa. There never was," Connor whispered as he eased forward, not wanting to startle her into taking an unintentional step off the end of the dock, and brushed her cheek with care with his fingers.

Alyssa's eyes widened. She teetered on the edge of the dock. Connor lightly grasped her around the waist and drew her away from the edge. She didn't resist, but she didn't relax, either.

"Alyssa, your father had no right to do what he did. Your grandfather should have yanked you away from your father when he first saw what was happening. But he didn't. Your grandfather made a mistake. I make mistakes. You make mistakes. Everyone makes mistakes. It doesn't mean that there's something wrong with you. It just means that people are fallible. Somehow, you need to be able to work past that."

Gently, Connor cupped Alyssa's face in his hands and gazed into her eyes. "Not for me. Not for Grand. But for yourself and your own happiness. You have to learn to trust that no matter what happens, you will survive. You've been through all this shit and *you're still here*. You didn't dissolve or disappear because of the bad things that have happened in your life.

"You are a living, breathing, human being with special gifts and talents, deserving of happiness. But you have to trust yourself before you can trust anyone else. Whatever happens between us, I want you to know that I will be your friend, first, last and always. You can tell me anything. And I will do my level best not to let you down." Connor's hoarse voice resounded with emotion as he tried to burn through Alyssa's pain to her mind and soul.

Alyssa stared at the man who pleaded, cried for *her* life. She could barely believe that she was hearing these words, from a man no less. Her concept of men had always been rather two-dimensional. It didn't include emotional and spiritual depth and integrity. The realization disoriented her. "I don't know how to *be* any different. I've *tried*. It always feels fake."

"That's because you didn't believe it, sweetheart. It felt fake because you didn't give it enough time to feel real. That takes a lot of time. It's not a mask you can drop into place and remove later. It's a whole mind-body thing. A paradigm shift in your perceptions of yourself and the world."

Alyssa's chest went cold as a new panic rose in her mind. She shook her head and opened her mouth to speak. Quickly, Connor brushed a thumb over her lips, silencing her. "You need time to think. I'm here if you need me."

Alyssa gawked at him with huge, burnt eyes, her mascara running down her cheeks. She let out a harsh breath through her mouth. She pulled her face out of Connor's hands and ducked around him on the dock. She backed away from him, not taking her eyes from his face, before turning and fleeing toward the house.

Chapter Eighteen

Alyssa closed the bathroom door behind her and leaned both hands on the counter, her head down, shaking uncontrollably. A jumble of raw memories and even more raw emotions flooded her mind. She worked so *hard* to stuff down all of those emotions and memories so they'd never surface. Apparently she hadn't worked hard enough, because it just overflowed the toilet of her life.

Again.

Alyssa lifted her head and stared into the reflected horror of her eyes in the mirror. She barely recognized herself, the calm veneer stripped from her appearance. *Damn him.*

She had been doing just fine before Connor, with those piercing eyes and amazing body, catapulted into her life. She shook her head even as the thought materialized. She hadn't been doing fine. She'd been hanging on by her fingernails and Connor wanted to pull each finger away from the edge she held on to so desperately. Just what that edge actually was, she wasn't sure. All she knew was that she had spent her entire life hanging onto that ledge and now it was crumbling from her grasp.

Alyssa straightened up and wrapped her arms around her body. Her head tilted back, eyes closed, as she tried to calm herself as she had done thousands of times throughout her life. Breathe in, breathe out, breathe in and breathe out. Over and over again until she gained some measure of composure. She slowly opened her eyes and let her head drop forward so that she was once again staring at her reflection.

In the silence of the bathroom, the shrill peal of her cell phone echoed off the hard surfaces and she jumped in surprise. Heart pounding, she dug through her small handbag, pulled out the phone and snapped it open.

"Hello?" Her voice sounded gravelly to her ears.

"Alyssa, dear, is that you?" The breathless voice of Mrs. Brody, Grand's next-door neighbor, crackled over the airwaves.

"Mrs. Brody? It's two in the morning. What's wrong?"

"Oh my dear, it's so horrible," Mrs. Brody cried.

Alyssa's body went cold, a huge lump formed in her throat. Swallowing past the lump, her voice projected calm even though she was a mess, she asked, "What's wrong? Is it Grand?"

Mrs. Brody sobbed hysterically over the phone. Alyssa sagged against the countertop for support and covered her eyes with her free hand. Alyssa snapped, "Mrs. Brody, what the hell is going on?"

"It's…it's your grandfather. He's gone."

"Gone? What do you mean *gone*?" Alyssa demanded.

"No one can find him."

Alyssa closed her eyes in relief and took a steadying breath. "Mrs. Brody, you know as well as I do that Grand's always wandering off on his own. Why has it got you so upset now?"

"You don't understand, Alyssa. His office in Calgary caught fire four hours ago. He's not at the house. The police have been searching for him for three hours now. Oh my dear, I'm so sorry. I didn't want to be the one to tell you. I tried to hold off as long as I could before I called," Mrs. Brody sobbed.

A bitter cold knifed through Alyssa. The cell phone slipped from her numb fingers and clattered to the floor. She shuddered. *It can't be true. It can't. He was fine a day ago. He can't be gone.* She stared down at the phone. Mrs. Brody's sobs emanated from the tiny speaker. Awkward, her body stiff from emotional shock, she managed to lean down to snag the phone. She lifted it to her ear and with all the calm she could muster, she said, "Mrs. Brody, I don't believe Grand is gone. I'm coming home. I'll sort everything out."

Alyssa cut the connection, severing the sounds of weeping. She dropped the phone on the counter and leaned her hip against the counter before covering her face with her hands. *Oh Grand, where are you?* Fear clutched her heart and tears squeezed out of her eyes, dampening her fingers.

It was just too much of a coincidence. The near fatal crash her first full day in Colorado, the run-in with the intruder at the office, the attack on her yesterday. And now Grand had disappeared. A small sound of grief managed to work its way out of her constricted throat.

A soft tap sounded at the door.

"Alyssa? Open up." Connor's voice drifted into the bathroom.

Alyssa jolted and stripped her hands away from her face. She stared at the door. She swiped at her face, wet with tears, with one hand and took a deep breath before opening the door. Connor leaned against the wall, one arm above the door with his hand pressed against the doorjamb.

"I'm fine," Alyssa enunciated with great precision. Any strong current of emotion would tear down the precarious control she had on herself.

Connor studied her tearstained face without speaking. The woman was unpredictable, somewhat unstable and nearly out of control. A proposal shouldn't have scared her that much even though he knew now there was a whole shitload of emotional baggage looped like an albatross on her back. Connor bit back the comment, knowing he'd just antagonize her further.

"I have to leave."

Connor rolled his eyes. "We're not back to this again, are we?"

Alyssa's eyes turned to glittering green ice. She answered him through clenched teeth. "Grand is missing. His office has burned down to the ground. I have to leave."

Connor stared at her, unmoving. Couldn't she see all this might be related?

Alyssa backed up a step and leaned against the countertop again. She whipped out the cell phone and dialed directory assistance. A tired operator's voice came across the line. "Residential or business listing?"

"Business, taxi services," Alyssa said, her voice clipped, terse.

Connor took two long strides across the room to her. He grabbed the phone from her hand and cut the connection. He looked down into her startled eyes. "I'll take you back to Alberta. There's no need to call a taxi."

"I don't want to put you through any more trouble than I already have." Alyssa eyed him as if unsure of him, of his intentions.

Connor wished he knew what Alyssa was thinking. It hit him again how little she actually trusted him. He knew it wasn't him in particular she didn't trust, but it still hurt. At the first sign of trouble, she was ready to claw his eyes out. At the second sign of trouble, she was ready to cut and run.

Connor could tell Alyssa was almost frantic about Grand, although she had clamped down on the fear. A guilty feeling stole through his chest. His hand reached out to lightly tug upon a silky tendril of hair.

Alyssa flinched back before she stopped abruptly to stare at his hand, now frozen in midair.

Connor's mouth straightened into a frustrated, flat line, and his hand dropped to his side. He spun away from her and walked out of the bathroom. "We leave in fifteen minutes. Be ready."

"What do you mean *we*?" Alyssa asked, her voice sharp enough to cut ice.

Connor turned on heel and strode back to her. Whatever she saw on his face caused her to jump, as if she would back up, but she was already smack dab against the counter. "When I said 'we', I meant '*we*', not just '*you*'. You may not trust me, but there's no way in hell you're going back alone."

"I'm perfectly capable of taking care of myself."

"I don't think you're *thinking* clearly. This past week has been a mess of near misses. During *any* of which you could have died. You can bury your head in the sand all you want, but your ass is target practice."

"My *ass* is none of your concern!" Alyssa fired back.

That's it. Connor grabbed her by both arms and jerked her up from the counter. Her eyes widened. Before she could protest, Connor's mouth came down on hers, opening it savagely and pulling her against his hard body. His tongue invaded her mouth, demanding a response. She tried jerking her head away from him, but he caught her head with his hand and kept her where she was. His other arm clenched around her waist. *Mine.*

There was no gentleness in him now, no patience. Just as quickly, Connor released Alyssa's body and mouth and stepped away from her. She staggered back before finding her balance again. She wiped the back of her hand against her mouth, as if wiping away the taste of him on her lips.

"Your ass *is mine,*" Connor spat. "Until further notice. Period."

"Like hell," Alyssa sputtered, her voice growing louder. "Look, we may have had sex, but you are not my keeper. Or my commanding officer."

"No, I'm not your keeper. I'm the man who's going to make sure that you stay alive." Connor spoke the words with a harsh edge. "If you don't like it..."

"I don't l—".

Connor's spoke over Alyssa. "That's your problem. Not mine. Get ready. Twelve minutes. You're wasting time."

Alyssa glared at Connor. With a muttered curse, she brushed by him into his bedroom, avoiding his glowering eyes. Connor left the room.

Alyssa stomped over to the walk-in closet and dragged out her single suitcase. She began shoving clothes randomly into the bag, not bothering to fold anything. When the bag was stuffed full to overflowing, she tried to close the case. She couldn't quite get the clasp to fasten.

With a muffled curse, she dragged the suitcase off the bed and it slammed onto the floor with a loud whomp. She dropped her ass onto the suitcase, her legs straddling the snap closure on the top of the bag, swearing to herself. She was going to get a freaking modern suitcase with wheels and zippers, dammit, as soon as this was over. Not this ancient piece of crap she'd owned forever. She reached down between her legs and, with some wiggling and tugging, managed to snap it shut.

Alyssa looked up from the bag and saw Connor standing in the doorway to the bedroom, watching her. Predatory. "What?"

"You ready?"

Alyssa struggled off the suitcase and got to her feet. She flipped it into an upright position and lifted it off the floor. It was a lot heavier than she remembered. She walked toward the door with the suitcase hanging from both her hands to her side.

With a grace belied by ease, Connor took the suitcase from her and held it as if it were full of feathers.

Alyssa made a grab for the handle of the suitcase. "I can handle it," she growled.

Connor pulled the suitcase away from her. "You can barely lift the damn thing. Don't go all hard-core feminist on me now." He stalked down the hallway toward the front door with Alyssa staring daggers at his back.

Alyssa felt like smacking him into the floorboards. Realistically, she knew that she didn't have a hope in hell of doing anything of the sort. She balled her fists up in anger and frustration. She didn't want to deal with all this.

Not now. Not later. Not *ever*.

Alyssa wished that Connor would just buzz off so that she could close this chapter and get on with the desert-like conditions of her life. Connor constantly reminded of all those things she told herself she didn't want. Almost believed it too.

Alyssa pushed all thoughts of Connor to the back of her mind with a determined effort. Mrs. Brody needed her. Grand needed her. She took a deep breath and followed Connor.

When Alyssa got outside, she abruptly realized that it was still the middle of the night and she was still wearing the skimpy outfit from the party. She shivered as the chill night air hit her overheated skin. There was no sign of Connor at the front door. Wrapping her arms around herself to ward off the cold, Alyssa turned down the side of the house and found Connor leaning against the green Jaguar, waiting for her with glittering eyes.

Wordless, Connor righted himself. He walked over to the passenger side of the car and opened the door. He didn't move aside. Alyssa ignored him as she tried to brush past him to sit in the car.

As soon as she was between the car and Connor, he pressed forward and pinned her to the car, his arms on either side of her, leaning against the car. She had no place to go.

Alyssa shoved at him. She might as well have pushed a mountain for all the good it did her. "Get off me! What's wrong with you?"

"*You* are what's wrong with me," Connor said in a low, savage voice. "You're ready to go off all hell-bent on finding Grand without even a thought to your own safety. Well, *honey*, think of me as your full-time bodyguard until all this crap is over. Don't even *think* of trying to lose me. You won't like the consequences."

Alyssa glared up at Connor, her breath caught in her throat. Anger swept through her body like wildfire. "Fine," she said, forcing the words from her numb lips.

Connor stared at her for a moment more. With a muttered curse, he lifted his hands from the car and moved back. When Alyssa continued to stare at him, he arched his eyebrows. Alyssa rolled her eyes and dumped herself less than gracefully into the passenger seat.

He checked to make sure that he wasn't going to shut the door on any extraneous body parts before slamming the door shut.

Hard.

Alyssa flinched and gave him a sidelong glance through the window. She exhaled in an uneven series of spurts. She wasn't looking forward to being around him for the next while, but short of taking out a restraining order against him, she didn't think there wasn't much she could do.

Alyssa ran her tongue along the inside of her teeth, her mouth slightly open, and breathed out, trying to contain her irritation with Connor. And the fear that she'd lost Grand forever. She slumped against the door and leaned her head against the cool window, suddenly exhausted. She closed her eyes to try to blot out the whole ungodly mess.

The driver's side door opened and Connor lowered himself down into the car seat. He looked over at Alyssa and guilt washed over him. She looked small, exhausted, stretched to the very end of her rope and he was harassing her. He shoved the feeling aside.

In this game, people who were led around by their emotions died. Fast. Connor had no intention of being one of those people. He wouldn't let Alyssa be one of those people either.

Alyssa might hate him by the end of it, but by God, she'd be alive.

Chapter Nineteen

Calgary RCMP Headquarters

"Let me see if I understand you correctly, Officer," Alyssa said very softly, very distinctly to the young Royal Canadian Mounted Police officer in charge of Grand's disappearance. "You've sifted through the wreckage of the office and didn't find a body, but you think he's dead anyway." Alyssa's voice fell an octave, vaguely threatening. "Explain why *again*."

Alyssa sat across the desk from the hesitant young officer, her arms folded across her chest. Hips balanced on the edge of the chair, legs outstretched in front of her, she glowered at the man. The flight from Colorado had been less than pleasant and her last nerve had already snapped. Aware that Connor leaned against the wall behind her, she studied the man.

The RCMP officer from Calgary couldn't have been any older than twenty-five and, to Alyssa's annoyance, this was his first "murder" investigation. Just less than six feet tall with a thin build to match his already thinning sandy blond hair, the man's watery blue eyes and pasty skin advertised the vestiges of a wicked case of adolescent acne. His pointy, oversized ears gave him an almost alien appearance. Maybe he was Vulcan, without the logic or emotional control. He looked uneasy—apparently dealing with upset women was not his thing.

"Please, Ms. Tiernan, call me Cedric." Cedric flushed as Alyssa continued to stare at him. "Cedric Waddington."

"Okay, Cedric, Cedric Waddington," Alyssa said dryly, lifting her eyebrows in query. She gave him her patented black look, the one guaranteed to make the most ornery person think twice about screwing with her. "*Speak.*"

Cedric cleared his throat for the tenth time since ushering Alyssa and Connor into his small, cluttered office. "Well, Miss, as I said, the fire department managed to douse the fire before it spread to the neighboring buildings in the industrial park. Unfortunately, your grandfather's building burned to the ground. We've had arson investigators combing through the wreckage since late last night and they say there are no human remains. They did find evidence of an incendiary device that was used to start the fire."

"Incendiary device," Alyssa repeated in a flat voice. "You mean someone set the fire intentionally."

"Yes," Cedric replied.

"And this means that Grand is dead?" Alyssa asked, sarcasm clear in her voice. "I would have thought it meant he was alive, but what would *I* know."

Cedric's throat took on a faint pink hue that proceeded to wash upward to the top of his de-forested head. The words spilled from his lips as he leaned forward across the desk. "The…the fire chief said that the fire burned for so long and at such a high temperature that human remains were unlikely to be found. Your grandfather's house was ransacked and now he's unaccounted for. We think it's likely that he didn't survive. Someone wanted your grandfather dead, like yesterday."

Alyssa gritted her teeth together. The man had absolutely zero tact. "Did it ever occur to you *rocket scientists* that maybe he's hiding? Or that he could be staying with someone? Have you even asked any of his friends if they've seen him?" Alyssa said, falsely sweet. She gave him wide, innocent eyes.

"Well, just Mrs. Brody, she told…"

"*Just* Mrs. Brody?" Alyssa interrupted, fighting the impulse to snarl at Cedric. She stood up, placed both hands on the desk and leaned very close to Cedric, her nose almost touching his. "Mrs. Brody, while a very nice woman, hasn't got two functioning brain cells to rub together. And apparently, neither do you," she hissed at him through clenched teeth and glared. "Get your supervisor, *junior*, I've had it with you."

Cedric blanched. He hastily placed his hands on the edge of desk and shoved back while he stood, nearly overturning his chair. Running a shaky hand through the remains of his hair, he scurried to the office door, yanked it open and sprinted to freedom.

Alyssa's head dropped as she leaned against the desk, her hair brushing the metal surface. For a moment, she stared down at the hair teasing the hard planes of the desk, trying to control her fear. She wasn't successful. Taking a breath, she slowly straightened her body and tried to calm her mind.

"You know, you catch more flies with honey than vinegar," Connor remarked mildly from his position behind her, leaning against the wall.

Alyssa swung around to face Connor. "Fresh out of honey, sport." As she made fists out of her hands, struggling with her emotions, she whispered harshly, "What is your problem anyway? I'm going through *frigging* hell and all you do is make it worse. Why don't you just get the *hell* away from me? Just *go away,*"

Yeah, no problem for him, Alyssa thought. His entire world hadn't been yanked from beneath *his* feet. Where the hell did he get off? Offering *her* advice. Unwanted, unwelcome, unsolicited advice, at that.

Yet, even as Alyssa stared at him, the familiarity of his presence, his heady masculine scent, reached out to her, tempting her even through the haze of rage fogging her mind. Her chest ached with a desire to be held, to be comforted and soothed.

Alyssa bleakly surveyed the man who attracted her like a very stupid moth to a very hot, dangerous flame, and yet unnerved her like no other man. She drew in a quivering breath and slumped against the desk, forcing herself not to throw herself into his arms.

Connor eyed Alyssa, compassion in his eyes. "I can't go away. Not now. You're half out of your mind with fear over Grand. And you're going to snap. Soon. "

Hesitant, he stepped close to Alyssa and wound his arms around her. Alyssa stiffened. Placing her hands against his chest, she tried to push him away, but she couldn't. He was too strong. And she was too damn tired.

Tears filled Alyssa's eyes. "Why are you *torturing* me?" she whispered, despair coloring her voice, as her arms went limp. She trembled with the effort of trying to remain calm.

Connor's only response was to draw her closer to the warmth of his body. She was so cold to his touch. His lips brushed against her hair, unfelt and unknown, his heart contracting in sorrow, her unhappiness magnifying his own.

"Alyssa," he whispered against her hair, "I'm trying to keep you alive. And the best chance of doing that is to ensure you're thinking calmly and rationally."

"So, driving me up the wall, around the bend and down the road is supposed to make me calm?" Alyssa's voice shook. "*Geez, thanks*. What *would* I do without you? You're making me nuts. Not calm. Not rational. *Nuts*."

"I'm not leaving."

Alyssa's voice trembled. "Why the hell have you been so awful to me since you found out about Grand? Like to see me squirm? Payback for turning you down? Is that it?"

Connor pulled away from Alyssa enough to look her in the eye. One eyebrow arched in question. "Is that what you think?"

Alyssa's chin went up a little. "Maybe," she said, eyeing him warily, her heart rate increasing. Even though she knew it was childish, she wanted to hurt him, to lash out at him for his high-handedness once the Grand situation had blown up in her face. She wanted to rattle his calm. See a break in the rock-solid armor of his casual nonchalance. So far, she hadn't seen even a nick, and it was driving her crazy to see him so calm while she fell apart.

Connor gripped Alyssa's shoulders and shook her once lightly. "Alyssa, last night you were ready to run off and handle this all on your own. Doing that will get you *killed*. And despite what you think of me, or what you say you think of me, I'm not enjoying your pain. You're too close to the situation. That's why I'm here. No payback. No ulterior motives, except to make sure you get through this in one piece."

Just then, a tall man with a husky build and sandy brown hair opened the door. Upon seeing Connor and Alyssa's current entanglement, the man jerked up one straw-like derisive eyebrow above an icy blue eye as if wondering if he'd interrupted a tryst in progress.

Alyssa jerked herself out of Connor's arms at the imposing RCMP officer's appearance. Running shaking hands through her hair, Alyssa turned to face the man, her own eyebrows raised in question.

The man half-smirked and flicked his eyes over to Connor, who regarded the man impassively.

The man turned his attention back to Alyssa and spoke, "My name is Captain David Hendricks. I'm Cedric Waddington's superior officer. I understand that you weren't too pleased with our Cedric."

"Your Cedric is an idiot. He tried to tell me that my grandfather is dead without even seeing a body and without speaking to any more than one person. You call that a thorough investigation? And quite honestly, his bedside manner sucks. Where did you get him from anyway? 'Morons 'R Us'?" Alyssa spoke with a hard edge to her voice.

"Why don't you sit down and we can discuss this?" the captain said in a soothing voice, as he gestured toward a chair.

Alyssa gave the captain a strained look before edging around Connor to take the proffered seat. The captain gestured to Connor to take a seat as well, but Connor shook his head. The captain sighed theatrically, blowing out his cheeks in response and took up residence in Cedric's vacated chair. He leaned forward, resting his elbows on the desk. "Alyssa," he said as he smiled charmingly at her. "May I call you Alyssa?"

"No." Alyssa looked at the captain with exaggerated patience. "Captain, you can dispense with the charm. I can do without it. What I can't do without are *answers*. Why did Cedric tell me that my grandfather was dead?"

"Cedric must have misunderstood your question. He's young and inexperienced and sometimes lacks tact."

"He lacks brains," Alyssa said flatly. "And he did *not* misunderstand my question. What are you going to do about my grandfather?"

The captain looked at her sharply. "Do? I am going to do my job. Just like Cedric, just like everyone else here." The charming façade faded as he looked at her. "Ms. Tiernan, we are a very busy police department. Aside from the fire at your grandfather's office last night, we've had multiple stabbings, a couple of robberies and one missing child.

"At this point, we don't have a lot of information for you because we are still *investigating*. Unfortunately, we've had a lot of cutbacks in the past year, and we don't have enough to manpower to spend on each case. I know this involves your grandfather and he is your priority and I promise you that we will get to it as soon as possible," he said on a more conciliatory note.

"As soon as possible might be too late—you don't know what you're dealing with."

"Okay, Ms. Tiernan, why don't you tell me what we're dealing with?"

Alyssa stared at the man, a little taken aback by the question. She doubted if the good captain would believe her if she told him that terrorists were involved. So she went to the next best truth.

"Captain, my grandfather is involved with oil sands research in northern Alberta. He's cultivated a brand-new technique for extracting the oil. It'll cut the cost of recovering oil to a fraction of what it is now, as well as eliminating the environmental damages caused by current extraction techniques. His competitors are worried and I believe he has been targeted by some of these people." Alyssa's voice rose as she spoke.

"Conspiracy theorist. Wonderful," the captain muttered underneath his breath. Alyssa decided she wanted to club him to death. In a normal tone of voice, he said, "Ms. Tiernan, don't you think you might be overestimating the threat? Perhaps you have evidence or proof of this alleged threat?"

Alyssa regarded him as her temper rose like a leviathan rising from the deep. With a monumental effort, she managed to calm herself before it got messy. With a shock, she realized he was baiting her and that he was not going to help her or Grand, not immediately anyway.

"My grandfather is missing. His office building has burned to the ground. His body has not been found, nor has a proper investigation been done," Alyssa repeated icily. "*None* of that is imagination. Those are cold, hard facts. If you are *not* going to help me, then let me know *now*. I'm sure the local and national media would be *fascinated* with why a possible murder is a low priority, *Captain*."

The good captain waved her threat aside. "Ms. Tiernan, of course we're going to help you. You'll just have to be a little patient with us. I'm afraid there's nothing more we can tell you at this point. As you have so keenly pointed out, we have not yet done a full investigation. Why don't you leave your number with the front desk and we will call you if we need something from you?"

"That's it? That's all you have to tell me? Why aren't you asking who Grand's friends are? Why aren't you asking me what I think? Why are you so damn cavalier about my grandfather?" Alyssa had never encountered police officers like this before. Why was this man being so totally unhelpful? So totally callous? She shook her head in disbelief and tried to choke down the feeling of panic that was wrapping around her body in tight bands, making breathing difficult.

Alyssa abruptly tried to stand up, but she found herself held in place by Connor's hands descending on her shoulders. She twisted around in her chair to look up at Connor. Before she could speak, Connor squeezed her shoulders slightly in warning, willing her to be silent.

"Captain Hendricks, I'm sorry. Alyssa is overwrought by the disappearance of her grandfather. I'm sure whatever you can accomplish will be much appreciated. We'll leave our number with the receptionist on the way out, and if we can be of any help, please don't hesitate to call us."

Connor looked down at Alyssa, who felt like ripping out his throat. The "poor, hysterical, little woman" bit rankled, even knowing that he was probably up to something. "Sweetheart, why don't we leave and let the captain do his job? I'm sure he doesn't need us getting underfoot. You're tired and upset, so let's just go back to your place and you can lie down."

Alyssa caught the warning in Connor's eyes before she retaliated with the scathing retort that burned on her lips. Her lips thinned as she pressed them together and bit back an angry torrent of words. Stiffly, she nodded, not trusting her voice.

Alyssa gave the captain one last black look before getting to her feet and stomping out the door. Connor caught up to Alyssa in the sun-drenched parking lot where she paced by their rented car. As he approached, she swung around to face him, a storm cloud on her face.

"Why the hell did you do that?" Alyssa demanded, the urge to kick his shin for the "little woman" speech almost overwhelmed her.

"Not here, Alyssa. There are too many eyes watching us," Connor said in a low voice, his eyes searching hers.

"Eyes? What are you talking about?" Alyssa asked, her voice a mix of bewilderment, frustration and anger.

"Just get into the car and we'll talk about it. Not here, not in the open," Connor responded, taking Alyssa by the elbow to guide her toward the passenger side of the car.

Alyssa momentarily resisted before acquiescing to the gentle pressure at her elbow. His hand was warm and reassuring on her chilled flesh. Gamely, she forced her attention away from the heat emanating from his body, tempting her away from her fear and sorrow. More than anything, Alyssa wanted his heat. She wanted anything he was willing to give her.

And that scared her. As always, the fear of trusting someone closed in on her. Connor had gotten closer to her than anyone, ever. He had climbed over the walls of her angst and found her soul, ignoring the signposts of distrust, dismissing the scarecrows erected around her heart.

Connor deposited Alyssa in the front passenger seat of the car and strode around to the other side. As they drove off, Alyssa studied Connor out of the corner of her eye. His midnight black hair glinted in the sunlight pouring into the car. The pupils in his blue-gray eyes were a pinprick of midnight. The tense line of his jaw made him look every bit as dangerous and unyielding as she knew him to be. And then he glanced at her and her heart nearly skidded to a halt against her breastbone.

He always had this affect on her. Even the thought of him was enough to make her heart go thumpity-thump. She was a little frightened of him. And a little attracted to him. Hell, *who* was she kidding, a lot attracted to him. She wasn't sure what she was more afraid of—losing him or not losing him.

Her feelings were a jumbled mess where Connor was concerned. She didn't know up from down anymore. Sanity from insanity. Love from hate. Want from need. Her feelings vacillated between the extremes—always searching for the logical medium, but always coming up irrationally short.

She loved him. She hated him. She needed him. She wanted him gone.

Alyssa wanted to tear her hair out, in the hope of yanking him out of her mind. But she couldn't. He had sunk so far into her skin, settled so deeply into her soul, that she would never be free. She wasn't even sure if she wanted to be free anymore. Fleeting moments, yes, but forever?

Alyssa brushed back her hair from her face and closed her eyes, leaning into the warm leather of the bucket seat. Taking a deep breath, she tried to clear her mind as the endless Alberta sun flooded the car.

When Alyssa first went to live with Grand, he had taken her out to the massive wheat fields of Alberta and Saskatchewan. The circle of life, he had told her. A beginning. An ending. And the continual rebirth of the land. This was life in all its complexity and simplicity. The richness and the starkness of nature's bounty.

Behind her closed eyes, Alyssa could see the fields of golden stalks of wheat, wheat kings, motionless beneath a big, blue sky. As far as the eye could see, only seeing burnished gold and clear, brilliant blue. In her mind's eye, she remembered turning to him. She had been so angry, radiating rage and fear.

Old man, you have no idea what life is about. You think it's about stupid plants and stupid land. How can you be so blind? Alyssa had spat the words at him. Her pain had been so vast that even after her father's death, she had rejected Grand out of hand. It'd taken time for her to realize that he loved her in his own way. It may not have been the way she wanted to be loved, but it was love just the same.

It occurred to her that she was doing the same thing to Connor. He loved her. He'd even said so, even wanted to *marry* her. And what had she done? She'd acted like a total head case and run away from him. Rejected him. Just like Grand.

Alyssa felt tears well up behind her closed eyes. The trip down memory lane, though unintentional, made her lungs contract painfully. She would give anything now to take back those angry words and angry actions of her youth.

And now he was gone. Lost. Maybe forever.

Alyssa's throat tightened painfully as she tried to push the fear down. The harder she pushed, the more her throat tightened until a tiny sound of grief escaped.

Though barely audible, Connor heard it.

Connor pulled the car over to the side of the road and reached for Alyssa, capturing her face between his hands.

Alyssa's eyes flew open, "What?" she croaked, her eyes reflecting wild grief.

"Sweetheart, we're going to find Grand. I promise." Connor searched her eyes.

Alyssa cleared her throat. The fear and anger in her face accompanied by the grief reflected in her eyes would have brought Connor to his knees if he'd been standing. She looked at Connor with accusing eyes. "Why did we just leave like that? You know as well as I do that they're going to be of no help whatsoever."

Connor let out a long breath and released Alyssa. She wouldn't accept any comfort from him. She needed it like oxygen, but she wouldn't take it from him. It stung and he told himself that it shouldn't matter, but it did. "I have a strong feeling that the police are either in on what happened to Grand or they've been told to stonewall us."

"Told to stonewall us?" Alyssa asked, her eyebrows sweeping upward.

"I may not be experienced with Canadian cops, but no cop I know would ever act like a possible murder or kidnapping was a low priority. The good captain is hiding something."

Chapter Twenty

"Do you want some coffee or something?" Alyssa called out from her tiny kitchen to the living room where Connor snooped around her stuff.

Connor was pleasantly surprised by Alyssa's home. He'd expected a darker feel to her home, reflecting her inner demons. But that wasn't what he saw here.

Brilliant sunlight flooded into the living room from enormous, west-facing windows, burnishing already gleaming maple floors. Walls painted a light whipped butter color offset the stylishly comfortable furnishings, without being hard or cold. At the far end of the room was an immense stone fireplace, a luxurious sheepskin placed on the floor before it as if to invite lovers to roll around on it. To one side of the windows stood an oak studio piano, sheet music overflowing onto the floor with careless abandon.

A numbered lithograph of the Group of Seven's Tom Thomson's "Sunset, Canoe Lake" graced the wall beside the fireplace. He stepped closer to the picture to study it. The gold-flecked sky outlined black pine trees furring a distant shore. It was a simple piece, but powerful, evoking feelings of serenity, untouched beauty and tragic sorrow. A fitting piece for Alyssa. And with any luck, not her requiem.

A sick feeling in his stomach gnawed at his nerves. She would not die. *Not* die. Not while he protected her. Which, as far as he was concerned, was forever. She was *his.* She just hadn't realized it yet.

Unsettled, Connor swung away from the print to survey the rest of the room. Her house was a pleasant surprise. A feast for the senses, from the warm browns and creams of the floors and walls to the simple, yet exquisite furnishings, testifying to the tastes and personality of the woman who'd chosen them. Yes, she was a sensual woman, but he hadn't expected to find that sensibility permeating her home. He wondered if she was even conscious of her sensuality. Probably not.

Connor realized that Alyssa was waiting for an answer. "Uh, yeah. Coffee would be good."

Alyssa didn't particularly want Connor wandering around her home. She knew that he'd be making parallels between her house and herself because that was the sort of mind he had. And quite honestly, she didn't need another person dissecting her mind, thank you very much.

Alyssa pushed aside her annoyance and settled into the mindless task of making coffee. As she scooped the coffee grounds out of the canister, her hand shook a little. Frustrated, she gripped the scoop tighter to force her hand into steady submission. Her hand shook more. Lips pressed together, she flung the scoop into the canister and snapped it shut with a loud crack.

"I'll take tea." Connor leaned against the kitchen door, no doubt observing her little hissy fit.

Alyssa flinched at the sound of his voice. The man moved like a shadow, damn him. *Why does he always see the things I don't want him to see?* Alyssa grimaced. She snuck a peek at him out of the corner of her eye as she reached for the tin of tea bags on the countertop. To her escalating embarrassment, she fumbled the box and it fell to the floor. *Just shoot me now and put yourself out of my misery, for God's sake.*

"Why don't you sit down? I'll make it," Connor said quietly as he filched the box off the floor and stood close to Alyssa, looking down into her eyes. Alyssa stared at him, not knowing what he saw in the depths of her eyes. He seemed to fill the tiny kitchen, making her feel surrounded, but not threatened. In fact, a frisson of excitement coursed up her spine.

Damn. Couldn't my hormones take a break, just for a while? Please?

Alyssa dragged her eyes away from Connor's enticing masculinity. If she kept looking at him, she'd be running her hands over his body and doing more than just being anxious about Grand's safety. She nodded and skirted around Connor to leave the kitchen.

Connor watched her leave in surprise. He *had* thought she'd sit down at the kitchen table and they'd talk a little. Obviously, Alyssa wasn't in the mood to talk. As he filled the electric kettle with water, the piano burst into sound. The music filtered throughout the quiet house and echoed off the walls.

It was not happy music. Nor was it sorrowful music. It was angry music, pouring out of Alyssa's fingertips into the keys and out of the strings. Beethoven's Fifth Symphony. Those outraged, powerful notes filled the house and slammed into Connor, rocking him with the knowledge of the extent of her grief. The music spoke for her. He suspected it always had and always would. Maybe, in his wildest dreams, she'd play happy music for him, for herself, someday.

Connor plugged in the electric kettle, slipped into the living room and sat down to listen. Alyssa beat at the piano ferociously, apparently trying to exorcise the demons plaguing her. As he watched, her fingers curled almost as if gouging the keys and she closed her eyes.

She abruptly stopped playing. She slammed her hands against the keys, discordant notes erupting noisily. And then again. And again, until the air was filled with dissonance and discontent, echoing off the walls. She leaned her elbows on the piano and cradled her head, shaking.

As soon as Alyssa had stopped playing the piece, Connor had jerked himself up out of the chair and had gone to stand behind her. Watched helplessly as she had flayed the piano keys in frustration. When she finally stopped and laid her head in her hands, he placed gentle hands on her shaking shoulders. He didn't speak, didn't utter a sound. He just stood there, caressing her shoulders, wanting her to feel better, secure. Safe. But she wouldn't. Not with Grand still unaccounted for.

Alyssa's agony seemed to go on forever, her despair limitless. The shaking gradually ebbed away and she melted against the piano, flotsam and jetsam on the beach of her life. To Connor, she seemed too fragile to weather the storm that was now upon them. Her very bones felt like they would snap beneath his hands. He knew, however, that beneath that fragility lay a core of steel that would not bend, that would not break and that would not allow her to stop until her dying breath.

Connor shook his head. A stubborn streak ran through this woman. He remembered her words to him after they'd almost been run off the steep mountain road near the compound. *Connor, one of the things you'll learn about me is that nothing knocks me down for long. I may bitch and complain and whine to no end, but I get back up and brush myself off. Every time. I promise.*

"Sweetheart, you're exhausted," Connor murmured. "What you need is sleep. You're white-knuckling it and if you don't rest, you're not going to be any help to Grand. Or to yourself."

Her shoulders tensed under his hands and she raised her head from the piano to glance back at him. The brief moment when their eyes met told him everything he needed to know—she wanted him, but was afraid to go to him, to ask him to hold her, to make love to her, to light her on fire. Conflicting desires warred in her eyes.

Connor pulled Alyssa to her feet and draped an arm around her waist. She felt boneless, weightless to Connor, ethereal. With a swift motion, he picked her up and cradled her in his arms. She closed her eyes and leaned against his shoulder. Her flesh felt icy in his arms. He cuddled her closer to warm her and she relaxed more into his body.

"Where's the bedroom?" Connor said in a hushed voice as he nuzzled her hair, breathing a soft kiss through the silken skeins.

Alyssa's eyes drifted open to gaze up at him. As her eyes locked with his, he felt a shiver make its way up her spine. "End of the hallway. On the right," she answered, her voice husky and low as she closed her eyes again.

Her husky response made Connor harden in a flash. He felt like swearing. She was frightened, exhausted, at the very end of her endurance, and all he could think of was burying himself so deep within her sultry depths he'd never come up for air. Not that *that* particular appendage needed air.

Careful not to bump her head on the hallway wall, he carried Alyssa to her bedroom and sat her on the edge of the feather duvet of her bed. He knelt down in front of her and stripped off her socks and shoes. Another shiver rippled through her body, her nipples tightening.

Jesus. I can't win. Or lose. It was all Connor could do to not look at her response to his touch. He snatched his hand away from her foot. *You can't take her when she so off balance. It's not right.*

Composing himself, Connor spoke with care, "Just have a bit of a lie-down and when you're awake, we'll talk." His voice sounded stilted even to him. Touching her, even in the most casual way, drove him to the edge of his restraint. Connor rose to his feet to make his escape when Alyssa caught his hand.

"Don't go," Alyssa whispered, lifting her eyes to his. Fear and yearning, in equal portions, glazed over her eyes.

Connor stared down at her, feeling each and every pulse of blood in his rigid flesh. "You need rest," he said, even as he sank down onto the bed beside her, powerless to stop himself.

"I need you," Alyssa said softly.

"You've got me."

"That's not what I meant."

"I know." Connor smiled ruefully as he stroked her hair. "Sweetheart, I don't want to force anything here. You're emotionally off balance right now. I don't want you to look back on this and think that I took advantage of you when you were at your most vulnerable."

Alyssa's responded by crowding closer to Connor, winding her arms tight about his waist. She placed her lips against his neck, as if to draw his warmth, his presence, into her body. Connor groaned as he shivered in sensual response. If she wasn't going to worry about it, then neither would he.

She shifted onto her side to reach one hand up to cradle his neck, bringing his lips down to hers. No languishing flower, her lips demanded that he relinquish himself to her. Seemed like a good idea. He braced his arms on either side of her, sinking into the mattress, and licked into her open mouth. She tasted of desire—and desperation. Whoa. Whether or not that desperation was for him or because Grand had disappeared, he didn't know. Didn't care.

Really.

He only knew he wanted her more than his next breath, more than anything he'd ever had before.

She pulled him down, maneuvering his body to lie atop hers, cradled between her thighs. It hurt to think she wanted him only to blot out the scary reality. He wanted to cry, be angry, be inside her—inside all of her.

A crazy mix of emotions fled through his mind and his thoughts must have translated into his hands—his grasp on her had tightened. She wriggled against him and gasped. He was holding her too hard. What was wrong with him? Did he want to hurt her? This was crazy—he never hurt women. He loosened his hold on her and let his head drop down onto her shoulder.

"Alyssa, I...you were going to leave me in Colorado. If we do this, are you still leaving? Does this mean *anything* to you? Because it means something to me," he choked out. And what was he? Insane? About to turn down sex with the woman he craved more than oxygen because he wanted more than just physical satisfaction and she didn't? And talk about sounding needy. God. For the first time in forever, he knew himself to be totally out of control and vulnerable. His former enemies would laugh themselves blind. He lifted his head to look into her eyes.

"Please. Connor," she whispered now, tears gathered in her eyes, magnifying them. "I need you."

"Do you, Alyssa? Do you really? Or is this just a way to block out Grand?" He couldn't keep his emotions from hitting his hoarse voice. He knew they were all plastered on his face. Frustration. Anger. Hurt. Want. Lust. Love. He felt tears pricking at his eyes but he blinked hard and beat them back. "What is *this*, Alyssa?"

Her tears ran down into her ears to make tiny puddles in the whorls. "I don't...know what this is. I can't separate...everything that's happened," she whispered. "Can't we just have right now? Whatever it is?"

He stared down at her. Her physical need of him could be enough to start. If that's all she'd give him right now, then he'd take it. And then he would change her mind about leaving—chain her to him with a driving passion. The subtitle of his every action designed to tie her to him mind, body, soul, heart. Every touch, every breath devised to capture her entire essence. He could do it. As an operative, he'd seduced women into loving him when he hadn't loved them. With love on his side, he would do it again.

Starting now.

"Yes," he growled and dove back into their kiss. He tasted surprise, yearning and more desperation from her lips.

She recovered from her surprise and struggled to pull her t-shirt over her head with his help. He shifted his weight off her a bit, pulled off her jeans and panties in one smooth, fast yank. She got him naked while he de-bra'd her. He sank back down between her legs and she arched against him. The wetness at the junction of her legs dampened his abs.

She pulled him down to her, wrapped her arms around him and levered him over onto his back. She pushed up into a sitting position on top his lower abdomen, looking pleased with herself. Tracks of tears still stained her face as she looked down at him. Her hands glided over his face, neck, spread her fingers over his muscular chest, and petted him. Her butt cheeks cradled his erection. Oh *man*. It felt like paradise, heaven, nirvana, all twisted together into bliss. He groaned and clasped her buttocks in his hands, squeezed and caressed.

She hitched herself up and, holding him up, sank down onto stiff penis, taking him into her soft, wet core in one, long, excruciatingly slow descent. She stopped only when her body stopped against him, totally enveloping him tip to root. They both let out slow breaths as she stayed motionless.

"I've heard…that if you're excited enough that…you barely have to move…to orgasm," she whispered, more air than sound coming from her lips. Her gaze locked with his. She rocked against him a touch and they both gasped at the sensation. His hands clamped onto her hips to keep her with him. And he thrust up into her. Only a little. Only a millimeter. Shock waves rippled through her body into his.

The urge to move, to plunge fast and hard into her slick heat, was almost impossible to deny. Seconds passed and it *was* impossible to deny. He held her hips down and inched his hips up, gathering speed, increasing in depth, thrusting faster. She was shaking apart in his arms, right now, her climax slamming into her at warp speed. Throwing her forward against him as he spent himself in her. The milking action of her tight walls triggered his orgasm. Rocked him back against the bed, bucked against her. She toppled onto his body like a house of cards blown over by a breeze, boneless, limp.

"You cheated," she groaned, her body still twitching in the aftermath of her climax, her sheath contracting wetly around him at random intervals.

"I know."

Chapter Twenty-One

Connor didn't want to awaken Alyssa. She was finally asleep, fitfully, but at least asleep.

Connor had lost whatever objectivity he'd hoped to gain by keeping emotionally distant from Alyssa. He had been trying to disengage himself from the power of her emotions. Not to be cold or callous, but to ensure her safety. One person emotionally tied up in a dangerous game could be managed. Two people emotionally tied up were invariably dead. The situation was deteriorating rapidly and the danger was escalating just as quickly, given the events of the last few days.

Connor carefully disengaged himself from the tangle of limbs and sheets that held him close to her. Dragging his boxer shorts on, he leaned down to softly brush away an errant lock of hair that fell over Alyssa's face. She smiled in her sleep and turned toward his caress-like touch.

The corner of Connor's mouth kicked up in amusement. They might fight like hellcats while she was awake, but she coveted his touch in her sleep. Connor leaned down to brush a kiss over her warm cheek before tucking the blankets around her sleeping form.

"Sleep well, angel," Connor whispered to her unhearing ears and slipped out of the room.

Late afternoon sunlight poured through the large kitchen window. It felt wonderful on his bare chest. Connor searched for a coffee cup and made the pot of coffee that Alyssa had attempted previously. He had work to do.

Sitting down at the kitchen table, Connor picked up the telephone and started dialing. His first call was to Liam at the compound. On the fifth ring, Connor was about to give up when the call was answered.

"What?" Liam sounded pissed off.

"Nice. Very nice," Connor said, amused. "You always answer the phone like that?"

"Where the hell are you? I've been trying to get a hold of you for hours!" Liam snarled.

"Hold on. Just hold on. What's going on?" Connor asked, no longer amused.

"What's going on? What's going on, the man asks. I'll tell you what's going on. All hell's broken loose here! People are dead, Connor. Dead."

Shocked, Connor rocked back in his chair and asked, "Who?"

"For one, the Israeli Roy was holding down at the station. You know, the Mossad guy you were talking about."

"So he was actually Israeli?" Connor dragged his fingers through his hair, trying to gather his thoughts. Damn it all. The whole situation had spun out of control like a rogue tornado. The end result would be a swath of humanity cut down in its prime. Although in the eye of the storm right now, he and Alyssa would soon be battered by fierce and potentially deadly winds.

"Yeah. Go figure." Liam took a steadying breath. "Some kind of commandos forced their way into the station early this morning, shot the place to hell, killed the Israeli and two of Roy's guys." Liam's voice shook. "Connor, they didn't have a chance, not a fucking chance in hell. No warning, no nothing."

The line was silent but for the sound of Liam's uneven breathing.

"Li, do they have any idea who did this?" Connor slipped in the affectionate nickname he had for Liam as a way of calming him.

"No, man. No idea. The feds have been called in. They're asking where you are, saying how convenient it is that you went missing during all this. The Israelis are screaming about their man. All the fingers are looking for a place to point, and right now, that's you."

"Shit. *Sh*it," Connor swore with heartfelt emphasis.

That was the problem with international politics—the feds would offer up the easiest scapegoat they could find and try to shove the rest of the mess under the carpet. If the chump who got caught in the crossfire wasn't smart enough to duck, he'd be mowed down with the rest of the grass.

Precision wasn't the name of the game. Grapeshot more accurately described the investigative style the feds would use now—take a scattershot at everyone and see who got hit. Whoever got hit *must* be the responsible person.

"What have you told them?" Connor asked.

"Told them? I've told those fuckers nothing. Officially, I don't know where you are and since you actually haven't told me where you are, I won't be lying when I say it. What do you need me to do?"

That's one of the things that Connor loved about Liam—no screwing around, loyalty up the wazoo and always willing to lend a hand. "For now, nothing. This conversation hasn't happened."

"Connor, this line could be bugged. *Crap.* Sorry, man, I didn't think about that."

Connor smiled bitterly to himself. "Not a problem. I installed a telephone bug deactivator on the phone line last year."

"Last year? And you didn't tell me?"

"Sorry, old habits die hard. Anyway, we're safe. For now. Though if the feds find that thing, there'll be hell to pay. You'll have to get rid of it."

"Where is it?"

"It's near the junction box in the basement. The lead that exits the junction box goes to the deactivator. You should be able to unplug it and re-attach the wires without losing the signal."

"What exactly does this unit do?"

"It sends a tone down the phone line that triggers any voice-activated recorder so it'll eventually run out of tape."

"Cool. Let me know next time you do something with the security so I don't inadvertently lead the cops to it."

"Sorry. Won't happen again. In the meantime, I'm going to buy a cell phone here with a local number—I'll send the number to you so we can keep in touch."

"How will I get the message? Everything is being monitored."

"I'll send it through a public e-mail service. Mailinator dot com, account name *dufus*. I should have the phone in a couple of hours, so just keep trying to access the account. The e-mails are erased every couple of hours, so it shouldn't be too much of a security problem as long as you access it from a public internet site."

"Dufus? You're going to name your account *dufus?*"

"Hey, it's better than using my own name or anything else associated with us. Besides, I was thinking of my little brother when I chose it," Connor said. The moment of levity quickly passed as his head began to pound, the frustration he felt with the whole situation now camped out in his brain. He ran his fingers through his hair and pulled hard, relaxing the muscles under his scalp.

Liam snorted. "Man, I hope you know what you're doing. This is just waiting to fall down on us like an avalanche."

"Tell me about it." Connor closed his eyes, exhausted already. The game was in full play now and he was right in the middle of the whole ungodly thing.

Again.

Connor opened his eyes and stared out the kitchen window in wonder—amazed at how normal things looked while everything went to hell. "Look, Li, I have to contact some people to find out what the hell is going on. I'll talk to you later. Call me when you get the cell number off the Internet."

"Fine." Liam paused for a moment, and then said tightly, "Watch your back, bro."

"Always do. You watch yourself."

Connor rang off. He leaned back in the chair, tipping it so it was precariously balanced on its back legs. He stared up at the ceiling, arms akimbo behind his head and frowned.

It didn't make sense.

Why would someone break into a police station and target a prisoner? Although the prisoner may have been an Israeli Mossad agent, but still. Unless…

Unless the man from Mossad had been telling him the truth. The Mossad had actually been sent to protect Alyssa. By Joe Taylor.

But who the hell were the other two guys in the compound who got away the night Alyssa zapped the Israeli? The ones who actually tried to kill him and Liam. And Alyssa. So many dead people—and virtually no viable information.

Connor let the chair bump down to sit on all four legs. He had to get a hold of Joe Taylor. There was no more time left—he needed answers and he needed them now. He just hoped to hell that Joe Taylor knew what was going on. If not, then they were all screwed.

"What's wrong?" Alyssa asked from behind him, taking him unawares, and he spun around in the chair. Despite the worries gnawing at him, he smiled a little sadly at the picture she made.

This is how he would always remember Alyssa. Sleepy, all soft and cuddly looking, hair mussed up, sexy as hell without realizing it. She wore a short silk cream dressing gown and probably not a stitch on beneath. He studied her intently for a few moments, trying to imprint the image of her on his brain.

Pain sliced through him. She didn't want to be with him, not really. She didn't trust him—not with her mind, her emotions, her fears or her hopes. She trusted him with her body, but not herself. She had carefully built her life around herself, not wanting to be beholden to anyone, anywhere, anytime. And she was afraid to renovate her careful construction to allow Connor a place in it.

The hell of it was that he could imagine what their children would look like. They would be beautiful, talented and loved beyond all reason. Their children would be stubborn and proud and probably more than a handful. He shook his head in despair.

It shocked him—the depth of his feelings for this emotionally scarred, beautiful woman for whom he waited to turn away from his love. Their love.

Leaving him alone.

Again.

Chapter Twenty-Two

"What's wrong, Connor?" Alyssa repeated, a little freaked by his quiet, anguished scrutiny. She moved forward and ruffled her fingers through his silky, jet hair. Her hand slid down his cheek, feeling the scratchy stubble under her fingers, and tilted his face to hers. As she leaned down to brush a whisper of a kiss across his lips, his arm came around her and pulled her close between his spread thighs. He brushed his hands over her pliant body, as if trying to memorize every curve, every texture.

Alyssa reveled in the sensation of Connor's big hands caressing her body. She tipped her head back as he pushed his fingers up through her hair and fisted his fingers in the softness there. He pulled her down to straddle him on the chair, nipping with his teeth at her jaw line and neck. Alyssa shuddered. Connor traced his hands down her neck and pulled the dressing gown apart to free her breasts. He carefully gathered up her breasts and lightly rubbed them against the stubble on his cheeks.

"We don't have time for this right now," he groaned. With an evident effort, he released Alyssa's breasts and drew her dressing gown together, shielding her ripe body from his sight.

Alyssa's eyes flew open in dismay. He had her halfway to heaven on earth and now she was left without the heaven part. "Connor..." she whispered in confusion, looking down at him with impassioned, dark eyes.

If Connor hadn't been sitting down, the look in her eyes would have dropped him. Hotter than lava. Her fully dilated pupils, with just a knife's edge of deep green around them, attested to her aroused state. He took a deep breath to calm his wildly beating heart and his stiffly rigid flesh now straining against the thin fabric of his boxer shorts.

"We need to talk." The words came out unintentionally harsh, his voice honed by the fierce cravings that Alyssa drew so effortlessly from him. To soften his words, he lifted a gentle hand to push a stray lock of hair that had fallen forward over Alyssa's face as she looked down at him. His fingers traced her cheek, trailing down the side of her neck, making Alyssa shiver in response to his caress.

Alyssa's eyebrows drew together, puzzled. He drew her hands into his and settled her more securely in his lap. Tears sprang into her eyes.

"It's Grand, isn't it? Something's happened to Grand," Alyssa whispered in a low, stricken voice. She hung onto Connor's hands, desperate for some sort of reassurance. Her fingers bit into his hands. The strength in her grip surprised him—her knuckles turned white under the fierce pressure.

Connor stared at Alyssa uncomprehendingly for a split second. "God, no. No, no, honey. I haven't heard anything about Grand." He freed his one hand from her grip to stroke her arm, horrified that she had misinterpreted his words. He pulled her into his arms and held her close. "God, sweetheart, I'm sorry. I didn't mean to scare you like that."

Alyssa stared at Connor. "Then what is it?"

"Last night, a team of commandos stormed Roy's police station and killed Ari, plus two other cops," Connor said in a voice devoid of emotion, his eyes watchful, unsure of how she would take the news.

In the past couple of weeks, he had seen every emotion under the sun from Alyssa, and given her current state, he wasn't sure what to expect next. She'd been under so much strain and stress, he worried that every new horrible thing that happened was pushing her closer and closer to the proverbial edge.

Alyssa drew a ragged breath and held it, fixing her eyes to his. "No."

Spoken so softly that Connor barely heard it, the word echoed tumultuous leashed emotions.

"That's it. No more," Alyssa said, her voice flat, angry. She pushed off Connor's lap and backed away from him, shaking her head. She breathed out through her nose, nostrils flaring, her pupils so dilated that her eyes appeared black and remote, like an animal trapped in a hunter's snare—an animal willing to chew off its own limb to be free.

"It's over. If these fuckers want the damn process so badly, they can have the damn thing," she hissed, eyes narrowing.

When will I learn? Alyssa bleak mood suffocated her, piled more dirt on top of a growing grave of filth and decay. People were dying, again, because of her stubbornness and pride, her blindness. *How many people have to die before the truth sinks into my thick, fricking skull? How many lives destroyed? Taken before their time.*

She could barely believe it as it was. A month ago, the last thing on her mind had been the thought of more people dying because of her. A couple of weeks ago, she'd only been concerned about a worrisome hacker in Grand's system. Now, the situation was the *definition* of FUBAR—fucked up beyond all recognition.

"Get out. Go home. Pretend you've never heard of Grand or me. Because it ends right here. Right now. I'm posting the whole process on the goddamn Internet and letting the Devil take the spoils, because this is all freaking bullshit." Alyssa's voice shook.

The first thing to focus on—prevent more people from being harmed, from being murdered. The second thing to focus on—prevent Grand and Connor from being sacrificed to the twin gods of greed and hatred.

The thought of the people for whom she cared desperately dying for a damn formula nearly paralyzed her. Bits and bytes. Money. And the politics of a few lunatics who would stop at nothing to possess the knowledge. Or destroy it out of hand—and destroy the people who knew how it worked.

Then it hit her.

Even if she posted the process on the Internet, it wouldn't be enough. The people responsible for these outrages wouldn't stop until everyone associated with the process was dead. They wouldn't stop—they would make examples of the people who were smart enough or brave enough to set the status quo on its ear. It wouldn't stop until everyone was gone and there was no one left who could tell the real story—a mystery in which people would eventually lose interest and ultimately forget.

"It's not enough, is it." Alyssa's dead voice intoned, her eyes jerked up to meet Connor's steady blue gaze.

"No. It's not," Connor responded quietly, squeezing her upper arms lightly.

"Oh, God." Alyssa speared her fingers through her hair and pulled hard on the silky mass. Dropped her head back and screwed her eyes shut. She freed her hands from the tangles of her hair and pulled the hair to the ends. And let go. Awash in pain, she opened her eyes to study her trembling hands—they seemed so foreign to her. Turning her hands over, she traced the lifeline on one palm.

"I always wondered why that was so short," she whispered.

Connor's hands shook as he grasped her cool hands in his fingers. Her hands disappeared into his very large, very warm mitts. Leaning into her, his lips brushed her forehead and he whispered, "Sweetheart, *you* are going to have a very long life. I promise."

Alyssa pulled back and looked up into his eyes. "You don't...can't know that." Her eyes filled with unshed tears. She pulled her hands free from his and gripped his hard muscled biceps. "And what about Grand? He could be hurt or even dead. He could be gone forever. I'll never get to say I'm sorry I made his life a living hell while I was growing up. I'll never get to say 'thank you'. I'll never—"

Connor raised her chin with one hand and covered her lips with his, stopping the pain in her voice.

Alyssa surrendered her lips to him, hungry for comfort, hungry for him and his ability to make her forget everything. She pulled closer to him, fitting her soft curves to his hard angles. Connor eased from the kiss, trailing his lips up her temple and forehead. "It's too soon to know, Alyssa. We don't know everything yet."

Alyssa nodded her head and let out a ragged breath. But she didn't let go of him—she just burrowed in deeper into his warmth. She was so cold. Icy fingers of dread had wound themselves around her heart. Her eyes closed as she felt herself drift. Down toward the abyss of her mind. As she reached the edge of that abyss, mocking words drifted through her psyche.

Look at you. You're ready to quit, to curl up and lick your wounds. Pull yourself together and do something to help Grand. If you don't, you might as well die. For God's sake, it's now or never. Stop sitting on the fence feeling sorry for yourself. It's your life—make something of it. Do you want to be miserable for the rest of your life? Clinging to a miserable excuse of a life? Because you're afraid of living, afraid of feeling, afraid of being hurt, afraid period. Aren't you tired of living in fear? Yet? What is it going to take for you to make that last step into the light? Into your life?

Claim it—it's yours.

Alyssa went stock still in Connor's arms, not breathing, lost in her head. In the past, she had erected a wall around herself. Whenever in contact with other people, it had always felt as if she were looking in on herself from a distance. Watching and waiting to mask her reactions, her emotions. Evaluating the intentions of others. Never joining herself, not only because she hadn't trusted others, but because she had never trusted herself. It had been so easy, so safe, to separate body from mind.

It reminded her of a type of computer system design called object-oriented design. The interface, her wall, her physical body, had certain attributes and functions designed to transmit information to the database, her mind. The interface protected the database, making sure that data that could hurt the integrity of the database didn't get written into it.

Her problem was that faulty information had been written to her mind, her neural pathways and thought patterns subverted to cope with the realities of her dysfunctional childhood. The interface hadn't and wasn't deflecting erroneous and unreliable information. That left her with one solution.

Rewrite her interface and clean up the database. Easier said than done. She needed to seek out the inaccurate data and prevent other damaging information from being written in the first place. She would have to take the step of listening to her feelings and her thoughts to decide if they were valid and reasonable. Being very much a perceptive person, she combined intelligence with intuition.

Professionally, it was a perfect mix. Gut feelings often guided her through the complex world of systems and fuzzy logic. Personally, it was an explosive combination. She out-thought her feelings, divorcing reason from emotion and coming up with the wrong conclusions. Always trying to second-guess the people around her, always trying to discover what they thought and taking small gestures and small talk as the whole truth and running with it.

Scary stuff. Especially now that everyone she valued depended upon her. Depended upon her thinking clearly and rationally, unencumbered by out-of-control emotions. She had to let it all go—the anxiety, the humungous chip on her shoulder, her fear, her pain and especially her low self-esteem.

Let it all go and jump into the abyss—free-fall toward her destiny and toward her true self. And let serendipity find its way to her since she couldn't find her way to it. She would have to accept whatever it gave to her. The only way forward appeared to be giving up control.

The phrase thrummed in her mind. The only way. The. Only. Way. She felt her pulse increase as she surfaced from the depths of her mind and took a huge gulp of air.

Connor didn't know what the hell was happening. One minute she'd had a meltdown in his arms, plunged into panic and grief, and the next minute she froze, her breathing slow and shallow. Her silence echoed like a shriek in the dark, unseen and unheard by anyone except him.

He could feel her thinking.

And then, finally, a deep breath. The rapid beating of her heart felt clearly through his chest. His heart rate sped up to match hers. He closed his eyes as she drew away from him, afraid to look at her. Afraid of what he would see—the end of their relationship. He gathered his courage and he opened his eyes.

And stared.

To his utter amazement, although she looked at him intently, hope illuminated her beautiful eyes, a lightness he'd never before seen.

It was mesmerizing. Seductive. And absolutely and totally unexpected.

He took a closer look, wondering if she had lost her mind.

Nooo. She was all there.

Maybe more there than she had ever been before.

Chapter Twenty-Three

Connor sat in the living room, listening as Alyssa tried to explain the last five minutes of her life. The first five minutes of her life.

"I don't know if I can really put it into words. It was as if a light bulb just flicked on," Alyssa said. She paced, gesturing wildly. "I just realized that I had to let everything go if I was going to help Grand. And me. And you. And everyone else involved in this mess. I don't have the luxury of holding back anymore. I can't live my life based on fear anymore. I don't know if this is making any sense to you or not, but right now I don't think we have the time for me to explain it properly."

Connor smiled uncertainly, still baffled and unsure of Alyssa's self-proclaimed enlightenment. He had seen stranger things happen. Pushed so far, people either broke or became stronger, making peace with their God, their devil and their souls. Alyssa apparently belonged to the latter category. She'd made the first steps toward her future and away from the past that had held her hostage for so long.

Connor hauled himself out of the chair and gave Alyssa a nearly bone-cracking bear hug. He felt the excitement surge through her body—she could barely stand still. Smiling into her hair, he said, "Perhaps this is enough self-discovery for one day. Especially since we need to pick your brain now."

"What do you need me to do?"

"I need to you re-link to the satellite to see if Joe Taylor has left any messages for me."

"No problem." Alyssa trailed her fingers down his sculpted abdomen, teasing the waistband on his boxer shorts.

She gave him a wicked smile and walked away from him toward the hallway, the decided sway of her hips beckoning him to follow.

Talk about a bird dog, he thought to himself ruefully. Later. It would have to be later.

Down the hallway, she made a left turn into another room. He followed and stood in what could only be described as the computer room. Three computers stood quietly against the wall along with three computer monitors. The incoming and outgoing cables between the beige boxes had been neatly and efficiently organized and tucked out of the way. An expansive mahogany workstation faced the window that looked out over Alyssa's small garden.

Alyssa walked over to the three servers and brought them to life. Crossing the room, she seated herself in a high-tech ergonomic chair loaded with all the hydraulic gizmos.

Tapping away at the keys, she took only a few moments to link to the satellite. With Connor peering over her shoulder, they scanned the target directory for an indication of a response from Joe Taylor.

"Bingo," Connor murmured into her ear as he pointed to a file on screen named Dawg.

"Dawg?" Alyssa asked, amusement clear in her voice. She downloaded the file onto her desktop, closed the connection.

"Don't ask."

"I'm just to scan it for viruses," she said as she opened another program window. After a moment, she added, "It looks good—only clear text. Joe doesn't believe in encrypting his data?" Alyssa asked, sounding suspicious. "That's really odd. Anyone could have read the message."

"Normally, yes. Maybe he thought I'd forgotten the decryption codes," Connor said, uneasy about the lack of security protocols employed for the message. There could have been a reason, but…

"I sup-pose," Alyssa said, doubt coloring her voice. She shifted in her chair and grimaced. She looked back at the monitor and read the message. Her jaw dropped.

"This can't be right," Alyssa said, her voice faint, shocked.

"Alyssa, let's just finish reading before jumping to conclusions," Connor cautioned her, but his stomach rolled in a sickening wave as he read the words.

Dawg,

Disassociate from the woman ASAP. Old man has agreement with Middle Eastern business interests. Old man has okayed any and all actions-stands to gain financially once competition eliminated.

Helpful if you find old man and report back. We're still looking – has gone to ground.

J

"There is no way on God's green earth that this is true!" Alyssa swung her eyes away from the damning electronic words to stare wide-eyed at Connor.

Connor returned her stare, deciding on how to proceed. Reading between the lines, Grand had been declared a clear and present danger to America's best interests. At best, Grand would be considered a traitor to Canada. At worst, Grand would be considered a terrorist plotting the downfall of the world's largest single economy.

Joe had never steered him wrong before, but the message had been sent in the clear with no identification. Anyone with access could have written it.

"Please tell me that you're not thinking something stupid like actually believing this crap." Alyssa fought to keep her voice steady. Grand would *never* be involved with something like this. Yeah, the old man had his moments, but he was no traitor—and he most definitely was not a terrorist.

"Sweetheart, Joe has never..." Connor said slowly, evidently treading carefully.

"Oh. My. God." Alyssa's mouth hung open in disbelief, shaking her head. She felt one edge of her upper lip curl in disgust. "You *do* believe it. *You do*. I can't believe it."

Connor's expression hardened. "Alyssa, it doesn't matter what I believe or don't believe. The only thing that matters is that we need to find Grand *now*."

Alyssa bit back the angry words the sprung to her lips. All the old insecurities reared their ugly heads—she couldn't trust anyone, no matter the circumstances.

"You're right," Alyssa responded tightly.

Connor looked sharply at her, his eyes swiftly evaluating her response. He looked distinctly displeased.

She grimaced inwardly. Damn, she really needed to take acting lessons. He probably knew that she might be agreeing with him, but she wasn't actually *concurring* with him.

Alyssa arched her eyebrow at him, daring him to contradict her when she'd just agreed with him. It was nearly impossible to argue with someone who was acquiescing to your viewpoint and Alyssa knew it.

"I'm right," Connor repeated, a hint of question in his voice. He narrowed his eyes at her, doubtless suspecting something off kilter.

"Absolutely. I have to find Grand before anyone else does."

"*You* have to find Grand? You mean *we* have to find him. Us. Together."

"Of course. What else would I have meant?"

"Alyssa, don't play games with me," Connor warned, his ice-blue eyes drilling into hers, giving her a look that had no doubt reduced hardened men to knee-knocking compliance.

Alyssa smiled sweetly at him and blinked, hoping to appear brain-dead, or at the very least, not deviously plotting to bury her kitchen cleaver into his thick skull when he turned away.

Ah, damn. He'd been shut out and Connor knew there was fuck-all he could do about it. Anything could come out of her mouth, but he could no longer count on Alyssa to tell him the truth. He didn't know if she would willingly include him in the next steps she, they, needed to take.

The only thing he could do now would be to keep in very close physical proximity to her. It wouldn't be beyond her capabilities to take off and leave him high and dry.

"Well, then, *we* need to buy a cell phone. I told Liam that I'd get one and leave a message on Mailinator for him. We need to do this *now*." His voice hardened measurably from even twenty seconds earlier.

"I'm hardly ready to go. I need to take a shower and get cleaned up. It's already four o'clock. Why don't you go out and get the phone? We'll go from there," Alyssa said the words with nonchalance, nodding encouragingly with a smile.

Not fooled, Connor's low voice brimmed with menace. "Alyssa. Don't try to get rid of me. I swear, it would be a bad experience for both of us, but I will guarantee right now that you will end up with the short end of the stick."

Alyssa stiffened. "Are you threatening me?" she asked softly, warily.

"I'm trying to keep you safe."

"How are you going to keep me safe? By making me believe that Grand is in league with God knows who? Because I am telling you right here and right now, it won't happen."

"I believe that you believe that, but can't you even admit it's a possibility?"

"No."

"Alyssa..."

"*Don't.*" Alyssa held up her hand, her eyes blazed with betrayal and hurt. "I don't need this bullshit. Not from you. Not from anyone."

Alyssa turned on heel and headed for the hallway. Connor took two large steps and grabbed her by the arm to swing her around to face him.

"Where do you think you're going?" Connor asked sharply, unsuccessful in his attempt to keep his frustrated anger to himself.

"*I* am going to take a shower, and by the time I get out, *you'd* better be gone."

"Don't count on it."

"You'd better make it happen, because the next thing I do is call the cops and have you arrested for trespassing." Alyssa wrenched her arm from his grasp. She backed away from him, shaking her head. "Just leave. *Now.*"

Alyssa turned around, headed down the hallway, stomped into the bathroom and slammed the door behind her.

Now *that* was a resounding success, wasn't it, Connor thought in disgust. He listened as the shower came on. Well, let her call the cops, because he wasn't leaving. When she got out of the shower, he would either drag her kicking and screaming to the store or tie her to him. With rope, if need be. Connor walked back out to the living room and dropped, like a boulder shoved off a cliff, into a chair to brood.

He had mishandled the situation. Badly. She had reacted exactly the same way as he had when she'd suggested that Liam might not be trustworthy. He didn't know what it was, but when he was around Alyssa, his higher brain functions shut down and the caveman came out. *You – mine. Me – protect you.* Complete with the Tarzan voice, he felt like a Neanderthal, for chrissakes.

God, normally he was a cool-thinking, fast moving machine. She brought out all the overprotective tendencies he usually only displayed to his family. His family knew how to deal with it—they just humored him out of it. Alyssa got angry. He had to rein in this tendency, at least outwardly, before he drove her away for good.

He rested his head on the chair back and closed his eyes as he waited for Alyssa to emerge from the bathroom. Minutes ticked by and still the shower ran.

Five minutes. Ten minutes.

Suspicion filtered through his mind. What was taking so damn long? He waited another few agonizing minutes. Finally at the end of his patience, he strode down the hallway and rapped peremptorily on the bathroom door.

No response.

"Alyssa, what's going on?" Connor spoke through the door, a cold pit forming in his stomach. God, what if she'd tried to kill herself or something? He hadn't thought she was suicidal, but then he'd been wrong about Alyssa before this.

Still no response.

Connor twisted the locked doorknob to no avail. He backed up and kicked the door, the wood splintering around the lock. The door gaped open, crooked on its hinges. Steam poured from the bathroom. He forced his way through the door and got the shock of his life.

The bathroom, except for the slowly clearing steam, was empty.

Chapter Twenty-Four

It was amazing what stayed with you from your youth. *I guess I'll always be able to pick locks and hotwire cars,* Alyssa thought with a rueful smirk. Well, as long as it was an old-fashioned type car—not the new cars with the key matched to the engine turnover. But even then she'd be able to hotwire it, given enough time.

For the fourth time in ten minutes, she checked the rearview mirror. No headlights followed her in the darkness on the road leading through the foothills of Alberta to the majestic Rocky Mountains.

She glanced down at the face of her watch. Nearly ten at night. Bone tired, she pushed the hair out of her face and tried to concentrate on the road. She fought against exhaustion, but it inexorably yanked her down. She shook her head to clear her mind to think. It was hard to believe that only last night…

Only last night had she danced enthralled under the moon and the stars. Only last night had Connor asked her to marry him. Only last night had her fragile world spun off its axis, with Grand missing and possibly dead. Today she had finally begun to understand the intricate workings of her emotions and tried to make some sense of them.

She nervously smoothed her hair over her scalp. The action, however small, diverted her attention enough that the front right tire of her car momentarily caught in the gravel by the side of the road. Instantly alert, she wrestled the car back onto the asphalt.

All righty then. That was a wake-up call, or at least a "time for a nap" call.

She'd had precious little sleep in the past twenty-four hours and what she'd had were more like catnaps, not deep, desperately needed oblivion. Alyssa had seen a rest stop about five kilometers back, so, taking a careful look behind and ahead of her, she slowed down and pulled a U-turn on the deserted highway.

She pulled into the rest area and parked a short distance from the washrooms. Turning off the car, she extricated herself from her seat. She staggered from her seat and leaned against the car for a moment. Her cramped legs and cricked neck testified to the relentless tension of the past hours.

Leaving Connor had been difficult, but not impossible to do. She had to find Grand before anyone else did. And that included Connor. Instinctively, she knew that she could trust Connor. Logically, she knew she couldn't chance it. The fact that Connor's company matched Grand's needs on a business level could have been due to some sort of subtle manipulation performed by parties unknown, even the American or Canadian governments. Who knew?

God, she didn't know what to think. And until she had Grand in front of her, she had no idea what was hurtling toward her. Grand could only be in a couple of places, she told herself. If he had escaped dying in the fire and knew someone or many someones had gone after him, he'd go to the most unlikely place out of Calgary of which he could think.

Hence the impromptu trip to the Rockies in a car she had "borrowed" from a member of the symphony. Rutger. She didn't think that Rutger would mind the appropriation of his vehicle. She'd left her salsa red Toyota Camry, with all the bells and whistles, in his garage with a note and the keys.

Rutger's car was more of the beater variety—an ancient Chevette hatchback, originally silver, but now a muted shade of sad gray. And a stick shift on top of it. She hated stick shifts. Cars should do their own shifting—it was a proven technology. She didn't need to reinvent the wheel.

Alyssa hoped Rutger wouldn't mind.

However, she had no doubt that Connor'd had a fit when she'd taken off without him. In fact, she could envision what his precise reaction had been. If she hadn't been afraid of Connor before, she had definite qualms about seeing him now.

Her easy escape had been a little surprising. Once the bathroom door had been shut, she'd turned the water on, grabbed a pair of jeans and t-shirt from the clothes hamper, dressed quickly and then wriggled out the small frosted bathroom window. Then she waited.

When Connor broke down the bathroom door, she opened the front door, grabbed her purse and laptop and RAN. Her car had been in a neighbor's garage two doors down since she didn't have one and she didn't like leaving her baby exposed to the damaging Alberta elements.

Once in possession of her car, she'd driven over to Rutger's house, picked the lock to his front door, grabbed his car keys and exchanged vehicles. Of course, he hadn't been there. He was off on tour. It had been easy. She hoped. A description of her Toyota may have been broadcast in an effort to find her. *Ergo,* the reason for the switch, her Toyota safely locked in Rutger's garage.

No problem.

In spite of the fact she'd been shaking so badly, she'd dropped her keys three times before managing to insert the correct one into the lock of ancient car. In spite of the fact that she expected Connor to catch up with her at any instant and raise holy hell. In spite of the fact that she almost *wanted* Connor to catch up with her and raise hell.

The thought made her wince. She'd always been extremely independent in a bid to avoid any situation where she couldn't at least partially control the outcome. As she had been as a child. Defenseless.

She sighed as she stretched out her limbs beside the car. She wanted Connor, but she didn't want to depend on him, didn't want to trust him with anything except her body. Sure, like that wasn't a messed-up thought process. She shook off the thought and, looking up to the star-bright sky, headed for the washroom.

As she was about to leave the restroom, a tingle of alarm made her stop. She peeked around the doorjamb to peer at the car. The car had company.

A man strolled around the car, taking a very close look as he prowled. She froze in place, evaluating the newcomer. The single light standard cast a ghostly pool of light around Rutger's heap. The man stooped to peer into the driver's side window. At least, she presumed it was a man. He wore a dark hooded pullover fleece jacket with the hood up, his back to her.

Yeah, definitely a man. Well over six feet tall, the man had a muscular build, narrow hips and broad shoulders. If it had been any other time and place, she would have taken a good, long, appreciative look. As it was, she could barely drag air into her now-seized lungs.

The man walked around her car, surveying it, his face always in shadow. A long minute later he walked back to his car, shrouded in the shadows outside the lone circle of the light, climbed in and took off toward the mountains, his wheels kicking up a cloud of dust and gravel.

Now *that* was weird.

Icy fingers of premonition skittered down her spine. Taking a nap here no longer appealed to her, not now. The man's unsettling presence had fully awakened her anyway. She took a last glance at the highway that led to Calgary and, not seeing any more headlights, ran to the car, jumped in and followed the direction of the departing car. She didn't see taillights in the distance and she heaved a relieved breath.

Alyssa would just have to hang on until she arrived at her destination. A friend of Grand's had a cabin on the outskirts of Jasper, nestled on the valley floor at the foot of the mountain leading up to Marmot Basin, a ski resort. They'd both been to the cabin more times than she could count. They'd been given carte blanche to stay whenever and for however long they wanted. Grand might have been hiding somewhere else, but this place seemed to be the most likely.

Twenty minutes later, she reached the now-dark and quiet main drag of Jasper. She drove past the old Canadian National Railway station and the huge black-and-white statue of Jasper the Bear. The corner of her mouth kicked up—as a child Grand had bought her a candle of Jasper the Bear. She'd loved it to distraction and it was still somewhere in her house. She'd never had the heart to burn it, even though the black-and-white paint on the bear had mostly flaked off, leaving a grayish bear-shaped lump of wax.

The smile disappeared from her face as images of Grand, dead or dying and needing her help, flooded her mind. Her eyes filled and the streetlights almost blinded her with the refracted brilliance. Alyssa wiped her eyes, impatient and irritated with herself, and took a deep breath.

You don't know anything yet. Don't jump to conclusions.

Alyssa passed quickly through the town—it was a small town, not much to it. Fifteen minutes later, she pulled off the highway onto a gravel road that led into a grove of spruce trees. The headlights of her car shone into the oily blackness of the night, illuminating little but the road. She felt a momentary spurt of panic. Under normal circumstances, if someone were in residence, the yard light would be on.

But these were hardly normal circumstances.

The headlights picked out the old log cabin in the woods. As she swung toward the lodge, the twin beams of light picked out small, glowing eyes from the dark. Probably chipmunks or raccoons. Still, a small tremor rippled through her body.

Pulling up to the small, two-bedroom cabin, she turned off the car. Not even a flicker of light showed in the cabin. She grabbed a flashlight from the glove compartment and prayed that Rutger had been as anal-retentively perfect as usual—he changed the batteries in his car flashlight every six months like clockwork. She pointed the flashlight out the windshield and pressed the button.

Thank God. It worked. *Rutger, I'm buying your predictable ass dinner. In fact, I may kiss that ass.*

Exiting the car, she swept the beam of light over the cottage. The light reflected off the two windows at the front of the cottage. The cabin looked asleep with the curtains drawn. No signs of life. Trying not to jingle her keys, she fumbled to find the one that would open the front door. And promptly dropped the keys onto the gravel. *Damn.* As she crouched down to pick them up, something at one of the curtained windows caught her attention. The curtains had shifted slightly in the breeze, revealing….

The barrel of a shotgun. Jesus.

"Grand? Is that you?" Alyssa called without standing up. "Grand?"

"Hell, girlie! What are you doing here? I damn near blew your head off!"

Relief flooded her body, leaving her lightheaded. It was a good thing she was already crouched on the ground, because she had a definite need to sit down before she fell down. She abruptly plopped her butt into the gravel as the front door opened. She didn't even mind that he'd called her "girlie" again. "Girlie" was something he'd called her when she'd annoyed him beyond belief during her puberty-from-hell stage.

It sounded like music now. She swore she'd never get upset at being called "girlie" again.

There he was. He stood in the front door. The interior lights, now blazing, flooded around him, silhouetting his frail, stooped frame, a shotgun hanging from one hand. He had a bald pate, but a shock of white hair grew long and wild at the sides. Alive as anything and totally pissed. No one had ever looked so good.

She watched as he propped the gun by the door and came to stand over her, gazing down into her upturned eyes. Her eyes filled. He frowned first and then his mouth quirked in tender amusement.

"Didn't you know, girlie? You can't get rid of me that easily," Grand spoke gently, even though he'd used "girlie". He brushed her cheek with a paper-dry, emaciated hand. She detected the slight odor of the Ben-Gay he used on his arthritic elbows to relieve the ache.

Alyssa scrambled to her feet and threw her arms around him. "Oh God, Grand. I was so scared. I thought you were *hurt*. I thought you were *dead*." She backed up and scanned him with a critical eye, holding both his hands. "You *are* okay, aren't you?" She asked anxiously, brows furrowed, as she surveyed him for damage.

Grand snorted. "Don't wind yourself up. I'm fine, Lyssa. Just *fine*. Come inside—it's too cold out here."

Alyssa released one of Grand's hands as he led her into the cabin. Everything seemed a little unreal—finding Grand in one piece in the exact place she'd thought he'd be. Looking exactly as he should look. His mass of white hair stood up at right angles to his head—Albert Einstein hair. Those piercing, light blue eyes that could still tell her thoughts at a glance.

Alyssa stumbled over the threshold of the post-and-beam log cabin. Still unnerved by the episode with the rifle, she glanced around as if she'd never seen the lodge before.

There was one main room, with a bathroom to the rear, which was sandwiched between two tiny bedrooms. The musty-smelling room attested to the fact that the cottage had probably been out of use for months. She swiveled to face Grand as he shut the door. He half turned from the door and slanted a glance at her out of the corner of his eye.

"You look like you could use some tea, Lyssa. Absolutely exhausted, you are."

Alyssa giggled and slapped one hand over her mouth. Normally she wasn't the giggling type, but under stress, she turned into a giggler. He sounded like Yoda from the *Star Wars* movies. He actually looked a little like Yoda, with the riotous hair substituting for big ears, and the huge, bobbly eyes. She wondered a bit wildly if his irises would bounce around his eye sockets if she shook him. She could paint him green too. The thought made her laugh a smidgen more hysterically.

Grand surveyed Alyssa with a critical eye. "Perhaps you need something a little stronger than tea? You're about to split down the middle and fall apart."

"Jeez, thanks, Grand." The giggles departed as quickly as they had come and she snapped at him, "I've just had the most awful twenty-four hours of my entire life and you're upset that I'm tense. I thought you were gone. Why didn't you call, for God's sake? I was having a *bird*."

"I didn't want to lead anyone to you."

"You didn't want to lead anyone to *me*? Grand, it's a bit late for that."

Grand stared at Alyssa. "Maybe I'll have something to drink too while you explain that last statement."

With that, he clumped over to one of the kitchen cupboards and took out two small, cloudy glasses. He moved over to the refrigerator and, from the cupboard atop it, took out a bottle of single malt scotch, Glenfiddich, his favorite drink. He unscrewed the cap and poured a dram into each glass. He motioned her over to the kitchen table with one of the glasses.

Alyssa took the chair across from Grand, who pushed a glass toward her. Delicately fingering the glass, she shot a look at Grand. "Why don't you start? You're the one who's hiding out in the mountains and have been presumed dead by the RCMP."

Grand considered her for a moment. Then he took a sip of the scotch. "It started happening after I found Energy Unlimited a couple of months ago. Little things in the Calgary office seemed to be moved. Footprints in the gravel around the building that shouldn't have been there. Feeling that someone was watching me. Nothing that I could really put my finger on." He grinned at her. "I'm an old man. After all, I could be developing Alzheimer's or something. So I dismissed it. "

The grin disappeared. "Last night I was working late and I thought I saw something outside the building. I went outside and—"

"You went outside? By yourself, Grand? Why didn't you call the police?" Alyssa interrupted heatedly. He thought he was invincible. He drove her to distraction—he never did the expected thing. Two months ago she'd found him on the roof on his house, replacing some asphalt shingle that had been damaged in a windstorm. She'd almost had a heart attack when she drove up—her eighty-three-year-old grandfather hanging off the side of the roof with nary a safety precaution in sight.

"I'm the one telling the story here. Your job is to listen, not to pass judgment." Grand scowled at her for a moment before continuing. "I went outside and didn't see anything. I wandered over to the garage to check that the car was still there. It was. I was just about to go back in when I heard the explosion in the building.

"The door leading into the garage was blown clean off its hinges. The lights went off. The external garage door wouldn't work, so I had to use the manual crank to open it. It was difficult, but I managed to open it just enough to get the car out. As I left the garage, I saw a car leaving."

Grand took a deep breath before continuing. "There's one more thing. I've also been receiving some very unpleasant letters telling me to stop my oil sands research. That started about three weeks ago."

Alyssa's jaw dropped as she stared in disbelief at him, flabbergasted. She took a large slug of the thus far untouched scotch in her hand. Her first instinct was to shriek at him for being a total moron. Her second instinct told her that her first instinct would get her nowhere. She tried to take the appalled anger out of her voice before she spoke. It took a full minute before she could respond in an even tone.

"So you knew there were problems *before* you sent me to Colorado and you said *nothing*?" Her voice rose and shook a little as she bit out the last word. She swiftly got it under control. "Why, *may I ask*, did you not bother to relate this little tidbit of information before I left?" she asked in a deceptively soft voice, knowing the softness would not deceive him into thinking that she didn't want to scream at him.

Grand stared back in the face of her barely controlled fury and leaned forward.

"Alyssa, I didn't want you to be hurt. I knew that Connor Donnelly would protect you. I found him for you."

"You *what*?" She felt her eyes bulge out of her skull.

Grand's eyes closed before opening to stare at the tabletop. His eyes flicked to her face and he took a breath. "I, uh…Connor would protect you."

"Nuh uh. Not that part. The next part."

"Oh. I, er, found him for you." Grand dropped his eyes to his glass and swirled the amber liquid around the tumbler.

"You *what*?" Alyssa repeated as her voice rose to a high-pitched squeak and her eyes widened.

"Well, I checked out his company and I hired a private investigator to see what kind of person he was. I thought his company was perfect for the co-venture and he was perfect for you."

"You were playing *matchmaker*?" Alyssa choked out the words. Oh God. How totally mortifying, to be marketed as a part of the deal. "Was Connor in on this?"

"What do you mean?"

"Was Connor aware that you were setting me, *us*, up?" Alyssa asked in an aggrieved tone of voice.

"Heavens, no, Lyssa. I swear." Grand reached over and took Alyssa's hands in his and squeezed lightly. "I know you think I'm a doddering old man at times and hopelessly old-fashioned, but you need a man. A man who will be your equal. A man you can depend on. More than anything in the world, I want you to be happy. I think Connor could be the one to make you so."

Alyssa closed her eyes and tipped her head back. *Oh man. My eighty-three-year-old grandfather plays matchmaker and I miss it entirely. I must really be losing it.*

Grand continued, rocking her hands in his, emphasizing his words. "I met the man. I know what kind of person he is. I know that you both have an Intelligence background. I know that two years ago you left that world and I know that something terrible happened. To you. That's why you left CSIS. I know you can't tell me the details, but Connor will be able to help you because he's probably been there. He'll be able to love you. You'll be able to love him."

Alyssa's lips moved, but no sound came out. She stopped trying to speak and instead tried to gather her thoughts—it was all going to come out very, very wrong if she wasn't extremely careful with her next words.

Grand cocked his head to one side and surveyed his mute granddaughter. Slowly, a small smile played across his face and his eyes sparkled a little wickedly.

"You made love with him, didn't you?"

Now Alyssa felt thoroughly absolutely dumbstruck—how had he guessed? Slack-jawed, she gazed at him numbly.

"You were careful, weren't you? Condoms and all?"

Alyssa finally found her voice, yanked her hands from Grand's grasp and exclaimed, "Grand! For God's sake, just stop *talking*." She felt her skin flame like a wildfire from her neck to engulf her entire head. Her face felt like it was on fire. At this rate, if she stood on a shoreline, she could substitute for a lighthouse. Not the reaction of a woman who hadn't been having raw, hot sex for the past week, she realized belatedly.

Oh, God. Oh, God. Oh, God.

Talking to Grand about sex was the last thing she'd ever wanted to do. It ranked right up there with yanking off her left arm and beating herself to death with it. Yeah, it was high up on the list of things to do in her lifetime.

Alyssa shoved back from the table to stand and walked away from the table, pulling her hair back from her face with her hands. "I don't believe this," she muttered to herself as she headed toward the front door. She desperately needed some air. She cast a look back at Grand as her hand held the doorknob and she shook her head.

Swinging the door open, she turned around and ran into a wall of muscle. Said wall of muscle had its fist raised to knock on the door. She muffled a surprised shriek as she felt hands grasp her upper arms to steady her.

She tipped her head back to see the owner of the hands and muscles—Connor. And looking none too pleased. With his ice blue eyes emanating shades of anger and frustration and his shock of midnight black hair, he looked like the devil or an avenging archangel come to life. And it looked like that vengeance was about to be directed at her.

Wonderful.

She should have known he'd be able to track her. It was, after all, something he used to do. And still did. Apparently with the utmost of ease, she thought disgustedly.

She wrenched her arms out of Connor's grasp and glared up at him.

"*You* can talk to Grand about our sex life because I'm not!" Alyssa snapped as she pushed past him to go outside.

Connor gazed after her in consternation. Stunned enough to forget how angry he was with Alyssa, he turned his head to watch her stalk out to the dilapidated Chevette and he then turned back to see Grand.

Grand looked like the proverbial cat that swallowed the canary. Very satisfied with himself. Almost smug.

Connor had definitely walked in on Act Two.

Chapter Twenty-Five

Alyssa shook her head as she leaned her back against the door of the Chevette, her butt on the ground, her elbows resting on her bent knees, as she tried to absorb the quirkiness of her whacked-out life. It felt like she had an angel on one shoulder and a devil on the other, each whispering words to sway her next actions, her next thoughts.

Quite honestly, she didn't know what to make of the unexpected turn of events in the past half hour. She had thought that she'd left Connor behind. She hadn't. She hadn't thought that Grand could play matchmaker without her knowledge. He had. It appeared the only delusional one was her. Totally oblivious to the motivations of the people surrounding her. She swore soundly at her lack of perception when it came to the men in her life.

Startled, she stared into the woods. The Man In Her Life. When had she started thinking of Connor in those terms? Probably since she couldn't seem to get rid of him, she thought sourly. She wondered whether or not she was purposely allowing him to find her, unconsciously making mistakes so that he could. Maybe she didn't want to see him go.

Alyssa came abruptly to her feet and swung back to face the cottage. She started violently. She wished he'd stop startling her. It was getting on her nerves. Connor leaned against the wall of the cottage, arms folded in front of him as he watched her with unblinking eyes, their color washed to silver by the moonlight.

Swearing beneath her breath, she took a belligerent stance, hands on her hips, legs braced apart, and glared at him. "What?"

"What *what*?"

"What are you doing here?"

"I thought that would have been obvious," Connor said evenly, his eyebrows rising in response.

"Nothing about any of this is obvious. Did it occur to you that I took off because I don't want you involved with this? With me?" Alyssa waved a hand near her head, fingers outstretched.

"No."

"Oh, really. Then, pray tell, what conclusion did you come to when I took off and left you in Calgary?"

"That you were angry and you needed some time alone."

"Most people avoid me when I'm angry. And giving me five hours alone has not made me less angry," Alyssa said, annoyance ringing in her voice. "Maybe you should trot off to Calgary and give me some more time. I'll call you when I've cooled off." She flicked one hand in the direction of Calgary.

Connor was not a man easily dismissed. "You don't want that," he responded calmly.

"Why is it that when I tell you what I want, you tell me it isn't what I want?"

Connor considered the question for a moment. "You're one of those people who have their poles reversed—you know, confusing north with south. You only think you want to get away from me." Connor lowered his voice seductively, his voice flavored with honey and whiskey. Temptingly sensual. Intoxicating. "From us. I know it's not true."

Alyssa shivered reflexively at his tone. A tingling sensation started in her chest and moved outward toward her toes and fingertips. Frustrated and thoroughly disgusted with her body's reaction to him, Alyssa dropped her head into one hand, covering her eyes, and sighed. Loudly.

Damn, but the man was annoying beyond belief. What was even more annoying was the sneaking suspicion that he was also right.

Alyssa didn't want to get rid of him. She worried that the Big Bad Boogeyman would hurt him if he continued on with her. She worried that she'd be hurt once he figured out she wasn't worth the extra effort it took to deal with her emotional problems. She worried that he would stay. She worried that he would leave. She worried that she'd spend the rest of her life looking for another Connor. Trying to find the exact mix that was Connor.

Tied up in knots, her guts roiled, protesting the indecision that was making her mentally sway like a palm tree in a hurricane.

Grasping onto the last of her reserves, Alyssa asked, suspicion clouding her voice, "How did you find me?"

"How do you think I found you?" Connor countered.

Connor had been pulled through the wringer, forward and backward. The last twenty-four hours had been a rat's nest of torturous ups and downs. For no other woman on the entire planet would he have gone through the total hell of the past day. Apart from his family, only one woman had ever worthy of enduring such torture. Worth his time, worth his effort, worth his devotion, worth his love. Only one. And she wasn't even on the same wavelength. All his efforts, the meaning behind his efforts, went unknown and unappreciated.

Gazing at her eyes, shadowed by the dark, Connor felt despair chilling him to the tips of his hair. Trying to draw Alyssa in was like trying to bait the hook for an extremely skittish fish. She'd swim up to his bait and peck at it, maybe even mouth it a little. The difficulty lay in trying to pinpoint when he should set his hook. Too soon and she'd be off like a light. Too late and she'd be gone for good.

But he had come too far to quit now, even though she said didn't want him. At this point, he could only try to prevent her from dying some horrible death. The only thing she'd left him to accomplish. The thought of Alyssa not in this world spurred him on. If she drew breath, he could hope to be with her, a part of her life. If she didn't draw breath, then there would be nothing but foul ash filling his life.

"When I went to the bathroom, *where you were supposed to be,* I heard the front door open. It was easy enough to follow you. I grabbed the rental car and followed you. Simple as that," Connor stated flatly, eyes narrowing.

"But I never saw you," Alyssa insisted. She paused, her eyes narrowing, before asking, "It was you at the rest stop, wasn't it?"

Connor knew there was no point in lying to her. "Yes."

"Why did you stop?"

"I wanted to make sure you were all right, but I wanted to get away before you came back from the bathrooms."

"But you took off ahead of me, where did you go?"

"I went a couple miles up the road and pulled over to wait for you to pass. Once you went by, I followed at a distance."

"So, what do you intend to do now?"

Connor gave her a withering look. "I intend to make sure you stay alive while we sort out this whole mess. What did you think?" He bit out the last words.

Alyssa almost took a step back, but he saw her eyes fire and pure obstinacy starch her spine, which impeded the movement. "Connor, most men would be heading for the hills by now. Most men would have taken the hint and left me alone."

"I did head for the hills—these mountains—and I'm not most men."

"No shit," Alyssa said, as her body drooped and she scraped her eyelids with the heels of her hands.

Connor cocked his head to one side to take an appraising look at Alyssa. "What did you mean when I came in, that I should talk to Grand about our sex life?" He been taken off guard by that one—it was one of the reasons he'd lost his head of steam when he'd arrived.

"Oh, you didn't know? You probably did, what am I talking about? Seeing as everyone can pull the wool over my eyes. Let me spell it out for you," Alyssa gestured, overly dramatic, to herself with one hand, as if showing off a prize on a game show, "Grand said that he'd decided that you were the man for me. That's one of the reasons he picked your company. Your company was good for him and you were good for me."

"Did you tell him about the sex?"

"Yeah. Right. What d'you take me for, a total idiot? He just looked at me and asked me, *no,* he *told* me we'd made love. And then he asked if we'd had safe sex, for God's sake. And…and… Why the hell are you smirking like that?" Alyssa snapped.

Connor wished he could have been a fly on the wall when it had happened. The wily old bastard might be cantankerous, but he loved his granddaughter more than anything on the planet. He could imagine the scene—Grand asking Alyssa about her sex life, Alyssa's horrified reaction. He'd caught the tail end of the drama, with her charging right into his arms at the door.

He started feeling decidedly happier. She hadn't been able to hide her feelings from Grand. If he had meant nothing to her, she wouldn't have reacted so strongly. For that, he had to thank the crazy old bastard. The past week had worn her down to the point where someone who loved her without reservation could easily read her.

It gave him hope—he had a champion in his cause for Alyssa's heart. The person who knew her best thought Connor was The One. From Alyssa's point of view, it would seem totally archaic and probably insulting, determined as she was that she never be dependent on anyone.

His breath whistled as he forced it out between his teeth. It never got any easier. She threw up so many walls that as soon as he managed to breach one barrier of the inner kingdom, another barricade was slapped up. He knew fear created the walls, fear of intimacy and fear of being hurt, but *damn,* it was frustrating.

Obviously frontal assaults would not work with Alyssa. Confrontation just exacerbated her wall-building tendencies.

He stepped around the Chevette and held out his hand to her. His voice deep and calming, he said, "You don't need to fight me, Alyssa. I'm not your enemy. I only want you safe. With or without me." He wanted to say, "Come with me, let me take you away, let me cherish you, let me laugh with you, let me cry with you, be my life, be my love."

All that and so much more did he want to say as he stood mutely awaiting her decision.

The subtle intonations in his voice made Alyssa want to close her eyes and surrender up to the halcyon gravity of his presence. Pulling her in. Pulling her closer. She swayed as she focused on his outstretched hand, somewhat surprised to find it there in front of her. She was so tired. So tired of running, so tired of falling. Of failing.

Alyssa's eyes sealed shut as she cast about blindly for his hand. He easily caught her hand and drew her close, cuddling her like a prized puppy or a loved woman. He rested his cheek against her hair and brushed a kiss near her ear. His nearness smoothed a soothing balm on her frayed nerves. Although she tried to deny it, she felt safe in his arms.

"I never said that I thought Grand was guilty of anything. I wasn't trying to hurt you or make you angry. I was just trying to look at all possibilities. Nothing more," Connor breathed into her ear. "Let's go back inside. It's kind of cool out here."

Chapter Twenty-Six

Connor watched Grand with growing affection. This guy could be his grandfather-in-law any day. He loved the guy.

"Grand," Alyssa growled at her grandfather, drawing out the name into two syllables.

Grand glanced at his granddaughter and gave her a conspiratorial wink. "You must allow an old man his dreams, my dear." He sighed theatrically. "There's so little time left in my life. You can't take my hopes away from me *now*."

"You are an incorrigible old man. And a troublesome matchmaker." Alyssa scowled and pointed a finger at him. "And you're a long way from death's door. Hell, you're the one who keeps telling me you're going to live forever. You've got plenty of trouble left in you."

"I'm so glad you understand, Lyssa. So when's it going to be?"

Alyssa crossed her eyes at her grandfather and dropped her head down to the table where all three of them sat. Connor saw Grand try to suppress a chuckle and Grand threw Connor a knowing look, his blue eyes sparkling roguishly.

"We haven't decided when yet," Connor offered innocently.

Alyssa's head snapped up off the table and she raised an eyebrow at Connor. "Don't encourage him. We're not getting married."

"Yet," Connor inserted with a smile.

"Can we please get back to the issue at hand, please?" Alyssa said, sounding a little desperate.

Grand gave up. "I *am* very sorry about involving you in all this." He spoke gravely to Connor, having repeated this particular sentiment about five times since Connor's unexpected arrival.

"I know, Douglas. Look, this may not be the best situation I've ever been in, but it's not the worst either. I just wish you had told me of your concerns in the beginning. We could have made plans to ensure Alyssa's safety." Connor was getting a little tired of the stream of apologies from Grand. He knew that Grand had no idea that he had endangered Alyssa with his reticence even before her trip to Colorado. Connor also knew that Grand was no terrorist. It wasn't in the man's mindset.

"I knew you were the right man for my Alyssa," Grand uttered fiercely, almost as if the words had been catapulted out of his mouth by a cannon. He looked slightly surprised at the vehemence of his outburst and dropped his eyes to the table.

Alyssa's creamy skin tinged with a rosy pink at this latest declaration. "Am I invisible or something? You two talk about me as if I were. I'm right *here*," she growled. She took a deep breath. "What has happened is history. The question is, what do we do now?"

Connor answered first. "Obviously, my contact at the CIA has been compromised. Eventually I'll find out what happened, but for now we'll concentrate on the facts.

"Both you and Grand, and I by extension, have been targeted by someone. We have to assume its Grand's process they want. It's the only connection between the three of us. Our culprits could be one of three groups that we know of—the natural gas producers, other oil-patch competition or terrorists." Connor counted off the suspects on his fingers.

"If it were one of the first two, then the Mossad wouldn't be involved. Unfortunately, that leaves us with the terrorists. I don't think we have much of a choice—we have to go either to CSIS or to the CIA. Probably CSIS since the focus of the problem is here in Canada. We need to go back to Calgary in the morning." He paused before adding, "At least I'm assuming that's the location of the nearest CSIS office?" Connor raised his eyebrows at Alyssa.

"The main prairie office is in Edmonton," Alyssa replied. "It's about a five-hour drive from here, but there's an airport just outside of Hinton, we passed it on the way to Jasper. Air time is an hour, more or less."

Connor grinned at her. "Perfect. I'll call my pilot in Calgary and get him out to Hinton in the morning, then."

Grand leaned back in his chair and gave a somewhat unconvincing performance of yawning and stretching, as if he hadn't slept in a month. He smiled impishly at Alyssa. "Time for bed. I'll leave you and Connor to figure out your sleeping arrangements."

Alyssa cast a jaundiced eye toward Grand at his transparent machinations. "You must really want great-grandchildren badly. We're on the run and you have your mind on this…this relationship, instead of thinking about what we're going to do next."

Grand's eyes sparkled, apparently interested in hatching more mischief. "Now, Lyssa, you can't tell me that you're not interested in Connor. And he can't tell me that he's not interested in you. You're the iron attracted to his magnet. I might be old, but I'm not blind. Not in both eyes, anyway."

Grand rose from his seat and clapped Connor on the shoulder as he passed by him on the way to one of the two bedrooms.

"Goodnight, children," Grand murmured as he closed the door.

Alyssa stared with ill-concealed disbelief at the closed door. After a moment, she shifted her eyes to stare at various parts of the room.

Connor watched her watch everything but him. Eventually, her gaze made it to him. She even seemed sort of surprised to find him still there. What did she think? That he would disappear as magically as he had appeared? He shoved his frustration down. Losing his temper would not get him what he wanted. He wasn't even entirely sure what compelled him—aside from the fact that she was gorgeous, smart and passionate. And he loved her.

In spite of the fact that she was always trying to get rid of him in between bouts of exhilarating jungle love, she captured his attention no matter what she did. He mentally sighed—probably hormone related. Him, not her.

"You take the bed. I'll sleep on the couch," Alyssa said coolly as she pushed back from the table with both hands and stood.

Connor glanced over at the couch. Springs stuck up through the tattered fabric. "You can't sleep on that. Those metal things will be poking you all night."

"It's not a problem, I've done it before."

"It may not be a problem for you, but it's a problem for me. Look, we're both adults, so there's no reason we can't share the bed. "

Alyssa narrowed her eyes at him.

"I won't touch you." Connor raised both hands in a hand-off gesture. "I just want you close and I can't keep an eye on you if you're out here."

"What? You think I'd take off again?"

"It wouldn't be the first time."

"For God's sake, fine then. Okay? Happy?"

"Happy doesn't have anything to do with it," Connor lied. "Relieved is more like it."

She shot him a wary glance before taking the long way around the table, avoiding him in the process, and headed for the bedroom. He sighed and got out his cell phone to have his pilot meet them in Hinton the next morning. Flipping the phone closed, he wearily dragged himself to his feet and ambled in Alyssa's direction.

The small bedroom had a double bed, two bedside tables and one ancient chest of drawers. Alyssa was in the process of struggling out of her lacy white bra without removing her tee shirt and stepping out of her jeans as Connor entered the room. She hesitated before continuing to undress. She kept the tee shirt and panties on and she slipped between the cotton sheets.

Without a word, Connor dispatched all of his clothing and slid naked into the bed beside Alyssa, who had scooted as far over to her side of the bed as she could without falling off. Unfortunately, a six-foot-two man in a double bed with a five-foot-five woman did not have any extra space. He turned out the bedside lamp and turned to face Alyssa's body in the inky darkness. She breathed shallowly, as if careful not to disturb an ornery bear that had crawled into a cave with her.

With a heavy sigh, Connor reached over and dragged her into the warmth of his body. She stiffened and pulled slightly away from him.

"I thought you only wanted to keep an eye on me," Alyssa whispered, her voice hoarse.

"It's so dark that keeping an eye on you is impossible. Just relax, you're cold, I'll keep you warm. Nothing else will happen unless you want it to." Connor snuggled her more firmly into the curve of his body.

"Connor…"

"Just sleep, Alyssa. That's all. Close your eyes."

He knew that, for appearances' sake, she probably felt the need to argue with him over the latest liberty he was taking with her personal space. However, her cool skin seemed to appreciate the warmth of his flesh and her body slowly relaxed as her skin temperature rose to match his warmth.

"That's right, sweetheart, just let it all go," he purred into her ear as he settled her closer yet. Her mind might be saying "no", but her body said a definite "yes". At least to this minor encroachment on the borders of her comfort.

Tomorrow would be a new day. He'd have to see how much further he could push those boundaries.

Chapter Twenty-Seven

The morning sun rolled over the mountains and splashed down on the tarmac of the Jasper Hinton Airport as Connor's Gulfstream taxied to a halt near the small terminal building. The sun dazzled in a cloudless, deep blue sky.

Alyssa lifted a hand to shade her eyes and breathed in deeply, enjoying the fresh morning air of a new day in the Rockies. She cast a considering glance at Connor and felt a flutter seize her stomach.

Earlier, Alyssa had been aware of nothing but an overwhelming sense of warmth and contentment as she slowly emerged from the gloaming of her dreams. She gravitated toward the source of that toastiness, only to realize that the toaster had grown a very prominent hard-on.

Her eyes shot open, only to fall into the depths of Connor's blue irises. Sleep still fogged her brain, making it difficult to think straight. Gazing into his intent eyes, a subtle shiver worked its way down her body. Connor drew her even closer and then, oh so slowly, lowered his lips until they were a breath away from hers, giving her every chance to escape.

"Yes or no?" he murmured seductively, his eyes drawing her into his world, daring her to see what he wanted for the both of them. Of them naked and wild together, her fingernails scoring his back as he claimed her body. Of her soft body aching, arching to meet his hardened body.

The answer had been a resounding "yes".

Another shiver racked her body and her eyes rolled back in her head as she thought about their hushed early morning detente. Not one square inch of her body had been left untouched during their interlude. She felt like a woman who had been well and completely loved. And not just physically beloved. But loved in her entirety—mind and body, soul and spirit.

She knew why she had run the day before. For all the indignation over the satellite missive, it hadn't been the reason she had decamped so fast. Yes, she'd been worried out of her mind about Grand. And yes, she'd been royally pissed off by the message and Connor's reaction to it. But she had wanted to make sure that she broke up with Connor on her own terms. She hadn't wanted to wait around for him to leave her. She had siege mentality when it came to men in general. Get them before they get you.

Words to live by. Or die by, as the case might be. And as much as she was determined to live her life on her own terms, she wasn't so sure she liked those terms any longer. Those terms kept her isolated for her own protection, or at least that was how she had rationalized it in the past.

Now those terms could get all three of them, Grand, Connor and herself, killed. Now she could no longer allow anger to be the only emotion she gave free rein to, that she allowed to control her. Now she no longer had the luxury of sequestering her emotions, keeping them at a safe distance in her psyche.

Now standing on the airstrip, Alyssa became aware she had been gazing vacuously at Connor when a sudden jolt of awareness hit her in the form of Connor's now-smoldering eyes drilling into hers. Her face heated and her eyes darted away from him like a startled school of fish, only to have her eyes stray back to him as if he were a lodestone.

Connor's lips curved into a satisfied smile, cognizant of at least some of the turns her mind had taken. Truth be told, their early morning activities had been occupying his mind too. Surely he must be winning the skirmish for her heart and soul.

He reached out to snag her hand, drawing her close before planting a thorough kiss on her pliant lips. She wound her arms about his neck and kissed him back before realizing they had an audience.

Much to Alyssa's chagrin, judging by her grimace as she attempted unsuccessfully to pull away. Much to Grand's approbation, his eyes twinkling.

"Don't get any ideas, old man," Alyssa warned, her lips twitching in what seemed to be the start of a smile as she finally fought free from Connor's possessive grasp.

"*Moi*?" Grand blinked ingenuously, pointing to himself.

Alyssa knit her eyebrows and tried to look displeased, but nothing could hide the light in her eyes. She arched an eyebrow at Grand before she glanced at Connor, who also attempted to look nonchalant, but he knew he failed miserably. It seemed that everyone was having a problem with looking more pleased than they wanted to this morning.

Sighing, Alyssa turned back toward the terminal building and did a double take as the door opened out onto the tarmac.

Darcy Myers, CSIS agent extraordinaire, in the flesh.

Now there was one person she would have been happy to never see again. Darcy exuded sexual confidence. Over six feet tall, his slim physique, honed by a love of fencing since university, had attracted many women over the years. He reminded her of a Greek god, except instead of brown hair, he had dark blond hair laced with silver streaks that glinted in the brilliant sunshine.

The fact that he was here, thirty-eight hundred kilometers west of Ottawa, was not a good sign. And it would be too much to expect that his presence was a coincidence. He was here because she was here.

Damn it all to a thousand blazing hells.

And at least one of those hells was striding toward them, accompanied by a posse of sunglassed black suits exuding attitude.

"Shit," Alyssa said almost inaudibly. Her apprehension evolved from two distinct areas. One, Darcy was the CSIS agent with whom she'd had a brief fling three years ago. And two, the only reason he'd be here now was why the rest of them were here. Terrorists.

Connor jerked around to face the newcomers at her breathed epithet. His eyes narrowed as the pack of penguins approached.

"What? The men-in-black having a convention?" Alyssa said derisively, loudly enough for it to carry the ten yards that now separated the two groups. "Isn't it too *uncivilized* out here in the wilds for you people?"

"Alyssa, darling, put your claws away," Darcy purred, his voice dark and dangerous as he advanced, catlike. Not mincing, but smoothly and powerfully. Absolutely assured of his place in the food chain. On top. "Why don't you introduce us?" Darcy indicated Grand and Connor.

"Oh, I'm sure you already know who they are, so let's just cut the crap, Darcy." Alyssa kept her voice steady and her eyes unflinching.

"Well then, let me introduce myself since you're too rude to do it yourself. I'm Darcy Myers. Alyssa and I used to work together at CSIS." He held out a perfectly manicured hand first to Connor, who shook it firmly, and then to Grand, who took it as if he were handling a venomous snake. "You, of course, are Connor Donnelly and Douglas Tiernan."

Alyssa couldn't figure out what had ever possessed her to get involved with Darcy in the first place. Drop-dead gorgeous in a fake, plastic-y kind of way, yes. Relationship material, no. He was one of the most self-involved, conceited persons she'd ever known. Now she found him revolting. She thought cryptically that she must have been clinically brain dead at the time or her genetic predisposition to finding his type attractive must have been in high gear.

"What are you doing here, Darcy?"

Darcy winked at her. "You've been a busy little bee lately, haven't you? And I can only assume that it runs in the family, since your grandfather has been busy too."

Grand bristled at his words. Alyssa laid a calming hand on Grand's arm.

"Darcy ..." Alyssa growled, her teeth clenched and hands fisted. Head ripping was a definite possibility.

Darcy nodded in a conciliatory fashion, trying to placate her. "Okay, okay... We've been hearing rumblings lately that there's a new technology that could revolutionize oil sands extraction techniques. We've also been hearing that some Middle East sorts are less than pleased with the advent of this new technology. Short and long of it, we've been observing your grandfather's activities for the past four weeks. After the last night, we put out the word that Douglas had been killed."

"You knew he wasn't dead?"

"Our man saw him leave the scene. He tried to follow, but he got caught at a level train crossing and lost him."

"So, you thought you'd just use Grand as bait, is that it? Flush out whoever was hanging around?"

"It's how the game is played, Alyssa."

Alyssa snorted. "Yeah, it's how *some* people play the game."

Darcy gave her a long, almost pitying, look. "We've been trying to find your grandfather since yesterday. We got the break we needed when Connor's pilot filed his flight plan late last night. We figured that if Connor's plane was here, so was your grandfather. We've been in contact with the CIA regarding the circumstances in Colorado and we're trying to put together a joint initiative."

Darcy flicked his eyes over to Grand. "Mr. Tiernan, you've got everyone quite excited over this process of yours and I'm here simply to ensure your safety. And that of Alyssa, as well."

"They wouldn't send you out here for a little babysitting job, Darcy. Why are you really here?" Alyssa asked, annoyed with the chit-chat—Darcy wasn't a small talk kind of guy.

Darcy's eyes slid to Alyssa. It was all she could do to prevent the outright revulsion from coming through on her face. The man looked at her like a juicy piece of steak displayed in the window of a butcher's shop—ready for his taking. His eyes took on a distinctly predatory look and he took one step toward her.

Connor stepped between Darcy and Alyssa, stopping Darcy's approach to Alyssa. In a menacing, low voice, Connor growled, "Don't."

A look of mild surprise crossed Darcy's face as he focused on Connor. Darcy raised one eyebrow as he said softly, "So that's the way it is between you and Alyssa."

"Don't forget it. I would take a lot of pleasure out of reminding you of it," Connor answered evenly.

Darcy shrugged as he took a step back and smiled coldly at Alyssa. "As Douglas Tiernan is by all accounts alive, we're here to charge him with conspiring to commit terrorist acts on Canadian soil."

Alyssa's blood, already simmering, erupted into a full-scale boil. "Don't play games with me, Darcy," she spat out in a low, harsh tone. Her eyes narrowed. "Don't you *dare* use Grand against me. I don't play by the same rules anymore. It won't be as easy to get me to shut up and go away as it was two years ago. This time, you ass, this time I'll go to every newspaper and television station I can find and blow the whole deal."

"The real Alyssa Tiernan just stepped forward, I see. Welcome back, lover." Darcy's smug grin grated on her nerves.

Which of course pushed all the wrong buttons in her head, making her want to beat that smirk into the ground, along with Darcy. "Oh go screw yourself!" Alyssa snapped. "And while we're on the subject, you were a piss-poor lover. *Really* pathetic."

Darcy's self-satisfied simper dissipated slightly before rebounding.

"You know as well as anyone that Mr. Tiernan is not a terrorist. Why don't you just lay your cards on the table and tell us what you want," Connor rumbled. He stepped back toward Alyssa and drew her nearer to him, seemingly eyeing Darcy up for a body bag.

Alyssa registered the possessiveness implicit in the gesture and, for the first time in her life, it didn't bother her. Her deep-seated aversion to being under anyone's power or influence was overridden by the knowledge that Connor wasn't seeking to hurt her or prevent her from doing what she wanted. It was a statement of solidarity.

Darcy considered the two of them for a moment before speaking to Connor. "I know your reputation. You *were* renowned for being able to pull off the near impossible, using both brains and brawn. It's regrettable, really. All that talent gone to waste." Darcy sighed and shook his head. Then his mouth quirked up at one end and his eyes sparkled. *Now what?*

Darcy continued, "We've been able to track Internet usage in Canada by the World Islamic Jihad. We think they're responsible for the blast in Fort McMurray and in Saudi. We know that a faction of the WIJ is here in Canada. We know that they're using encrypted transmissions to communicate with each other over the Internet. We even know their Internet provider here in Canada, but they don't use a regular landline to surf.

"They've been using WiFi wireless technology to hook up in coffee houses and the like. We've been able to intercept the encrypted messages, but we need the key to decrypt the messages." He paused. "That's where you come in, Alyssa."

"Darcy, you know the drill. You get the ISP to tip you off when they're on and hack their laptop for the decryption key." Alyssa spoke as if to a particularly slow first grade child, the snarling in her gut driving her snaky with anxiety.

"Easier said than done. They've got a killer firewall that's stymied all our attempts. We invariably alert them to our presence and they bolt before we can get anything." Darcy paused before grudgingly adding, "We need *you* to hack them. You're still one of the best—no one we've hired has been able to replace you."

"I'm not one of yours, in case you hadn't noticed."

"You are now. It's the price of admission, kiddies. We play my way or no way. Take your pick—you help us or we help ourselves to your grandfather."

Chapter Twenty-Eight

"Back off," Alyssa said in a low, steely voice to Darcy as he hovered over her shoulder, watching her work on the computer.

It was bad enough that CSIS had sent a former lover to "ask" for her help, but it was even worse that he insisted on standing not two inches behind her chair, leaning over her, effectively caging her between his body and the computer. She could actually hear him sniffing her hair, for God's sake. He had always had a thing for the smell of her hair. It was weird. Mister God's-Gift-to-Womankind—a hair sniffer.

She detected the faint aroma of the clove cigarettes he loved to smoke—that, and the faded scent of sandalwood in his favorite cologne. Alyssa used to think that the combination of odors emanating from him was very masculine. Now it was all she could do to keep from gagging on the stench.

Alyssa marveled at her past choices in men. How had she ever found this man even remotely attractive? It wasn't like she had been drunk or anything when she dated him. Nothing chemical had been impairing her judgment at the time. A small shudder of revulsion worked its way through her body. She felt like throwing up, preferably right onto his Italian leather shoes. And she would too, if he didn't back off soon.

Connor had left the Edmonton headquarters of CSIS to scout out a decent cup of coffee ten minutes earlier and hadn't yet returned from the *Second Cup* coffee shop down the street. Before Connor left, he gave Darcy a blatant warning—*you do anything to upset her, asshole, and you will be talking out of the other side of your mouth for the rest of your short life.*

Immediately after Connor left, Darcy had started slowly circling around Alyssa, like a shark scenting blood in the water right before a feeding frenzy. Alyssa supposed it was part of his genetic makeup to act like a totally self-involved asshole, but that didn't make him any easier or more pleasant to deal with.

Darcy slithered right up behind her and leaned over to take a look, a very close look, at Alyssa's progress. That she'd told him to get away from her seemed to be of no consequence. Darcy's hand drifted down to rest very lightly on Alyssa's exposed neck.

Apparently he didn't count on Alyssa's almost instantaneous knee-jerk reaction. She shoved her hands against the desk and wheeled around in the chair, knocking Darcy off-kilter. Before he could regain his balance, she hammered the heel of her hand upward and connected like a bulldozer with Darcy's nose. She heard a crunch as his nose wedged a little further back into his skull. He clutched at his nose and staggered back, blood pouring from between his fingers.

As he backed up, Alyssa leaped to her feet and, with the ball of her foot, brutally rammed that portion of his anatomy he prized the most. He hit the bricks with a high-pitched shriek and alternated between clutching at his genitals and his nose, swearing soundly between ragged heaves for air.

"What the fuck did you do that for? Goddamn it!" Darcy gasped from his prone position on the floor.

Connor arrived to see Darcy swearing on the floor and Alyssa standing menacingly over him. Connor took one look at the scene before him and had two distinct reactions. His first reaction was, "I'll kill the son of a bitch". His second reaction was, "that's my girl". Connor put down the two vanilla bean lattes he'd brought and dragged Darcy to his feet by his lapels. Darcy still gasped in pain and, although he struggled, he couldn't extricate himself from Connor's grasp. Connor jerked Darcy once to get his attention and looked over at Alyssa.

"Should I kill him, darling?" Connor said with a slightly bored air. "Now? Or would you prefer later?"

Alyssa shoved her hair out of her face with one hand and smirked. "Now, if you have the time."

"I have all the time in the world." Connor paused. "Perhaps you could tell me the exact reason why he's dying—I'll have to explain the bloody carpet stain to the CSIS director."

Alyssa recounted the incident before Connor shook Darcy again. Darcy could at least stand now, but he continued to drip blood onto the carpet Connor shoved Darcy out of the room, down the hall and propelled him into a nearby office without knocking.

Myles Collins, the Operation Chief, looked up as the two men barged into his office, but maintained an inscrutable air at the interruption. A scar about an inch long cut through his right eyebrow, giving him the look of a very tough stevedore. His black eyes flicked over Darcy's physical condition and then slid to Connor. In opposition to his very fearsome demeanor, he had a soft voice, but it contained a hint of icy disapproval.

"Gentlemen, do we have a problem?"

Connor answered. "Just so that we understand each other, if this asshole comes within fifty yards of Alyssa, I will personally see to it that he feels the after-effects for a very long time."

Myles leaned back in his chair, rested his elbows on the arms, steepled his thick, stubby fingers and watched Connor with the patience of a hawk tracking its prey. His bushy eyebrows rose in admonition. "Be very careful whom you threaten, Mr. Donnelly. Myers is a prized member of CSIS and we would be distinctly displeased if anything untoward happened to him."

"Myers is a prize bastard. And I will happily neuter him if he even breathes in her direction again. This asshole put his hands on her. If he goes near her again, we're out of here. In fact, we're out of here now," Connor said evenly. He shook the now limp Darcy by the collar before he walloped Darcy in the backside with his foot, propelling him toward the couch at the side of Myles' desk. Darcy stumbled, hit the front rail of the couch with his knees and toppled onto it. Darcy gave Connor a venomous look.

"Mr. Donnelly, you might recall a certain charge we're not making against Douglas Tiernan because of Alyssa's cooperation," Myles said, unperturbed.

Darcy interrupted, "I want to press assault charges."

Myles glared at Darcy. "The only thing you're going to press is your feet into the pavement. You're a total asshole. Just couldn't keep it in your pants, could you, dickwad? Those morons in Ottawa couldn't find their cocks with both hands and they sent me a halfwit." Myles rose to his feet and towered over Darcy. "You fucked up. Get your sorry ass out of my fucking jurisdiction."

Darcy gaped at Myles—Myles' voice, though nearly inaudible, was even icier than it had been when speaking to Connor. Now it condensed the air into ice crystals, which was no small feat given the desert-like humidity levels in the prairies. "Now wait a fucking minute, *sir*. I was sent out here to secure her cooperation. I got it. You've got no reason to dismiss me."

"Wrong. You were specifically warned not to involve yourself with her personally. I warned you myself and she told you to 'back off'."

Darcy gawped at the chief before swallowing hard. "There were surveillance cameras in the room?" he squeaked as he blotted his bleeding nose with the sleeve of his silk shirt.

"Of course. When I deal with turds like you, I like to be prepared. Get your stuff and get out. I'll have to clean up your mess."

Darcy got to his feet unsteadily as two armed guards appeared in the office. Myles spoke without taking his eyes off Darcy. "Please escort Mr. Myers out of the building. He won't be returning."

The guards came forward to stand right behind Darcy. When they'd been summoned, Connor didn't know. With a look of disgust, Darcy shot Myles a furious glance and stomped out of the office, the guards shadowing him.

Myles looked back at Connor. "Where were we?"

"You were in the act of dropping the bullshit. You can't charge her grandfather with anything and we both know it. She's here to help. If you people are going to be a bunch of assholes, then the deal is off. Go find yourself another guinea pig." Connor turned on heel to leave the office.

Before he reached the door, Myles said, "You'd kill for her, wouldn't you? In fact, you *have* already killed for her. You'd do it again in a heartbeat to protect her."

Connor swung around to glare at Myles. "Your point?"

"My point is that emotions, in this line of work, are dangerous. Rampant emotionalism has killed more damn good people than I care to remember. My point is that all this anger, all this passion is going to get both you and Alyssa killed. My point is that Alyssa and her grandfather need us just as much as we need them. You walk out of this room, out of these offices, and you know that none of you may survive.

"You'll all have a better shot at survival if Alyssa stays and helps," Myles continued, his voice monotone, but his black eyes glittered with emotion.

"You should have just asked for help in the beginning, instead of opening with threats," Connor said, his voice soft and icy. "That would have gone a long way. You know that she wouldn't have refused to help."

"Yes, I knew it, but Ottawa didn't know that and it was their call," Myles responded in kind.

Connor stared at the man. He wanted to dislike Myles but he couldn't. In many ways, Myles matched the type of people Connor had admired in the CIA—tough and pragmatic. Unfortunately, with the tough and pragmatic came the calculating and cold. The calculating and cold part had almost stripped Connor of his humanity six years earlier and so he'd left the shadows and ghosts to prevent losing himself in the dark. No, he didn't hate Myles. He admired him, but he also pitied him.

"What's going on?" Alyssa asked from the door, her voice sounding suspicious. Connor turned to look at her.

Myles answered her question. "Myers is gone. He won't bother you again. I'd appreciate it if you would stay and help us."

Myles' directness startled Alyssa. She stared at him, wide-eyed. Candor was something she'd never expected to receive from anyone at CSIS. Her eyes narrowed warily. "What about my grandfather?"

"Your grandfather will not be prosecuted for anything in connection with this business. Myers felt it would be best to have a bargaining chip with you and the folks in Ottawa okayed it. It was a ruse."

Alyssa fell into speechlessness. The man was not typical CSIS material. He called a spade a spade and let the chips fall where they may. But then again, it might be an act. She had difficulty in gauging others' motivations and truthfulness. Partially because her first reaction was always to tell the truth as she saw it.

"I want to speak to my grandfather. Now. Before anything else," Alyssa stated.

"No problem. We've shifted him to a nearby safe house. I'll call and you can speak to him," Myles answered, gesturing for them to sit down on the chairs in front of his desk.

Myles picked up the telephone and asked for the safe house. "Ms. Tiernan would like to speak to her grandfather. Can you put him on the line?"

A pregnant pause later, Myles' outward appearance had not changed, but something boiled beneath the icy cool exterior. Alyssa tensed. Myles flicked his eyes over to Alyssa before he disconnected the call with the sharp jab of a stubby finger.

"Your grandfather's gone."

Chapter Twenty-Nine

"Gone?" Alyssa whispered, shocked. Her voice strengthened. "What do you mean *gone*?"

"Myers dropped by the safe house a few minutes ago and told the agent on duty that he was bringing Mr. Tiernan to the CSIS office. The agent had no reason to doubt Myers, so he let your grandfather go with him."

For the first time since she'd met Myles, she saw some glimmer of emotion from the man. Although his tone of voice betrayed nothing, nothing could hide the stone cold anger flashing in his black eyes. "Fuck it all to bloody hell. This situation was bad enough without this bullshit. Just...crap," Myles finished, as if he had run out of expletives, or didn't want to swear anymore in front of Alyssa and Connor.

Myles snagged the telephone handset from its cradle. "I want an APB put out on Darcy Myers and Douglas Tiernan. Last known location was safe house four. Get Myers' personnel file and find out the make of his car. Get the request out to the city police and all RCMP detachments in the area *now*. Send Briggs and Johnston out to sweep the area. He couldn't have gone too far. I want this guy yesterday." Myles replaced the receiver with a soft click, the action in stark contrast to the grim fire burning in his eyes.

Alyssa riveted her gaze at Myles' face. Fear made her skin clammy as the ability to form full sentences deserted her. She lurched forward and slammed her hands on Myles' desk. The report reverberated throughout the office as Alyssa struggled for composure. Myles didn't even flinch. He simply waited for her to speak. Or scream, as the case might be.

Connor came up behind Alyssa and grasped her shoulders just as Alyssa pushed back from the desk. She would have staggered without Connor's hands on her shoulders, her eyes glued to Myles' face. It just didn't make sense. Why would someone like Darcy throw his whole career away in the blink of an eye? Darcy was the job. The job was Darcy. They were two sides of the same flawed coin.

Flawed…hmmm. The question was how much more flawed had Darcy become in the past two years since she'd last seen him. Most people in the field eventually burned out. They took desk jobs in an effort to restore the balance in their lives, both emotionally and physically. The job could suck out every last bit of humanity and leave a smoldering shell of a person in its wake, unable to distinguish the good guys from the bad guys.

A chill racked her body as the pieces of the puzzle slowly clicked together in her mind. She closed her eyes, concentrating on grasping those that hovered on the outer edges of her consciousness.

CSIS would normally have sent a low-level errand boy to pick them up at the airport, not someone like Darcy. CSIS had a full psychological profile on Alyssa. And they probably had a whole whack of information on Connor.

They would have known that Alyssa would be open to any reasonable entreaties they made. And even if she hadn't, knowing Connor's background, she most likely would have been persuaded to help. There would have been no need to send a full-fledged seasoned agent. No reason to send Darcy. Unless…

Unless Darcy had screwed up so badly that his last chance at redemption had been to facilitate Alyssa's re-acquisition by CSIS. Perhaps Darcy had been one of those agents who managed to skirt the regular psychological assessments demanded of all field agents. Darcy could slip into, and out of, personalities in a flash. The job demanded multiple personalities. The strain could have been enough for

Darcy to reach his breaking point, leaving him incapable of rational thought or action.

The only other possible reason for Darcy being sent to pick her up would be if he had crossed over into the shadowy world of playing both sides of the game. The draw, she knew, could be powerful for some agents. Lies, double-crosses, theft, murder and seduction—all legally sanctioned. Very appealing to some. He could have convinced the brass at CSIS that Alyssa would be difficult and, given their joint history, he would be the logical choice to pull her back into their orbit. All the while setting her up as a sitting duck in a two-bit sideshow.

Or it could be a combination of the two theories. At this point, she knew only one thing—she wanted Grand back.

"Who decided to send Darcy?" Alyssa breathed the question, her voice barely audible.

Myles, the master of the soft icy voice, responded in kind. "Darcy convinced CSIS that he was the only person who could bring you in. Why?"

Connor answered the question for her. "Because it's probably been a setup all along. Darcy's probably a double hitter, playing both sides against the middle, waiting to see who will be declared the winner before choosing a side. His hand has been forced a little earlier than he expected and he needed to make a hasty move. That would be Douglas. His target the entire time."

Alyssa jerked her eyes up to Connor's face and then her gaze hit Myles. The nightmare of the past few weeks bubbled up in her mind and she snarled at Myles, "CSIS couldn't discover a plot hatching in their own backyard if it there were blinking yellow arrows pointing directly it. *Jesus*." She spun around and stormed out of the office.

Yup, Alyssa would have made a crappy field agent, Connor thought somewhat bemusedly as he stared at the empty doorway. He heard the door of the ladies' washroom, a few doors down, open and close gently behind her. No doubt Alyssa would have slammed if it she could, but the door was one of those slow closing types that ensured it didn't hit you on the ass on the way in or out.

Connor turned back to Myles to see him cock his head to one side like a befuddled dog. Probably not too many people had the balls to cuss Myles out and then walk off in a huff.

Lord, when that girl crosses those bridges, she burns every single stick down to the cinders and then pulverizes the ashes. Connor shook his head, somewhat amused, somewhat bewildered. Alyssa evidently did not believe in graceful or strategic exits.

Connor watched as Myles lost the befuddled look, replaced by a somewhat amused look. Myles caught Connor's eye and smiled. "A real firecracker you have on your hands there."

"You already knew that," Connor stated.

"As a matter of fact, I did. I have her personnel record. Thought it might come in handy dealing with her."

Connor's eyebrows arched in inquiry at Myles, but Myles shook his head. "Can't divulge specific information, but I will say she's known for her technical expertise, creativity, short fuse and believing in what she does. No patience with bullshit, politics, incompetence or laziness, so unfortunately being a government employee was never a good fit for her. Too many shades of gray."

Connor nodded and started for the door, but Myles stopped him.

"It might be best to leave her alone for a couple of minutes to calm down. We should come up with an action plan."

"You're not pissed that Alyssa reamed you out?" Connor asked, eyebrows raised, arms akimbo on his chest.

Myles chuckled. "More surprised than anything else. Even I get tired of dealing with yes-men all the time. Every once in a while, it's refreshing to hear an uncensored opinion." The small smile on his face disappeared. "You tell anyone that and I'll have your balls for breakfast," he growled.

Connor and Myles batted around a few ideas before Connor left to knock on the women's bathroom door. Alyssa didn't respond.

"Alyssa, are you okay?" Connor called out, his head bent to place his ear nearer to the door, listening for any activity within. He heard only silence. He knocked again, louder this time. When still no response came, he shoved the door open. As he entered the bathroom, his gaze fell upon Alyssa leaning against a long row of sinks staring at the floor, her face ashen and her lips nearly colorless.

"Sweetheart? Are you okay?"

Alyssa dragged her focus away from contemplating the tiled mosaic floor to look blankly at Connor, her eyes haunted. Dark and shadowed, her eyes showed a purplish bruising beneath them. One hand held her cell phone, flipped open as if she'd just been speaking to someone.

"What's wrong?" Connor demanded as he closed the distance between them and picked up her free hand, which hung limply by her side. Her hand felt icy cold. He laid his other hand softly on the curve of her cheek. Cool. Too cool.

She was emotionally shut down. Alyssa's thoughts whirled like leaves in a vortex as she stared at Connor. Her stomach roiled sickeningly. If she had to face any more of these moments-of-truth, she swore she would seriously throw up. Decisions, decisions. Always these damn decisions. She wanted to retreat into a nice, safe cave and roll a big boulder over the entrance to hole up for the rest of her unnatural life.

With a determined effort, she tried to shake off the funk her mind had wandered into when she had received The Call.

The Call to Arms or Retreat. The Call to Vengeance or Defeat.

The question had become, which call would she answer? And would anyone ever really know what happened? The truth could die with Grand, die with her. And what purpose would have been served? Fear or Justice, Courage or Cowardice. She didn't know which course of action would be worse. She just wanted Grand back, she wanted Connor. Now she wanted so much.

And now she would never have any of it.

She became aware of Connor standing before her, saying something to her, caressing her cheek with his hand. She stared at him—his lips moved, but she couldn't hear his words. Her eyes filled with tears and she launched her body into his arms, making him stagger with the force. His arms surrounded her to steady both of them. She twined her arms about his neck and glued her body to his. Her body shuddering, she buried her face in his neck and breathed in his uniquely masculine scent.

Decision made.

Chapter Thirty

“I’m in the air now,” Alyssa droned into her cell phone, her voice icy and distant.

“I’m happy to hear it, darling,” Darcy responded with the velvet voice that she knew he knew pissed her off. “No doubt you got rid of Prince Charmless?”

“I’m sure you already know that.”

“As a matter of fact, I do. I know that you and he had a stupendous blowout at CSIS headquarters in Edmonton. He left you high and dry, darling. Brava! It must have been *quite* a performance. I would have loved to have seen it.”

“I’m sure it’s all been reported to you in gory detail.”

“Don’t ask, don’t tell, darling. By the way, how did you convince Connor’s pilot to bring you to Fort McMurray? Without Connor?”

“I’m sure you know that too.”

“A little birdie told me you went to the bank to withdraw a very large sum of money. The birdie said you bribed Connor’s pilot. You were always resourceful. I admire that in a woman.”

“Exactly how many people do you have on your payroll anyway, Darcy?”

“Curious little cat. You know what they say about cats, don’t you? Ah, but of course you do,” Darcy chuckled and the sound made the hairs on the back of Alyssa’s neck stand on end. “‘Twenty-questions’ is over. You’ll land in Fort McMurray in forty-five minutes. Someone will be there to escort you. Don’t put up a fight, darling, or your grandfather will pay the price for it. Am I being clear?”

"Crystal," Alyssa snapped.

The connection went dead. Alyssa stared at the phone. Maybe if she crushed it and then stomped on it, it would, by some freak of nature, kill Darcy. Somehow she doubted it. Technology wasn't that advanced yet.

Too bad.

Connor reached over and filched the phone from Alyssa and flipped it close. "I have to agree." Sitting on a comfortable leather couch in his jet, he popped the earphone out of his ear and snuggled her in closer to his side. "Excellent acting."

"You think he bought it?" Alyssa asked anxiously, turning her head to search his eyes.

"Hook, line and sinker. And speaking about lines, I just want to make sure that the wire and tracking device CSIS outfitted you with are functioning properly." Connor looked at her, his lips tightening into a flat, grim line. He had objected vociferously to using Alyssa as bait, but in the end, Alyssa had prevailed. She'd given him no choice.

Post-"launching-herself-into-Connor's-arms-like-a-rocket" in the CSIS ladies room, Alyssa had blurted out her conversation with Darcy. After leaving Connor and Myles for the bathroom, Alyssa had splashed a few handfuls of water onto her hot face. She'd stood there breathing heavily, her hands resting on the vanity as she leaned forward to stare at her reflection.

A chirping noise emanated from her purse, jolting her out of her reverie. It took a moment for her to realize that the noise was her phone. Not many people called on her cell. She nearly let it go, but on the fourth ring she picked it up.

"What?" she barked.

"Darling."

The one word sent shivers down her spine. Darcy. Bloody Darcy screwing with her bloody mind. She nearly threw the phone against the tiled wall. A number of seconds passed before she could even attempt to speak.

"Darcy, you goddamn son-of-a-*bitch*. Where the hell is my grandfather, you piece of shit?"

"You should be more polite to the person who has the power of life and death over your grandfather."

That made Alyssa pause. Every nightmare she'd ever had materialized in living color.

"What do you want?" she asked icily.

"Very little actually. I want you to get rid of CSIS, and Connor, and get to Fort McMurray within two hours or your grandfather is dead."

"Fort McMurray? Why Fort McMurray?" But Alyssa had already known the answer. She started trembling, barely able to hold the phone without dropping it.

"*You*. It was you. All along. You're the one who tried to run Connor and me off the road. You're the one who arranged for the attack on me. You torched Grand's industrial unit." Furious, she hurled the words at him through the phone—she regretted again that words couldn't kill. He would have been dead in a nanosecond. She settled for strangling the phone in a death grip. She heard a sharp crack as the plastic case of the phone complained against being mangled.

Darcy laughed and, with a note of pride in his voice, said, "Well, I arranged for it, darling, I didn't do it personally. Except for the last one. I very much relished setting fire to your grandfather's business. Too bad he got away. That complicated matters somewhat. In any case, you've got two hours to get to Fort McMurray."

"Two hours?? It takes at least four hours to drive there!"

"I would suggest that you charter a plane, darling. You can hire a plane at the Edmonton City Centre Airport to take you to Fort McMurray. "

"Filing a flight plan takes a minimum of thirty minutes. And that's if they're not busy."

"Details, details. Just be there. Tada, darling."

"Wait, wait! Where I am supposed to find you?"

"At the airport, of course. Make sure you're alone, or your grandfather dies. If you try to pull any fast ones, your grandfather dies. If you do anything I don't like, your grandfather dies. Are you picking up a pattern here?"

"Yeah, Darcy, I've got it," Alyssa responded coldly.

"Good. Later, babe."

And then Darcy was gone, leaving Alyssa staring at the phone in her hand. A wave a sheer panic scattered her wits, blood rushed insanely through her head. As she slowly became aware of her surroundings again, she realized Connor stood in front of her, holding her hand and stroking her cheek. And she launched herself at him. Clung to him, literally glued herself to another human being for the first time in her life.

Connor wrapped his arms around her shaking form. When her trembling subsided to a minor quaking, Alyssa tipped her head back and gazed up him, her eyes filmed with tears. She spilled the entire story in a rush of words. Unable to pause—afraid to stop—afraid that she couldn't go on if she did. As the torrent continued, the floodgates in her mind broke irrevocably. There was no going back, not now, not for either of them.

"I have to go, Connor," Alyssa said, her voice shaky, as she swiped at her eyes with the back of her hand. "Grand…Grand needs me… I… I…" Alyssa patted her hands frantically against Connor's chest, as if trying to get his attention or to infuse him with the sense of urgency she felt.

"What do you mean?" he asked, his voice neutral, his eyes watchful.

Connor captured her hands in his, holding them to his chest. "He'll kill you. He'll kill Grand. We'll have to figure something else out." He enunciated each word.

"Then we have to figure something out *now*. Because I have to go, Connor, I have to go *now*. I have to do something. Now, Connor, *now*." She pushed her captive hands against his chest to underscore the desperation of the situation.

"And we will. I promise," Connor vowed, as he pulled her once again into a crushing embrace.

After a very private meeting with Myles and a carefully orchestrated, very public, knock-down-drag-out fight with Connor, Connor came through for her. They rode in a jet that now winged its way toward Fort McMurray.

"I need to check your wire again," Connor said in a low voice that sounded very close to a growl.

"Again? Myles checked the wire twice before we left and you've already checked it once during the flight."

Connor grasped the bottom of her tee shirt with determination and hauled it upward until he saw her underwire bra. "Again. No chances taken—not with you—not for a second. It's bad enough that you've already been in the line of fire. It's worse knowing that I won't be with you. I'll hear everything that's said, I'll know where you are, but I won't be in visual contact with you all the time."

Back at CSIS, they'd managed to thread the wire of the surveillance device through the same opening where the actual underwire for her bra was located. It would be very difficult for Darcy to detect on a casual search of Alyssa's body. The thought of Darcy touching Alyssa while conducting a full body search was enough to make Connor's blood boil. Unfortunately, boiling blood wouldn't extract Alyssa from the very dangerous situation at hand. Cool, calm reason would hopefully do that. That, and a lot of luck.

Connor had a momentary mental flash of ordering his pilot to turn around and take them both back to Colorado. He could keep her safe there, but he also knew that Alyssa would never forgive him.

Even frightened to death, she would do what she thought she needed to do. She knew she could die. Life could be so fleeting. None of the emotions bubbling beneath his surface were detectable in either the motion of his hands as he checked the wire or in the set of his face as his eyes searched for any telltale bumps in the bra.

As she watched him work on the bra, watched him carefully touch the smooth skin of her breasts and chest, she shivered as his dexterous fingers inadvertently, or maybe not so inadvertently, brushed against her heated skin.

This is ridiculous, she thought wildly. *I am about to take the biggest risk of my life, I might die, Grand might die, Connor might die, and the only thing I can think of is making love to Connor, right here, right now.*

Connor sat in front of her, apparently not thinking anything of the sort, so concentrated was he on the wire. For heaven's sake, here she was sitting in front of him half-naked and he may as well have been inspecting a turnip.

And then he looked up with those amazing blue-gray eyes and she knew she was wrong.

His eyes, the color of a midnight storm, were savage and primal. Fear. She saw fear and blind need warring in his eyes in matched portions. The need to have her and have her need him. She reached for him as he seized her in his arms.

He pushed her down on the couch as he swept the tee shirt over her head and went to work on the fly of her jeans. She raised her hips so that he could drag the denim and the silk of her panties down her legs. The jeans and panties prevented their complete removal, so he yanked off her sneakers first and followed with her panties and jeans.

He ran his hands up her legs, between her thighs, opening her. A stab of pleasure centered in her womb and radiated outward and she trembled. Mindless, she whimpered as he slid a finger into her soft, heated sheath, stroking her already slick flesh. Her hips jerked and kept on jerking as he found an amazingly sensitive spot and massaged it. He was the rock thrown into her pond, the exquisite sensations rippling outward, tightening her around his cleverly inquisitive fingers.

"Oh God, oh Connor, please..." she moaned and shuddered, her finely drawn, taut body on the rack of pleasure. "Now. *Now.*"

Connor fumbled with the fly on his jeans with one hand, his fingers shaking so much they kept slipping off the metal tab, while keeping the fingers of his other hand in intimate contact with Alyssa's body. He wanted every second he could possibly steal from the coming hours, spend himself in her living fire and have or be something to remember if anything went horribly wrong.

He couldn't believe he'd finally found Ms. Right—*damn, even my mother would like her*—and now fate insisted on conspiring against him to rip her away. The injustice of it strangled the breath in his throat. His eyes glazed over with tears he refused to shed. She would not die. She would NOT die. Not if he had breath left to take, strength to spend, love to give.

Finally freeing himself from his jeans, if only having shoved them down around his knees, he lowered himself between her trembling thighs and slowly thrust into her welcoming heat.

As he thrust all the way in and fully seated himself, she relaxed with a tremor, as if reassured by his fullness within her, and she closed her eyes. His hands snaked down to her hips and tucked her pelvis in toward him, enabling him to deepen his thrusts. He buried his head in her neck, absorbing the sweet scent that was Alyssa, and groaned.

Alyssa wrapped her legs around his hips and her arms around his body as he strained to join their bodies, fierce in his possession of her. The sound of flesh wetly meeting flesh filled the cabin. She jolted against him with each thrust he made, met him and urged him on.

She gasped, unable to catch her breath, aware of the precursors of release building exponentially, unstoppably within her body. She fought to get closer to him, twisting fiercely under his unrelenting subjugation of her body, heightening the sensations for them both.

Her world tilted on its axis and she cried out, a prelude to the coming climax. Without warning, he pulled back an inch from her, looking down on her as his thrusts stilled.

Alyssa's eyes opened in surprise and she made a questioning sound in the back of her throat, her body pulsing on the razor's edge. His face drawn, graven, as his eyes searched hers.

Connor spoke, his voice low and shaking. "I love you, Alyssa. I love you so damn much it hurts. I wanted you before I even knew you. He can't have you because you're *mine*. And I'm yours. Always. I want you to say the words. Even if you don't mean them. I need to hear them."

Alyssa's chest constricted as she stared up at him. This hard, proud, *gentle* man loved *her*. And with a shock, she knew she had fallen completely in love with him. When, she didn't know, couldn't care. Blinking back the tears of emotion that blurred her vision, she gave him a shaky smile and gasped. "I love you too. I want to be with you. Now. Tomorrow. Forever." She brushed her lips against his, once for each of her last three words.

Connor groaned and fastened his mouth over hers, using his tongue to parry and thrust with hers, an aggressive game of advance and retreat, both his tongue and his erection penetrating her body. Irrevocably possessing her in every way a man could possess a woman. His hands roamed over her body, as if wanting to know every last inch of skin before it was time for her to face Darcy. Alone.

She cried out as he brought her to a fast and stunning climax and then tipped over the edge to follow her down. Gasping for breath, he collapsed on top of her for a moment before trying to shift his weight off her, but she wrapped her arms and legs around him and refused to let him go.

"I'm crushing you, sweetheart."

"You feel wonderful," she sighed, clinging to him.

The intercom from the flight cabin pinged on, startling both of them, returning them to reality. "We're fifteen minutes from landing, Mr. Donnelly. We're starting our descent."

Truer words could not have been spoken.

To hell they descended.

Chapter Thirty-One

As the Gulfstream jet landed on the single runway at the Fort McMurray airport, a minivan waited at the far end of the landing strip near the terminal building. The jet roared past the van and disappeared around the corner of the terminal. The driver of the van shifted the vehicle into gear and chased after them.

The occupants of the van arrived in the hangar in time to see Alyssa exiting the craft.

Alyssa alighted from the aircraft in time to see Darcy leap out of the rear passenger door of the van before it halted beside the airplane. A menacing giant of a man exited the front passenger door of the van to stand by Darcy. The man was quite possibly the largest, nastiest looking man Alyssa had ever seen.

He must have been at least six-seven or six-eight, carrying a minimum of two-hundred-eighty pounds on his mountainous frame. Black spiky hair erupted from the top of the man's head, an evil Bert-brow slashed across his forehead above beady black eyes that looked downright psychotic. Dark, swarthy skin completed the package. Hell, his *hands* were a good six times as large as Alyssa's hands.

She gawped at the man in semi-horror. What mad scientist had screwed up the medical experiment that brought this monster into being?

"Search it," Darcy barked to Monster-man.

Monster-man was amazingly fast on his feet, faster than Alyssa would have thought possible. She held her breath as he brushed by her and he stooped to get into the jet.

"I told you no funny stuff, Alyssa." Darcy's eyes drilled into hers, malevolence dripped from his voice, as he wrapped his hand tightly around her forearm.

"What?" Alyssa fought to keep her facial features as bland as possible. Acting wasn't her strong suit, but desperation could work miracles. Right? "I haven't pulled any *funny stuff*."

Darcy narrowed his eyes at her, but said nothing. Instead he waited for Monster-man to come out of the jet dragging the pilot behind him. Monster-man shook his head at Darcy.

"You're sure no one else is in there?" Darcy asked.

The man answered in a deeply accented, baritone voice. "Yes. Only pilot." He shook the pilot by the collar for effect. The pilot looked suitably terrified and the poor man half stumbled as he was yanked from the craft. Monster-man's face split into a grin, enjoying the pilot's fear. Or at least Alyssa thought it was a grin. He could have been preparing to eat the pilot for all she knew.

"Excellent," Darcy purred with a smile and turned back toward Alyssa. "Very good, my dear. For a moment I thought you were playing games with me."

Alyssa allowed her eyes to glaze over at his comment. Darcy wrenched her toward him, his fingers digging razor-sharp into her flesh. "Respect, Alyssa, *respect*."

"You're hurting me, Darcy," Alyssa hissed through her clenched teeth.

"Not like you hurt me. And believe me, you'll be in a whole world of hurt soon enough."

Alyssa couldn't prevent a shiver of dread working its way up her spine. Sucking in her breath, she asked, "Where's my grandfather?"

"He's safe and secure. He's very anxious to see you," Darcy responded in an extremely reasonable tone of voice. It dropped suggestively for his next words. "But first, we need to dispense with the formalities."

"Formalities?" Even to Alyssa, her voice sounded apprehensive.

"A search. Of your person. Well, your body, to be exact." Darcy's eyes glinted dangerously. "Hands on the van, Alyssa. Spread your legs." He shoved her toward the van hard enough that she whacked into the side of it with her shoulder.

Oh *shit*.

Connor had warned her that she'd be subjected to a search and she'd tried to steel herself against the thought of it before emerging from the jet. But preparing for it and actually having it done were two very different things.

As she assumed the search position against the van, she tried in vain to stop her trembling. She felt Darcy breeze up behind her. She let out a strangled stream of air through pursed lips. For long moments, as she stood against the van, she waited anxiously for Darcy to begin his search.

Every second he delayed made each passing moment an abomination—and the bastard knew it. She tried to focus her mind on Connor, on her love for him. On his love for her. She had to make it through this, she had to. For herself and for Connor.

She knew that Connor was nearby. He'd jumped from the jet as it had slowly taxied to a stop and now he hid somewhere in the hangar. She tried to concentrate on that, knowing that he would protect her, die for her, if need be.

But he couldn't protect her from Darcy's search. And she didn't want Connor to die for her. Desperately, she wished that they'd spoken more extensively about her and Grand's almost certain death sentences. She hadn't told Connor that if it came to a choice between her life and his, he shouldn't sacrifice himself, that the thought of him dead would be more than she could bear. She fought back the tears that threatened to spill and tried to focus on the frightening realities she now faced.

A search won't kill me. Think of Connor. Think of Grand. A litany of phrases ran through her agitated mind as it fumbled for reasons why she'd survive this. She closed her eyes to block out as much distraction as possible.

"Wider, darling. Spread your legs wider," Darcy whispered into her ear.

She felt his hand caress her buttocks through her jeans. Her body condensed into ice, stiff and rigid. Her breath came out in short, compressed spurts. Fighting down panic, she complied by shuffling her feet a bit wider. Her whole stomach felt like it was going to fall out of her abdomen to lie quivering on the concrete.

"That's better. You used to like it when I touched you, Alyssa. You remember?"

"No," she hissed through clenched teeth.

"Ah, now you've hurt my feelings," he simpered and bit her neck hard. The unexpected pain zinged through her and she flinched. *Damn, any reaction is a bad reaction, even if it did hurt.*

"Myers," Monster-man growled. "Not have time for this. Have whore later."

Alyssa nearly looked at Monster-man in surprise. It hadn't occurred to her that Darcy wasn't running the show, but evidently he wasn't. It would have been much easier to unravel the threads of this intrigue if Darcy had been the main culprit. *How much bigger did this conspiracy go?*

Darcy sighed and murmured into her ear. "Unfortunately, he's right. Fun and games will have to wait." Darcy moved his hands over her body. Not just a simple pat down, but touching her body inch by inch. When he reached her bra, she made a Herculean effort to not change the tension in her body. His fingers stroked up the underwire of her bra and stilled.

Oh *hell.*

"What's this?" Darcy murmured to her.

"It's the underwire in my bra," Alyssa managed to say in an almost normal sounding voice.

"Are you sure?"

She swung her head to the side so that she could glare at him out of the corner of her eye. "You want my bra, you pervert? You can have the fucking thing. You know, I didn't think you were such a *freak,* but I guess I was wrong."

If he called her bluff and actually took her up on the offer, she was so screwed. If he found the wire… If he removed the bra and threw it away, Connor would have no means to track her. No way of knowing if she were in imminent danger. She held her breath, counting the heavy beats of her heart. It was a horrible gamble and the words couldn't be unsaid.

He stood so close that Alyssa felt, more than heard, the chuckle deep in his chest. A few but long seconds later, his fingers moved on and soon concluded the search.

"I do believe that you've complied with my conditions." Darcy grabbed her about the waist and shifted her around so she faced him. Thighs to hips, chest to breasts. Waaay too close for comfort. She hoped her face held up to scrutiny. Her best bet was to look absolutely disgusted and, given the fact that she was, she thought she succeeded admirably.

She kept the look of absolute revulsion on her face—the slight sneer that pulled the left side of her mouth upward, her narrow eyes blazed with unmitigated hatred.

If only looks could kill… Actually, now that she thought of it, she wished that a lot of things, including Darcy, could be killed with a word, a look, a thought. Anything other than having to deal with Darcy now.

Darcy grabbed her left upper arm in a vise grip and swung her around to shove her into the rear passenger sliding door. She narrowly missed hitting her head on the roof of the van as Darcy propelled her into the vehicle. The van didn't have two sliding passenger doors. Her stomach sank. She was trapped. Literally.

Monster-man grabbed a long length of rope from the front passenger side wheel well, swiftly hogtied the pilot and slung him over his shoulder as he climbed into the jet, whacking the pilot's head against the hatch frame in the process. A minute later, Monster-man emerged, looking very amused. The van dipped to one side as he climbed into the front passenger seat.

A swarthy dark-haired man, about half the size of Monster-man, drove the van. He spoke not a word, wheeling the van around in the hangar, picking up speed as they exited the hangar doors and disappeared into the long, low light of the coming Alberta night.

As Alyssa cast her eyes longingly out the window, she felt a sharp prick in her wrist just above where Darcy held her hand in a death grip. Panicked, her head whipped around to look wide-eyed at Darcy. He had a coldly amused look on his face. Actually, there are two of him now, Alyssa mused groggily. Great. Double the pleasure, double the fun. *Too bad he isn't gum that I can chew up and spit out into the garbage.* She wanted to giggle and her chest quaked as she suppressed the urge.

"Why?" she managed to grind out. A cascade of colors flitted in and out of her field of vision and she felt a frost creeping up from her throat into her mouth.

"It's a surprise, darling," Darcy responded with a grin. "Night-ee-niiiight," he singsonged.

She heard him as if from a long distance, felt him pull her near and put his arm around her like an old friend or lover. She didn't have the strength to fight him and her mind spun away from consciousness, away from reality. She tried to hold on to the feeling of panic, but it slipped away from her, replaced by a feeling of contentment. Her last coherent thought was of Connor. Of the time she'd squandered.

And her world went black.

Chapter Thirty-Two

As soon as the van disappeared, Connor rocketed out from behind the boxes where he had watched the unfolding events. He bounded into the jet to find his pilot tied up and fastened to one of the reclining chairs in the cabin.

Connor flipped out a switchblade and swiftly cut the man's bonds.

"Are you okay, Chris?" Connor demanded.

"Yeah," Chris answered, sounding disgruntled. "What now?"

"Stay here and wait. Keep your cell phone on. We may need to leave quickly."

"Will do," Chris responded. "Good luck."

"Thanks."

Connor grabbed his laptop computer and bolted out of the jet. He hurtled toward the back of the hangar where he had arranged for a Ford Taurus SHO sedan to be stashed. Totally nondescript in appearance, the hood hid a supercharged engine—four-hundred-and-fifty horses under the hood—helpful, given the circumstances. The doors were open and the keys were in the ignition, as requested. CSIS could apparently be very resourceful.

He jumped into the driver's seat, turned the key in the ignition and the car growled to life. He flipped the lid on the laptop, hit a few keys and the tracker program pinpointing Alyssa zapped on. The program showed Alyssa, or her bra, moving along a superimposed map of the area. As long as the satellite didn't go haywire, he would have a link, albeit a tenuous one, to Alyssa.

There she was, blipping her way up Airport Road, turning north on Highway Sixty-Nine toward Fort McMurray. Connor jammed the five-speed manual shift into gear and wheeled out of the hangar, determined keep up with the van. Ideally, he'd be able to stay just out of visual range of the van until they arrived at their destination.

The surveillance device in Alyssa's bra was part GPS—Global Positioning Satellite—technology and part audio transmitter. The GPS pinpointed Alyssa's location to within one meter, something for which he would be eternally grateful. Even if he couldn't see her, at least he'd know her location. He shoved an earphone jack into the laptop and lodged the earpiece in one ear.

He faintly heard Arabic being spoken by at least two of the vehicles occupants. He had suspected, they had all suspected, a Middle Eastern connection of some sort and the surveillance device just confirmed it. He dialed up the volume on the bug to see if he could catch what they were saying.

"Old man! Why do we need him, anyway? We should just kill him. Now. And the whore," one man spoke angrily in Arabic.

Another man answered in the same language. "We need information before they die. And Myers wants some time alone with the whore."

"Ach! We have only two hours. We do not have time to waste. *Insh'Allah,* this will go as planned."

"It will. Be patient," Darcy answered in Arabic.

Connor's fingers clenched the steering wheel as his growing frustration with the whole hellish situation caught up to him where it counted—in the heart. That son-of-a-bitch would die if he hurt Alyssa. If any of those bastards harmed her in any way, shape or form, he would have the last word. Fuck the legal crap—old-fashioned justice would be his form of retribution.

Connor berated himself for not nixing this plan when he'd had the chance. Or chances, as the case might be. He could have derailed the whole plan at CSIS. He could have turned the damn jet around before they landed. He could have...he should have...dammit, he could have done *something*.

He had done nothing.

Because Alyssa would never have spoken to him for the rest of her life, he castigated himself. He should have done it anyway, but fighting Alyssa on this one had been like battling a Sherman tank with a pitchfork. There was no give in that woman on the subject of Grand. She would gladly die to save Grand. No matter that Grand had lived a full life, while Alyssa had been waiting for, afraid of, her own life.

Christ, this could turn into a total cluster fuck without any effort at all. Damn if he did, damn if he didn't. Well, he was just going to have to "cowboy the fuck up" and deal with it. Whatever *it* was or turned out to be. And right now, that was keeping track of Alyssa.

Keeping her alive.

Connor flicked his eyes down to the display on the laptop on the seat beside him. The van turned north on Highway Sixty-Three to head toward Fort McMurray. Connor remembered that oil sands production surrounded a tiny hamlet by the name of Fort McKay located on the west bank of the Athabasca River, thirty-seven miles north of Fort McMurray. Minutes later, the van passed over the Ralph Steinhauer Bridge and rocketed northward away from the small city.

North to the oil fields.

Connor knew that Grand's claim lay just to the east of Fort McKay, in what was, for all intents and purposes, the deep bush of northern Alberta.

Connor flipped out his cell phone, pressed a speed dial button and held the phone to his ear.

Even before the first ring had ended, the receiving party had snatched the phone off its cradle. Myles. For a man who never appeared to hurry, he sure had grabbed the phone awfully fast.

"Collins," Myles barked.

"Donnelly," Connor responded. "They've got Alyssa. It looks like they're driving north on the Sixty-Three toward Fort McKay. Douglas' research facility is just east of the town. My guess is that's where they're headed. Do you have any people up here?"

"No. You're the nearest one, but not for long. We just came into some disturbing intel. It looks like Darcy is working with a man in the States who is connected with a radical Islamic fundamentalist in Saudi Arabia. The man's name is John Hughes. Do you recognize the name?"

"Hughes? No. Why?"

"Do you recognize the name Joseph Taylor?"

Icy fingers of premonition climbed up Connor's chest. "Yeah."

"He's been found dead at his home in Washington. John Hughes went AWOL as soon as the body was found."

Connor closed his eyes for a second and pushed aside the grief for a man he had called friend. Taking a deep breath, he quietly asked, "What's the connection with Hughes?"

"Hughes is an intermediate member of Taylor's staff. Not a field op. An analyst. I'm not privy to all the details as it's a CIA matter, not a CSIS matter. And the CIA wasn't particularly forthcoming with a lot of information." Myles paused. "This has gone straight to the highest echelons of both the Canadian and American governments."

"Why?"

"On Hughes' laptop computer, the CIA came across plans for detonating a nuclear device. And not a small one either. We're not talking about a dirty bomb. We're talking about a full-scale strategic nuclear warhead. A one-hundred kilo-tonne yield."

"Christ. How did they get a hold of something like that?"

"The former Soviet Union. The possibility has been there since the breakdown of the communist stranglehold in the early nineties. Everyone's worst nightmare has come true."

"Shit."

"Yeah—shit. The fallout from a weapon of this magnitude is enough to contaminate a large portion of Canada and America. The devastation would be horrific. It turns out that Hughes' laptop is the computer that's been sending encrypted messages to the World Islamic Jihad faction here in Canada.

"There was a whole whack of information on Douglas' activities in the oil sands. And anyone connected with him, mostly Alyssa and you. The logical conclusion is that WIJ is planning on detonating the warhead at Douglas' research facility. It would be perfect—right in the middle of oil sands country. Shut down Alberta oil production and then finish off the Saudi oil fields. Very little oil for anyone left over."

Connor's breath hissed in through clenched teeth. "Total anarchy. The world economy comes to a grinding halt. Just what any red-blooded terrorist would die for or kill for. The end of the current world order."

"You got it."

"Fuck," Connor said disgustedly. "What's the brass going to do?"

"They're scrambling all anti-terrorist units specializing in the disarmament of nuclear warheads, both American and Canadian. Fighter jets are heading to the Mildred Lake airstrip just south of Fort McKay and to Fort McMurray as we speak. The nearest Canadian Forces Base is Cold Lake, but there is no anti-terrorist unit stationed there. They're bringing in the Canadian Special Forces Joint Task Force Team Three from British Columbia, who have dealt with nuclear weapons.

"We can't risk bombing the target because that could set off the warhead. Unlikely, but it's still a possibility. We need to know the specific location of the weapon so that it can be disarmed. If the trigger for the weapon hasn't been activated for the launch sequence, then all that is needed is to remove the trigger. If the launch sequence has been activated, a specialist will be needed to disarm it.

"Your job is to find that damn weapon. Your government has requested your help since you know the situation and you were their operative. They have full confidence in you and so do I. If you can't find the nuke, the other teams will have to. All other considerations are secondary." Myles paused, and then added quietly, "Including Alyssa."

Connor's stomach rolled. He knew it had been coming, but to actually hear it spoken aloud laid waste to his soul. Alyssa could only be saved as an adjunct to finding and disarming the weapon.

Fuck. *Fuck.*

Connor's hands tightened on the steering wheel, eyes fixed on the road ahead of him, spruce trees on either side whipping by as he drove on autopilot. Old ways of dealing with situations flooded his mind, searching for a way out of the morass.

The plan had been to get a location on Alyssa and Grand and get them out of danger. Straightforward and simple. The plan had been turned inside out and backward. Everything had changed in the blink of an eye. They were no longer just dealing with Darcy or a few terrorists.

They were dealing with unspeakable horror of the blackest kind. Just like the oily pitch extracted from the sticky sands, dark was the evil in men's hearts.

Chapter Thirty-Three

Alyssa lay gripped in the throes of a drug-induced nightmare. Grand was dead. Connor was dead. She blundered through a strobe-lit corridor, the bursts of light making it impossible to get her bearings, searching for a way to escape from Darcy. The corridor turned on one side and then the other, coming closer and fading away at intervals. She could hear him laughing, chilling her soul, the sound echoing through the halls of her mind.

"Alllysssaaa." His voice spun out from all directions and chilling laughter followed, freezing her into immobility. Helpless. Alone. Her chest heaved as she vainly tried to force air into her non-functioning lungs.

"Alyssa." The voice seemed to be right next to her ear. She lurched away from the voice, clawed away from the hated sound.

Awake.

Her eyes flashed open to see Darcy's face hovering over hers. She lunged toward him only to realize that she had been tied hand and foot to a cot. The ropes bit into her wrists and ankles as she strained against them. She flopped back down on her back. A piece of her hair tumbled down into her eyes as she stopped fighting against her bonds, breathing heavily.

Darcy laughed. "Not this time, lover." With a finger, he brushed aside the offending lock of hair and sat beside her on the narrow cot. She glared at him as he stroked her hair.

"Where's Grand?" she spat.

He ignored the question. "We're going to get to know each other all over again, lover." He stroked a wandering finger down the side of her neck and lightly brushed the side of her breast. Her breath locked in her throat.

"I love your fear—turns me on," Darcy whispered, his eyes glinted as they swept over her body. In a normal tone of voice, he said, "Your grandfather is in the other room. I'll have him brought to you." Darcy lifted off the side of the cot and strolled away. He took a few steps before turning back.

Before Alyssa could respond, Darcy bent down and brought his lips down brutally over hers. She threw her head back and forth to dislodge him, but he just laughed, held her head down with both hands and forced her mouth open with his thumbs before shoving his tongue into her mouth.

Alyssa reacted without thought. She bit him. Hard. And refused to let go of his tongue even as he yelped in pain and tried to pull back. The faintly metallic taste of blood filled her mouth, making her gag. Enough so that Darcy could pull away from her. His hand whipped out and slapped her hard across the face, snapping her head to the right and bloodying her nose. Tears of pain and fear trickled down her abused face.

"Bitch!" Darcy breathed as he wiped the blood from his lips with the back of one hand. He gazed at the blood on his hand and then skewered Alyssa with a jaundiced eye. "Do anything like that again and I'll kill the old man. Slowly. Do you hear me, Alyssa? Very, very slowly. And you'll watch every second of it."

When Alyssa didn't turn her head to look at him, Darcy stalked from the room and slammed the door behind him. She let out a shaky breath and tried to ignore the throbbing in her left cheek and nose. Biting him hadn't been the most brilliant thing she'd ever done, but it had all happened so fast. She had to start thinking instead of only reacting. Reacting without thought was going to get her and Grand killed before Connor could find them.

She swept her gaze around the semi-dark room where she lay. It sort of looked like one of the storage areas in Grand's research facility, lit only by a tiny window in the upper corner of one wall. It *was* the research facility, she was sure of it! She tried to remember the layout of the building, the mental exercise taking her mind off her pain.

The main entrance to the small two-storied building faced west. A bubble-like tent, about one hundred yards wide by 300 yards long, protruded from the back of the building. The tent contained Grand's research area. Huge warehouse lights attached to the top and sides of the structure and flooded the tent with brightness.

The room she was in was on the second floor of the building. If she'd been able to get to the window, she'd have seen the white bubble tent billowing out the back of the building like a huge marshmallow.

Alyssa remembered in a flash that Connor could hear her. God. She could tell him where she was. She started speaking, her voice low, but clear.

"Connor, I'm at Grand's research facility twenty kilometers west of Fort McKay. I'm in the second floor storage room on the northeast corner of the building—not in the tent, but in the building itself. Darcy said that Grand is here. I don't know—"

Alyssa's jaw snapped shut as the door hit the wall beside it with a resounding bang. Monster-man pushed Grand into the room. The old man stumbled and almost fell as the door slammed shut behind him. As he righted himself, he took one look at Alyssa and tears filled his old eyes.

Grand limped over to her and placed a featherlight hand upon her now-throbbing hot cheek as tears streamed down his leathery face. "Oh God, Lyssa, my dear. I'm so sorry. So very, very sorry," he whispered. He looked at her bonds and reached to untie the ropes at her wrists. His hands shook so that he had a little difficulty with the tightly tied rope.

Grand's tears were Alyssa's undoing. In all the years she'd known him, he'd never cried, never even come close to crying. Not even at his son's—her father's—funeral. He was the rock—she was the one always going to pieces.

The few tears she had shed now intensified. The tears filled her eyes and spilled down her face. "It's going to be okay, Grand. You'll see. It's going to be okay."

When he had untied both hands, she sat up and threw her arms around his shaking shoulders. His arms came around her and held her with a strength that surprised her. She had never thought of Grand as a physically powerful man, but now he nearly squeezed the breath from her lungs. He stroked the back of her hair and he wept with abandon.

Alyssa pulled back from him and gave him a watery smile, gripped both of his hands and spoke softly, urgently. "Grand, it's going to be okay—I've got a surveillance device hidden in my bra. Connor knows exactly where we are, he can hear us too. I've already told him where we are. We..."

Grand patted her thigh, his watering blue eyes sad beyond measure. "Alyssa, you don't understand. They've got a nuclear weapon here. They're going to detonate it and end any oil sands research for a very, very long time. I overheard Myers talking. It's not just about you and me anymore."

Alyssa gaped at Grand as she tried to absorb the impact of the bombshell he'd dropped on her. "A nuclear bomb?"

"This is bigger than just us. Although I've yet to figure out where we come into the picture. I mean, they could just set off the bomb without us. Why have us around at all?"

Grand had a point. There was no point having her and Grand die—unless Darcy was royally pissed off at her and just wanted to kill her. But still, Darcy wasn't given to fits of pique. Darcy's style was more like a scalpel—in fact, he prided himself on getting his jobs done cleanly and with a minimum of fuss. His actions had always been well thought out and planned down to the nth degree. There must be some reason that she and Grand had been brought here.

"I don't know, Grand. I just don't know. Nothing is making sense right now." Alyssa leaned down to untie one of her ankles. Grand took the hint and untied her other ankle. "And while we're at it, why would Darcy tie me down just to bring you to me? He must know that you would untie me."

"Myers told me about your little run-in with him. Maybe he was trying to prevent a repeat."

"I guess, but—"

The door to the room swung open again. Outlined by the massive frame of Monster-man, Darcy leaned against the doorframe, arms akimbo over his chest.

"I see you're getting reacquainted. It's very touching—grandfather and granddaughter. What a picture you make." Darcy smiled coldly at them and spoke over his shoulder, not taking his eyes from his two captives, "Get them and bring them to the tent for our surprise." Darcy turned away from the door and strode off.

Monster-man, with a short stocky man following behind him whom she automatically dubbed Mini-Monster, wedged through the door. Mini-Monster looked like a miniature version of Monster-man. Monster-man grabbed Alyssa to haul her out of the cot while Mini took Grand and shoved him on ahead. The old man stumbled and fell to the floor. Grand cried out in pain, grabbing his right hip with one hand.

"No!" Alyssa shouted at Mini-Monster, grappling with her captor, her hands flailing. "He's an old man—he can't take that kind of abuse!" Monster-man quelled her struggles with ease, dragging her up the front of his body and wrapped his long arms around her and squeezed the breath out of her.

White flashes and yellow spots streaked through her field of vision as lack of oxygen affected her brain. She stopped fighting. Her vision cleared when Monster-man stopped his boa constrictor act. She gasped to fill her lungs with oxygen.

Mini-monster yanked Grand up by his elbow and pushed him toward the door. Grand limped badly, his breathing strained. He shook his head at Alyssa, a warning in his eyes.

Her captor flung her over one shoulder like a roll of carpet and left the room. Grand and Mini-Monster followed. Alyssa braced her hands against Monster-man's enormous back, pushed up and craned her neck to get a look at Grand. He still limped, but he gave her a strained smile of reassurance.

It had been a while since Alyssa had visited the facility. Large sliding doors that allowed machines to enter and exit the area sat at the east end of the tent. Alyssa saw what looked to be a military type truck, parked to the far right of the huge enclosed area, with a canvas top over the back and sides of the truck bed. In the center of the tent lay a very large wooden box surrounded by at least ten shouting men. The men swarmed around the crate, wielding crowbars to rip the box open.

Monster and Mini deposited Alyssa and Grand next to where Darcy stood ten yards from the box watching the melee, an Uzi machine gun dangling negligently from one hand. Darcy glanced over at his unwilling guests and smiled.

"I just wanted you to see this before..." He didn't finish the sentence, as he spied something that was evidently not to his liking. He strode off in the direction of the teaming men, shouting in Arabic and waving his hands. The men looked scornfully at him, or at least that's how it seemed to Alyssa, but they stopped what they were doing.

Darcy leaned his machine gun against the box, the butt of the weapon resting in the earth, and grabbed a crowbar from one of the men. He worked with care on loosening the lid. After few minutes, he succeeded in releasing the top from the rest of the box. Six men lifted it and dumped it on the dirt floor.

A sandy-haired man Alyssa hadn't seen before sidled up beside her. "You should feel honored that you'll be a part of history, Alyssa," he said in a calm voice.

Alyssa looked at him in surprise. He was of medium height, with thinning sandy-blond hair and blues eyes so light they were transparent. His eyes shone with a zealot's maniacal glow.

"Who are you?" Alyssa asked bluntly, not bothering to soften her tone.

The man gave her a sidelong glance. "John Hughes."

"You sound American."

"I am. To my everlasting shame."

"Shame?" Alyssa echoed.

"Shame to be a member of the nation that has brutally suppressed Allah's truth and will and defiled the holy land of Arabia. But Allah is great and he has seen fit to charge me with the task at hand."

"Task?" Alyssa echoed him again.

"The end of the dominance of America and the West over Islam. It will be a whole new world. Islam will reign supreme. His will shall be done, His words shouted from every corner of the world. *Insh'Allah*."

Alyssa went cold—she'd never met an actual terrorist before. An ideological convert to terrorism in the name of Allah. He's mad, Alyssa thought, as she stared at him in ill-veiled horror. The man caught the look in her eye and chuckled.

"Come. Let us see what Allah has given us," Hughes commanded.

Two of the men dragged Grand and Alyssa over to the container for a look-see. Alyssa's eyes dropped to look in the box and she choked, coughed in shock. The theoretical, now real, bomb looked like a very fat rocket with a snub nose.

As she watched, Darcy pried open a hatch on the rocket, revealing a control panel of switches and lights. He flipped a switch and the control panel lit up. Hughes pointed proudly to a yellow plastic knob attached to the control panel by a thin ball chain. "This trigger shall restore Islam to its former glory." He repeated himself in another language for the other men.

The men cheered, raising their hands in the air in jubilation.

Darcy gazed at the weapon for a moment before he lifted his eyes to a horrified Alyssa and spoke softly. "This will be the end of the world as we all know it. Something far superior will take its place."

Alyssa stared at him in disbelief. His eyes did not appear to be crazed like those of John Hughes. As far as Alyssa knew, Darcy wasn't the sort of person to turn into a crazed terrorist, but evidently she was wrong. He must have converted at some point. He must know that this device would kill everyone here as well as himself.

"Looking for your just rewards in paradise, Darcy? Seventy-two virgins to accede to your every whim?" Alyssa sneered. "You know, the Koran was mistranslated from its native Aramaic into Arabic. You don't actually get seventy-two virgins when you murder and die in the name of Allah—you get seventy-two *raisins*, you moron. A German professor, Luxenberg, retranslated the text."

Darcy laughed. "Do you actually think anyone here believes that? It doesn't matter what you believe, it's what they believe that matters."

"But it's what you believe, isn't it?" Alyssa spat out.

Darcy regarded her for a moment before smiling. "Of course."

Aside from the fact that I'm standing in front of a frickin' nuclear bomb, something's wrong. She just couldn't put her finger on it. Darcy wasn't a joiner. He never had been. At least not the Darcy that Alyssa knew and despised. What angle was he playing? He was probably the least suicidal man she'd ever known.

Darcy motioned to one of the surrounding men and spoke to him rapidly in Arabic. The man had a small digital camcorder and motioned for everyone to stand in front of and beside the weapon for picture time. Two of the men forced Alyssa and Grand to their knees in front of the container and bound their captives' hands with thick rope, while another man took video footage of the spectacle

Darcy laughed and motioned for the cameraman to give him the camera, apparently so that he could get all the soon-to-be-dead-martyrs in the shot. Darcy moved from beside the container, slung the machine gun over his shoulder and grabbed the camcorder with one hand.

Darcy plucked Alyssa from her position on her knees to drag her with him until he stood a number of yards away from the crowd. He motioned to the rest of the men to sit in front of the container. They crowded around Grand and smiled as if Darcy was taking pictures at the company picnic.

Darcy spoke to Alyssa. "We can't have a woman in the final shot. We're sending off the film to Al-Jazeera television in Qatar before the weapon is detonated." He forced her to her knees again a short distance from where he would take the final shot.

Darcy rested his machine gun against one leg and fiddled with the camcorder for a moment. Instead of taking a video clip, though, Darcy dumped the camcorder to the dirt, snatched up the weapon and opened fire on the group of men in front of him.

Alyssa screamed as she saw Grand collapse to the ground. The bodies of other men piled on top of him. It was all over in a matter of seconds. No one had a chance to escape the screaming rounds pouring out of the Uzi.

"Oh God oh God oh God oh God," Alyssa moaned over and over again as she wobbled on knees that had turned to jelly beneath her body. She couldn't even see Grand anymore, buried beneath all that dead and dying humanity.

Alyssa finally managed to tear her eyes away from the carnage in front of her and shrieked at Darcy. "Why? God*damn* you, why?"

Darcy looked over at her and smiled. "You didn't really think I'd join that ragtag bunch of idiots, did you? My poor Alyssa, still in the dark. Let me enlighten you.

"I'm still going to detonate the weapon. You and I, however, will not be here to see it. The Alberta oil sands will be inaccessible for a very long, long time. My associates in the Middle East will kill all oil production in Saudi. Your late grandfather's extraction process will be mine and you're going to give it to me.

"There are oil sands in Venezuela—I'll live like a king, Alyssa. A king. The king of oil. Did you think I didn't remember that computer-like mind of yours? You have the process. I know you do because you told someone else about the process. Do you remember who?" he asked, his voice silken with menace.

Realization dawned on her. Roy. The sheriff in Colorado. She'd told him and Connor about the process she'd memorized. "Roy," she whispered.

"That's right—Roy," Darcy confirmed with a smirk.

"I won't give you the process. You'll have to kill me."

"My dear, you know as well as I that there are 'veys' to make you talk," Darcy said the last words with a German inflection. "You won't last long. Not against the drugs you'll be pumped with." He flicked his eyes over to the pile of dead. "Say your goodbyes." Darcy sauntered toward the truck on the right, Uzi in hand.

Alyssa's mind whirled like a dervish in all directions. Grand was dead. A nuclear weapon lay in front of her. As the thoughts in her mind wheeled around, they slowly coalesced into a single purpose.

The trigger.

From what little she could remember of the CSIS seminar on the construction of nuclear weapons, they couldn't function without something to trigger the explosion. This had to be a thermonuclear fusion device. A fission explosion would trigger within the bomb and heat the interior of the weapon, causing the tamper to burn away. The resulting explosion would exert an inward pressure on the volatile cocktail contained inside to set off the fusion explosion.

She watched as Darcy approached the truck and climbed into the canopied truck bed. She staggered to her feet, her bound hands pulling her off balance, and tripped toward the pile of dead men and the container. She rested her tied hands against crate, leaning over to peer inside the trunk.

She peeked over to look at the truck where Darcy disappeared. He was still inside. She propped her body against the crate and reached in awkwardly with both hands to yank on the chain that connected the trigger to the bomb, her hands slick with sweat. Her fingers slipped off the chain and the chain held fast.

She grabbed the chain again, gave it a harder yank and it snapped free. She stumbled against the container, knees collapsing against the hard wood and stared in shock at the thing in her hands for a few seconds.

Reality kicked in. She had the trigger. She pushed back from the container with her knees shaking.

She stumbled toward the east exit as fast as she could.

Chapter Thirty-Four

Connor was going out of his mind.

Literally.

He had heard everything that Alyssa had been through since leaving the relative safety of his jet. With the exception of the last five minutes. His vehicle had been rumbling over the dirt road that led to Grand's facility when the audio died. The surveillance device's acoustics shorted out to the sounds of Alyssa's screams fracturing his psyche. Frantic, he rifled through every frequency he could think of. And no matter what he tried, he couldn't bring it back online again. The GPS part of the device still functioned, even though the blip on the laptop hadn't moved, but the no sound thing drove him nuts.

The car hurtled over the ragged dirt road until he came to within two kilometers of the facility. He made an abrupt right turn and shoved the car off-road, mowing down whippy young trees as he bulldozed through, jarring every bone in his body and every cell in his brain. He killed the engine twenty yards from the road.

He got out of the car and stuffed the laptop into a backpack. He adjusted the straps as he silently tramped through the swampy muskeg. His feet sank into the damp, decaying matter of the forest floor, making movement slow and difficult. Mosquitoes the size of bats feasted on his unprotected flesh. The branches of dead trees slapped his face as he advanced toward the facility.

Snap.

Connor hunkered down in the inadequate cover of the surrounding bush and froze. *Shit.* Someone else was out here.

He noiselessly extracted his .357 Magnum from the back waistband of his belt and his eyes drifted unfocused over the thick landscape, looking for anything out of the norm in a forest. An out of place color, a shape, a movement.

"Don't move." A quiet voice drifted down to Connor as something hard butted up against the back of his head just enough to get his attention, but not enough to harm.

Crap.

"Drop the weapon," the voice commanded. "Slowly. No sudden movements."

Connor released his grasp on his weapon and let it swing from his index finger. He raised his other hand to shoulder level and reached down to deposit his hardware on the damp ground. He slowly raised the other hand to shoulder level. A team of men in full camouflage and combat gear materialized out of the woods, their weapons pointed at his head.

"Lace your fingers behind your head and stand. Carefully."

Connor did as the man instructed. Fairly certain that he stood amongst Canadian Special Forces Team Three, he relaxed slightly. Unfortunately, they didn't know who he was—a good guy or a bad guy.

"Who are you?" the lead soldier snapped.

"Connor Donnelly. I know where the bomb is."

Silence.

The lead man spoke again. "Where's your ID?"

"Back right pocket in the wallet."

The man behind him withdrew the wallet and tossed it to the lead guy. The lead guy opened the wallet and glanced once at the driver's license and then up at Connor.

"It's him," the uber-warrior declared to the men with him. His team backed off a bit, but didn't lower their weapons. "I'm Lieutenant Carter—we've been keeping an eye out for you. Where's the bomb?"

"It's in the research facility just east of here. I was in audio contact with a woman who was taken hostage by Darcy Myers over an hour ago. The audio died, but she has a GPS transponder on her. She's here somewhere. She's confirmed the existence of the device and its location. There were terrorists with her as well as Myers. I heard machine gun fire and screaming before the audio died."

"Where's the GPS display unit?"

"In the backpack."

Carter motioned for the man behind Connor to retrieve the laptop from rucksack. The man unzipped the pack and snagged the laptop. Connor lowered his hands as the man placed the laptop on a tree stump and flipped it open.

The soldier studied the display for a moment before speaking. "L.T., whoever has the GPS on them is moving toward us—coming from the east."

Connor's head jerked toward the man. Jesus, she's alive, he thought. He just barely kept from collapsing to his knees in relief.

"On the road?" Carter asked sharply.

"No, through the bush," the soldier answered.

"Everyone down. Take cover and move toward the target," Carter barked. He looked over at Connor. "You too. *Move*."

Connor scooped his Magnum up from the ground and hunched down in the brush with the other men. Carter glanced at Connor, who had the weapon in his hand, and smirked. "Nice to see that you're prepared."

Alyssa made it to the far exit of the tent when she heard Darcy shout at her to stop. She made a sharp right turn as she left the tent and headed for the front of the building, shoving the trigger clumsily into her jeans front pocket with her tied hands. Realizing that staying on the dirt road would only help

Darcy find her faster, she headed for the deeper bush beside it. If she could just keep her bearings and keep ahead of Darcy, eventually she'd end up at McKay, twenty kilometers away.

The leaves on the trees filtered out the light of the sun and she worried that if she lost sight of the road, without the sun acting as a compass, she might lose her way and never be heard from again. She ran on, gasping from both fear and exertion, and tried to put the vision of Grand dying in front of her eyes out of her mind.

"Allyyssaaa, Allyyssaaa, you can't get away from me," Darcy called out to her. The sound bounced off the trees of the forest, making it hard to tell how close or how far away he was.

She stumbled on the damp ground and ended up sprawled out inelegantly on the collected leaf and twig refuse of the forest floor. She staggered to her feet and took a step. She bit her lip to avoid crying out as her ankle shot fiery pain into her leg and she fell again.

Damn. *Damn.*

Gasping, she struggled to her feet again and limped away unsteadily. She gritted her teeth against the pain burning in her ankle and hobbled on, her breathing labored. At this pace, Darcy would quickly overtake her. And take the trigger.

The trigger, oh God, the trigger. She glanced around wildly, looking for one of the small streams or sloughs that dotted the area. If she could just find one, she'd throw it in.

"Allyyssaaa," Darcy called out again and laughed ominously—he sounded much closer, pushing her nearer to total panic. "When I fiiind yooouu …"

The bastard sounded amused as she lurched onward, grinding her teeth to distract herself from the pain in her ankle. She finally lurched to a deep gully, lined by a small creek and full of half rotted trees swarming with mosquitoes.

Alyssa was fumbling through the pockets of her jeans for the trigger when someone grabbed her from behind.

Darcy.

She hadn't even heard him approach. She opened her mouth to scream when his hand clamped down over her mouth. She struggled against his implacable grip. "Now, that wasn't a very nice thing to do," he hissed into her ear and gripped her around the waist even harder, making breathing even more difficult. "Where's the fucking trigger?" He moved his hand from her mouth.

"I...I threw it into the gully," Alyssa gasped.

"Myers!" A roar came from the nearby brush and a man in camouflage peeked out from behind an enormous spruce tree. "You've got nowhere to go. Put the weapon down."

Darcy swung the Uzi toward to man, keeping Alyssa as a human shield and laughed. "I don't know who the hell you are, but you take a step toward us and I'll kill her."

Alyssa screamed, "He's lying! If he kills me, he won't get the plans to the process. If he finds the trigger, he'll detonate the nuclear weapon." She paused and her voice quavered on the next words. "Shoot me and it's over!"

Shit. *Shit*. Whoever these people were, they would probably kill her to nullify the bomb threat. Her life meant very little in the balance and she knew it. She closed her eyes and waited for bullets to rip into her body.

"Myers! You're surrounded. There's no way out. Give it up and everyone will live."

Darcy laughed. "Fuck living. If living means spending the rest of my life in prison, I'll die here and now, but she'll die too."

Darcy shoved Alyssa away from him hard and raised the Uzi to annihilate her. Alyssa stumbled and hit the soggy ground hard. A single shot rang out, echoing in the trees.

Something hit Alyssa in the back. Her head whipped around to see Darcy still standing—a huge piece of his skull had been blown out of the front of his head. A huge crater carved into his face where his right eye used to be. He wavered slightly on his feet, a dazed look in his remaining eye. The skull fragment had hit her. He fell toward Alyssa, but she was too stunned to move.

His body hit her legs and she cried out as pain rocketed up her leg from her injured ankle. Her stomach heaved and she gagged, but nothing came up, as she hadn't been able to eat for at least a day. Still, she felt like crap warmed over, between the pain in her leg and the nausea.

Once the retching fit stopped, she raised dazed eyes from Darcy's dead body to see Connor standing two yards behind Darcy, his weapon gripped in his hand. He stared at Alyssa like a man dying of thirst staring at an oasis. He tucked the weapon into the back of the waistband of his jeans, strode over to Alyssa and kicked Darcy's lifeless body off her legs.

And then she was in his arms, her feet dangling far the ground, being held so closely, so tenderly. She closed her eyes and wrapped herself around him, looped her tied hands around Connor's neck and latched on, sobbing and hyperventilating. She became aware of Connor murmuring over and over again, "You're all right. You're okay. I've got you."

"G-Gr-Grand. He…he's d-dead. D-Darcy killed him. He killed everyone. Grand's gone," she sobbed.

"Oh, baby. I'm so sorry," Connor whispered and murmured comforting sounds into her ear. "I'm so sorry, sweetheart." He rocked her back and forth. "I need you to stay with me for a little longer, honey. Can you do that for me?"

Alyssa hiccupped and nodded and Connor set her down on her feet. Alyssa cried out as the pain in her ankle roared to life and would have fallen if not for Connor's arms holding her up.

Connor scooped her up and strode past the phalanx of warriors toward a fallen tree and gently lowered her to sit on it. As he untied her hands, he raised his voice and asked, "Is one of you a medic?"

A tall, lanky, red-haired man with soft brown eyes stepped forward. "I am." The man walked over to Alyssa and squatted down in front of her, smiling reassuringly. "I'm Sergeant McGraw. At your service, ma'am."

Sergeant McGraw had a definite Newfoundland brogue. His hands carefully touched her ankle here and there to determine the amount of damage. "You're in luck—it's not broken, but you do have one hell of a sprain." He shifted his eyes up to her bruised face and bloodied nose. He gently pressed his fingers to her cheek and nose. "Don't think anything's broken there, either." McGraw turned his head to speak to another man. "Lieutenant Carter, she's going to be fine."

Lieutenant Carter asked, "Ms. Tiernan, do you *have* the trigger? You told Myers you threw it in the gully."

She managed to focus her eyes on the tall blond man with the slight Alberta drawl. "I have it. I grabbed it when Darcy wasn't looking and ran." She dug into the front pocket of her jeans and extracted the trigger. "Here. Take it." She handed it to him as if it were a venomous snake.

"Where's the device?" he asked.

"It's in the research facility tent behind the building just east of here. My grandfather," Alyssa's voice cracked but she held on, "my grandfather is in there with the others. They're all dead."

"We'll go check it out," Carter said. "Donnelly, take Ms. Tiernan back to your car and stay there until we come for you. Understand?"

"Yeah."

The Canadian Special Forces team dissolved like mist into the forest, aimed toward the facility. Connor carried Alyssa the distance to the car. He climbed into the backseat of the car with her, folded her up in a blanket and held her as she wept.

Finally the crying turned into tortured hiccups, racking her tired body. Connor pressed his lips to her temple and gathered her closer.

Night had almost descended on the forest. The sun had almost been chased out of the sky by the moon. Soft sounds of crickets and chirrups of foraging squirrels drifted through the open windows of the car along with the calm night air.

Exhausted by sorrow, Alyssa finally drifted off to sleep in Connor's arms. Connor felt tears pricking at his eyes. He would have given anything to spare her the whole ordeal. But it was over and done now. Grand was dead. His love, his heart, was alive. And for that he would be forever grateful.

The sounds of military helicopters and ground vehicles shattered the stillness of the night. A powerful searchlight aimed from a helicopter illuminated the car, blinding Connor and jerking Alyssa awake in his arms.

"The gang's all here," Connor said to her, in response to her unasked question.

A man's face appeared beside the window. Myles Collins. He gripped the open window ledge and surveyed them for a moment. As Alyssa stared at him, a slow smile broke over his broad face and he reached for her hand through the window.

Alyssa stared at him, a confused look on her face.

"Your grandfather's alive."

Chapter Thirty-Five

At the Fort McMurray Hospital, Alyssa sat in a wheelchair beside Grand's bed and stroked his hand. Her injured foot was wrapped in an elastic bandage and propped up on the leg rest of the wheeled chair. It ached, but it would heal. Just like Grand. Grand's surgery, to remove the bullet from his leg, had left him groggy and tired.

"Your grandfather is a tough old guy. When the shooting started, he hit the ground and the bodies of the other men piled on top of him," Myles said from the entrance of the room.

Alyssa started in surprise at his voice. He hadn't been there a minute ago. She looked over at him as he entered the room. "When the team found him, he had mostly managed to dig his way out from beneath the heap. Angry as hell. All he wanted to know was where you were and if you were okay. He was ready to take on the whole unit."

Alyssa smiled at him. "That's Grand. Always ready for a fight."

"Sounds like his granddaughter," Connor replied from his position on the chair at the foot of Grand's bed.

"Me?" Alyssa replied, mock incredulity in her voice. "I'm as meek as a mouse."

"Yeah, right, I totally forgot. Ms. Meek here telling the Special Forces team to *shoot her*. That's meek, all right. Insane is more like it. I aged ten *years* in five seconds," Connor said, his voice rich with sarcasm. "I swear I'm going to lock you up for your own protection."

Alyssa harrumphed, but let her eyes laugh at him.

She turned toward Myles. "Will we ever know the whole story?"

Myles considered her for a moment. "I can tell you a little." He settled into another armchair and dragged it toward the bed.

"As far as we can tell, John Hughes converted to a radical version of Islam and was recruited by the World Islamic Jihad ten years ago. He traveled to the Middle East after graduating from college in the States with a specialty in foreign languages and we're guessing that's when the conversion took place. He came back to the States and procured an entry-level position in the CIA as an analyst.

"A year ago, he was promoted to a senior position in Joe Taylor's area. By all accounts, he was a model employee. He never expressed any political views, no anti-West or anti-American sentiments and ostensibly lived a quiet life. He married six years ago and had two children.

"Six months ago, a faction of the World Islamic Jihad in Canada got wind of a brand-spanking-new experimental process that would revolutionize the extraction of oil from the oil sands. Which, in turn, would lessen the West's dependence on Saudi oil. And that's when we think WIJ brought Hughes out of the deep freeze. We know that Myers had been tracking the WIJ in Canada and we think Myers presented himself to them as a convert. We're guessing that WIJ had the nuclear weapon for five years or so and was waiting for a chance to use it, formulating their plot as they went.

"Disable the Saudi oil producing machine and wipe out any possibility of the world turning to Alberta for oil. WIJ gathered its forces in Saudi and a week ago bombed a Saudi oil facility. They also organized the first strike against a major oil producer here on the same day."

"What about Roy?" Connor asked.

"It looks like Sheriff Jenkins was blackmailed into helping the terrorists. He gave the terrorists the layout of your

Colorado home and the security measures that you'd taken. The terrorist threatened to kill his wife and daughter if he didn't comply."

"Are there charges pending against him?" Connor questioned.

"The US authorities are still sorting everything out. At this point, it's an internal American matter."

"How was Taylor involved?"

"Taylor was tracking WIJ activities in the States, but he didn't realize that one of his own people, Hughes, was keeping an eye on his progress. We think that when Taylor got close, Hughes murdered him, assumed his identity online and left the country for Canada."

"How did the Israelis become involved?"

"We think that Taylor leaked information to the Israelis before he died and they sent two of their agents to Colorado to see for themselves."

"So they *were* there to protect me?" Alyssa asked, eyebrows lifted high.

"Sort of. They were lucky enough, or unlucky enough, to arrive at Connor's compound at approximately the same time as the terrorists. It was just dumb chance. You were never meant to encounter the Israeli agents. You disabled one and the other took off before he could be discovered. And then the terrorists showed up. Connor killed one. The other terrorist escaped. The surviving terrorist came back with his cohorts and murdered two police officers and the Israeli agent to tie up all the loose ends."

"Then who was the hacker? Grand's system was targeted and Connor's system was physically breached," Alyssa asked.

"Probably Hughes and his associates. A lot of the funding of these terrorist organizations comes directly from the Saudi government, so cash would not have been an issue," Myles replied.

"But why go after Alyssa and her grandfather?" Connor asked. "If they were going to nuke Alberta anyway, why bother with them?"

"We think this was Myers' idea. He had evidently planned on double-crossing the terrorists as soon as he got the bomb and the person who knew the extraction process. Darcy would have ended up a very rich, very powerful man. Everyone who knew him would think that he, Alyssa and Douglas were dead. WIJ would think that their people who died in Alberta were martyrs. No one would be any the wiser. An excellent cover for starting a new life."

"I think I'm getting a headache," Alyssa mumbled as she rubbed her temples.

Myles grinned at her. "It's enough to give anyone a headache. Including me. But thanks to you and a lot of lucky breaks on our side, we've emerged as the victor this time." Myles glanced at his watch. "Well, it's five in the morning and I'm bushed. I'm going to crash. I'll see you both back in Edmonton in a few days."

Myles heaved himself out of the chair and shocked the hell out of Alyssa by giving her a big bear hug. She hugged him back gingerly.

"If you ever want a job at CSIS again, let me know," Myles said with a smile in his eyes, as he drew back from her.

"Uh, sorry, I've got other plans."

Myles smirked. "I'm sure you do. Can't blame me for trying though." He held out his hand to Connor and the two men shook hands.

And then Myles left.

Alyssa and Connor stared at each other. She flushed at the raw look in his eyes. She flicked her eyes to Grand and stroked his head for a moment before she turned back to Connor. "I'm sorry about Roy and your friend Joe, Connor."

"Thanks. So am I." Connor blew out a breath. "I just thought that this part of my life was over."

"And then I waltzed into your life and dragged you back into it," Alyssa said bitterly.

"You waltzed into my life and changed it forever, Alyssa," Connor replied quietly. He rose from his seat and came toward her with an outstretched hand. "Come outside with me."

As she grasped his hand, Connor's heart did a flip-flop. He swung her up in his arms and carried her out of the hospital through the Emergency department exit. The nurses tittered in their wake.

The eastern sky showed the barest signs of light in the distance, but the stars and the moon still decorated the sky. A time of transition.

He sat on a picnic bench under a tree on the hospital grounds with Alyssa in his lap. He wrapped his arms around her and rested his chin on her head, wondering how to broach the subject he wanted to pursue.

Before he could speak, Alyssa whispered, "Connor, back in the jet you asked me to tell you that I loved you, that you didn't care if it was a lie, you just wanted to hear the words. I said the words to you."

Connor closed his eyes. *Christ, she's going to rip my heart out right here, right now.* He'd lost her after all. After all the terror. After all the joy. "It's okay, Alyssa. You don't have to say it. I was a little out of my mind. I know—"

Alyssa cut him off, her words rushing out as if afraid she would chicken out, "I want you to know, they weren't just words."

For a moment, Connor's heart stopped beating. He couldn't absorb her meaning. His heart roared back to life and pounded against his chest. His head snapped back and he pulled away from her slightly, his eyes searching hers. Alyssa took a deep breath continued.

"I love you. You mean more to me, are more precious to me, than anyone I've ever known." Alyssa paused and then said in a shaky voice, "I know that I'm screwed up. I've always known I was different. But when we're together, it doesn't seem so insurmountable. It's like I've got a fighting chance to be normal."

"So, Grand was right?" Connor smiled at her and tucked a stray lock of her hair behind one ear.

Alyssa flushed and gave him a rueful smile. "I suppose so. I'm never going to live this down."

"Will you marry me?"

Alyssa studied him in the approaching light of dawn and tears welled in her eyes. Her heart expanded exponentially in her chest and seemed to move upward. "It's only been a week," she managed to whisper, heart in her throat.

"We'll have a long engagement, whatever you want."

"I want." She threaded his arms around his chest and clung to him. She tilted her head back to see his face. "I'll marry you."

"So, uh, how many kids do you want?" Connor asked, his voice overly casual. "Since we're getting to know each other better…"

"I want my own baseball team."

Connor shook his head as if to wake himself. He grinned, lowered his lips to within a hair's breadth to hers and whispered, "Maybe we should have a shorter engagement."

"Okay, engagement's over, let's get married."

About the Author

Ten days after Brooke's last exam at university, she took off for a three month tour of Australia and New Zealand. No, the SS Minnow was not lost. A year and a half later, after adding Singapore, Malaysia, Thailand, India and Britain to the itinerary, she returned to her snowy home town of Sherwood Park, Alberta, Canada. Deciding that she wanted a change of location, she flipped a coin to decide whether to live in Vancouver or in Toronto. Toronto won (or lost, depending upon how one looks at it).

After working at stockbrokerages for three years, she went back to school to learn how to program computers. Her current job, when not writing, is as a project manager/business analyst for a leading IT integration firm.

Brooke is a member of the Romance Writers of America and the Toronto Romance Writers.

Brooke welcomes comments from readers. You can find her website and email address on her author bio page at www.cerridwenpress.com.

Tell Us What You Think

We appreciate hearing reader opinions about our books. You can email us at Comments@EllorasCave.com.

Why an electronic book?

We live in the Information Age—an exciting time in the history of human civilization, in which technology rules supreme and continues to progress in leaps and bounds every minute of every day. For a multitude of reasons, more and more avid literary fans are opting to purchase e-books instead of paper books. The question from those not yet initiated into the world of electronic reading is simply: *Why?*

1. ***Price.*** An electronic title at Ellora's Cave Publishing and Cerridwen Press runs anywhere from 40% to 75% less than the cover price of the exact same title in paperback format. Why? Basic mathematics and cost. It is less expensive to publish an e-book (no paper and printing, no warehousing and shipping) than it is to publish a paperback, so the savings are passed along to the consumer.
2. ***Space.*** Running out of room in your house for your books? That is one worry you will never have with electronic books. For a low one-time cost, you can purchase a handheld device specifically designed for e-reading. Many e-readers have large, convenient screens for viewing. Better yet, hundreds of titles can be stored within your new library—on a single microchip. There are a variety of e-readers from different manufacturers. You can also read e-books on your PC or laptop computer. (Please note that

Ellora's Cave does not endorse any specific brands. You can check our websites at www.ellorascave.com or www.cerridwenpress.com for information we make available to new consumers.)

3. ***Mobility***. Because your new e-library consists of only a microchip within a small, easily transportable e-reader, your entire cache of books can be taken with you wherever you go.
4. ***Personal Viewing Preferences.*** Are the words you are currently reading too small? Too large? Too... ANNOYING? Paperback books cannot be modified according to personal preferences, but e-books can.
5. ***Instant Gratification.*** Is it the middle of the night and all the bookstores near you are closed? Are you tired of waiting days, sometimes weeks, for bookstores to ship the novels you bought? Ellora's Cave Publishing sells instantaneous downloads twenty-four hours a day, seven days a week, every day of the year. Our webstore is never closed. Our e-book delivery system is 100% automated, meaning your order is filled as soon as you pay for it.

Those are a few of the top reasons why electronic books are replacing paperbacks for many avid readers.

As always, Ellora's Cave and Cerridwen Press welcome your questions and comments. We invite you to email us at Comments@ellorascave.com or write to us directly at Ellora's Cave Publishing Inc., 1056 Home Avenue, Akron, OH 44310-3502.